Second Bloom

Second Bloom
Eve Matthews

Eve Matthews

Second Bloom

EVE MATTHEWS

Edited by Emily Hainsworth

Digital ISBN: 979-8-9879005-0-5

Paperback ISBN: 979-8-9879005-2-9

Dedicated to my parents.

*For catching me inappropriately chatting on AIM with my boyfriend
in high school and making me break up with him.*

Rat Bastard

SHE'S GOT YOU - PATSY CLINE

YOU DON'T OWN ME - LESLEY GORE

A CASE OF YOU - JONI MITCHELL

THE WANDERER - DION DIMUCCI

ESCAPE - RUPERT HOLMES

HEARTBREAKER - MARIAH CAREY (FEAT. JAY-Z)

COSMIC LOVE - FLORENCE + THE MACHINE

SMOKE AND ASHES - TRACY CHAPMAN

SAY MY NAME - DESTINY'S CHILD

WHOSE BED HAVE YOUR BOOTS BEEN UNDER - SHANIA TWAIN

TRUTH HURTS - LIZZO

I LOVE IT - ICONA POP

GIVES YOU HELL - THE ALL-AMERICAN REJECTS

FLAVOR OF THE WEAK - AMERICAN HI-FI

UNDERNEATH IT ALL - NO DOUBT

EDGE OF DESIRE - JOHN MAYER

COMING HOME - LEON BRIDGES

BY YOUR SIDE - SADE

*** TRIGGER WARNING : CHEATING SPOUSE ***

PROLOGUE

"RAT BASTARD"

Clara swiped a tear off her cheek and hit save. She scrolled through her music, voraciously adding anything and everything to the playlist that fit her mood. Her face was streaked with salt, illuminated by her phone. Tipping her bottle to the sky, the last drop sloshed between her lips and she scowled, crawling out from behind a pair of suit pants. She hit play.

Patsy's voice shook the house, flooding around her, taking up every bit of space for air. Clara's fingers slid along the carpet, meeting the cold silver of the ice bucket. She frowned. The etched monogram beneath her touch was like Braille. The peaks and valleys meaning more than they ever had any right to. Dipping her hand into the polar slush, she reveled in the prickling pain.

"Shit."

Last call. Clara searched, spotting the bottle opener, nearly hidden by a shiny pair of loafers. A small graveyard of empty beer bottles surrounded her as she stretched, snagging the metal contraption. The sound of release was a salve, smoothing over the pain in her chest. She took a long pull and lay back, letting her eyes fall closed. The chandelier glowed above her eyelids, warming her skin. Transporting her somewhere far, far away. A tropical beach. No, a cabin in the mountains. No.

She sighed. *The lake.*

Tears bubbled like shaken champagne, and she looked up as tiny rivers forged a fresh path, disappearing into her hair. She stood, squaring off with the clothes in front of her face.

Her hand inched along the prism of pressed shirts and she halted, clutching the silky fabric between her fingers. She swallowed at the knot in her throat and tugged hard, the seal on her sanity busting with the pop of each hanger against the rail. One by one Clara pulled, yanking until everything lay in a heap on the floor. A sob ripped from her chest and she twisted, falling to her knees.

Her breath rushed past her lips in hot, heavy bursts. *"She's got you."*

Grabbing a button-down off the ground, she stumbled from the walk-in closet, out of the bedroom, and down the hall to the study. Music followed her. The sultry hum like a slow-burning flame, inching closer and closer to gasoline. Clara eyed Mark's prized stash of cigars tucked in the humidor on top of his desk.

She tugged her ratty pajama top over her head and tossed it on the floor. Setting down her drink, Clara slipped the cold, blue dress shirt over her naked skin. A soberness washed over her and she pressed her nose against the stripes, tears springing to her eyes.

After a moment, she straightened and popped the stiff collar at her neck, forcing the tears back, just like her feelings. Clara flipped the weighted lid in front of her and reached in, touching the expensive paper ridges. Plucking a cigar from the box, she rolled it between her fingers, snatching her beer off the dark mahogany.

She halted, staring at the water ring left behind. A huff of air shot past her lips as she turned, marching toward the door, defiance in every step. At the threshold she glanced back, her eyes lingering on the circular splotch of water. She gritted her teeth. "For fuck's sake." Clara trudged over, swiping her crisp cotton elbow across the water ring before slinking away. She was drunk. Not irresponsible.

Clara returned to the closet. She scooped up the expensive pile and marched back out to the landing, beer and cigar in tow. With a swing of her hips, she spun, hoisting the belongings over the rail of the second-floor staircase. Beer splattered below. She cringed, peering over the edge. Sucking in a breath, Clara swayed and raised her bottle, toasting her invisible audience. "One for the homies."

She balanced the unlit cigar between her lips, fluffing her hair from her eyes. Going up to her tiptoes, Clara sauntered down the hallway, the ornate Turkish runner cushioning her every step. Straying off course, she bumped into the wall and clamped her eyes shut, begging the room to stop spinning.

She settled the cigar between two fingers and grabbed hold of the rail, waiting for her cue. She stepped down, tread by tread, belting the lines off-key. With a roll and flick of her wrist, Clara snapped her fingers like heavily bolded punctuation. A showgirl descending the stage. The music licking her heels.

Tightening her grip along the shiny polished wood, Clara chugged what remained of her drink. She sank, observing the pile before her. Her chest rose and fell and she stared, taking in all the bits and pieces of Mark, now jumbled and unwanted.

She rested her head against the banister. Clara pushed a hand through her hair, listening as the song played out. A very unladylike belch escaped her, and she stared at the shiny puddle of beer splattered across the marble foyer. Mark's clothes were currently sopping it up. A smile lifted the corner of her mouth. *Oops.*

Clara's gaze traversed the entryway, landing on a framed photo from their wedding day. Her stomach lurched, twisting like a spinning teacup at the carnival. She felt hot. Too hot. Hoisting herself up, she raced for the back door, shoving her way onto the porch. The air was thick with dew and she gasped, drinking it down, breathing through the pain.

Clara grabbed the wooden rocking chair beside her and slumped down, peering into the solitude beyond the screened-in porch. The windows to her bedroom were shoved open, and music continued to tumble, falling around her. It was the only sign of life for miles. The pads of her fingers dragged against her arms in warm, damp strokes. A curl of peeling paint rustled beneath her bare feet and she pushed back, rocking herself in the dark.

She stayed within the confines of the mesh. Protected from swarms of mosquitos that had undoubtedly come out to play. A lighter lay beside a nearly empty citronella candle, and Clara sat back, igniting a flame beneath the end of the cigar.

She stilled. Even amidst the music, she could hear the peaceful hum of summer. Frogs croaked and cicadas screeched, their calls filling the darkness. It was a noisy kind of peace that could drive someone insane. Digging into her pocket, Clara met the edge of a bit of paper. It was crumpled and uncrumpled within an inch of its life.

I don't really know how you're supposed to write something like this. It's a warning—I wish someone would have given me one.

Mark is cheating on you. I thought he was cheating on me but I saw your name on some old mail at his apartment and now I know he's married. Fucking disgusting. I confronted him and he didn't even deny it. We met in February and I've never even seen him with a wedding ring and I've never heard your name—and you deserve to know that. I doubt he would have ever told me about you, but I needed you to know about me.

The messy cursive blurred as Clara wiped a streak of snot on the sleeve of Mark's button down. She inhaled, embers blazing in the pitch black of the porch. Her lungs filled with smoke and she sputtered, coughing uncontrollably. Leaning forward, she reached for a barren pot by the wall, dragging it to the center of the floor. Clara balanced the cigar between her lips, staring down at the letter in her hands. The edges no longer crisp, but soft with wear.

Fucking disgusting.

With a flick of the lighter, fire danced along the words she had memorized. The flame grew, and she dropped the paper into the clay pot at her feet. She shrugged hard, and the silky cotton fell from her shoulders, exposing her to the night. She held it up, lighting a flame at the cuff, waiting as it slowly began to catch. The porch glowed for a moment, and Clara sat back in the rocking chair, her knees folded beneath her chin. As the warmth died, a chill drifted across her skin. The cigar burned red between her fingers and she cast it into the pot, slipping into the darkness, letting the night swallow her whole.

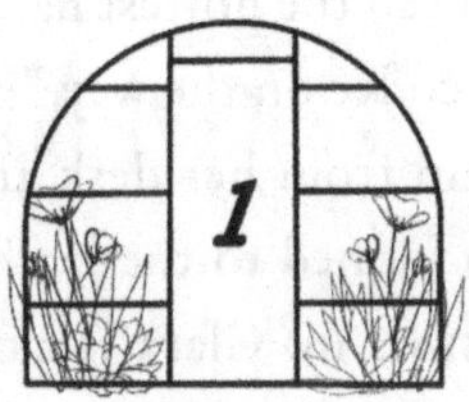

"Clara?"

The fog was translucent. Morning light shot through the clouds, slicing between the mountains. The view made her feel... tiny. Rubbing her palms against her pants, she felt a chill fall across her cheeks. She noticed the hint of a path in the distance. Her hair rustled against her rain jacket and she turned at the sound of her name.

"Clara Monroe—"

Clara tore her eyes away from the photograph. Her gaze darted to the receptionist, sitting at the frosted glass window. She knocked back the last sip of coffee from her travel mug and collected her purse from the empty chair to her left. Clara walked from the waiting room across the hallway to Eileen's office.

"How are you doing today? Would you like a tea or a water before we start?"

Eileen Strong had a perfectly styled bob that was an unrealistic shade of auburn. It was pin straight, but Clara knew it was naturally curly on account of days like today. Over the past few months, Clara had caught glimpses of wavy frizz during the late afternoon, when all of her morning sessions were already taken. She was here today for a seven thirty a.m. slot, but it was pouring. Clara could see the bends and waves that even the hottest flat iron couldn't fight.

"I'm fine. I drank a coffee on the way."

Eileen had gotten up from her desk and walked with Clara into the room. She motioned to the leather armchair opposite her and they both settled in. Clara felt comfortable with her. She had actually started to look forward to their sessions. As a self-proclaimed know-it-all, it felt good to have someone push her right to the edge. It was a bit of a drive into the city, but she'd rather die than divulge anything to anyone with a zip code in Silas Grove.

"How are things between you and Mark?"

"Things are... the same. He still comes by the house to pick up his stuff." Clara shook her head. "He just shows up."

Eileen nodded. "How do you feel about that?"

"It's frustrating." Clara let out a bitter breath. "It's been six months and he won't sign the papers. It's his house, so..." She hesitated. "I know I'll have to move out when it's all over." Clara swallowed thickly, running her tongue over her bottom lip. "Sometimes I wonder if he's taking his time just to annoy me." She rolled her eyes and then closed them for a moment. When she refocused, Eileen's gaze narrowed. Still nodding.

"Why would he want to do that?"

Clara thought before answering. "He's selfish. And territorial." She glanced at Eileen and shook her head. Reluctant to utter her thoughts out loud. The leather squeaked beneath her as she shifted. "Sometimes, I think he wants a reason to drop by and poke around... to see if I've had anyone over."

A brief pause. "Have you?"

A heavy laugh shot between Clara's lips. Eileen sat stoically. Still gently nodding. Still gently provoking. Clara cleared her throat and watched as rain pelted the window outside.

She composed herself. "No... I haven't had anyone over." The truth had seemed a little less pitiful before she spoke it into existence. "There's no way I'd date anyone in town, and... honestly, I don't know if I'm ready." Clara frowned. "And his mom still calls."

Eileen's gaze widened and her eyebrows raised ever so slightly. "She's still calling you." A question lingered in her tone.

"Not as often... but, yeah." Clara held Eileen's eye for a moment. "I feel bad for her." She looked down, picking at the fabric of her pants. "Mark and I were together for nine years. I'm sure she just wants it all to go away and for things to stay the same." Clara shrugged before looking up. "She probably imagined things would go differently."

Eileen pursed her lips, lightly rolling the pen in her hand. "Have you given any more thought to the boundaries we discussed?"

Clara sucked in a measured breath. "That's one of my goals this summer. I need to be more consistent. But Bonnie... I don't have the heart to tell her about Mark. It hurts, but I think her accusing me of breaking up the marriage just has a lot to do with her fear of the 'D' word."

"Divorce."

"Right."

<hr>

Clara swung into the stormy lot and shoved her car into park, the wipers jumping like her pulse. All she could see was the pained look on the receptionist's face at Eileen's office, handing

Clara her credit card. *Declined*. Reaching for her phone, the screen lit the dull gray of the car. It was pouring. Her thumbs hovered over the keyboard.

CLARA: Did you cancel my credit card?

MARK: Depends.

CLARA: ?

MARK: You're the one who wants to split up.

Clara thought of the porch and the crumpled note. How the corners had gone fuzzy and limp after a year of hiding in her purse. A secret that she had carried with her everywhere until she couldn't take it anymore. Until she had to drain her savings, hire a lawyer, and serve Mark with divorce papers. *Fuck*. It didn't make a difference that it was nothing but a pile of ash now. She still felt it.

CLARA: SIGN THE PAPERS

She hit send and covered her face with her hands, letting out a muffled scream. Depleted, she slumped against the headrest. The image of the dark lot outside went from blurry to crystal clear. Back and forth. Over and over. She looked up at the ceiling, listening to the lines that trickled through the speakers. The chorus climbed, and Joni's words got louder and louder, rivaling the rain outside. The lyrics slipped between her ribs and she turned up the volume, letting it slice her soul in two. Her nails left tiny crescent moons on her palms as she unclenched her fists.

Her eyes slid to the clock on the dash. Nine a.m.. *God, it was too early for this*. Her musical choices were manic. They always had been. She huffed a breath and wiped her face. Lately, all she craved was angst and melancholy. She envisioned herself with long, pin straight hair, driving along a dark highway just like Nicole Kidman in Practical Magic. Only she wasn't a sexy man-eating witch escaping from the wrath of an ex who just refused to die. *On second thought.*

The rain on the roof became deafening. Staring at the front door of the sad, four-story building in front of her, the fluorescent lights glowed an unnaturally bright white. Like a bug zapper just waiting to snuff her out. She wanted nothing more than to drive home, crawl into bed, and hide from the life she didn't want.

———⁂———

"**1**-800-BOUQUET. How can I help you today? Yes—I understand that you have our *Warm Sunset* arrangement in your cart... and you are trying to apply a coupon to the order? Well, sir, that coupon code doesn't apply to orders less than fifty dollars..."

All the cubicles hummed with a forced, energized chatter. Walking to her desk, Clara passed a series of uneventful customer service conversations that were a string of varied complaints. She rounded the corner to her cube, sliding into her swivel chair. Picking up her headset, Clara glanced over to the supervisor's window as she logged into the server. Sharon looked pissed. A paperclip flew, thumping her on the shoulder. When she glanced over at Ryan, he covered his mic. "She was asking for you half an hour ago."

"*Great.*" Clara turned to smile at their boss from across the sea of cubes. "She hates me."

Ryan nodded, his eyes never leaving his screen. "She really does."

She pushed back from her desk. "Wish me luck."

He raised his hands from his keyboard, fingers crossed in silent solidarity. Ryan was her only confidante in this hellhole. Standing, Clara walked through the mouse maze, making her way to their boss's tiny office. Sharon had windows on all three sides so she could survey her peons. Watch them toil away, making sure they hated every second after they clocked in.

"Hey Sharon. Ryan said you needed me?"

Sharon held up her hand, silencing her. She hugged her phone to her ear, and Clara bristled. She thought about her session with Eileen. *Was she, in fact, as terrified of divorce as her mother-in-law? Why did she care what Mark thought?* She watched Sharon's acrylic nails tighten around the phone and Clara shifted where she stood. *Why hadn't she packed up all his shit and delivered it herself? Curbside service at its finest.*

"Clara—where were you this morning?"

Her gaze jumped to Sharon's. "Oh. I—uh..." she tucked her hair behind her ear. "I had an appointment. I mentioned it to you at the beginning of the month... and the beginning of last month... and when you initially hired me."

Clara knew Sharon wasn't listening. She watched as her boss wrote down some bit of pertinent information that just couldn't wait.

"Oh yeah. This is your standing *mental health* appointment, right?"

Her jaw dropped. Clara took a deep breath and glanced around. She was certain she could bore a hole into the top of Sharon's head, since she was still committed to scribbling rather than looking Clara in the eye. "Yes, Sharon. It's a *standing appointment*. First Tuesday of every month. I didn't think it was going to be an ongoing issue—"

"Oh, it's no issue. I guess I just forgot about it." Sharon interjected. She was enjoying this. Anything that hinted that Clara's life was a mess made Sharon happy.

"You know, since you're only working the bare minimum, I sometimes lose track of where you are... or if you're even coming in at all." An icy stalemate filled the air of the tiny office. Clara narrowed her gaze and pushed her shoulders back, straightening her spine. The phone on the desk between them rang and Sharon swiveled away, dismissing her. Heat flamed Clara's face, and she turned on her heel, striding out of the room. Her boss knew absolutely nothing about her life.

———eee———

The day droned on, as expected. Her only reprieve was when Ryan briefed her on his latest love interest. Ryan was tall and slender with a permanent scruff of five o'clock shadow and thick, sooty lashes. They bonded instantly in the breakroom the week Clara started work. He was brooding after a recent fling and she attempted small talk, divulging that she was newly separated. Entranced by her situation, Ryan understood why misfortune brought her to work in such a sad, sad place. They were kindred spirits. And they were broke.

Unlike Sharon, Ryan's delight in her misery felt more like camaraderie. They bantered, learning about each other through a heavy veil of sarcasm. Ryan had gone to school for interior design, successfully securing a contract for a string of boutique hotels his first year out of school. He was even in a serious relationship before they broke up, tragically. After the split, he left the design world, and had been crashing at his mom's house until further notice.

Having grown up bouncing from state to state with his parents, he was used to constant change. Clara remembered that day in the breakroom, and how his expression had softened when she mentioned Silas Grove. His grandmother had lived there her whole life. He was adamant that his current accommodations were temporary, and that his mother, Trish, was actually more fun now that he was an adult.

"Got any hot plans?"

Clara glanced over at Ryan in her peripheral. "Yeah, super steamy."

"*Do tell.*"

She laughed. He was always ready to entertain the mundane. Every Friday he asked about her plans, and every Friday she had absolutely nothing interesting to offer. But he always held out hope for her. He would leave that small metaphorical window cracked just in case.

"I have to go to Eli's tomorrow to complete some orders. The flowers arrived yesterday and I need to get the centerpieces made so I can drop them off in the afternoon."

"Riveting. I've never asked... but is Eli nice looking?"

Clara snorted. "I'd say he's a catch if you're in the market for a wholesome, married, seventy-year-old with dirt under his nails."

Ryan scrunched his nose. "I wouldn't say that seventy isn't an option. I just think if you're going to widen the net for your potential pool of suitors, you should consider upping the threshold to *sugar daddy* level."

"I'll keep that in mind next time I'm at the pharmacy and I spot a cutie sliding into that *very* sexy blood pressure cuff."

He swiveled to face her. "For God's sake, at least make sure he's picking up the name brand Band-Aids. None of that generic crap." Ryan waved his hand through the air. "How will he keep you in the lifestyle that you've become accustomed to?"

She shook her head and smiled.

He pinned her with a pointed look. "You really need to know your worth."

Despite the theatrics, there was something soft in Ryan's voice. They powered down their computers and the two of them made their way to the elevators along with everyone else in Customer Service. Clara glanced out the window. Gray clouds hung low in the sky and rain continued to drizzle.

"I don't understand why you're even living in that house."

Clara frowned, eyeing the brick entrance in the distance. Her mother's disapproval was unyielding, like the iron gate in front of her. She hit the clicker on her visor and rolled forward, passing the mailbox, disappearing into the lush tunnel that lined the drive. She'd deal with the bills later.

"You should just come home."

Clara grimaced. It was impossible to ignore how bad the property looked. The shrubs needed to be pruned, and the grass was full of weeds. Rain flowed in heavy sheets across the pavers and she slowed.

"Mom, I can't just leave—" *Can't as in won't.* She heard a scoff and Clara tensed, approaching a maidenhair grass that she failed to cut back the season before. And the season before that. After she had gotten the letter, it seemed everything had begun to suffer. The fresh growth mixed with the old and it looked stifled, just trying to push through.

The yard was always a point of contention. Mark preferred having a crew come out twice a month to hack everything back. He never understood why she piddled around, trimming stuff all throughout the year. He would come out of the house, ruffle her grungy sunhat, and ask why she even bothered.

What she wouldn't give for someone to take care of it now. Clara averted her eyes when she walked to the car each morning. Everything begged for the attention she wasn't ready to give, and all the things that usually brought her joy felt dull. These days she survived off takeout and she could sleep away an entire weekend if left to her own devices.

"Anything would be better than living under that roof. If it were me—"

Clara pulled up to the house, parking as close to the overhang as possible. Mark had stored their boat and his old mustang in the garage, leaving not an inch of space. She grimaced.

"I *know*, Mom." She closed her eyes and pinched the bridge of her nose. "You would have never stayed to begin with."

Clara groaned, listening as rain overflowed the gutters and shot out from the downspouts below. "Look, I'm working on it, okay?" She cut the engine. "And, I'll—uh… I'll send you another check soon." She swallowed, looking longingly at the front door from where she sat. There was a lengthy pause. Clara envisioned the pinched look of her mother's lips on the other end of the line, strung tight with disappointment. Her face heated. "I have to go." They mumbled a curt farewell, full of all the things that didn't need to be said out loud.

The garden center only paid minimum wage, so she split her time between there and The Bug Zapper. Every week she counted down the days until she got to work in the fresh air with Eli and Gloria. They were the only ones in town who didn't seem to be put off by her mere existence. Or by the idea that she had run Mark Monroe off his beloved family estate.

She looked out her window at the tiny streams flowing between the pavers. She'd have to make a run for it. Swinging the car door open, her first step landed in a huge puddle. "*Shit,*" she muttered, followed by a string of other profanities.

Clara fumbled through the pavers and up the front steps. Water squished between her toes, and she caught her breath, squaring off with the front door. Her stomach dropped. She pressed her forehead against the frosted glass inlay and scowled. Her keys and her purse were still sitting in the front seat of her Lexus.

"You've got to be fucking kidding me." Clara glared at the ceramic squirrel by her foot, where the spare usually sat. She had gotten rid of the hideaway key after Mark had come over unannounced a few too many times since moving out. It had been her first attempt at setting some boundaries. Her nostrils flared, and she picked up the stone rodent, catapulting it into the yard. It landed with a heavy thud and Clara marched forward, trudging back out into the storm.

⸎

She kicked off her ruined flats and darted upstairs, not bothering with the lights. What remained of the gray, dim daylight filtered in through the oversized windows. Her feet met the tile of the bathroom and she shivered. Turning the heavy silver valve, Clara paced, waiting for the water to warm. She glanced around and frowned. Her vanity had become littered with junk and the jute area rug on the floor curled in one corner—a death trap just waiting to happen.

Like the yard, she sometimes believed that if she just kept her head down, all the unpleasantness would disappear. Lately, she had felt conflicted, teetering between indulging the sadness and trying to make believe that things were just fine. She stared at the other side of the bathroom, sterile and untouched.

Her emotions were on edge. It felt like Eileen was right there, encouraging her to confront her fear. "Do the work," she would say when Clara was being avoidant.

She approached, trailing her finger along the beveled edge of Mark's vanity. Clara examined the dust and pulled on a tiny silver knob. Sure enough, the drawer was still full. Everything left behind wasn't deemed a necessity. *Like her*. A watch Clara gifted him years ago sat pushed to the back, surrounded by a half-opened pack of Q-Tips and a pair of toenail clippers.

She noticed his old Dopp kit and unzipped the main pocket. Her heart lurched. The backs of her eyes burned and she placed her palms on the cool stone counter. Steam drifted around her from the shower. Clara picked up Mark's travel-sized cologne and the font on the front blurred as unshed tears balanced on her lashes. She was playing with fire. She didn't need to unscrew the top to know how it smelled.

She had washed the sheets a million times the week he moved out. That scent was woven into every good memory between them. Now it lingered behind like an unwelcome guest. The glass vessel made a small clink as it met the marble countertop. Opening the shower door, Clara kept her eyes on the vanity. The steam got thicker and the glass finally fogged. She closed her eyes and let the hot water wash over her salty tears, wondering if her mother-in-law was right. If it would be easier to just pretend the whole thing had never happened.

"Excuse me, Clara? Do you have these zinnias in pink?"

She was still standing outside her car and had barely tied her smock before being bombarded by Kenny and Steve, who were regular customers at Grady's Gardens.

"Uh, yes... We were supposed to get a delivery earlier this week." She grabbed her purse and her coffee, shutting the door with her hip. "Give me just a moment, and I'll check with Eli."

They made their way toward the main entrance. The two men hadn't made it ten feet before they halted at a display of coreopsis and the bickering ensued. Clara found them endearing most days. Occasionally, she overheard their hushed whispers and her ears would burn, catching bits and pieces of gossip, wagering whether she'd ever move out of the *Monroe Mansion.*

"Give me the tag thingy for the orange flowers. THERE. NO. TO YOUR LEFT. NO—YOUR OTHER LEFT—"

"Hold on, give it back! I need to see how much sun they need—"

"Wait, I thought you hated orange."

"Usually orange looks garish, but *these* aren't garish, right? And look, they take full sun."

Clara sipped her coffee and stood in silent observance through her sunglasses. Saturday garden debates and the smell of fertilizer wafting through the air. *Marital bliss.* Kenny loaded up their cart with an array of bold, tropical colors. Clara wondered if her bitterness would ever fade. It'd be nice to see in Technicolor again.

She inserted herself into the squabble. "If it's no trouble, I'm going to head inside. Come on in whenever you're ready and we can check on those zinnias for you."

They nodded in unison. Never missing a beat, they moved on to arguing about planters and potting soil.

Clara ducked out of the rising sun and felt a rush of cool AC as she stepped into the main building of the nursery. The smell of grass seed and bird feed laced the air, and she spotted Eli in his office with the door open, chatting with someone. The customer was sitting with his back to the threshold, and her eyes flitted over the wide span of his shoulders at the top of his chair. The men angled the computer monitor between them, taking turns pointing at the screen. Clara propped her sunglasses on top of her hair, piled into some semblance of a bun.

Sliding her phone from her back pocket, she connected to the sound system Eli had installed a few weeks ago. He'd given her a hard time, teasing about the peace and serenity of nature. But she won him over after playing the greatest hits of the sixties for an entire afternoon. He folded like a cheap suit.

Spotting the raggedy clipboard with her name on it hanging behind the counter, she filtered through her orders for the morning. Clara glanced through the doorway at the workstation Eli had thrown together out in the greenhouse. She was going to need more dirt. Eli and the customer had walked off, taking their discussion outside. Clara tucked the clipboard under her arm and drank a large swig of coffee.

The lazy rhythm of *The Wanderer* started up overhead and she smiled, pushing through the doorway to the greenhouse. Clara surveyed the pots Eli had pulled for her. Some of the inventory was already organized, and she walked back and forth, counting containers of greenery. Clara retrieved a tray of orchids. Several orders were for porch planters, and some were for table arrangements.

She smiled to herself. Every spring, Gloria's creations popped up all over the town. Hanging baskets overflowed outside the shops, and wraparound porches preened with color, waking up from the cold. With Gloria's recent health problems, she had taken Clara under her wing so they could continue to fill orders as business picked up. Double checking her list, Clara grabbed her hat off the old hook by the register and headed out to collect everything else she needed.

∼✦∼

Clara had worked her way pretty far from the greenhouse. She stood squinting down a row of three-gallon boxwoods, thankful she slathered on sunscreen before leaving the house. The dolly was jam-packed. It was going to be a beast to haul back to her workstation.

She noticed Eli and the customer from earlier over by the fountains and water features. *What were they doing?* Maybe he was redoing his entire yard. Maybe he was a designer? It never ceased to amaze her how much money people dropped on outdoor living spaces. From where she was, the two men looked about the same height. Clutching the metal handle of the cart, Clara's eyes lingered. There was something familiar about the way he stood.

Sweat dripped down the nape of Clara's neck. Her mouth felt like gummed up sandpaper. Parking the dolly, she remembered the soil for the planters. *Damn.* She needed to get a move on. Sonny and Brandon could handle delivering the larger items, but Clara wanted to help with the smaller planters herself. She got satisfaction out of making sure everything looked just right upon arrival.

Cutting through the main building, she soaked up as much AC as she could and popped out the side door where Eli kept pallets of dirt, mulch, and gravel. Clara looked around to check for any ripped or damaged bags. She'd learned to use those for the planters and baskets and to save the good bags for the customers. She spotted one in the back buried three layers deep. *Bingo.*

Clara worked methodically, taking her time. A dance of pulling and shoving—like Jenga with moderately higher stakes. She maneuvered it halfway out of the stack and felt soil fall into her boot. Sweat dripped into her eye and she winced. Clara propped her foot up at the base of the pallet for more leverage and pulled hard.

"Need some help?"

A deep voice came from behind, and her arm jerked violently. The front of the bag tore and Clara stumbled, clutching whatever came loose in her arms. She slammed into the body behind her and took them both down somewhere between the pea gravel and red mulch.

"Sir—I am so sorry..."

Clara grimaced as she sat up to assess the damage. The guy had hit the ground awkwardly behind her and her face went up in flames. He had more or less broken their fall when she slammed into him—*clutching a ripped bag of dirt.*

Brushing her hands together, she turned to see if he was okay. Her stomach twisted. He was stretched out on the ground, and with his attention averted, she sat there frozen on her ass. Like a cartoon burglar caught under a spotlight, her eyes darted around, desperate for an escape. As he redirected his focus and looked her straight in the eyes, his gaze narrowed and a small huff of air left his chest.

"Clara Saunders."

His tousled hair was sweaty, and a lock fell to his forehead. She couldn't tell if it was the scorching heat of her embarrassment or the sun beating down, but she couldn't catch her breath. She was parched. Irresponsibly dehydrated.

Clara cleared her throat and moved to stand. "Uh, *Monroe*... It's Monroe now."

"Oh, yeah—sorry. I should know that. I was there, after all." He offered her a hand.

His eyes skimmed over her, and she adjusted her smock. Her humiliation was palpable. The last time she had seen Connor Kent, she was in a wedding dress, marrying Mark.

Clara brushed dirt off her shirt and ran her hands over the backs of her legs. Connor had picked up a backpack and was taking inventory of its contents. Clara noticed his beat-up Chucks, shorts, and faded T-shirt. He wasn't dressed for yard work. Serious customers showed up in long sleeve shirts and dusty work boots. As if he could feel Clara's eyes, he turned to face her, zipping up his backpack.

"No harm done."

"Glad to hear that. Look, I'm really sorry about—" Clara motioned to the debris on the ground.

He put his hand up. "It's fine."

His curtness caught her off guard.

"I was looking for Eli and I saw you. Looked like heavy-duty stuff, so I thought I'd offer a hand is all." At first glance, he appeared friendly, but his words were short.

Questions raced, lighting up the switchboard in her brain. Whatever he was saying began to fade. Of all people—why was *he* here? Didn't he live in Denver? Or was it Chicago? Through her sunglasses, she took inventory. Her eyes flitted over him, scanning in facts. He was tan—*he likes being outdoors*. She could see the flex of a bicep peeking out from his shirt sleeve as he held his backpack. He was lean—*was he a runner*?

He motioned to the building behind them. The corner of his mouth lifted, but his words dissolved in a hum of static, clouding her good manners. She glanced back and forth between his eyes and his lips as he spoke and her robot-brain started smoking. Those damn dimples. Clara glimpsed his hand. No trace of a tan line circling that very symbolic finger. But that didn't *really* mean anything. She, of all people, knew that. Realizing she hadn't heard a word he was saying, she stood mortified—brutally aware that she was staring.

"... And then I saw you, but I didn't realize it was *you*."

Clara paused, blinking several times before speaking. "I'm so sorry Connor, I think I'm just a little light-headed." *Reboot*. "What are you doing... *here*?"

"I'm working with Eli." The cadence of his voice insinuated that he was repeating himself. He seemed... irritated.

"*He's my uncle*... I'm back in town and helping him out."

Clara stared, dumbfounded.

"I was just going to help him with his website, but I realized after I got here that the place could use a little help."

Help? Her stomach tightened.

Connor motioned to the bag in his hands. "Anyway, he mentioned that the new signage should get delivered at the end of the month, but I figured it'd be fine to knock out some shots while I was here for the initial consult."

Photography. Clara nodded her understanding. "Right. Eli has been talking about doing that forever. I totally forgot that you take pictures—"

Connor winced. His lips tensed into a flat line.

Clara dabbed at the sweat on her face. "*Shit.* No—that's not what I meant. I mean, I know you used to take pictures. I guess I just didn't realize you're *still* doing photography."

Seconds ticked by. What she wouldn't give for an oncoming car she could jump in front of.

"I mean, I know you helped our photographer at the wedding—but I didn't know you did it as your *job.*"

Connor straightened his shoulders and sighed—letting Clara make an ass of herself. The sun was insufferable, and so was her very embarrassing attempt at conversation. Sweat dripped down her back. She took a hard pivot.

"So, you're back in Georgia. I could have sworn you were living somewhere else—"

"*Chicago.*" He glanced down at her smock. *Grady's Gardens* was printed in a bright cheery shade of green across her chest and his eyes skipped up to meet hers. "I moved back to be closer to Eli and Gloria." His expression softened.

Clara shifted her weight. Eli was his uncle. His *family*. A million more questions washed over her. An apology sat lodged in the back of her throat. Just as she was about to speak, Eli popped out the side door.

"Ah! There you are! Connor, I should have introduced you to Clara. She is my right-hand gal. Sometimes I think she knows the place better than I do." He turned to her with a warm expression. "Clara, this is Connor, my nephew."

An awkwardness floated between the three of them. Clara offered Eli a small smile. She wanted to erase the annoyance that tinged Connor's eyes. *Had he always been this surly?* Eli continued to glance back and forth between them. Connor cleared his throat. "You know, Clara and I actually went to college together. We were just talking about how I shot her wedding—"

Surprise washed over Eli's face. "I didn't realize you knew Mark's wife."

The air left Clara's body.

Connor shrugged his broad shoulders, a look of indifference in his expression.

Hearing her name slip from Connor's mouth had sent her into another trance. A portal to a past life. He looked like a sexy, angsty ray of sunshine. Clara was sunburned with dirt stains on her ass. *And* she had offended him.

"Ex-wife." She swallowed thickly. "I mean... we're *separated.*" Clara's pulse thrummed as their gazes held.

Eli's eyes widened and jumped to Clara's. "*Right*—I'm sorry."

Connor kept his expression steady. He glanced at Clara with—what was that? *Pity?*

She looked down at her shoes. She couldn't bear to see it. "Well, I'm going to grab whatever is left of this potting soil and I'm heading inside. Connor, it was nice running into you." Clara motioned a small, informal wave in his general direction. Keeping her gaze averted, she slid past him.

There was a brief pause. She could feel his eyes on her. "Yeah, you too."

The second Clara dodged inside, she locked herself in the restroom and splashed her face with cold water. She looked up in the mirror, little water droplets racing down the strands of hair that had escaped from her hat. She was beet red, with remnants of dirt smudged all over her clothes. *Excellent.* Between the ratty hat and sweat stains, she was a far cry from the girl she used to be.

The rest of the afternoon flew by. Clara chained herself to the workbench. And by eleven o'clock, everything had been loaded up and delivered. Gail Walker was delighted with the large concrete planters bursting with color and trailing vines, along with the six orchid centerpieces she had ordered for her charity luncheon.

"Everything looks beautiful, Clara. You guys always do such a wonderful job." Mrs. Walker continued to gush over the flowers and complain about the catering while digging out tip money from her purse. Clara felt her phone vibrate in her back pocket. She said her goodbyes and handed the cash to Sonny and Brandon, the two guys who did all the heavy lifting and drove the nursery's delivery van. They loaded up as Clara slid into the passenger seat and pulled out her phone.

RYAN: How's the sugar daddy?

Clara smiled to herself.

CLARA: Just finishing up a delivery. What's up?

RYAN: Dinner and drinks tonight?

She hesitated, hearing the faint sound of her fuzzy robe calling her name.

RYAN: MARGS.AND.CHEESE.DIP.

Her fate was sealed.

"Hold up. So how do you know this guy?"

It was exceptionally crowded, even for a Saturday night. The Mexican restaurant was a dive that Ryan and Clara had discovered one day on a lunch-break excursion. He knew her rule, understanding that if they ever went out, it had to be anywhere but Silas Grove.

The waiter arrived with their second round of margaritas and they shuffled the plates and chip basket, accommodating the booze. A band played in the next room and Ryan looked at her, waiting. Clara licked salt off the rim of her glass before a wave of sticky sweet slush skated over her tongue.

She took a deep breath, raising her voice over the music. "In college, we had this big group of friends... I could have sworn he majored in *business* or something..." The vinyl booth stuck to her skin as she shifted. "Definitely not *photography*."

The tequila had worked its magic, and she found herself thinking about Connor's lips. She wondered what his drink of choice was. Her memories were filled with tailgates and kegs galore. Years of innocent flirting. She sucked back another swig. *The lake.*

"What—so you guys were just friends? When was the last time you even saw him? The wedding?"

Clara stared down into the chip bowl, willing it to tell her the future. "Something like that."

Ryan scooped a chip into the cheese dip and quickly dunked it in salsa. He chewed and gave Clara a pointed look. He wasn't buying it.

"Well... He wasn't invited as a friend. We had a falling out." She watched as Ryan's eyebrow lifted. "I mean—*he* had a falling out." She nodded emphatically. "*With the group.*" The band changed songs and Clara averted her gaze, observing as couples swayed across the dance floor.

"Anyway, I have no idea how it happened, but he showed up at our wedding with the photographer we booked." She winced.

"That's awkward as hell," Ryan shouted across the table.

One of their phones started buzzing. Ryan mouthed an apology and plugged his ear while answering the call. Clara sat back with her drink, goosebumps appearing along her arms. She thought back to that carefree time of her life. When her only problem was pulling an all-nighter before finals or picking out an outfit during football season. When her entire world revolved around Mark.

Her smile fell. Connor seemed like a completely different person. He had always been so carefree. She remembered him painting himself from head to toe for every game, dressing like a lunatic. He was always flashing those dimples. Their conversation from that morning crossed her mind, and she cringed.

People clapped for the band and they announced that they'd be back after a quick break. A playlist started and Clara rested her chin in her hand.

"Yeah, just send me the link... No, you are not bothering me. We're getting Mexican food." A smile stretched across Ryan's mouth. "Whatever. Bye"

Clara grinned from across the table.

Ryan dug around in the chip basket, avoiding her gaze. "Jonah can't remember the name of the empanada place we went to last time I visited."

She nodded her head, taking a sip of her drink.

"He said I need to eat something other than nachos." Ryan waved his hand. "He's ridiculous. What were we talking about?"

Clara sighed. "I believe your exact words were '*that's awkward as hell*.'"

"Right... So what happened at the wedding?"

Clara sank against the booth, glancing at the ceiling. "It was a blur. I remember being surprised to see him, you know—" She tucked her hair behind her ear. "Because we weren't really friends anymore." She watched as Ryan checked his phone, smiling before replying to a text.

"Back up." Ryan set his phone down, catching her eye. "There's something you're not telling me."

The waitress arrived with their dinner, and Clara breathed a sigh of relief. They did another dance of rearranging the table before Ryan glared at her from his seat.

She sighed. "We kissed once."

Ryan sat up straight, a smirk stretching across his lips. "*Oh hot damn*. Keep going."

Clara shook her head, scowling. "It was a million years ago. We were really drunk." She touched the rim of her glass, flakes of salt falling to the table. "I doubt he'd even remember it." Her smile faded and she raised her drink to her lips.

Ryan dragged the chip basket to his side, shoveling it down like popcorn. His eyes held hers. "Do you remember it?"

She swallowed the last of her margarita. Clara bit the inside of her lip, exhaling. She nodded, dropping her hands to her lap.

Debauchery shone in Ryan's eyes. "It was good, huh?"

She twisted the hem of her shorts under the table. She glanced over, watching as the band returned to the stage. The music cued up and Ryan followed her gaze, annoyed by the disruption. Memories flooded and Clara breathed deep. Peppermint and heat. Loud music and dancing in the dark. Connor's hands over her dress, pressing her against the wall.

Her lips parted.

"*Shit.*" Ryan fell back against the booth, chip bowl depleted.

The haze cleared and Clara blinked, oblivious.

He motioned to the look on her face, his smirk pulling into a very dangerous grin. "It must have been really fucking good."

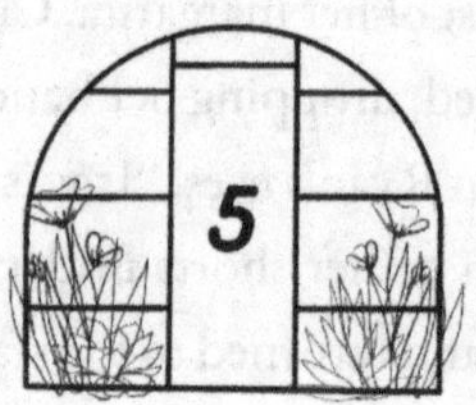

Weeks stretched by with unremarkable regularity. Clara woke every day, drove to a job that she hated, and came home every night to an empty house. Ryan and his mom had gone away for a trip to Palm Springs, so Clara was left to stare at his cubicle, awaiting his return. It was the first time in their six months of working together that they'd been apart, and she felt his absence like a giant gaping hole.

Before the separation, she and Mark had lots of friends in town. Once the marriage was officially on the rocks, she found it difficult to spend time with any of them. Turned out no one was surprised by Mark's indiscretions, which made her feel impossibly alone. As if it were her fault that she married him. *Maybe it was.*

Her only solace was the garden center—but even there, things had been unusually quiet. Up until now, she had been busy filling special orders, but as spring stretched into summer, customers retreated from the heat. Leaning across the register, Clara frowned. If things got any worse, she'd have to consider working more days in The Bug Zapper. What it lacked in zest, it offered in pay.

She drummed her fingers along the counter, staring at the small cluster of framed photos that hung by the front door. How many times had she looked at them and never knew Eli was Connor's uncle? Now, when she walked past, she couldn't help but steal a glance. She particularly liked the one of Connor climbing the magnolia just out front. Eli posed beneath him with silver touching his temples, sporting the same wide smile he wore every day.

Connor was all string bean limbs and freckles. Several baby teeth were missing and his haircut was in the shape of a bowl. Clara reached over, straightening a row of wildflower seed packets on display, and pushed back from the register.

Eli had asked Clara to man the main building as he and Connor took on repairs day after day. Which meant she was chained to this very spot. Front and center. Today, Connor had been with Eli all morning, discussing the website layout and tossing around ideas as they replaced the ancient irrigation lines in the greenhouse.

She found herself transfixed, watching for any sign of movement through the doorway. Any indication that Connor was standing next to her workbench, near her leather gloves, touching her pruners. She bit the inside of her cheek.

After rearranging the wind chimes for the millionth time, Clara let out a dramatic sigh. Moving to hover by a shelf of patio couch cushions, she glanced at Eli's office door. They were inside, chatting, and she studied Connor from behind. He was seated in front of Eli's desk and today he wore a hat, worn-out T-shirt, and shorts. Same Chucks as usual. Just as her mind began to wander, Eli erupted in laughter.

Knocking lightly on the open door, she popped her head in. *Just be cool.*

"Hey—if it's okay, I'm going to run out and pick up lunch real quick... Y'all need anything?"

Their laughter tapered off, and Eli smiled at her from behind his desk. Connor didn't even look up and instead checked his phone. He scratched his stubbled jaw and turned his baseball cap backward. Her stomach did a flip-flop.

Eli chimed in, "Sounds great! Where are you headed?"

"The Slice." Clara's eyes darted over Connor. "It's a sandwich place over on—"

"I know what *The Slice* is." His expression shifted.

She clamped her mouth shut and took a breath, facing Eli.

With a tilt of his head, Eli observed his nephew. Confused, he turned to Clara and rattled off his order. "I'll take my usual—Italian sub, extra banana peppers."

Clara nodded and glanced back at Connor. She waited as the seconds rolled by. Connor finally glanced up at Eli and looked over at Clara.

"Oh... You don't have to buy me lunch."

"I'm not buying you lunch... I mean, I'm just picking up *my* lunch and figured I'd let Eli know I'd be out in case the phone rings or something." He continued to stare up at her as she rambled. "You could just give me some cash and tell me your order. Or you could pay me later—"

"All right, then." He reached for his wallet. "I'll take a turkey and cheese on white."

Clara paused. "So just turkey... and cheese... and bread." She furrowed her brow. "Nothing else?"

Connor shrugged. "Yeah, I know, kinda boring."

"Do you want it toasted?"

"Nope, cold is good."

"So… just a cold, dry sandwich with no condiments." She looked at him deadpan. *Yikes.*

His eyes narrowed, and he gave her a curt nod. She was judging him for sure.

And with that, she reached forward and took Connor's credit card, sliding it into her pocket.

"Be back in a bit."

The old deli was just five minutes down the road from the nursery. Clara walked in and heard the chime of the bell perched above the door. The red and white checkered floor was slightly sticky underfoot and the fluorescent lights lit up the chalkboard menu behind the counter. Clara was thankful for the slow trickle of air conditioning.

"Hey, Mike—I've got three orders. An Italian with extra banana peppers, a Reuben, and a turkey on white."

Mike punched in the orders. "What else on the turkey?"

"Oh! Cheese—I forgot the cheese."

The old phone behind the counter rang. It was avocado green, and even the sound itself had some age to it. The chord was tangled so tight, Clara doubted anyone could successfully lift it from the receiver without ripping the entire thing off the wall. Mike looked up. "What kind of cheese?"

Shit.

What kind of cheese? Connor didn't say. Five other customers waited behind Clara. The lunch rush was picking up. She panicked and picked the most boring cheese that came to mind.

"American."

Mike tried to hide his disappointment, but Clara swore she clocked a frown.

"Anything else on the turkey? Do you want it toasted?" The phone continued to ring, and he turned, glaring over his shoulder.

"Nope. *Cold*."

Mike grimaced. Clara tried not to smile.

"$24.25. Right now we're *cash only*." Sensing her confusion, he pointed to the little paper sign on top of the card reader.

OUT OF ORDER

Double shit.

Clara dug around in her purse. She had planned on picking up the tab for Eli because she owed him, but she panicked, hoping she had enough to cover the rest. She thumbed through her driver's license and a punch card for a coffee shop that had closed two years ago. Someone cleared their throat behind her and her stomach dropped.

Coins clattered to the counter and heat rushed to her face. Piecemealing a wad of cash and a quarter, she let out a sigh of relief, pushing the pile of money toward Mike. The line behind her had doubled in size. As he handed Clara her change, he shoved a to-go bag in front of her.

"Have a good one. NEXT!"

By the time Clara got back to the nursery, Eli and Connor weren't in the office anymore. They were over near the garden sculptures and patio furniture outside. Eli waved her over, and they took a seat at one of the modern wrought-iron tables under an awning. Clara handed the bag of food to Eli and plopped down, starved and sweaty.

"Sorry that took so long. I got stuck behind a utility truck coming back." She sighed. "Oh... and the card reader was out of order." She slid Connor's credit card over to him without further explanation.

"Wait—so what do I owe you?"

Clara kept her eyes on Eli as he opened the bag. "Don't worry about it. Really."

Eli interrupted. "Well, I hope you didn't pay for the whole meal... Mike shorted us a sandwich."

Clara's eyes widened as she shook her head in disbelief. "There's no way—I was so...*specific* when I placed the order." A flush crept up to her cheeks. "I'll run back over and pick up whatever we're missing." She quickly glanced at Connor and started to stand.

Eli motioned for her to sit back down as he stood. "I'll call Mike right now, so he knows he owes us the next time we order from there. You two stay here and eat." When he walked away, Clara and Connor looked at each other and then down at the two wrapped sandwiches on the table.

Clara's stomach grumbled loudly, and the corner of Connor's mouth lifted. *A sign of life.* They opened the sandwiches and discovered his was the one that got left behind. Doing a little ceremonious dance in her seat, she peeled back the foil wrap to reveal a toasted, melted, salty confection designed by the gods. She took one half of the Reuben in her hands and hovered, preparing for the mess that was bound to ensue.

Clara sank her teeth into the rye. *"Damn—that's good."*

She glanced over at Connor, who was watching her. She could see the amusement behind his sunglasses. Deflecting, she motioned to the lunch in front of him with her elbow. "Aren't you hungry?" Connor looked at her mouth, undoubtedly covered in 1,000 Island. *Flip-flop.*

The humor in his eyes faded. "To be honest... I'm not sure I'm a fan of *extra banana peppers*."

Clara chewed thoughtfully. Surely he was starving. He and Eli had been there since before eight o'clock. Clara had been close to gnawing her hand off when she got stuck behind that utility truck.

"Well, I agree that extra banana peppers can be a little... *aggressive,* I suppose." Before she knew what she was doing, she plucked a napkin out of the paper sack and slid the other half of her sandwich across the table. He lifted his hands up in a small gesture of defense.

"No, Clara. That's your lunch."

She wiped her mouth and insisted. "Connor. I don't think you understand the magnitude of what's happening here in front of you."

Connor ceased to protest. The moment grew serious.

"You see... This is my *favorite* sandwich. It's the best Reuben within a fifty-mile radius. The ratio of meat-to-kraut-to-bread is perfection. The 1,000 Island isn't overpowering, and the bread is *magical.*" Her sunglasses were slipping, and she lifted her chin, holding his gaze. "Also, the pastrami is paper thin, which is a work of art in and of itself."

Connor's reserve cracked. He broke into a smile and looked down, uncertain.

"I'm offering to share it with you."

With dramatic resignation, he studied Clara's form. She had her elbows up on the table and she sat hunched over. She was committed to the meal, but not the mess. Leveling her with an equally serious look, Connor raised both arms as if to force his make-believe cuffs back from his wrists.

He inched forward in his seat, caught her eye, and took a huge bite. Clara stared, captivated. Through a mouth full of food, he let out a deep hum of approval.

Clara tipped her head back and laughed. Meeting his gaze, her breath caught. A relaxed smile played at his lips, and his dimples deepened.

Flip-flop.

Clara looked down at her lap and sucked in a breath. Scrunching up her dirty napkin and the foil wrapper, she tossed them both into the empty paper bag. Clara cleared her throat and sunk more comfortably into her seat. She watched as he scarfed down the rest of her favorite sandwich. "So... you like it."

She saw him pause briefly. Without looking at her, Connor smiled to himself and nodded.

"What would you have done? Just starved all afternoon while Eli and I ate right in front of you?"

He wiped his mouth. "I'm sure I've got a granola bar or something in my car. Maybe even in my backpack." Connor cleaned his hands as much as possible before tossing everything into the sack, along with Clara's trash.

"It's no big deal. A lot of times when I'm out shooting, I just eat whenever I get a chance." He smiled at her. "It's more about necessity, not indulgence."

Clara looked at him, incredulous. Connor laughed. "If I'm out hiking and something catches my interest, I don't like to stop unless I have to. You learn to be patient."

Clara pondered aloud. "So... you're taking photos for things like *National Geographic*?"

A burst of laughter escaped his chest. "No—not quite. Web design and marketing are my main gig. As far as photography goes...

the stuff I actually get paid for is more commercial. The trips I take are really just for me."

"I see." Clara looked over at a couple walking toward a section of ornamental grasses. "So, you don't normally shoot weddings?"

Connor's smile flattened. He didn't answer right away, and he shifted, crossing his arms at his chest. "You know, that was my first trip home after I moved to Chicago. I came back to see my family and pick up the rest of my stuff when Sam called me about the job."

Silence stretched between them. Memories crept in. Like a cloud crowding out the sun. She thought of her wedding day and how happy she had been. *And so incredibly stupid*. She looked down, pressing her fingers against the hot iron beneath her.

"I heard about what happened. With you and Mark."

Clara's head popped up.

"I mean, I had heard about it before the other day. You know..." He glanced her way. "With the dirt."

"Oh." Clara nodded, not quite sure what to say. Her face warmed, his gaze steady on her.

"Eli told me about a girl who was working here at the nursery... but I didn't know it was you." Through his sunglasses, Clara felt his expression soften. "I'm sorry it happened the way it did. You know, you guys splitting up." Their eyes held.

Clara's brows knitted together. A huff of breath shot past her lips and she shook her head. "I'm not."

Now it was Connor's turn to look away.

Thunder rolled overhead, and Clara looked up to the sky. A breeze passed over the table, pushing the paper bag over the edge. Connor reached out, crumpling it before it fell.

Her gaze dropped to his. His mouth was set into a hard line, and he looked pained.

"You're better off, you know."

Clara felt her pulse quicken as the air, thick with humidity, continued to push and pull around them.

Raindrops pelted the table. They grabbed their stuff and dashed for the main building, weaving between rows and rows of plants. Reaching the door, their clothes were soaked. The air conditioner was on full blast and cold air skated over them. Clara recognized the song playing overhead, and a smile broke across her face.

Catching his breath and taking off his hat, Connor stood in confusion. "What's so funny?"

The storm had darkened the windows, and rain echoed beneath the tin roof. Clara ran her hands down her bare arms. Even though it was summer, she was chilled to the bone.

"Eli." She smiled, rolling her eyes. "He loves this song."

As if on cue, Eli hung up the phone at the front register and hurried over to the sound system, turning the volume all the way up. Music poured through the speakers, enveloping them in the dark, empty building.

Clara was laughing and shaking her head, already swaying to the familiar beat. Connor watched as Clara transformed in front of him. Her hair was soaked from the rain and her wet shirt clung to her.

"It's pretty clever."

Connor's eyes jumped to hers. "What is?" Her smile was bright and had reached her eyes. She looked like a different person.

She pointed up. "The song."

Eli summoned them both. Connor hung back, watching as Clara danced to the other side of the room. He'd tried to dry off when they dove inside, and when he turned, he'd seen her. Drenched and beaming, Clara had looked up at him and it was like the world stopped. Watching Eli with Clara—they looked like two old friends. Something constricted in his chest.

The phone rang again and Eli reached to grab it off the hook. The music continued to blare and Clara boldly sang and danced alone. She was completely content. Like Connor wasn't even there, mesmerized by every single thing about her.

He steadied himself against the door and listened. The words told a tale of missed opportunities and cheating. About second chances and not realizing what you had all along. Connor's smile fell. Through the glass, he saw his car parked at the far end of the lot. Fishing his keys from his pocket, he could hear the heavy sound of rain falling at his back. Clara's laughter resounded in the empty building, intertwining with the music and the lines of the song. His curiosity piqued.

Connor thought of the droplets on her arms. He wanted to feel the texture of her chilled skin against his lips. He thought of her breasts pressed against her wet shirt and his grip tightened on the metal handle. Just then, she turned, catching his eye. Her gaze was like warm honey and everything slowed, suspended in a lazy golden sweetness, beckoning him from across the room. Sucking in a breath, Connor shifted and pushed out into the rain.

Clara got home from the nursery and yanked off her wet clothes. She showered and pulled on her favorite pair of briefs, sweatpants, and an oversized long sleeve shirt. It was June, but Clara kept the air conditioning at a crisp seventy degrees. With a sheet mask balanced on her face, she pulled open the freezer drawer, feeling around for a fresh container of Rocky Road.

Checking her phone, she noticed a new voicemail from Bonnie. Clara glanced up, catching her reflection in the decorative mirror on the opposite wall. She looked ridiculous. Like a modern Mrs. Doubtfire. She hit play and her mother-in-law's voice filled the kitchen.

"Clara, dear, Mark says you just need some time to *yourself*... but don't you think it would be best if Mark was home with you?" Clara's nostrils flared and she eyed the display of porcelain plates adorning the wall in front of her. *Monroe family heirlooms.* "I think it'd be just lovely if you two could make amends and put this little *thing* behind you before you do something you'll regret. Hope you're faring well at the house by yourself. Speak to you soon, honey. Bye-bye."

Spoon hanging out of her mouth, she hit delete and trudged to the living room. Clara sank to the couch and looked around, realizing how much of their home wasn't actually hers. She glanced down at the blanket stretched across her lap.

The chenille throw wasn't even her choice. Everything screamed *Bonnie*. With a newfound fury, she began chiseling away at the pint and turned on the TV. Sarah Jessica Parker's face filled the screen and Clara smiled, dropping the remote. *Sex and the City* reruns were her kryptonite.

Bonnie obviously still thought this whole situation was her fault. Like she was punishing Mark. *Was she punishing him?* Clara drew in a meditative breath while excavating a marshmallow chunk lodged in the icy cardboard. If she was truly over him, she *should* be seeing other people. Shoveling a heaping scoop into her mouth, she scanned the room. Small clusters of dishes and cups had taken over all the horizontal surfaces, and the shades were drawn.

Chocolate ice cream coated her tongue, and she studied the TV screen as the four best friends crowded together at a diner in the middle of the night. Clara swallowed past the knot in her throat, pressing herself deeper into the couch, feeling like a lonely speck of dust.

She sighed. These were the friends she wanted. Glancing over at the big leather chair in the corner, her stomach lurched. The backs of her eyes burned and Clara sat up straight.

She supposed Ryan was kind of already her Carrie. Playful and full of life. She sniffled. Miranda would kick her in the ass and berate her with how men were actually obsolete. Her eyes widened as breathy moans floated from the screen, and her spoon scratched at the bottom of the container. She glanced down in disappointment.

Savoring the very last bite, she poked her arm out of the blanket, propping the empty carton on the cushion beside her.

If Clara was honest with herself, it had been a while since she'd had sex. Like—*good sex*. Mark had been her first, *and only*. When they were in college, she had felt so close to him. Her heart would race every time she saw him, and when they fought, she felt like her insides were in knots for days on end. There was this passion—always desperate to make up so they could tear each other's clothes off. Over the years, everything between them had become so mechanical. Like he was on autopilot. Like their life was on autopilot.

She *should* put herself out there. She glanced around at the clutter, and a frown pulled at the corner of her mouth. *Fine.* She'd clean the house first, *then* put herself out there. Five episodes in, Clara had gone horizontal, fixated on the screen, watching as Samantha and Carrie debriefed after their night on the town. Over the phone, Samantha staunchly advocated that Carrie try face-sitting *immediately*.

Wrapping herself in the throw, Clara laughed alone in the empty house. She needed a Samantha in her life. Someone to encourage a little mischief. She pondered. Maybe Ryan was actually more of a Samantha than a Carrie.

Wait.

Did that mean *she* was the Carrie? Mr. Big flashed before her eyes. The never-ending back and forth. All the tears.

Barf.

And they ended up together, even though he treated her like shit.

Double barf.

Throwing off the blanket, Clara stood. She wasn't Carrie. Snatching the empty ice cream container from the couch, Clara gathered all the trash and dirty dishes from the living room. She hoisted them onto the kitchen island and scoffed. Mark was *not* Mr. Big.

She dug her phone out from the pocket of her sweatpants and pulled up her never-ending playlist. Primal drums and rhythmic melodies blasted out, fueling Clara's animosity. Sliding everything into the sink, she turned the water to scalding and furiously scrubbed at a week's worth of cemented crud.

She was *not* Carrie. She had her life together. She didn't keep sweaters in her stove. And—unpopular opinion—she had always thought that Carrie should have picked Aiden. Clara yanked the trashcan over to the fridge and began chucking old takeout into the bin. Sniffing a questionable box of Chinese food, Clara gagged.

A knock rapped at the front door, and Clara jumped. She checked her phone. Ten thirty p.m. She slinked along the wall and made her way to the front of the house. Peeking out the blinds and onto the porch, she heard the thud of boots. *A man.*

"Clara!"

Damn.

Clara sank out of view from the window and touched the mask on her face. She looked down at her grubby clothes—no bra.

Double damn.

"Clara—turn that shit off!"

More furious knocking.

What the hell was he doing here? She peeled off the mask, smoothing out the hyaluronic goo. She grabbed the giant claw from her hair and gave it a quick shake. Maybe she looked dewy and radiant. She bit the inside of her cheek. She'd bet twenty dollars that she looked like she'd dunked her face in *Vaseline* and stuck her finger in a socket.

"Clara!"

Make it $100.

She took a breath and listened to Florence wail her heart out. So much soul. So much power. Clara drew in a breath and threw her shoulders back. He was not going to see her squirm. She strutted toward the door, and in a split second, ditched the baggy sweatpants. Panicking, she chucked them in the decorative basket, leaving her in briefs and the oversized long sleeve that hung to her thighs. Steadying herself, she whipped open the door in mock surprise.

"Okay! Okay! I hear you!"

Mark had his forearm up on the doorframe, putting them face to face. His cocky smirk was laced with fake irritation. His smile dropped.

"*Jesus,* Clara. When did you start answering the door for strangers in your underwear?"

Perfection.

"Well, Mark, I don't typically answer the door like this. I was cleaning and must have lost track of time." She looked up at him. "I heard someone beating down the door, so I came to see what the fuss was about."

Mark stepped forward and pushed past her. He walked into the foyer and glanced around. His eyes flitted over a box in the corner with his name scrawled across the side in bold, black writing. He looked out of place. What used to be their home had begun to shift. Every day that went by without him was like the universe removing him from their house, atmospherically. She hadn't really felt it until now. The raging, carnal music only magnified how unwelcome he was in her space. Scowling, he dragged in a breath. He felt it too.

"Can you turn that off?!"

Clara rolled her eyes. She marched past him to the kitchen. Spotting her phone by the sink, she hit pause. The drums silenced, and all that was left was tension filling the room like the stink of putrid takeout. Clara turned and grabbed a glass of water.

"Want something to drink?"

"Yeah. You got any beer?"

"Sorry, I don't." Clara smiled at him. "I've got some tea, though. And a never-ending supply of ice cold H2O."

Mark twisted his face and leaned his hip into the counter beside her. He was slick. His clothes were tidy, like he had just stepped out of a magazine. Never a hair out of place. Feeling brave, she turned to face him head-on. She noted the five o'clock shadow that dusted his jaw and winced.

The man had a chin like a superhero. She had always loved the icy blue of his eyes, but seeing them now, they looked cold and lifeless. Like a demonic husky. Even in all of her discontent, Clara could barely look at him. It was like staring into a fucking spotlight.

His ego had always been out of control. When he wanted to, he had a way of making you feel like you were the only person in the entire world. It was a sad realization the day she tried to remember the last time he had made her feel that way. He was studying her now. The silence stretched.

Clara could feel Mark's eyes on her, starting from the tips of her toes and wandering up her legs. Part of her felt self-conscious. He had obviously moved on. The other part of her, the cocky one, felt like he needed to see what he was leaving behind. Focusing on his shoes, she sent a wish out to the universe. She hoped, spitefully, that he was as lonely as she was. Who was she kidding? *It was a hex.*

"You know, your mom called tonight." Her eyes caught his. "She still thinks I'm the one to blame."

Mark pushed away from the counter and walked around the kitchen toward the living room. His eyes landed on an empty stretch of wall where one of their wedding photos had hung. "Is that right?"

The smell of his cologne swirled around them, and she grimaced. It used to be hypnotizing. Now, she couldn't remember why. "It's like she's just choosing to completely ignore the fact that *you're* the one who left."

With his back to her, Clara watched as he ran his hand through his hair. She followed, desperate to voice the injustice chasing her like the plague. "*You're* the one who moved on."

Mark stepped into the room and just as she gained momentum, he turned, sliding into his favorite leather chair. She watched, heart pounding in her oversized shirt. Crossing her arms over her chest, she stood as he folded his hands behind his head.

Mark grinned. His wide, arrogant smile lit up like a Cheshire cat. Like he hadn't heard a damn word. "Come to think of it... a water would be great."

Clara clenched her fists and bit the inside of her cheek. Turning on her heel, she strode from the room. Grabbing a glass from the cupboard, she pressed the button on the front of the fridge. Ice clinked, and she flipped up the tap at the sink, water shooting out from the faucet. As it neared the rim, she moved, letting the cool stream run over her wrist.

She closed her eyes and repeated every mantra she could conjure. *You are in control of your feelings. You are in control of how you react to the world around you.* She inhaled, letting her lungs swell with a stilled serenity. *He's a piece of shit and you do not want him back.*

God. She wished she was wearing pants.

Clara walked back toward Mark, handing him the glass. She shifted her fingers, dodging his touch. Propping his feet up on the ottoman, he set his water down without a coaster. Clara moved to the open entryway and leaned against the threshold, refusing to sit. Her proximity was just out of reach, but close enough that she hovered over him.

"So, how is the flavor of the week? Or have you moved on to another victim already?"

Ignoring her, he focused on his hand wrapped around the water glass. Finally looking up, he flashed a devastating smile. "What makes you so sure there's someone else?"

Her heart twisted. Clara's gaze narrowed, and she shrugged, casually. "I just assume old habits die hard."

Mark laughed. "You don't know what you're talking about." His wet fingers were now brushing back and forth across the soft leather of the chair. The hair on the back of her neck stood. "Clara—*honey*, there isn't anyone else. Not really."

The lie was bold. Like a slap across the face. Between the cheating, the blaming, and the gaslighting, Clara was incensed. She had been caught in a whirlwind of shit ever since Mark walked out and everyone in their life wanted to point the finger at her. He had said he needed space, but deep down, she knew he was sleeping around.

Their *friends* judged her for marrying him in the first place. And her mother-in-law accused her of kicking her beloved son out of their home. What Bonnie didn't know was that Mark had left long ago. His physical presence had just been a place holder. A cardboard cutout for a husband. The heavy smell of his cologne permeated the sanctity of the home Clara had been forced to create for herself—*alone*. She wanted to scream.

"You really must think a lot of yourself... showing up unannounced. I could have had *company*."

Mark straightened. Putting his feet down on the ground, his eyes locked with hers. "Yeah—*right*."

"I told you," Clara pushed her hair from her face. "I don't typically answer the door in my underwear for *strangers*."

Her insinuation hung in the air. Mark sat staring, the rise and fall of his chest quickened as he tensed his jaw. Satisfied, Clara moved from the wall. "It's getting late. I think it might be best if you get going—"

Mark's hand shot out from the chair, and his fingers clamped around her wrist. Yanking her down, she landed hard in his lap. Clara pushed at him with her free hand and tried to stand. His grip tightened, his face only inches from hers. A smirk pulled at his lips.

"Who are you opening that door for, Clara?"

The smug son of a bitch. She jerked her arms. Her confusion dissolved. She was pissed. Like a bout of rough-housing that had quickly gone south. "Mark, what's wrong with you?! You're *hurting* me—"

Still holding her wrist, he slid his other hand to her waist, locking her tight against him. "No one comes into this house. Do you understand?"

Panic mounted, and she sucked in a breath. Clara shoved at Mark's hand at her hip "You can't tell me what to do—"

Her movements became frantic as the tension escalated. His lips came down on hers and she flinched, turning away. His stubble scratched her lips and his cologne turned sour. She was trapped. He was never going to let her go. Twisting hard, Mark loosened his hold, and she elbowed him with all her strength. His grip released and Clara fell out of his embrace, scrambling to her feet. She wiped her mouth, staring as the pattern on the rug blurred below them, fury coursing through her body. "Sign the fucking papers."

Shoving a hand through her hair, she marched through the foyer and ripped open the door. "Sign the papers and you can kick me out if you want." Clara listened as Mark slowly rose. "Take what you came for and leave. *Now*."

Blood rushed in her ears as the heavy thud of his boots moved closer, heat radiating off his skin. Halting in front of her, he turned. She stared at the ground, drawing in a breath. Mark leaned in and she turned her cheek, staring at the staircase. His breath rustled against the shell of her ear. "Be careful what you wish for."

The second he passed through the doorway, Clara turned the deadbolt, the sound reverberating in the base of her spine. She looked at the stack of boxes, and her chest heaved. He hadn't taken a single thing. She turned off all the lights and made her way upstairs. Stunned, Clara washed her face and brushed her teeth in a haze.

She traced her fingers down the wall, killing the overhead light. Her hands were shaking. Pulling back the covers, tears dripped down the collar of her shirt. She needed a distraction. Something to calm her nerves and soothe the pain in her chest. She crawled into bed and buried herself under layers of blankets—like a fortress from the outside.

Clara reached for her phone and turned out the lamp on her bedside table. From the glow of her screen, she pressed play. The melody picked up where it had left off, resounding in the safety of her bedroom. Florence's voice no longer sounded like a battle cry. It sounded broken.

Under the numbing weight of loneliness, Clara began to accept that she had brought this pain upon herself. Big, hot, salty tears dripped from between her lashes, rolling down her cheeks and into her hair. Clara twisted onto her side and away from Mark's half of the bed. She couldn't stand the thought of him. Not here. Not tonight. Not ever.

Pressing her face into a cool, dry spot on her pillow, she gasped. Her eyes clenched shut, and she exhaled, hearing the sound of the wind in her breath as it passed over her lips. Over and over, she concentrated on the swell of her lungs as her pulse steadied. Behind her eyelids, the ridgeline came to view. She stepped up to the edge of the cliff and looked out into the distance. The breeze rustled her hair. The sun pushed through the clouds overhead. Clara placed her hand over her heart and swore to herself that she'd never go back. She whispered the promise out loud.

She was not a Carrie.

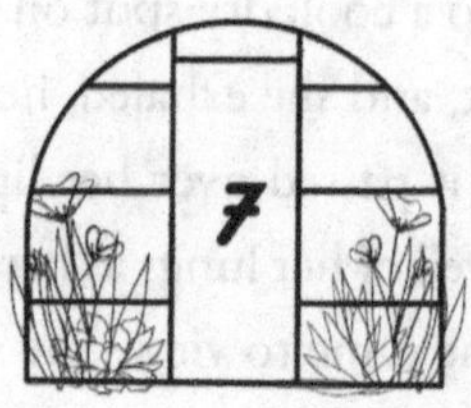

"Damn, girl. You look like shit."

Clara kept her head down as she sank into her cubicle next to Ryan. God, was she thankful he was back. Not so thankful for the brutal honesty.

"Oh, Ryan. I missed you, too!" Clara clasped her hands together and turned to him with mock enthusiasm and a huge, cheesy grin.

"Don't mistake me. I *missed* you. I *missed* you like crazy." He threw his shoulders back and hushed his voice. "I almost murdered Trish."

He reserved referring to his mother by her first name for the direst of occasions. "I'll have you know she lured me on that vacation under false pretenses. Once we got there, she not only had me schlepping *all* the luggage, *and* all the shopping bags, *but*—she ditched me for *a man* she met through an *online dating site!*" The last bit rushed out of his mouth in a screech as he turned to power on his computer.

Clara's puffy, red-rimmed eyes just about fell out of her head. "*No.*"

"*Yes.*"

"Trish... is seeing someone?"

"She has taken a lover... apparently." Ryan was typing on his keyboard and rolled his eyes for dramatic effect.

Clara heard her phone chime twice from the pocket of her purse.

Matching Ryan's disdain, she took an exaggerated breath. "So... did you check out this... *lover?*"

Ryan shivered, feigning disgust. "*Ew. No.* I don't want to know anything about my mom's lover... I'd rather die."

Stifling a smile, Clara patted him on the arm. "Oh, don't be so judgy. Maybe Trish is on to something. Maybe a *lover* is actually what I need."

A tiny grin pulled at his mouth. "A *lover* you say?"

Clara wiggled her eyebrows at him, attempting to curb the awkwardness of Ryan's failed vacation. She heard her phone ding twice more.

"Well... what on Earth has inspired you to take a *lover?*"

Leaning over and digging her phone out of her bag, she sat up and snapped her fingers, remembering her epiphany. "Hold that thought. I have a very serious, life-altering question to ask you."

"Well *shit,*" Ryan swiveled his chair so he was facing Clara, providing her with his undivided attention. "*Go.*"

"Am I..." Clara bit her lip, nervous to even utter the thought out loud. "Am I a *Carrie?*"

Ryan tilted his head and pursed his lips. His lack of instantaneous denial was an absolute betrayal. He quickly detected the importance of her question and pushed on.

"Well... Carrie is arguably the star of the show. And she is human. She makes a lot of shitty decisions, but I think that is part of her *essence.*" Ryan lifted his hands to emphasize the word. "She's relatable to the audience because she makes the impulsive choices that are covered in red flags."

Clara opened her mouth to protest.

Ryan shot his index finger out. "*But...* they're sometimes the choices we, as mere mortals, wish we could make in real life."

Silence hovered in the air, and Clara squinted at Ryan. She lifted her chin and her lips flattened into an irritated line. She couldn't disagree. Clara frowned, and Ryan leaned forward, patting her on the hand.

"Clara... there is no shame in being a *Carrie*. You're loveable. And bold. And more courageous than you give yourself credit for." He shot her an encouraging smile.

Clara let a deep breath escape. Like the pressure from a hot-air balloon. "Well, thank you for that. I'm sorry if I'm not taking the news well. I lived my whole life thinking I was a Charlotte... this is a big change." Clara punched in her passcode, checking her notifications. "Speaking of which... have you always known that you're a Samantha?"

Ryan grinned and spun his chair again, facing his desk. Flipping his non-existent hair over his shoulder. "*Obviously.*"

Laughing, she looked down. Four texts. Two from Eli. Two from an unknown number.

ELI: Morning Clara!

ELI: Sonny hurt his shoulder and Brandon is still on vacation with his family. Connor is going to help with the delivery.

Clara re-read Eli's texts twice. Her brow furrowed and her stomach flip-flopped. *Shit.*

555-624-8956: Hey Clara, it's Connor. Eli asked if I could help you on Saturday.

555-624-8956: Hope it's all right he gave me your number. I didn't know if you still had the same one.

Clara flushed. Her thumbs hovered over the keyboard. She thought back to their lunch at the nursery. It had been a good day. It felt like she and Connor had finally broken the ice. Then, out of nowhere, he had left. He hadn't even said goodbye... which was a little weird. She shook her head. *Don't over-analyze.*

CLARA: Hey Connor—Very nice of you to offer, but I can manage if you've got other plans!

Damn that exclamation mark. There should be an app where you could remove the exclamation mark in its entirety from your phone. She bit the inside of her cheek. Three dots floated across her screen.

555-624-8956: I'll be there. What time do you need me?

The word *need* in Connor's reply provoked an unsolicited tingle that she felt in the back of her knees. She should just ask Ryan if he could help instead. Glancing over at his cube, she frowned, watching as he cleaned a smudge from his shoe. The order for the Samsons was for a bunch of large stone planters. Also, Ryan had a very strict policy about sleeping in on Saturday mornings.

CLARA: The delivery is at 11. How about 9? That's enough time to load up and plan for traffic.

555-624-8956: See you then

Placing her phone face down on her desk, she looked up at Ryan, who was watching her.

"So, are you going to spill about why—with all due respect—you look like shit?"

Sharon walked around the corner and was coming their way. They both turned back toward their separate cubes and started typing.

"I'll tell you about it later..."

"**W**ait—so are you *okay*?" Ryan peered through his sunglasses and over his water.

Taking in a breath, Clara shrugged. They were seated at a cafe table outside their newest favorite Italian bistro. The heat was barely tolerable, even under the shade of their umbrella. "Yeah, I mean in an existential sense... absolutely. I am here. I am technically unharmed. I'm fine."

Ryan frowned. "Then why do you look like you haven't slept since I left?"

Technically, it had only been six days. Even less than that if she counted the nap she took Sunday afternoon. Clara had tossed and turned after the incident on Saturday night, and then she paced around just about every night when it got dark out. She had developed a new routine.

Shut all the blinds and draw all the curtains... triple-check the doors and double-check the windows. She doubted Mark would come by again after the ass he made of himself. If it wasn't fear that kept her up, it was the crippling stress that he'd actually make good on his threat.

Clara had combed over her finances, counting and recounting. She had depleted her savings to pay her attorney, and begged her mother to cover the rest. She needed the divorce, but she needed a plan. If she didn't think of something soon, she was going to have to pack it in, skip town... *And move back in with her mom*. She shuddered at the thought.

Clara rubbed her forehead and cocked a weary smile. She scooped up the last bit of their antipasto, dabbing her lips with the cloth napkin. "Damn. I suppose I should add some more products to my skincare routine."

"For real, Clara, I'll come over tomorrow after work." Ryan leaned in and lowered his voice. "We'll make a plan."

She gazed through her sunglasses, studying the concern in his expression. Something about Ryan living with Trish felt acceptable. Transitional. Easy. Her hands twisted the cloth napkin below the table and after a moment, she looked down. There was nothing *easy* about her own mother. Clara's lips parted, wanting so badly to tell him everything... But she had long abandoned confiding in people. "So what are you and Trish up to for the Fourth of July?"

He rolled his eyes at her, annoyed. "Well, Trish has *plans*. Which I assume includes her *lover*... so she will be *ocupado*."

"Me and Jonah are going out, which will be fun. Crazy 8 is doing a Throwback Night..." Ryan shot up in his seat after the waiter took their payment. "Oh my God. If you're in town, you *totally* have to come with us. You haven't met Jonah yet and it'll be the perfect distraction."

Jonah was one of Ryan's oldest friends. He was visiting for the upcoming holiday, and Clara had heard little else other than Jonah—*this*, or Jonah—*that*. Clara looked down at her arm resting on the table. A sliver of skin near her elbow wasn't covered by the shade overhead. When she looked back up at Ryan, he hadn't moved a muscle. He was staring at her with the enthusiasm of someone who had just invented electricity. He knew she was dreading the Fourth of July.

She tried her best to muster something akin to his excitement. "I'll think about it."

He wasn't convinced by a long shot. The waiter brought their receipts back. After they put away their cards, they walked back to

Clara's vehicle and slid into what felt like a furnace. In the safety of the car, Ryan pried further.

"So... you swear Mark didn't hurt you? I didn't want to make a big deal, but that shit's messed up." He adjusted the AC on the passenger side so that it was at full blast.

Clara gripped the steering wheel as they exited the parking lot and pulled onto the street, hitting light traffic. Shifting in her seat, her fingers absently reached for her lip. She knew the answer was more than just gossip to Ryan. He was like the brother she had never had, but had always wanted. She wasn't threatened by Mark... and she knew deep down that Mark wouldn't actually hurt her. He had lashed out like a kid who didn't want to share his toy. He needed to grow up.

"No..." She sighed. "No actual bodily harm. It just freaked me out, you know? He's never done anything like that before and it just..." She adjusted her rearview. "It just surprised me."

"Well, please seriously consider my offer."

A smile rose at the corner of her mouth, conceding. "I'll consider it."

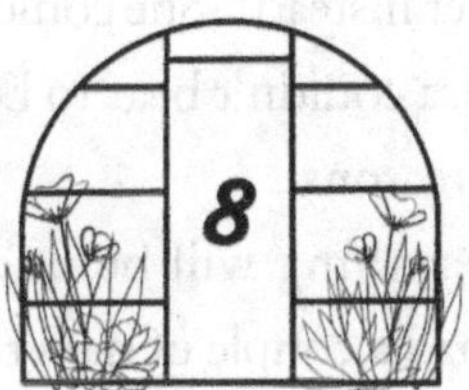

After dropping Ryan off, Clara's phone started ringing. It was Eli.

"Clara! Look, I hope it's all right... I was on the phone with Connor when Sonny stopped by with his arm in a sling. He overheard everything and offered to help right there on the spot." She could hear Gloria in the background.

Eli carried on. "Generous, but I don't know if he understands what he signed up for. We weren't doing these types of deliveries when he was a kid." Letting out a chuckle, he added, "Definitely not fun work."

Clara smiled, and then frowned a little. It wasn't fun work... and she was going to do it all with Connor alone. "You know, since Connor's never done anything like this... do you and Gloria want to meet us there? You two could chat it up with the Samsons while we unload everything. Might make things a little less awkward." Less awkward for her, at least.

"No! You're a seasoned pro! Besides, Gloria and I are meeting with her sister tomorrow so we can't be in two places at once..." Clara turned into her driveway and rolled to a stop in front of the garage.

There was a pause on the line. Eli sensed Clara's hesitation. "Unless you need us, then of course we could just reschedule. Maybe we could meet for dinner instead." She could hear Gloria protesting in the background. Clara couldn't bear to be a nuisance. Especially not for her own selfish reasons.

"Don't be silly. Everything will be fine." She took a breath, reminding herself she had a couple of days to plan before Saturday. "Give Gloria a hug for me, okay?"

"Okay, will do." She could hear the relief in his voice. "And you're still opening tomorrow, right? We have a doctor's appointment downtown, first thing."

"Yeah, no problem at all. I've got my key and I'll just see you whenever you come in."

"Thanks a bunch, Clara—you're a lifesaver."

She smiled to herself. "See ya, Eli."

～

Connor tossed and turned. Ever since he unpacked, he had felt restless. It had been a few weeks, and he had a grocery store he frequented, a coffee shop he liked, and a Greek place he ordered takeout from more than he should. He had even started taking the same route when he went for a run. His problem was that he visited all those places at irregular hours.

Lately, Connor worked for long stretches into the night. He'd put a podcast on and hit his stride around dinner time—then he'd fall into a slump around midnight or so. That wasn't unusual except that he was wired. He'd shower and try to wind down, but he'd lie awake staring at the ceiling for hours. He started grocery shopping at night and going for runs to exhaust his mind. Nothing was working.

He hated naps, but now he caught himself dozing, stealing an hour here or there. Connor pushed at the sheets and rolled over, thinking of Chicago. He had been tired of missing his family and was sick of missing out. He thought coming home would be the answer—but he couldn't shake the feeling that he didn't belong anymore. Like a pair of shoes that didn't fit the next year.

The only peace he felt was at the nursery, helping Eli. He sighed, thinking of work, cycling through a checklist of things to follow up on in the morning. *Or tonight. Who needs sleep?*

In the beginning, Eli spoke to Connor about building the website. After Connor had gotten back to town, he'd taken one look around at the nursery and noticed how run down everything had become. Eli told him how worried he was about the new signage getting delivered and how he wasn't as agile as he once was. It wasn't long before Connor started finding excuses to come by, chiseling away at Eli's to-do list. He had helped replace the drip lines in the greenhouses and stepped in when a shipment showed up late with slate pavers. Tomorrow, he'd be helping fill an order... *with Clara.*

He heard the disappointment in Eli's voice over the phone the day Sonny broke the news that he was temporarily out of commission. Without a second thought, Connor had offered up his Saturday morning on a platter. Connor sat up in bed, scrubbing his hands over his face. He pulled on a pair of running shorts over his briefs.

Clara was like a portal to the past. She brought up a lot of things that he had locked away when he left after school. He grimaced. Things he had chosen not to think about for a long time. Connor knelt down and tightened the laces of his Brooks, tucking his apartment key into the zippered pocket of his shorts. Before the front door clicked shut, he glanced at the time on his phone. Two a.m.

C onnor pulled into the gravel parking lot of the nursery, suppressing a yawn. He cut the engine and felt the building warmth of the car overtake the fading air conditioning. *God, he was glad it was Friday*. He was going cross eyed, staring at his computer all afternoon. Eli hadn't picked up when Connor called earlier, so he figured he'd swing by and grab dinner while he was out. He was trying something new. Dinner—early bird style.

In theory, it gave him time to take a power nap before his late night stride. He thought he'd maximize productivity rather than breaking to snack. He rubbed his eyes and glanced over at the front door. Seeing Clara's car, he sighed. He'd be quick. *Get in. Get out.*

His thoughts drifted. They had definitely been avoiding each other... or maybe he was just avoiding her. Connor didn't understand why the friction sat deep in his gut, but he felt himself tense whenever Clara crossed his mind. He had to fight the urge to be short with her. He tried to be cordial, but he only trusted himself with basic pleasantries. Fidgeting with the top on his water bottle, he couldn't suppress the yawn any longer. As his lips closed, he leaned back, resting his eyes. The drugging lull of slumber pulled him from the sunny summer day.

C onnor woke to an incessant tapping on his window. He was sweating profusely. Eli's face peered at him from the other side of the glass. *Shit.* How long had he been out? He popped the car door and stepped out, gravel crunching under his shoes.

Eli's confusion was obvious. "Connor—are you all right?"

Pinching his damp T-shirt, Connor felt the cotton fabric peel away from his chest and back as it billowed, offering temporary relief. It was almost golden hour. Connor scrubbed a hand down his face and smiled wearily at Eli as they walked toward the main building. "I was just catching a power nap."

Concern dropped from Eli's eyes as he patted him on the back. "Ha! Any longer and I would have broken the window to save you from heat stroke."

They passed Clara's car and Connor changed subjects. He looked around. "Any news on the sign installation?"

Clarity clicked across Eli's face. "*That's* why you called. Things got busy around four and I forgot to return your call."

His uncle looked apologetic. Connor couldn't fault him. His customers were his world. "Don't worry about it. I was nearby and figured I'd stop in."

"Nearby?" Eli's cell phone rang in his pocket and he stepped back, trailing behind. "Sorry, Connor. I'll be just a sec—it's Gloria."

As they approached the glass door, Connor saw Clara on the other side, flipping the *open* sign to *closed*. She glanced up and an easy smile spread across her face. They stood like that for a moment. Both of their hands resting on opposite sides of the same door. Their eyes held. He took his time, studying her as the slow rhythm of his pulse beat against the heat of the metal handle. Clara tilted her head, a question in her eyes. Who would budge first?

"All right, honey. Mhm, we're finishing up and I'm headed your way. Yeah, I can pick up your medicine on the way home... I know... yep. I love you, too. See you soon." Eli smiled and sidled up next to Connor. He set his hand on the horizontal bar near Connor's and gave a slight push. The small bell chimed overhead.

"Connor is a bundle of nerves!"

He turned to look at his uncle. Eli was speaking to Clara.

"He came by just to check on the big install." He motioned over in Connor's direction with his thumb. "All the suspense must've gotten to him because he conked out in his car."

"Oh... yeah. Like New Year's Eve." Connor nodded, ruffling his sweaty hair. "Just couldn't stay up." He raised his eyebrows and offered a hint of a smile.

Confusion etched Clara's face. "So... the whole time you were out there... you were *asleep*?"

Connor felt Clara's gaze touch him. Had she seen him pull in and park his car? Something about that thought made his hard edge soften. He looked over, offering a lazy smile. "I was up late and needed a few minutes. I do that sometimes." *Sometimes meaning every day this past week.* As she mulled over his words, he forged on. "I was actually going to grab dinner and thought I'd swing by... you know, just to see if there were any updates."

She nodded and looked away. *Was she disappointed?*

"Unfortunately, it looks like the delivery date got pushed back—*again*. Something about pieces being on backorder." Eli shook his head in frustration. "Anyway, I need to head out and pick up Gloria's prescription. The pharmacy was able to fill it and I'd like to go ahead since traffic is going to be busy." He started toward the counter to shut everything down. "What do you two have planned on this wild Friday night?"

Their eyes collided. Connor cleared his throat. "I've got a ton of work to do back at my apartment." He watched as Clara shifted from side to side, looking down at her own feet. He added, "I was just picking up some food to take back."

Eli walked away, turning off the fluorescent lights overhead. His voice rang out. "*Clara?*"

Connor watched her cringe in front of him. He smiled. She looked like a cartoon, frowning in anticipation of Eli's meddling.

"Uh—I'm just gonna head home!" Clara called out, answering so Eli could hear her from the depths of the building.

Eli continued to shout. "Clara! That is not what Fridays are made for!" Connor watched as color crept up from the collar of her shirt. She kept her eyes on her shoes. He felt bad for her. *Almost.*

Eli trudged back toward them with Clara's purse in tow. He held it out. "You can't keep doing this to yourself. You've got to get out there." Eli's eyes lit up. "Why don't you two go grab a bite—"

"I have plans," Clara interjected. "Yeah... I'm having friends over." Her gaze jumped between Eli and Connor. "When I said I was heading home, I meant I needed to tidy a little because... people are coming." The exaggerated way she was moving her hands, and the rapid cadence of her voice, said otherwise. "We're going to cook dinner and have some drinks." She had always been such a bad liar. His smile widened, and he rocked back on his heels, hands in his pockets.

Eli eyed her. "Oh, that sounds fun." The three of them walked out into the parking lot as Eli locked up. "Listen, everything should be set for tomorrow. Clara, you've got the keys to the van, right?"

"Yep." Clara's eyes darted over to Connor before she added, "and we've already discussed everything, so it's all sorted out."

"The Samsons don't live off of Broad anymore." He looked at Connor. "They moved to the city. Their address should be on the order sheet." He nodded once more, looking at Clara. "You guys call me tomorrow if you need anything. I'll be back in the afternoon once I drop Gloria and your mom off at the house." Eli gave a small wave and ambled toward his pickup truck.

They stood together as the dust from the gravel lot settled around them. Connor felt a knot tighten in his stomach. Witnessing Eli interrogate her made him take a step back. Clara's vulnerability made her seem less perfect... *more human*. Tonight, Eli was worried about her. And she was willing to lie so he wouldn't. Connor turned to face her and stopped. The setting sun outlined Clara's profile, casting her arms and legs with a golden glow. Strands of hair had come loose from her ponytail, framing her face in the dizzying heat.

"Come with me," he uttered.

Through her sunglasses, she turned to look at him straight on. Her eyes were hidden, but Connor studied the rest of her face, searching.

"Oh. That's... that's a really nice offer, but like I said—"

"We both know you don't actually have plans." He heard the severity in his voice and hoped he didn't sound like a complete asshole. Clara frowned. He watched the pull of her mouth as she stood, deep in thought. Connor looked at the straight line of her posture. Her shorts looked utilitarian. And drab. But *just* short enough that they weren't completely terrible. Her feet were tucked into shoes that most women he knew would consider an abomination. They weren't shoes... but not boots. Not exactly rain boots... they were... very unattractive.

"Okay."

His eyes traveled back up her legs and skipped to meet her eyes. Something in her expression told him she was just as surprised by her answer as he was. He nodded. "Okay, then."

He watched as she glanced at her own vehicle. "I can bring you back by after dinner." Connor motioned toward his car. "Just so you know—I was planning on pizza." He pressed *unlock* on his key fob and they opened their respective doors.

"So..." Her voice was flat and teasing. "You invite me to dinner, embarrass me by calling me out, forcing me to admit I have no plans... and then bully me into eating *pizza*?"

He looked at her seriously over the leather console between them. "Don't tell me you don't like pizza."

She stretched her legs out in front of her, taking inventory of the inside of his SUV. "No." Clara smiled at his frown. "I *love* pizza."

As they turned onto Laurel Lane, Clara pulled up the website, per Connor's request. He noticed she was scanning through each item meticulously.

"Are you trying to memorize the entire menu?"

"Very funny. I'm not about to squander this precious pizza moment and pick something lame."

Connor had no idea what a *precious pizza moment* was, but he enjoyed that it sounded like a rare occurrence. They came to a red light, and he tapped his fingers impatiently. "Well, it's only Alberto's. There can't be that many options." He glanced in his rearview and then over at her, nonchalantly. "How about we get two?" He was starving. Her eyes were still glued to the menu on her phone. "Just order mine and then pick whatever you want." Clara nodded absently, the weight of the pizza world on her shoulders. She gasped, shooting up straight in her seat. Connor tapped the brakes, jerking the wheel. "*Jesus*—"

"Sorry." She smiled, dialing the number. "They have a special tonight." After placing the to-go order, she hung up. He couldn't even begin to catch the name of what she'd picked.

Alberto's was slammed. He snagged a spot off of Main Street, not thinking about how busy downtown would be. Planters adorned most every shop along the way, bursting with flowers and lush greenery. As they approached the faded striped awnings, his heart warmed.

Opening the heavy wooden door, he stood back, motioning for Clara to step through. She smiled up at him, and he followed behind, glancing around. The smell of dough and baked cheese filled the air. The old pizza parlor still felt the same.

He and Clara stood shoulder to shoulder amongst the crowd of hungry customers. Half of Silas Grove was here, breaking bread and sharing pitchers. Connor took in his casual attire and glanced at Clara. He noticed the pink across the bridge of her nose and grinned, looking down at her work boots.

She seemed unfazed by how they stood out from everyone else. As the cashier walked back and forth behind the counter, gathering their order, Clara stepped forward and spoke to her, asking for extra containers of parmesan and crushed red pepper. Her chin tilted down as she thumbed through her wallet. Connor leaned in to put his credit card down on the counter in front of her.

His words hummed close to her ear. "Just so we're even." His arm came around her, brushing the fabric of her shirt. She looked back over her shoulder and up into his face. A smile pulled at the corner of his lips. The warmth in her expression quickly faded, and he felt her stiffen against him. He followed her gaze, meeting a booth of people looking in their direction.

"Order up!" The cashier took Connor's card and completed the transaction. She snatched up the cordless phone that was ringing, starting another pickup order. A swirl of paper zipped out from the printer and she slapped the receipt down with a pen.

"Connor!" A large man with a thick, dark mustache stepped out from the kitchen, his voice booming, drawing attention from everyone in the restaurant.

"Hey, Alberto." The man reached over the counter and shook his hand excitedly, giving him a hard pat on the shoulder.

"I was wondering when you were gonna pay us a visit." He chided him with a pointed look. "You've been away too long." He crossed his arms. Seeing the boxes on the counter, he pointed. "Is this you?"

Connor nodded, glancing down. "Yeah—we're just picking up a to-go."

Alberto suddenly noticed Clara, and his eyes widened, sliding back and forth between them both. "I was wondering who ordered the special. I didn't realize it was you." He was speaking to Connor, but his eyes were trained on Clara. She chewed her lip, glancing around.

"You two should eat here." He waved a hand, motioning beyond the bar. "Grab the pies, we'll get you a table." Walking away, he spoke over his shoulder. "What do you want to drink?"

Connor smiled warmly, and a large group came in the front door, standing right behind them. There wasn't any room for Clara to move. Connor stepped forward, pressing into her as he went to grab the boxes. He felt Clara freeze, trying to shrink into herself. Catching the lingering smell of her shampoo, he stood back to his full height. It was faint... a mix of fresh air and sweat. The combination made his knees buckle. Hearing a hush of whispers, he turned, catching several sets of eyes staring at them.

Clara cleared her throat and something inside of him hardened. He shoved his hand through his hair and sucked in a breath, slipping away from the counter. He hastened, catching up to Alberto as he made his way across the pizzeria, an apologetic smile balanced on his mouth. "Hey—sorry, but I think we're just gonna take them to go." He saw the confusion in the older man's face. "We don't want to hold up a table."

"*Nonsense.*" Alberto lowered his voice, moving closer. "You know, I had heard about her and Mark a while back." He glanced beyond Connor, frowning. "I didn't know if it was true or not."

They both looked back toward the register. Clara strengthened her hold on the boxes as she watched him, pleading from across the restaurant. His throat tightened.

"*Good for her.*"

Connor caught Alberto's eye, a question in his expression.

"I am a little surprised." He grinned, slapping Connor hard on the back. "But I'm glad she's seeing someone." Alberto waved at a customer over at the bar. "She could do a lot better than Monroe."

Connor stared, lips parted, his words lodged in his throat.

"Don't be a stranger." Alberto stepped away, leaving Connor frozen where he stood. "You bring her back, okay?"

Connor felt the heat of everyone watching and he squared his shoulders, walking through the crowded room toward the entrance. His eyes met Clara's. "Ready to get out of here?" He watched relief wash over her as he reached for the pizzas. Connor signaled for her to grab the rest of the containers and they walked in silence to his SUV, setting everything in the backseat.

"Um." Clara adjusted her purse on her shoulder, opening the passenger-side door. "Maybe I should just go home."

Connor slid on his sunglasses and looked at her through the cab, both of them standing outside the car. He motioned with a tilt of his chin. "You're not hungry?"

She shrugged, distracted by a group passing by on the sidewalk. Her voice softened. "I don't know if this was a good idea."

He grimaced, looking down the length of the old brick buildings surrounding them, thinking. "What about your *precious pizza moment*?"

Her head popped up, a smile tugging at the corner of her mouth. Clara took a deep breath. "We could go back to the nursery." She pushed her hair from her face and looked back toward the restaurant, frowning. "Or maybe we could just take the food to my place?"

Monroe Mansion.

Still reeling from Alberto's words, Connor's jaw tensed. Seconds passed. A heavy sigh left his chest and he slid into the front seat. Turning the key in the ignition, Connor looked at Clara, still standing in the street, cast in gold. Her eyes like pools of amber. "Get in."

They drove, winding down streets, in a silence that wasn't strained. Like a tiny crack had splintered in the wall between them. As they neared the edge of town, his eye caught hers, approaching the exit leaving Silas Grove.

She inched down in her seat and relaxed, smiling as they drove into the fading summer sun.

Clara looked at Connor down the length of her beer bottle. He was standing at the makeshift kitchen island, eyeing her pizza box with great trepidation. She couldn't suppress her smile. Setting her drink down, she felt the stainless steel countertop under her fingers. He had offered her the sole barstool, choosing to stand. Clara had tethered herself to her seat, feeling strange, surrounded by his things. Throughout dinner, she glanced around, assessing the space. It was a studio apartment with the kitchen right off the front door. She noted the giant open bookcase that stood as a partition in the living room, catching a glimpse of what she assumed was his bed behind it.

Clara got the sense that this dinner had truly been impromptu by the way Connor dashed around, tidying things as she set up the food. If what she witnessed when they walked in the door was proof of how he lived as an unsupervised, adult male... she was embarrassed. For herself. She thought about her most recent bout of rage cleaning. Connor's place was basically immaculate.

"So, you've got... pear... and prosciutto... and cheese?" Connor pointed at her pizza and frowned. He had spoken through a mouthful of his own standard pepperoni and sausage.

Clara chuckled. "It's gorgonzola, if you want to be specific." She reached in and lifted the smallest slice, moving it through the air, dodging empty beer bottles toward Connor's side of the island.

He shook his head in a slow and playful way. "There is no way that's good."

She gingerly laid the slice in his box, nestled in the open space where he had eaten three of his own. She licked her fingers and shrugged as she looked up at him. "I don't know, Connor... it might just be amazing."

"Pears on a pizza..." He tilted his head back and smirked, taking a long pull from his own beer. "You've lost your damn mind."

She liked the zing that passed between them. Easy and familiar. "Fine. I dare you."

His brows knit together as he lowered the bottle. It sat with a clink. "What are we, back in college?" He smiled boldly. She swallowed the lump in her throat. The warmth in his eyes toed the line to something more. Something heavier.

Clara's smile faded, and the zing fumbled. The openness of his apartment suddenly felt unnerving. The brick walls and exposed pipes did little to muffle the feelings bouncing around between her ribs. "No dare then. You can just try it and if you like it... you like it. If it's not the best pizza you've ever had—"

"Then you have to answer a Truth."

Clara's breath stilled. A heat crept up her spine as she watched him pick up the pizza from the cardboard. Not making eye contact, he lifted the slice and examined it. She peered up at him from her barstool, face flushed and skin tingling. Connor seemingly transformed into his old self right in front of her. Watching him now, he was completely oblivious to the wild thrum of her heart.

Clara polished off the rest of her drink as Connor took a large bite, chewing thoughtfully. His expression guarded. He stood in contemplation, looking off into the distance. She must have been staring, because his eyes caught hers and he grinned.

Her stomach fluttered at the flash of his dimples. Finishing another bite, he set down his slice. Clara bit her lip in suspense. Drum rolling along the stainless steel, he stopped, raising his arms in the air. A king making a grand announcement. "It's fucking delicious!"

Clara jumped from her seat, overcome with smug exhilaration. A series of victory dance moves ensued as Connor initiated a slow clap in her honor. Clara punched the air triumphantly. Both laughing, they stood together, enjoying the burst of happiness that filled the moment. Now side by side, barely touching, they basked in the shared, alcohol-induced levity. Clara broke away, grabbing their empty bottles.

"Do you recycle?"

"Yeah—if you'll just rinse them out, I can take it from there." Connor took her lead, closing the cardboard boxes. He opened the fridge and slid their leftovers into the middle shelf. Clara quietly made her way over to him after throwing away their dirty napkins.

"Mind if I have another?" she pointed at the drinks on the shelf below the pizzas. She didn't exactly wait for confirmation before grabbing one and twisting off the lid. She inched around him, feeling brave from her buzz, and ventured deeper into his apartment. Curiosity motivated her, but loneliness pushed her. Clara couldn't put her finger on why she didn't want to leave. She just knew she wasn't ready.

"So..." She drank from her beer, padding into the living room just off of the kitchen. "How come you didn't just get a place in Silas?" A leather couch sat positioned against the bookshelf, facing a flatscreen on the opposite wall. "I mean, since you come to town so much." She spotted his bed on the other side, behind the books. A spark skipped around in her chest, and she forced herself to turn and walk away.

"I don't know." He cut the water off at the sink. "Just felt like it might be good to have a little privacy."

Clara glanced over her shoulder at him.

He shrugged, sheepishly. "You know how it is."

His apartment was large and industrial. A desk sat in front of one of the three huge windows that ran almost floor to ceiling. She meandered her way around the coffee table, toward the notepads and equipment that littered his workspace. Connor's handwriting was scribbled in neat little lines, but the letters themselves looked indecipherable.

"Unfortunately, I do."

Her smile dimmed. Flash drives and memory cards were laid out along with his camera. She stood back, careful not to touch anything. Mark had always hated when she rearranged his things. She heard the quick release fizz as Connor opened another beer for himself. He followed Clara into the living room and took a seat, sinking into the depths of the couch. He leaned his head back, watching her. They stayed like that for a moment, deep in silence.

Clara spoke quietly. "Penny?"

Connor tilted his head.

She smiled. "For your thoughts."

He returned her smile from where he sat, comprehension reaching his eyes. He shook his head, bottom lip between his teeth, choosing his words carefully. "Just you. Standing there—looking at my stuff."

Clara straightened, realizing dinner was over. And she had opened another beer and pushed her way in. All because she wasn't ready to be alone. "I'm so sorry." She broke eye contact and looked down at the rug below her boots. "I'm completely imposing." She walked swiftly, carrying her beer back toward the kitchen, setting it next to the sink. She wondered if he had actually planned to work tonight. Maybe he had plans to go out with friends like other normal people. Maybe he had plans to meet up with someone... maybe a date.

She shook her head, got out her phone, and pulled up Lyft. Her palms were sweaty. "Don't worry about driving me back, okay? I can catch a ride so you can get to whatever you need to do." She clicked through several screens and rushed to confirm. The embarrassment she felt at overstaying her welcome quickly shoved her buzz into precarious inebriation. She turned, pressing her hand against the exposed brick for balance, and spoke out—more to herself than to Connor. "Is the bathroom back here?"

She was already closing the door and locking the handle before he could even answer from the couch. Clara turned on the light and looked up into the mirror, wincing at her reflection. She looked drunk. Repeated nights of minimal sleep were starting to show.

She couldn't even imagine how badly Connor wanted her out of there. Quickly, she peed, preparing for the car ride home, and turned on the water faucet to wash up. Steadying herself, Clara closed her eyes and leaned forward, splashing cold water onto her face, willing herself to sober up.

"Clara... you all right?"

The depth of his voice on the other side of the door startled her. "Yeah, just need a minute." She heard the embarrassing hitch in her voice. Too peppy. Transparent. She scanned the bathroom, failing to locate a hand towel. Water dripped everywhere, and she took an exhausted breath.

She clutched the bottom half of her shirt, pulling the hem upwards to blot her face. *Just grab your stuff, thank him for dinner, and get the hell out of here.* Opening the door, light from the bathroom sliced through Connor's room, illuminating his tall frame sitting at the end of the bed. He leaned on his forearms, looking down at his hands.

"Don't leave," he said under his breath.

She couldn't speak. Her anxious mind quieted, and her reaction to Connor's words felt purely physiological. She wanted nothing more than to bring herself close enough to melt at his feet. Connor stood and moved away from the bed.

"Don't leave." His mouth pressed into a hard line. "Not if you're upset." She felt his warmth, hovering with reserve. "Did I say something wrong?"

She looked into his eyes. Soft and honest. She pursed her lips, not trusting herself to answer.

At her silence, Connor ducked his chin. "I drank too much. I told you I would drive you back, and I didn't keep my end of the deal." His gaze touched every corner of her face, trying to read her thoughts. "I'm really sorry... I pushed you into dinner and then put you in a shitty spot." His expression shifted, now full of restraint. His eyes crowded with things he wanted to say. "I wasn't trying to get you to leave."

Her gaze dropped to Connor's mouth. In the midst of burying the messy remains of her marriage, she had no business getting wrapped up in another guy. Her pulse quickened and disappointment flooded her chest.

Connor studied her, his voice quiet. "Penny?"

The corner of her lips rose. When she brought her eyes back to him, his smile mirrored hers. Drunk and dizzy, she struggled to catch her breath.

—ele—

Connor reached forward and placed his palm on Clara's shoulder, fingers splayed wide. "How about we hit reset?"

He watched her sway and offered a gentle squeeze, steadying her. He couldn't believe he had screwed up so badly. "Look, I'm basically an insomniac... so I'll drive you back to your car after we've sobered up." Clara checked her watch and looked up at him like he was crazy. A pang of guilt twisted in his stomach.

He continued. "Seriously, we can just hang out and I'll drive you back." She started to protest, so he pressed. "Clara... even if you catch a ride home tonight, you'll need your car in the morning. I've got nothing but time to kill."

Connor watched her expression change. Saw her gently bite the soft flesh of her lip as she contemplated. He tore his eyes away from her mouth and caught her staring past him at his bed.

"I will need my car in the morning... and I'm pretty much a night owl, too." She tucked her hair behind her ear. "I really don't want to mess up the delivery."

"We won't." He offered a supportive tilt of his lips, and she gave him a weary smile. He looked at his hand resting on her shoulder and ran his thumb across her collarbone. The warmth of her skin under his palm felt electric. He took a deep breath and stepped back to a respectable distance.

"Take all the time you need." He walked back to the neutral safety of the living room, motioning for her to take a seat. "I'll make sure you get to your car when you're good to drive. No rush." Clara noticed two full water glasses sitting on the coffee table in front of the couch and she let out a sigh. A deflated smile rested on her lips and she sank down. Pressing the cold glass to her cheek, she glimpsed up, pinning him with a look.

"How did you know I was going to stay?" She glanced at the glass of water in her hand.

Connor shrugged, answering honestly. "I didn't." He motioned to the door. "I thought you might want it while you waited for your ride."

Clara's eyes went wide. "Shit." She dug out her phone, canceling her ride. "And you swear it's not a problem to drive me?"

Connor looked down at her and nodded once more. "I swear."

"All right." She let out a breath and returned to her phone. "I guess you're stuck with me."

He walked over to the other side of the couch and sat down, drinking from his own water next to Clara's. "So, what'll it be?" He checked the time. Eleven p.m. "Want to watch something?" He reached for the remote on the cushion between them. "Or just kill time with riveting conversation?"

"A movie could be good."

He glanced at Clara in his peripheral. She had sat back against the cushions, her posture still rigid. She crossed her arms across her stomach and crossed her legs as well. She watched the screen as he cycled through different options. "Maybe something old? So we don't have to finish it if we need to leave?"

Connor turned and gave her a quick smile. "In a rush?"

Surprise flashed across her face. "No, not at all... I just figure we pick something non-committal, right?"

Connor shook his head and faced the television again. "Slow your roll. You said it..." He slid off his shoes, pushing them under the coffee table. "I'm stuck with you." He watched Clara study his movements. She did the same with her work boots, leaving her in a pair of socks. He noticed the mismatched patterns and smiled to himself. They decided on *Catch Me If You Can,* and as the opening credits rolled across the screen, Clara tucked her feet underneath her, snuggling deeper into the couch.

Connor got up and refilled their waters. "Lights on or off?"

"Um... off?" From the couch, Clara asked, "So, this is based on a true story, right?"

Connor hit the switch with his elbow, and the only thing left was the ambient glow from the kitchen. "Yeah—I think so. It was in the seventies or something." Connor set both their glasses down on the counter and turned on the tap.

"Is Amy Adams in this? Or is it Jessica Chastain?" Her voice echoed through the studio.

Connor turned off the faucet. "You're talking about the one who plays Leo's wife?"

Clara took her glass from his hand and sat back again. "Yeah, I think it's Amy Adams... but sometimes I get them mixed up."

They were about an hour into the movie, and Clara had not stopped chatting. Normally, Connor couldn't stand anyone talking through a movie. Had she always been like this? Some of her commentary was strictly observational, and other times, she provoked an actual response from him. All of it was strangely entertaining.

"So, what's really the deal with the pinstripes?" Clara peered over at him.

"Well, it's the Yankees." He pointed as Christopher Walken filled the screen. "They also live in New Rochelle, which is in New York. So geographically, it makes sense for the storyline. And it's more than that—"

"It just seems far-fetched. To claim that the only reason the Yankees win is because of their outfits." She unfurled her legs, still keeping to her side of the couch. "I don't understand."

Connor smiled. "First off, they're not outfits. They're uniforms." He watched as the scene carried on in front of them. "And Walken is trying to teach the art of deception." He straightened in his seat. "You know... saying that the team only wins because people can't take their eyes off the pinstripes."

"That's terrible."

"Well yeah. He's explaining how a person can get away with stuff because people only focus on what they want to see, rather than what's right in front of them." He turned to face her. "Like if a person can just keep up appearances, the charade keeps going... and no one questions anything."

Clara sat face forward, eyes glued to the screen. From the dim glow of the movie, he noticed a tear running down her cheek. Clara stood and excused herself to the bathroom. "Intermission break," was all she muttered before she walked away.

With his heart in his stomach, he hit pause. "Dammit." His mind was racing. Retracing exactly what he'd said, Connor winced at the harshness of his words. He heard the faint sound of running water and Clara padded her way back through the studio. Connor got up. Surely she was ready to leave. Clara rounded the bookcase, saw him standing, and stopped.

"All set?" Her eyes were glassy and tinged with red.

"Uh yeah, if you're ready. Let's get you home..." He grabbed his phone and leaned forward to put on his shoes.

"Oh... I meant the movie?" She pointed at the screen and Clara gave him a tired smile. "Unless you're trying to get rid of me." The tightness in his chest eased and a short laugh escaped his lips.

Clara slid into her spot with her legs curled next to her. Connor leaned back and hit play.

⸺⁓⸺

After another half an hour, Clara's inquiries began to slow. Connor found himself sunken deep into the cushions, head propped in his hand, with his arm balanced on the arm of the couch. He sat up a little, taking the reins. "So, you actually claim to be a night owl?"

Clara startled. She rolled her shoulders and took a deep breath. "Uh... yeah. I barely sleep... I'm like Leonardo, I guess."

Connor turned his head. "DiCaprio?"

Clara fought a massive yawn and scooted down lower into the couch. She was basically horizontal except for her shoulders, neck, and head—which were somewhat still vertical with her arms crossed at her chest. At the tail end of her drowsy display, she laughed. "No. Da Vinci. He lived in four-hour increments or something crazy like that."

"That's insane."

Clara tilted her head back against the leather upholstery and rested her eyes. "Come to think of it, you're more like Da Vinci. He took naps all the time." He watched her smile to herself. With her eyes closed, he could see the darkness of her lashes fan across her face. "Plus, you're the artist."

It was his turn to smile. "Clearly, I'm not accomplished enough. You were shocked that I still do it as a job."

A crease furrowed her forehead, and she peeked one eye open at him from her side of the couch. "I shouldn't have said that."

"Don't worry about it." He knocked her ankle lightly with his elbow.

Abandoning the movie, Clara twisted in her spot. She was looking directly at Connor with her body stretched out, leaning her head against the arm of the couch. "Well, I remember all your stuff in college was really good." Clara paused. "And our pictures from our wedding were beautiful."

Our.

Connor's shoulders stiffened.

Clara nudged her toes against the side of his leg. "Connor?"

He looked over, realizing that she was staring right at him. He placed his hand over Clara's foot and encircled her arch. He ran his fingers along the underside of her toes, over her sock. Pulling his eyes away from hers, he looked down at the contrast of his hand on the cotton covering her skin. He pondered the mismatched pair. One was striped, the other solid gray. How could someone make such an obvious mistake?

"Can I ask you that *Truth*?"

— ✕ —

Clara focused on Connor's hand, trying desperately to temper the electricity tingling up her leg. His thumb brushed back and forth as they sat in silence. Clara's exhausted mind was racing.

She felt the weight of Connor's request. Truth was, she had too many truths. Too many things she was ashamed of.

She tucked her hair behind her ear. "Who says you get to ask a *Truth*?"

Something changed behind his eyes. Connor shifted, so he was now fully facing her end of the couch. His left foot stayed planted on the floor, the other loosely crossed beneath him. He draped his arm across the back of the couch, holding onto Clara with his free hand. He looked at her with intrigue.

"I reserve the right to ask a *Truth*—per the challenge."

Clara wiggled her toes, keeping her poker face strong. "If anyone won, it was clearly me... you loved the pear."

Connor raised his eyebrows, lazily massaging her arch. She wanted to feel the warmth of his hand in other places. She bit her lip, fighting to stay focused.

"I said it was delicious." He admitted.

Clara smiled confidently. "Right. Which means that I won."

"No. The wager was whether it would be the best pizza I have ever tasted."

Clara put her hand over her eyes, feigning dramatic frustration. "You're ridiculous. That's clearly a play on words... like a figure of speech." Another yawn overtook her. She was losing her edge. Clara fully extended her other leg down the length of the couch, stretching out like a cat. There was a momentary pause, and she sucked in a breath, feeling both of Connor's hands slowly wrap around her feet. She stilled.

With her eyes still covered by her hand, she leaned into the strength of his fingers, feeling her tension dissolve and resettle between her legs. Connor worked silently, moving up to her

Achilles tendon. He pushed and pulled, slowly dragging her muscles between his thumb and index finger.

"Oh my God."

The motion of his hands froze. She cringed, wanting to bury herself in the cushions. Better yet, maybe a sinkhole could open underneath them and swallow the entire building whole, leaving no witnesses. Seconds passed into minutes. She could hear Amy Adams and Leo getting hot and heavy onscreen—playing nurse and doctor. Lifting her hand, she blinked into the dim light.

Connor's eyes were focused on the apex of her thighs, sliding up to the sliver of exposed skin at her midriff, where she had snuggled into the couch. The way he looked at her body made Clara arch, strung tight from wanting. She watched his gaze climb her ribcage to the unsteady rise and fall of her chest. A warmth spread through her stomach—a delicious and infuriating reminder of what she was missing. What she couldn't ask for. Not from Connor. She swallowed and his eyes jumped to hers.

"Giving in that easily?" He smirked, dimples flashing.

Clara's breath hitched. "Excuse me?"

"Our debate." The low rumble of his voice issued a tidal wave of goosebumps. "Your last point wasn't very compelling."

Clara huffed. She was holding onto anything and everything, trying to keep a lid on the electricity racing across her skin. She could light up his whole damn apartment if he put a lightbulb in her hand. She wasn't in the mood to argue. She was in the mood for *something else.* Just then, Connor leaned forward and slid his hands up to the back of her calves. She let out a small moan of approval, and Connor smiled.

His request was firm. "Keep convincing me."

After a moment, his hands began kneading again. When she hesitated, he grabbed her by the ankles and pulled. The quick movement elicited a squeak from her chest. As their laughter quieted, he teased. "If you stop... *I* stop."

Their gazes held. She felt like her insides might combust as he took his time, working his hands back and forth over her skin.

"Well... I dared you because I wanted you to try something new." Her words carried across the space between them.

"Mm. So your stance is that you were trying to help me..."

Clara let her eyes close. "Exactly... To expand your palate." He had moved to the front of her shins, increasing pressure, dragging the pads of his fingers against her. Clara sucked in air between her teeth. Feeling the sharp ache dissipate into pleasure, she regrouped. "I don't know how you survive eating the way you do." She wiggled against the leather, tugging her shirt down. "There's a whole world of flavors out there just waiting to be explored, and you're choosing to limit yourself... It's like you don't even know what's good for you."

Connor slid his hands to the front of her thighs. Clara jumped. Jerking to a sitting position, her hand flew to her chest. Connor sat calmly across from her, reaching out with a soft gesture.

"Shit—I'm sorry." Concern emanated from his blue eyes. "Did I hurt you?"

Clara shook her head silently and let a breath pass her lips. A pained smile pulled at the corners of her mouth. "No. Not at all. I... I'm just really ticklish." She shrugged her shoulders and straightened. She reached for her water on the coffee table and took a large gulp. Setting it back down, Clara resumed her original position on the far end. Arms crossed. Legs tucked beneath her. "Let's just finish the movie."

Connor sat back and scrubbed his hand down his face. *What just happened*? He watched as Leo walked through a crowded airport, Trojan Horsing his way past cops and detectives, surrounded by beautiful flight attendants. Clara's reaction hit like a bucket of cold water. She was careened over the end of the couch. Any farther and she'd be on the floor.

It had been years since he'd felt this. He misread her. He couldn't remember the last time he had put himself in the position to misread someone. This is why it was easier being alone. The movie blurred and his thoughts tightened—like he was adjusting the focus ring on everything around him. Connor stretched his shoulders.

He was a different person now. He had a life that was completely separate from the world that Clara moved in. He frowned, fighting the urge to glance in her direction. His social life had been his entire world before it was obliterated, all for trying to do the right thing.

He heard a heavy sigh and checked his phone. One forty-five a.m. He needed this night to be over. As the final scene came to a close, Connor sat forward and grabbed his shoes. He wrestled them on, not bothering with the laces, and turned. Clara was tucked into a tight bundle, legs folded beneath her. Her body had sunk down to the arm of the couch where her head sat propped up in her hand.

All before succumbing to the unassailable lull of slumber. Another trailing breath escaped her, and Connor shook his head, absorbing the absurdity of Clara Monroe sleeping on his couch. The girl he tried every day to forget was now the woman he couldn't stop thinking about.

He hesitated, wanting to slide his hand over hers. He wondered what it would be like to stretch out beside her and pull her in close. Connor stood and ran his hand through his hair. He wanted to wake her up and tell her to get the hell out of his apartment.

He circled the coffee table, past her dozing silhouette. Without a second thought, he walked around to the other side of the open bookcase, just feet away from her. Starting at the opposite end of the couch, Connor dragged the crisp cotton of his duvet across her body.

She unfurled and twisted into its weighted comfort. Like the magnetic pull of the tide, unintentional and subconscious. Leaning over, he gathered their shoes, lining them up side-by-side next to the front door. He refilled her water glass one last time and placed it softly on the coffee table. As he pulled back the sheets and climbed into his own bed, Connor did some quick math before setting an alarm.

Tomorrow was going to be a bitch.

10

Clara rolled over and awoke to the sound of fabric crinkling. She squinted in the dark. A blaring sound was right by her head. *Where the hell is it coming from?* She sat up, patting the cover around her as realization hit her in seismic, tsunami level waves. "*Shhhhhhhh...*" Clara clambered around for her phone—desperate. She needed to plan her escape.

Did I sleep here? Above her, behind the couch, she saw the glow of a screen—the source of the cacophony. Extending her arm, she reached, fingertips grazing the slick screen. She used her other hand to pull on the shelf closest to her. *Almost.* The alarm screeched and just as she touched the tiny brick, it slipped out of reach. She grappled, knocking something over. A stack tumbled off the backside of the two-way bookcase, pelting everything below in a barrage of paper and sharp edges.

"*SHIT—*"

Clara ducked under the duvet, curling onto her side. Shame followed everything she touched, like some sick version of Midas. A string of expletives left the bed behind her while the alarm clock raged. *Why am I still here?* She heard the harsh thud of Connor's feet hit the floor, his steps skulking closer and closer until all the noise cut out at once.

Clara pulled the top of the cover down and was met with a direct view of Connor's very shirtless chest. The hazy gray of the early hour filtered through the massive windows of his studio. She lifted her eyes higher, wincing. Connor sat on the coffee table across from the couch, holding his hand over his eye.

His hair was rumpled and his voice left his body in ragged, angry breaths. "What... *the hell*... was that?"

Clara brought her arms out from under the cover and sat up. "Well. I-uh... the alarm went off on my phone—"

"That... was my phone," Connor interjected. Holding said phone in his hand.

She opened her mouth to speak, then snapped it shut.

He continued, still holding his left hand to his face. Still completely shirtless. "*Your* phone... is on the charger." He tilted his head toward the kitchen. Clara's eyes peeled away from his pecs and flitted to the counter.

"You plugged in my phone?" Clara pushed the blanket down to stand and Connor got up from the coffee table, walking back to the bathroom. Clara grabbed her cell. The screen glowed at 100 percent. Five o'clock a.m. She trailed behind him, hovering in the bathroom doorway as he leaned over the vanity. In the bright light, she could see every line of his tan, muscled torso. The cables of his biceps flexed and rolled as he checked for injury.

"You might have given me a black eye... maybe a paper cut." He tilted his face back and forth, assessing the damage.

Connor's shoulder blades shifted. Her eyes followed each vertebra down the curve of his spine until finally disappearing into the waistband of his sweatpants.

"You look incredibly apologetic." The flatness in his voice sent her plummeting and her eyes flashed to the mirror. Heat shot across her face and she stood up straight, pushing away from the threshold. He had been watching her the entire time.

Clara nearly stepped back into the door itself and smoothed her hair. "Did I sleep here?"

Connor reached for his toothbrush and she pressed her lips together, aware of how absolutely disgusting she felt. She should keep her words to a minimum. Maybe there was an app for sign language. Maybe she could mime.

He spit a mouthful of minty foam down the drain and rinsed. "Obviously."

Clara angled her body, turning to pick imaginary lint off her shirt, and breathed into the open air of his bedroom. "I need to get to the nursery to start that delivery."

The sound of the faucet continued behind her and she peeked, seeing Connor splash water on his face. Droplets rolled down his forearms and onto the counter. She felt hot and panicky. There wasn't an industrial-strength deodorant in existence that could cover up a full day of work outside... in the Georgia heat. *Put on twenty-four hours ago.*

She clenched her arms to her sides as he pulled a fresh hand towel from a linen closet behind the door. Why the hell didn't she see that last night? Clara checked her phone again and started mentally running the timeclock, accounting for everything that needed to get done. She let out a rank, frustrated breath. They were cutting it close.

His eyes connected with hers in the mirror again. "Can you repeat that? I couldn't hear you." He pointed at the faucet.

Clara pursed her lips and stepped away. "I don't think I have enough time to go to my house."

"You were sleeping pretty hard last night." He slid a drawer open, pulling out a bar of Speed Stick. "I figured it was late and since we both have to be there, I'd just go in early and help with everything. You know, I kind of owe you since I didn't get you home last night."

Clara couldn't remember the last time she felt so ill-prepared. She had just gotten drunk and slept over at a man's apartment—*an attractive man's apartment*—without overnight necessities. She had passed out in her sweaty work clothes. And after a full evening of carbs and beer, she had thrown dental hygiene out the window. She hadn't done anything this irresponsible since... *forever*. She rubbed her hand over her forehead, staring at the floor. "I feel disgusting."

Connor nodded. "Well, you look it."

Her eyes widened. He smirked and stepped back, reaching into the linen closet a second time. "I can get you some clothes if you want to shower here. If you don't care about being presentable, then I'm sure we can figure something out." He held out a towel and Clara reached for it, keeping her eyes locked on the floor.

"Shower sounds great. I'm sure I'm basically a troll at this point."

Ignoring her, Connor scanned the bathroom and pointed over his shoulder. "Right. Well, there's your towel... all the shampoo and stuff is in the shower." He stepped forward, and Clara hugged the terrycloth to her chest as he slipped past. After closing the door, she sighed. She grabbed the hem of her day old, sweaty shirt and yanked it up along with her elastic sports bra. Clara had barely worked the fabric over her nose when the handle rattled. She threw herself against the door as it cracked open, slamming it shut.

"Connor! I was... undressing, and I didn't..." Clara's naked shoulders sagged. Her shirt and bra bunched up around her neck like a dirty scarf. *A shitty infinity.* She heard him groan like a wounded animal.

She grimaced. "Are you okay?" There was a pause.

"I was just going to tell you I don't have a hair dryer."

—⁓—

Clara bit into the cold pizza slice, trying her best to keep crumbs from scattering to the floorboard. Her damp hair was already frizzing around her face and she looked down at the clothes Connor had loaned her.

She peeked across the console as he drove them to the nursery. She could see his profile more clearly with the morning sun darting across the dash. The faded cotton shirt he'd loaned her darkened in splotches where her hair rested. "Earth Day?"

Connor nodded, not taking his eyes off the road. "My sister left it by accident on her last trip to visit me." He glanced at her. "She made me swear not to throw it out."

She touched the billowy nylon of the borrowed shorts on her thigh. They were loose but snug enough that they stayed up at the waist. Standing in Connor's bedroom, Clara had considered reaching for her day-old work clothes. Just as she was about to rough it and go commando, she noticed these had built-in underwear. *Hallelujah.*

"I don't even care who left these behind." She popped the last chunk of crust between her lips and chewed. "Whoever she is, I am eternally grateful." She could have sworn she detected a hint of a smile.

Connor motioned to the cup holders between them, touching the water he had grabbed on their way out. "You're probably gonna want to drink that."

He pulled into the lonely gravel lot and parked by the front door. Something settled in his stomach seeing Clara's car this early in the morning. Like a strange walk of shame. Except nothing had happened between them other than a momentary lapse in judgment.

They grabbed their stuff, got out, and unlocked the front door before walking into the empty building. Connor moved to the back hallway, turning on light switches as he went. Clara walked to the front and grabbed her clipboard with the itemized order details. Connor stood opposite her, watching. Clara brought her gaze to his.

"Right. So how do you feel about going and pulling the plants that we need?"

Connor glanced at the expanse of rows outside and rubbed his neck. "You probably know where everything is way better than I do." He placed his palms on the counter between them and leaned in, combing over the list. "What else will you need to get started?"

Clara tucked her purse under the counter and stood back up. "Well, we are going to need potting soil..." Their eyes met briefly.

Connor nodded, looking back down at the sheet between them. "I know where the pallets are." He didn't acknowledge that day at the beginning of summer. The corner of his mouth lifted.

Clara bit the inside of her cheek and shifted her weight, using an elastic on her wrist to tame her waves into a bun. She looked at Connor's mouth. "There's also the planters the customer picked out... they're pretty big. We have them taped off, so if you could bring them over to the work area, then it would make the assembly process a little easier."

He straightened his shoulders and walked toward the side door. "Sounds like I've got my marching orders." Once outside, he turned and grabbed a pull cart, making his way to the pallets.

Clara followed close behind and headed out into the maze.

***

Clara shoved another five-gallon elephant ear onto the pull cart and noticed two baby boxwoods had fallen off the back. *Dammit.*

"I'll get those" Connor appeared at her side. He bent easily at the waist and grabbed them both by the thin black plastic of the containers.

"Wow, that was fast." Clara watched as he failed to find an open spot on the flatbed dolly. "I think we'll just have to carry those, if that's all right." She gave him an apologetic smile. "We've reached max capacity."

"No problem." His eyes scanned the full-hand truck. "Did you get everything?"

"No, unfortunately. I need to get a few more shrubs that aren't going into the planters."

"Well, how about you carry these guys?" Connor handed her the boxwoods. "I'll pull the cart. Then you can give me the list for the stuff you're missing so you can get started." He had already begun maneuvering down the narrow walkway and back toward the greenhouse.

"How many more do we need?" He asked over his shoulder.

Clara stared, watching his muscles jump as he pulled the load in front of her. His attention was straight ahead, giving her shameless access. The sun had crept higher and Connor's T-shirt was clinging with sweat. Clara walked ahead and placed her plants on the ground, reaching for the door to the greenhouse. "Four more, I think?"

With a labored breath, Connor pulled the cart through. They worked together, unloading everything. Clara wiped the sweat from her forehead and looked at her workspace. Connor had already arranged all the bags of potting soil and the planters into neat rows. She watched as he drained the rest of his water, standing in front of the industrial fan installed at the end of the run. Her palms felt hot and sweaty inside her leather gloves.

He raised his brow. "Got the list?"

She blinked "Oh. Yeah—here." Clara stepped forward, handing over the clipboard. "I put a star next to the ones we still need." He turned promptly and headed back out. She walked over, steadied her stance, and hoisted a bag of soil over her shoulder. After depositing it next to the first stone planter, she frowned at the track shorts. *No pockets.* Clara went to grab a box cutter from the workbench and sliced the ends of each bag, dumping the contents into the pot.

She began combining small shrubs with annuals and perennials. Creeping vines tumbled over the sides and contrasting colors shimmered in bright, cheerful hues. The oversized planters were going to flank the entry points of a home with large doors along a wraparound porch. Clara heard the greenhouse door open again and Connor walked in, carrying all four shrubs at once. Clara stayed hunched near the ground, stealing a glance at his arms.

He sunk into a tired heap. "*Damn it's hot.*"

She smiled, moving her eyes back to her work. "Eli keeps water in the mini-fridge in his office."

Connor went from sitting to laying in the dirt next to her as she nestled creeping jenny into the pot, liking the way the lemon-lime played against the base of the elephant ear. Clara chuckled. "Four shrubs isn't *that bad.*"

He turned his head on the ground and squinted at her. "No. Four shrubs isn't that bad... *however*, there are a million different kinds of the ones we needed." He returned his gaze to the ceiling.

We. Clara smiled to herself. She stood and dragged over the next pot.

"I thought you used to work here growing up."

Connor huffed. "Yeah, unloading stuff and working the register." He closed his eyes and wiped sweat from above his lip. "I was just like any of these other kids that work here in the summer... not exactly a master gardener."

She checked her watch. They needed to allow extra time to load. She felt something and looked down. Connor had reached out and placed his hand across the top of her work boot. Her throat tightened and their eyes held as he gazed up at her from the dirt.

"How are we doing on time?"

She swallowed, contemplating. "Not good, not terrible." She inched her foot away, a little concerned at how much she liked that he had reached for her. "I'm going to grab us some water."

When she returned, she saw that Connor had dragged over the last few planters and the rest of the potting soil so she wouldn't have to walk back and forth. A smile pulled at the corner of her mouth.

"I figured it would make it easier." He pointed at the supplies. "So you could work faster."

"Thanks, it'll definitely help." She grabbed a tray of flashy heuchera and sweet potato vine and knelt down at the next pot. She watched as Connor opened the cold water she brought him. He took a knee in front of the four shrubs he had carried back and frowned.

"Which ones did you grab?"

He paused. "Well. This tag says viburnum, this one an azalea, and these two are roses."

Clara chuckled. "*Okay*... could you be a little more specific?" She saw Connor squint at the fine print.

"All right—the first one is a Viburnum Awabuki... *Chindo?*" Connor looked in her direction.

She nodded, remembering the order sheet. "That sounds right. How about that azalea?" She ripped the opening of the bag of soil a little wider.

"Azalea Rhododendron *Admiral Semmes*..." Connor paused. "Who the hell is Admiral Semmes?"

Clara laughed, adjusting the plant in front of her so it wouldn't sit too low once the dirt settled. "I don't know who Admiral Semmes is, but that's definitely not right."

"How do you know?"

"*Because*. I can't remember the exact one they wanted, but it was an *Encore* variety." The one that Connor had grabbed looked more like a native azalea.

Connor shook his head. Clara continued. "And twenty bucks says the roses they ordered are Knock Outs."

She finally turned to look at him as he scanned the clipboard. She concentrated on his face... trying to see if she was, indeed, correct. He turned toward her, expression completely neutral.

"What makes you so sure?"

She tilted her head. "Because most people are fairly predictable." She motioned around them to the huge stone planters packed tight with showy foliage.

His poker face pulled into a smirk. "Care to expand on said *predictability?*"

Clara stood. "Well... Eli is known for keeping inventory that is a little hard to find, but nine times out of ten, people buy the trendy stuff. They want plants that are low maintenance... things they don't have to work too hard for." Clara brushed her gloves together. "And most customers are impatient. They want things that bloom all the time so they can have a grand spectacle all 365 days."

Connor walked over to a bag of soil. He tore it open, prefilling the last planter. "What's so bad about that?"

Clara shrugged. "It's not *bad.*"

Connor chuckled. "You definitely make it sound *bad.*"

She liked the sound of his laugh. "*No.* I just think people want perfection all the time. But it's not real and sometimes it feels... forced." She smiled to herself. "Seasons are the *ultimate* grand spectacle. Everything has its moment in the spotlight—you just have to be patient." She continued while working a five-gallon boxwood out of its plastic container. "Like, it's inconceivable that *waiting* for the magic is more rewarding than having it in your face all the time."

Connor walked away in silence and returned, carrying the last two trays of flowers and vines. "Mother Nature sounds like a tease."

Clara rolled her eyes.

"So you're a purist." He pressed. "Are you into growing things from those little paper packets?"

Clara dabbed the sweat from her face with the sleeve of the Earth Day shirt. "No, definitely not. Growing from seed requires *too* much patience. The water, the sun exposure... everything has to be controlled to a certain point." She was kneeling down and leaned over to her left, reaching for a bag of peat moss. Connor handed it to her.

"Thanks. Starting from scratch is a little intimidating... I don't know if it's for me."

Connor watched her, pursing his lips. "How do know about all this stuff?"

She kept her eyes on her work. "I've picked up a ton, you know, spending time with Eli and Gloria." Clara checked the container in front of her, making sure it wasn't too crowded. "I came here a lot after we got married—Mark and me."

Connor's shoulders stiffened. "I didn't realize he was into this stuff." The image of Mark strolling around with her, touching her, buying her things for their home—it made him nauseous.

"He isn't." Clara huffed. The sound was bitter and heavy. "I started coming by myself." Her throat bobbed, remembering the exact day she'd broken down. She had gotten the letter the night before and wandered around Grady's for an entire afternoon. Gloria sat with her for over an hour, smoothing her hair and wiping her tears. Clara sucked in a breath. "After a while, Eli offered me a job."

Connor sat back, perched on the edge of the table closest to her. Something had constricted in his chest. He thought the idea of her here with Mark made him sick. But the idea of her being left alone made him angry. He stretched his legs out in front of where she worked, taking a deep breath. He moved his shoe, touching the tray of tiny flowers in her hand. "And you're not into stuff like this?"

She shook her head, observing the muscles of his calves. "I hate annuals. All show and no go."

Connor smiled. "You realize you sound like Goldilocks."

She sighed. "They're good for a short while and then they're basically compost." Clara rotated the heavy pot in front of her, rather than get up and move. "In nature, things take time. Some things grow, some things die..." From the ground, her eyes traveled the vertical length of the arrangement in front of her, deep in thought. "Some things go dormant and wait to wake back up." She turned, gazing up into his face. "But when they do, you find yourself doing a double take. They might look more vibrant the next time you see them bloom."

Connor continued to sit above her, watching carefully. His gaze held a spark, ready to catch. "And you'd rather torture yourself by waiting than go for instant gratification?"

Clara broke eye contact, taking off her gloves. The faint line where her wedding ring used to sit was barely visible now. "There is gratification. It's just... delayed. But that doesn't make it any less beautiful."

Connor reached a hand down and hoisted her up. Clara's breath stalled at the feel of his hot, bare skin against hers. She cleared her throat. "Did you know there are bulbs that take years to bloom again?"

His eyes widened, mocking her. "You don't say—"

His dimples deepened. *He is definitely more handsome now.* She pushed at his shoulder and forged on, matter-of-fact. "Not like *regular* bulbs... there are some that take like a decade to come back."

Connor finally stood from the table, bringing them face to face. She studied the scruff bordering his lips. The tone of his voice carried in the quiet space between them. "I think you need a tree."

Their eyes collided quickly, and Clara let out a nervous laugh. She watched, transfixed, as those lips pulled into a smirk.

With a painful step back, she turned and walked away. Clara couldn't quite catch her breath. Dragging a garden hose back to the work area, she played along. "Trees *are* very resilient." She pulled the trigger and water shot out in a wide, even spray. "Maybe that's exactly what I need."

Connor contemplated her words. His eyes roamed her body, observing the graceful way she moved as she worked her way from pot to pot. "Word on the street is that weeds are pretty resilient."

She scrunched her nose at him. "They are not *resilient*. They're *persistent*... there's a *big* difference." Clara watched as water dripped from the base of each pot. "Trust me, *resilient* is something that withstands and endures." She frowned. "*Persistent* is something that wears you down."

He scoffed, entertained by her rebuttal. "I'd argue that *persistent* and *resilient* are definitionally adjacent."

Connor stood behind her, half listening, half looking at the way the loose hem of his shorts fluttered against her thighs. She turned, catching his eye, and her gaze grew serious. "Well, I can tell you from experience... you don't want anything that wears you down." She glanced at her watch and set down the hose. "*That shit's exhausting.*"

Connor sidestepped, moving out of the way as Clara strode past, eyes focused and tone sharp. Lifting a hand to his jaw, he scrubbed across his stubble. A breath shot over his lips and a lopsided grin stretched across his mouth, watching as she marched out of the greenhouse.

⚯

It took them forever to pull out of the gravel lot. They packed every nook and cranny between the giant stone planters with tarps and loose material to keep them from colliding. Clara twisted in her seat, looking into the back as they slowed to turn onto the road. She entered the delivery address into her phone and read the first few steps out loud to Connor. After about fifteen minutes, they fell into traffic. Clara let out a sigh as she craned her neck, looking out the window.

"God. I think there's a wreck up ahead."

Connor adjusted his seat and fiddled with the controls for the AC.

Clara sighed. An angry honk came from behind them, and Connor looked in his rearview.

"We'll get there. Just try not to think about it." After another five painful minutes of silence, Clara sighed again.

"Grab the cord out of the front of my backpack."

Clara's brow furrowed.

"I can't sit here and listen to you sigh constantly."

Clara resigned and dug around in his aforementioned backpack. Retrieving the cord, she straightened in her seat, grabbing Connor's phone from the cupholder.

"So what kind of music does Mr. Connor Kent listen to?"

"I was thinking a podcast could be good."

Clara swiveled in the passenger seat. "Don't tell me..."

"What?"

"*Spice Girls.*"

"Excuse me?"

"*Michelle Branch.*"

He stared at her in utter confusion.

"Ohhhhh... *Cher.*"

Connor shook his head. "Are you going to tell me what's happening?"

Clara nodded. *All-knowing.* "You're clearly hiding something if you're suggesting we listen to a *podcast*. No one in their right mind could be distracted by a *podcast* at a time like this."

Connor pinched the space between his eyes. "Fine—whatever. I didn't know I was sharing a vehicle with the authority on all things entertainment." He tossed her a look. "Just pick something."

Clara tapped Spotify, scanning his recently listened-to episodes. Economics? *Barf.* She searched for her own mega masterpiece and smiled, letting out a small squeal. She hit play and, after several silent seconds, frowned down at his phone. "Why isn't it working?"

Connor sighed, reaching over. "You have to plug it in—"

Shania's voice shot out, blasting their eardrums, ringing like the inside of a tin can.

"Oh, God—"

Heat flamed her entire body. Lyrics hit them—about beds and boots and where they'd been. Clara lunged forward and hit next, his phone dropping from her hands. *"Shit—"*

Fingers jumped along a piano, notes tumbling around the cab like Connor's phone. Lizzo's words pounded the air between them and her stomach twisted.

Yes—My name is Clara and I am in fact, 100 percent that bitch.

Clara reached down, smacking her head on the dash as she scraped along the floorboard. She fished the phone up by its auxiliary cord, mashing the screen until everything stopped. She froze, unable to turn. Clara caught a wave of Connor's *sport*-strength deodorant and she clamped her arms tight to her sides.

She may or may not have stolen a couple of swipes before they left. She should have swiped it all over her body, because she was definitely going to die in this van. People will ask... *Was it the heat? Was it from starvation? Was it because her butt went numb from sitting for too long, shaving off years of her already sedentary life?* No. She died after Connor Kent stole a glimpse into her angry, emotional, man-hating existence.

Another car honked from behind them. Clara cringed, peeking over at the driver's seat. Connor sat motionless with his wrist propped at the top of the steering wheel, his hand draping down. Clara followed the line of his arm, dusted with hair until it disappeared beneath his shirtsleeve. His expression was indecipherable.

Clara didn't realize she had been holding her breath and exhaled. Like someone had punctured a hole in a bounce house. Another song started and her hand shot toward the dash. Connor intercepted, grabbing her wrist. When she looked again, a grin stretched across his face, her heart hanging off a cliff.

His dimples deepened, and his smile glowed like a forty-watt bulb. It wasn't bright or blinding. It was warm and intimate. Like something rare, meant only for her. A spark hummed around them and Connor pushed her hand out of the way... turning the volume all the way up. His lips moved and his voice left his chest—a foreign sound fueled by nostalgia. Clara watched, transfixed, as the rhythm slowly traveled down his body and overtook the entire delivery truck. Before Clara realized what was happening, Connor had fully transformed into the star of her punk rock teen dreams.

She shouted over the music. "You like this song?!"

Connor looked at her like she was crazy. *"Abso-fucking-lutely."*

Clara tipped her head back and laughed. Connor's words rolled over her like the formidable heat of summer, wrapping her in that ever elusive happiness that always seemed just out of reach. She joined him, knowing every word. The bridge approached, and the drums halted. Connor stopped singing and took a backseat, giving Clara her chance in the spotlight. She grabbed hold of it. Squeezing her eyes shut, she belted the lines. It felt *so .damn. good.*

When she looked, Connor was right there with her. The beat dropped, and they shouted the lyrics together, Connor on the drums of the steering wheel. They erupted in laughter as the song flowed around them. Clara leaned forward, covering her face in her hands, in complete disbelief that this was the same man she had almost snuffed out under a pile of books. She beamed. Connor sat with his head leaned back on the seat, the electric blue of his irises focused solely on her. His attention wasn't hurried. It was like the years between them had melted away over the past four minutes.

Someone behind them laid on their horn.

Clara jumped. "We're moving!"

Connor hit the gas, and they took off. They needed to make up for lost time.

⎯⎯⎯e⎯⎯⎯

Clara's legs were shaking. They had been at it for the past hour. The order had failed to mention that the Samsons' wrap-around porch was situated atop two flights of stairs, half of them rickety and bowed within an inch of their life. The sooner they finished, the sooner she could collapse.

Connor saw the depletion in Clara's face. "Almost there."

"You said that already." Sweat dripped into her eye.

"Watch the railing..." He sucked in air. "Hey, let's just rest a sec—"

"No-Connor... I need this to be over." Clara groaned. She adjusted her grip on the handle of the harness they were using to carry the planters up Mount Olympia. Her knees buckled. "Oh, God—"

The pot swayed between them, the weight forceful enough to knock their tired bodies off balance.

"Whoa... Clara, *focus*." The cords of his arms tightened as he tried to still the movement between them. "Look at me." His voice was stern, "*Almost. There.*" Their eyes cut through the exhaustion. She nodded, trusting him.

"You good?" He watched her mouth soften as she exhaled.

"Can we get ice cream when we're done?"

A chuckle passed his lips. "I didn't know you performed manual labor for sweets."

"*Hell yeah*. And it better be good."

They broached the final stair, and together, rested the planter slowly. A smile broke across Connor's face as he tilted his chin to the sun. "Hard parts over."

Clara was leaning back against the rail. Exhaustion emanated from every part of her body, and his heart pinched. If he could finish the job without her, he would. He tapped her arm, and she nodded, signaling that she heard him. The Samsons waited patiently for them at the last door as they dropped the final pot into place. At Clara's direction, they lifted one last time, ensuring that the best side faced forward. Once it was over, Clara excused herself and pointed to the truck, motioning that she was going to go sit.

"Go ahead, I'll meet you down there." She waved over her shoulder and panted, grabbing the banister. Connor turned toward the elderly couple and asked if everything was to their satisfaction. They boasted their approval, pressing a wad of cash into his palm even though he had already politely declined. *Ice cream money.*

The Samsons retreated inside and Connor smiled, watching as Clara descended the steps in front of him, untying the tangled knot of frizz at the base of her neck. Shiny waves tumbled around her shoulders as she reached the first landing. She turned to look at him with mischief in her eyes. "All right, Kent! This ice cream better be—" Her legs buckled. Grabbing the railing, she twisted into a heap of sweat and swear words on the wooden stairs below.

He rushed down, stepping over a broken tread, and reached out to her. "What happened? What's wrong?"

"*Shit... I don't know... I heard this crack.*"

Connor winced. "I think that was the stair."

Clara's fingers were wrapped around the area above her boot. Her mouth pressed into a hard line.

He knelt down and pried her hands away. "Let me look." She leaned back and winced. The sun was beating down on them both.

"Can you try moving it for me?" He held her boot in his hands and looked into her face.

Clara attempted to flex and point her foot. He could see the sweat beading at the base of her throat.

Connor shifted his weight and went to stand. "Let's get you to the van."

"I think I need a second before I try—" Connor threaded his arms under her limbs, swinging her up close to his chest.

"*Connor!* You're going to drop me!"

He tightened his hold, their sweaty skin sliding, then fusing together. He took the remaining stairs slowly, and she groaned.

They reached the open doors at the back of the van. "I'm going to set you down for a second." Connor lowered her, watching as she put all her weight on her good ankle. She clutched the inside of the door with one hand and held onto his arm as she sat on the bumper. Connor wiped his brow.

"You want to ask if we can sit inside the Samson's for a bit?"

Clara glowered at the mountain of stairs and shook her head.

Connor sighed. "Do you want to go to Urgent Care?"

"I'd rather *die*."

"Well, that's a little dramatic."

"I just mean I don't feel like sitting in a waiting room for hours so someone can tell me to keep it elevated and to pop an extra strength Tylenol." Clara lifted her leg and looked at her ankle with disdain. "Can you just take me home?"

They sat in silence. Connor nodded. He helped her hobble over to the passenger door and supervised as she pulled herself up. He leaned into the cab, yanking against the tension of the seatbelt at her side. As he stretched it across her chest, he looked into her eyes, freezing at the surprise he found there. He glanced at her mouth.

"Connor... I'm not a complete invalid." She smiled and his voice caught in his throat.

"Suit yourself."

He straightened and stood back before circling around the van. Opening the driver's side, Connor slid in and cranked the engine, hot air tumbling out from the vents.

"Right." He turned in his seat and glanced back as they rolled in reverse. "Let's get you home."

Connor liked the way Clara felt against him. They reached the front door, where he begrudgingly set her down. He told her it'd be easier to run up the steps and unlock the door, then double back, but she insisted.

He kicked something by his foot and swayed, looking down. "Shit."

"Oh—it must be the blanket I ordered!" She kept one arm looped around his neck for balance as she perched on her good foot.

Connor's brows knitted together. "You realize it's like a million degrees outside."

Holding her purse, she stuck her arm in, fishing for the key—the smell of his deodorant filling the air. Connor fought a smile above her head. When he'd buckled her in after the delivery, the combination of her sweat mixed and melded with his own and he was overcome with this heady zing. Her pheromones were lethal. The clang of her keys broke his trance and the heavy door swung open.

She tutted. "Trust me. I'm well aware."

He leaned to pick her up again.

"I can manage from here."

"All right." Connor withdrew and stepped to the side. "I guess... just give me a call if you need anything." *She clearly wants space.*

Clara grabbed his arm, wobbling slightly. "Wait! I just meant I can manage getting to the couch... you know, without the whole *Tarzan* thing?"

He raised an eyebrow, and Clara rolled her eyes.

"Just give me your arm and I'll hop."

He did as she asked, and they stepped over the threshold. "And grab the package, will you?" She directed him into what appeared to be the living room and Clara flopped down on the couch. "Maybe you could just move a few things within reach? I won't keep you... I'm sure you've got stuff to do."

A chill from the air conditioning drifted over him. He shifted his feet and looked around, dropping the box on the floor. Spotting the kitchen, he walked away and dug around in the freezer.

He shouted, holding open the stainless steel door. "You got any dish towels?"

"Third drawer down! To the right of the sink!"

Connor grabbed a cloth along with an ice pack and headed back into the living room. Clara had managed to take the boot off her good foot and sat staring at her other one. She lifted her hips and pulled her phone from her back pocket. She was typing at lightning speed as he grabbed a few pillows from around the room and shoved them under her leg. "What are you doing?"

She didn't look up. "Just Googling whether I'm supposed to take the boot off... I think you're supposed to leave it on." She finally met his eyes. "It keeps it from swelling too much or something."

"You can take it off." He knelt down to the ground beside the couch and looked at the bruising that had already started. His eyes traveled up the smooth line of her leg, goosebumps appearing across her skin. His throat bobbed. "That only applies if you were in an emergency and couldn't get off your feet." He met her eyes again. "Like if you were out on a trail somewhere." Clearing his throat, he tapped the top of her boot. "You ready?"

She gave a quick nod. "Ready."

Connor pulled firmly, his eyes never leaving her face. His stomach tensed when he caught her wincing and with a quick motion, the boot released and fell to the floor. Clara flopped back onto the cushions. Connor smiled and peeled off her sock... well, *his* sock. He laid the dish towel across the deep compression lines embedded in her skin and placed the gel pack on top.

"That ought to do it." His eyes slid over her, laid out on the couch, and he looked away, glancing down at his hands. "Do you have any Tylenol?"

Clara yawned and made a noise that he assumed was a *yes*. "Top drawer in the powder room."

Connor caught her yawn, and she smiled up at him. It had been a long morning. He stood up and walked back out to the foyer. Passing the stairs, he rounded the corner, finding the bathroom.

"I checked all the drawers, but I didn't see—" He sighed, coming back into the room. Clara's eyes were closed and her head had lolled to her shoulder. He watched as she shifted, snuggling into the cushions, and he looked around, searching. Glancing down at the floor, Connor picked up the package at his feet. He walked to the kitchen and cut open the box, releasing an airtight ball of fluff that expanded into a giant cloud. "*What in the hell...*"

Connor shook his head and grabbed a piece of paper. Scribbling quickly, he tucked it next to her phone on the couch, draped the blanket over her, and grabbed her keys before slipping out the front door. He reached the bottom stair of the porch and something caught his eye. A stone squirrel lay face down in the grass and he raised a curious brow in the direction of the house.

It was only then that he looked around. A little messy, but impressive. The yard was sprawling and Connor's throat tightened, curious as to how much of this was Clara's work. The flowerbeds were full of weeds, the overgrown shrubs swayed, and he wondered, how many hours—how many days—had she spent out here... alone? He turned and got back into the van for what felt like the millionth time. Starting the engine, a smile tugged at his mouth. He shook his head. *So much for his Saturday.*

—⁓—

Clara awoke to her phone buzzing. Drenched in sweat, she frowned, shoving the giant blanket from her body. She glanced at the ice pack on her ankle and peered around the room. It was light outside, but it was quiet in the house. Drawing in a breath, Clara recounted the blur of events that got her there. The broken stair at the Samsons' and the early morning at Grady's. She shoved a hand through her hair. *Connor's apartment.* Sliding a hand along the cushions, she peeled her phone from where it had plastered itself to her lower back.

RYAN: What's on the itinerary this evening?

Clara zoomed in and took a picture of her ankle.

RYAN: Shiiiiiiiit.

CLARA: I know. It can't get any worse.

RYAN: What happened to you? Do you need rations?

Her ankle hurt like hell. Her stomach rumbled loudly, as if on cue.

CLARA: I do need rations... and a candy stripper.

CLARA: STRIPER***

RYAN: I'll bring dinner. I'll call to review options when I'm OMW.

RYAN: If I find a cute candy stripper, I'll bring him too.

CLARA: My Knight In Shining Armor.

Clara laughed and tossed her phone on the coffee table. A noise came from the porch outside. She jolted up, swinging her gimpy leg to the floor. "OW! Shit—"

Just as she clutched the sofa to try to stand, the lock turned. "Oh my God." She sank horizontally, more or less throwing herself to the floor in slow motion. Clara squinted at the shoes standing in the foyer.

"If this was a horror movie, you would definitely be the first to die."

Rolling on her back, she hinged at the waist, popping up above the table. "Damn you, Connor Kent."

He held her keys in one hand and a paper grocery bag in the other. "If you're not in the mood for sustenance or pain medication..." He tossed her keys on the table next to her phone. "Then I'll take this elsewhere."

"*WAIT!*" Clara struggled to get to her knees. "What did you bring?"

"You didn't see my note?" She shook her head. He walked toward her, looking down at her ankle. "Grab hold."

Clara hooked her arm in his and together they made their way to the kitchen. She pulled out her own barstool as he slid another next to her and patted the seat. "*Up.*"

"So bossy..."

He gave her a look, daring her. She resigned and carefully lifted her leg, resting her knee and calf along the top so her ankle wasn't bearing any weight.

He set the grocery bag on the marble island in front of them and unloaded the goods.

She wiggled her eyebrows at him. "So... whatcha got?"

"Well, you didn't have any Tylenol." He pulled a bottle out from the bag and shook it before setting it down and sliding it across the surface until it bumped into her arm.

"Where do you keep the glasses?"

Clara started picking at the childproof lid. "Upper cabinet by the fridge... left side."

Connor retrieved two and filled them with ice from the freezer and water from the tap. He glanced at her ankle. "How bad is it?"

She stayed fixated on the container in her hand. "Oh—uh. Bad, but not the worst?" The pressure released and the plastic top ricocheted onto the counter.

"So, on a scale of one to ten—one being *barely any pain* and ten being—"

"A Civil War limb amputation?"

Connor stared at her. The corner of his mouth pulled into a smile. "*Right*. What's the verdict?"

"Eh—maybe a four?" Her stomach rumbled again. Loud enough that Connor laughed.

"Well, I hope you like breakfast." He pulled out a box of pancake mix and set it on the counter, followed by a carton of eggs, butter, and bacon.

Clara tilted her head. "It's like, three p.m."

"Haven't you heard of breakfast for dinner?"

Clara amped up the puzzled expression on her face, "I repeat, *it's like three p.m...*"

"Ha. Ha." Connor turned and began pulling out pots and pans. "I might not have the most refined palate, but I haven't met anyone who doesn't like breakfast."

"Hm. Were there other contenders?"

Connor's back was to her. "Disappointed?"

"No. Not at all... I *love* breakfast."

"Good." Their eyes met over his shoulder. "No need to discuss the *other contenders*."

Clara looked down at the counter. "Mixing bowl is in the bottom cabinet... on your right."

Connor knelt down, following her directions. "Are you an active participant? Or are you in this for the show?"

She smiled. "I can help."

"Good. That'll make this go a little faster." He brought her the box of mix, along with the required ingredients. She watched as he dug out a measuring cup from the drawer in front of him, following his movements as he maneuvered around her kitchen. She bit the inside of her cheek, surprised at how much she liked seeing him there. Connor stepped toward the sink.

She cleared her throat. "Tell me... are you a *milk* or a *water* guy?"

His hand paused at the tap. "Is there a difference?" Clara's expression said it all. She leaned forward and put her face into the crook of her elbow. He rolled his eyes. "All right—we'll do milk."

Clara popped up with a smug smile and reached into the box of mix.

He set the measuring cup in front of her. "I'm really starting to see a different side of you."

"Oh, yeah?" She dumped the milk into the bowl and he watched as it spilled down the powdered mix. Connor felt its resistance as it trickled into tiny streams. He handed her the whisk. "Yeah, you're kind of a pain in the ass."

Before he turned, he caught the drop of her jaw and smiled. He moved to the stove and set two pans on medium-low.

"Well. That's not anything *terribly* new."

He raised an eyebrow, and she leveled him with a glint in her eye. He sliced open the package of bacon and laid a few strips in the pan, listening to the sizzle. "I don't remember you being this..."

"*Clever? Witty?*" She slid the bowl forward and used her hands to scrape up the stray particles of mix from the counter. "*Entertaining?*"

Connor pulled a pair of tongs from the utensil holder next to the stove. "No... you were all those things back then."

Clara went quiet, and he looked in her direction. There was a warmth in her eyes that caught him off guard. He reached for the bowl in front of her. Using a knife, he threw a pat of butter into the pan, watching it slide around before melting into a puddle.

"You seem..." He shrugged and met her gaze, searching. "*Strong.*"

"Strong." Clara's eyes widened in disbelief. "I'm beginning to wonder if you're remembering the right person."

"My answer still stands." Connor drizzled the first pancake. "It wasn't meant as an insult... Maybe you just don't see it."

He stole a glance. Clara was sitting up straighter in her chair, relief tinging her eyes. "Does my opinion matter?" He felt stupid for asking. Like he was fishing.

"It matters." Clara twisted her water glass on the marble. "Other than my mom, I don't have many people in my life that knew me back then."

He smiled. "We're not exactly dinosaurs."

"No, not quite." Clara laughed. "I just mean, you knew me B.M. and A.D."

He tossed her a look.

She chuckled. "*Before Mark*… and *After Death*."

Connor bristled. He didn't want to talk about Mark. Grabbing a plate, he began pulling pancakes off the stove. He laid another round of bacon in the pan. Hot grease hissed and popped.

"Wouldn't *Before Marriage*, and *After Divorce* be more appropriate?"

He felt her contemplating. "It seems bigger than divorce… more like a *death*," she said quietly. "It's weird to hear you talk about what I was like… and if I'm different now." She reached for the box that contained the pancake mix, fidgeting with the cardboard. "I don't know what *me* is supposed to feel like now."

He flipped a pancake with the flick of his wrist, and shifted, leaning against the counter. He studied her as she tore at the flap on top of the box.

"I don't think I realized how empty my life really was until he left." She looked across the island. "In the beginning, everything was so simple. I used to just look at him, and think *this is what love is*." Clara scanned the kitchen. "It never felt like I was giving anything up… I was just so caught up in being whatever I thought he wanted." Her eyes fell on a small photo of them on the fridge. One she had forgotten to take down.

"You were young." His words brought her back. He saw the sadness on her face. Connor pulled the last piece of bacon out of the pan and reached for the carton of eggs. He glanced over. "You gonna tell me how to do this, too?"

"Yes." She smiled.

———ele———

With Connor's help, Clara hobbled back to the living room. "Couch? Or chair?"

Clara glanced at the leather chair and frowned. "Um... couch, please."

Sitting together on the cushions, they ate in silence for a few moments, both voracious.

"Pass the syrup?"

Clara handed him the glass bottle and watched as he drizzled sticky, golden liquid onto his plate. "So... you really think I seem strong?"

He screwed the lid back on and smiled to himself. She was fishing—he didn't mind it. "You don't think you are?" He watched a blush creep across her face.

She picked up a piece of bacon. "I know experience is supposed to make you wiser... I guess I just wonder if instead of getting wiser, I've just been doubling down on my mistakes." She bit the piece in half.

"Maybe it's not over."

Clara's eyebrows shot up, and she turned to face him.

"I mean, maybe you haven't come out on the other side yet." Connor chewed a forkful of scrambled egg. He watched as she leaned back against the couch cushions, her shoulders sagging. His chest constricted at the sight.

He knocked her knee with his. "How bad was it?"

She looked up at the ceiling, exhaling. "*Civil War limb amputation.*"

An amused breath passed his lips, but Clara wasn't smiling. She sat back up in her seat and resumed picking at her plate. "You know, I got a letter from a woman..." Connor swallowed thickly. His food suddenly tasted like lead paint. He watched her push her food around as she spoke—the words like nails on a chalkboard. "She figured out that Mark was married, and she wanted me to know what he had done. Like she was looking out for me." Her smile twisted. "This woman left him the second she found out... and *I stayed*." Anger shook in her voice. "For so *fucking* long."

Connor studied her face. Tears wavered along her lashes as her confession sat between them, like a bomb waiting to be detonated. He never understood why she'd stayed... but she was obviously paying for it now.

"Well." He sighed. "You lived to tell the tale." Connor winced at his trivial tone.

Clara turned to face him, narrowing her gaze. Her eyes shimmered and he wanted to take it back. He wanted to intercept his own words and replace them with the right ones. Ones that mattered.

She stared at him in silence, taking in every inch of his expression. A smile broke across her face and he leaned in, counting his lucky stars as their laughter tumbled together in the quiet house.

"You're right." She nodded assertively, blotting her tears. "I lived to tell the tale. What matters is that it's done."

"See?" Connor's smile mirrored hers. She tilted her head, waiting. "You are strong."

Pleased, Clara picked up her fork. She couldn't wipe the grin off her face, and he couldn't stop thinking about how he had put it there.

"Aren't you the least bit interested to know if I think you've changed?"

Connor stuffed three layers of pancake into his mouth. He chewed slowly and mulled over her question. He *was* interested, and that bothered him.

She wiped her mouth with her napkin. "I think you're very different."

"Is that right?"

"Yeah."

"You're making me think this is gonna hurt."

"I'm sorry," she said. He could feel her looking at him. "It's nothing bad... just *different*."

Connor kept his eyes on his plate, attempting to appear unbothered. "If I had known that you needed a thesaurus this badly, I would've picked one up while I was out."

Clara elbowed him. Connor reached for a piece of bacon from her plate. He stilled, bracing against whatever she had yet to say.

"You're more reserved."

He nodded, but felt there was more. When it came to Clara, he was a glutton for punishment.

"I'm not a little kid." His eyes slid to hers. "You can say it."

A long silence stretched on and he waited patiently as she found her words.

"Sometimes you seem a little distant."

His mouth settled into a hard line as he considered her assessment.

"Sometimes, when we see each other... it's like you're irritated with me." She fiddled with the hem of her shorts. After a moment, she looked down.

He reached out and placed his open palm along her shoulder, the same way he had the night before. He focused on his fingers as his thumb brushed back and forth along the cotton ribbing. "It's strange being back." He found her eyes and hesitated at the vulnerability he saw there. He wanted to fall into that feeling so badly he could taste it. "When I left, I started over." he squeezed her shoulder lightly. "Eventually, I met people. Made new friends." Clara held his gaze. "But for a long time, I just worked... *a lot*." He watched her pulse thrum at the base of her throat. "And it was nice. I didn't have to worry about disappointing people. Or having to explain myself to anyone. It was just... easier being this way."

Clara stared at his mouth. At the gentle slope of his Cupid's bow and the way his words formed as he spoke. "Was there ever... anyone?" She felt every slide of his hand, knowing that if he moved even the slightest, his touch could graze the bare skin at her throat. "Anyone you *wanted* to explain yourself to?" Clara waited, sinking into the weight of his grip, holding her breath for his answer.

"If you're asking if I was *alone*, the answer's no." He shifted, loosening his hold. A trace of a smile formed, disappearing before it ever reached his eyes. "But no. No one special."

Clara covered his hand with her own. It was like she was back in his apartment, pushing her way into his living room. Not ready to leave. "I'm sorry."

Her palm slid over his skin, and Connor's eyes locked on hers. Their breathing stilled. His gaze traveled her face, taking in the frizzy waves framing her cheeks.

She ran her tongue along her bottom lip nervously. "I'm so sorry."

Connor swallowed. He pressed his fingers to the back of her neck and drew her close, his jaw touching her temple. Minutes passed and Clara exhaled, her body going limp. It was like they had been trapped, both struggling for the surface for so long. He pulled back and looked into her face. Her eyes were closed. He traced the arch of her brows, gently pushing strands away from her face.

He wanted to lift her chin and press his mouth to hers. Feel the weight of her lips against his. He smoothed his hand down between her shoulder blades as she relaxed against him. There was an imperceptible shift, like the perilous moment before an avalanche. He wanted everything, and could ask for nothing. He *wouldn't* ask. Connor withdrew, giving her a reassuring squeeze.

"Let me take these to the kitchen."

"You don't have to do that just yet—" Her eyes were soft and her voice pleading.

He did. He needed an excuse. *Anything.*

The doorbell chimed.

They looked at each other. Realization flashed across Clara's face. "Oh my gosh, it's Ryan—"

Holding their dirty plates in his hands, Connor stiffened.

She looked up at him. "Can you do me a huge favor—can you please get the door?"

Connor pivoted. The utensils clanged noisily as he slid them into the sink. Of course she was seeing someone. He heard a knock and shut the water off.

"Connor?"

"Be right there—"

Connor walked down the hallway, passing by the landing of the staircase, and wiped his hands on his shorts. He opened the door and was met with a very surprised set of eyes.

"You're not Clara."

He exhaled. "No, I'm not."

"I brought her food." The irritation in Ryan's expression dissipated. He was now assessing Connor with newfound fascination. "Is Clara here?" Ryan and Connor walked into the house, greeted by Clara, who was sitting with her foot perched atop a mountain of pillows.

"So, I brought you the rations you *so badly* wanted..."

Clara pouted. "I completely forgot, and we just ate... *I am so sorry*." Shrugging her shoulders high, she batted her eyelashes. "Can you forgive me?"

"Don't worry about it. I'll stick it in the fridge so you can have it tomorrow when I'm not here." Connor and Ryan stood together, looking at one another.

"Connor... This is my friend, Ryan. He and I work together."

Ryan extended his hand and looked at Clara with curiosity. "So *this* is Connor..."

She shot Ryan a look. "*Yes*, Ryan, this is *Connor*... Connor and I work together at Grady's."

Connor shook Ryan's hand, confused by their exchange. "Well... now that you've got a new nurse, I guess I should head out. Looks like you two can take care of everything from here."

"Wait! why would you leave? I just got here, and I didn't realize Clara had a guest. If anything—*I* should leave."

Connor's eyes met Clara's. "I wouldn't really say I'm a guest."

Clara looked at Ryan, filling in the gaps. "Um. Connor was there when I got hurt. He brought me home and made sure I didn't die."

Connor smiled. "That's giving me too much credit. At most, I made a grocery run and bought some very mild pain medication."

Carrying the takeout bag to the kitchen, Ryan spoke over his shoulder. "Well, since you two have already eaten, I'm going to dig in. I thought I was going to starve to death in the curbside pickup."

Clara looked at Connor. "You really don't have to leave. I'd like it if you stayed... unless you have plans."

"Yeah, I'll stay for a bit..." Connor bounced back on his heels with his hands in his pockets. "You know, just to make sure you're set for the night."

Connor was confused and intrigued.

Ryan and Clara bantered, breaking to laugh between every scene of the show, and he could barely get a word in edge wise.

"I don't understand. How do you guys know all the women *and* everyone they're dating?" Connor looked at Clara, who looked at Ryan. They shared a silent moment of knowing.

Ryan crunched a tortilla chip. "If you're a true *Sex and the City* fan, then you've watched it from the beginning." He held up his palm, covering his mouth as he spoke. "If you're just dipping your toe into the water, then, of course, you're gonna be lost."

Clara nodded in agreement as Ryan motioned toward the TV screen. "The way I see it... Each woman's storyline consists of one or two *major loves* and then all the *sex* that takes place is more or less for commentary."

"Okay." Connor bobbed his head, absorbing. "So, are any of these men here considered a *major love?*"

"No, no one here. This is just a sexy bartender-caterer-waiter that Carrie is talking to at the moment."

Connor popped a cold nacho into his mouth. "Doesn't one of them end up with a bartender?"

Clara and Ryan looked at Connor with surprise and delight.

He glanced at them innocently. "So, how did these women become friends in the first place? This seems like an unlikely group."

Ryan looked personally offended, addressing his question like someone explaining the meaning of life. "How they became friends is not the point... What is more important is how their lives intersect and bring meaning to the show as a whole."

Connor's eyes narrowed, a glint of disbelief hovering just below the surface. Clara grinned. She was growing attached to his sparring.

"It just seems unlikely that this art gallery owner—"

Ryan lifted his hand. "She doesn't *own* the gallery. She just *works* at the gallery."

"Okay—*whatever.* I highly doubt that this art gallery girl would be best friends with this attorney, who would also be best friends with a writer."

"Yes, yes. Who is *also* best friends with a PR queen..." Clara rolled her eyes, tugging her new throw blanket up to her chin. "What's your point?"

"I don't know... I guess I can understand how it makes the show more entertaining."

Ryan jumped in. "Half the fun is identifying with one of the characters. It becomes a game. Like *Friends,* or *The Golden Girls.*"

Connor laughed, reaching for another chip.

"For example, Clara and I were recently discussing how I'm a *Samantha.*"

Connor blinked a couple of times and then blinked some more. He looked back and forth from the TV screen as Samantha brought up *funky tasting spunk* while having lunch in a fancy restaurant. "So you're the blonde."

"Yes," Ryan confirmed. "And our sweet Clara here just came to the realization that she is a *Carrie.*"

Clara whacked Ryan in the head with a throw pillow. Seeing the confusion on Connor's face, she clarified. "I've spent my whole life thinking that I was a *Charlotte* and I came to the sad conclusion that I am actually more of a *Carrie.*"

He pursed his lips. "And that's a bad thing?"

"Some people don't find her character to be the most favorable," Ryan whispered.

Clara whacked him again.

"Okay, if you're *Samantha,* and you're *Carrie...* then who would I be?"

Ryan clapped his hands and sat up to a sitting position on the floor.

"That is the question of the hour." He looked up at Clara. "What is Connor's *Sex in the City* alter ego?"

Clara adjusted the ice pack on her ankle and smiled. She and Ryan both took their time staring, deep in assessment. They threw out subtle comments, talking as if he wasn't even there. It was revealing. And terrifying.

"He doesn't seem extremely worried about fashion, but he doesn't seem sloppy."

"No, not sloppy. But then again... none of the women are sloppy.

"But we agree that Carrie is probably the most likely to be sloppy if any of the women were going to be, right?"

"Right. But he's not sloppy, so what difference does it make? I don't think he's Carrie."

"No, definitely not." Ryan shook his head in complete agreement. Connor didn't know what to make of this. But he could tell from Clara's earlier reaction that he didn't want to be a Carrie. Whatever the hell that meant.

"He's not very Park Avenue Princess, but he's giving me a serious Charlotte vibe."

"Yeah, not prim and proper... But for sure a do-gooder."

Connor glanced at Clara, a smirk pulling at the corner of his mouth. She smiled back, and they both fell silent.

"Damn. I didn't know that helping you was a crime."

Clara blushed. "It *isn't*."

Ryan looked between both of them, sensing the zing. "Well, I think we should gather more data about said *do-gooder-ness*." He nodded, a serious tone lacing his words. "If we're to truly decipher Connor's alter ego... I'm going to need the facts to determine how far he ranks on the *Charlotte York Scale For The Pure Of Heart*."

Clara groaned, and Connor gloated.

She sighed. "Fine. I twisted my ankle and he helped me to the car."

Connor looked down at his hands in his lap, biting his lip, fighting a smile.

"What is that look for?" Ryan waved his hand toward his face.

Clara rolled her eyes. "He *carried* me to the car."

Putting his hand lightly to his chest, Ryan gasped. "Do continue."

Clara's eyes found Connor's, and she proceeded. "He buckled me in—"

"Mm. Mm." Ryan interrupted, shaking his head with his lips pressed together. "*Sorry*, keep going."

"Then he made me lunch and got me Tylenol." Recounting their day out loud, her heart pinched. What she didn't mention was his insistence. The way he not only offered his help, but conveyed that he wasn't in a rush to leave. That when she talked about things that could have been left unsaid, he pushed for her honesty. He didn't back down from her, but he didn't make her feel small. Somehow, he managed to do the opposite.

"Extra Strength," Connor clarified.

Her eyes shot to his. "Right... Extra Strength." Clara confirmed.

"*Extra. Strength.*" Ryan folded his hands in his lap, reaching a decision. "You, Connor Kent, are off the friggin' charts."

———

"**S**o, when did you move back to Georgia?" Ryan inquired.

Connor looked at Clara and then back at the television. "I moved at the beginning of summer. Tied up a few loose ends and came back to be closer to family."

Ryan nodded. "Well, I'm surprised I haven't seen you out and about. You're not exactly a forgettable face." He wiggled his eyebrows at Clara. "I think I would recognize you if I saw you out around town."

"I've been at the nursery whenever I have the time." Connor glanced in Clara's direction. "And this one has kept me busy over the past forty-eight hours."

Ryan's eyes darted between them.

"But yeah, I need to get out more. I've been pretty busy setting up my new apartment and, you know, trying to find a new routine."

"So, you have a new apartment?" Ryan's eyes connected with Clara's. A smile played at his lips. "Have you had a proper housewarming yet?"

"I'm actually thinking of having a few people over on the Fourth of July... but it's not a big thing."

Clara tore her eyes from Ryan and glanced down at her hands. Connor clocked her reticence.

"It's just going to be a few friends. I don't really know many people in the area anymore." The three of them fell into a lull as the television played in the background.

Before Connor realized what he was saying, he offered, "I don't know what your plans are for the Fourth... but if you guys are in town, you should stop by."

Ryan looked at Clara, eyes bright. "Yeah! We will definitely try to come."

"It's good being back," Connor said, still holding her gaze.

Something softened in her expression and he glanced at the spot on the couch where he had sat, holding her to his chest.

"I should probably get going. But it was nice hanging out." Connor smiled. "Hopefully, your ankle is feeling a little better."

"It sounds like you were an *excellent* candy striper..." Clara's eyes cut to Ryan's and he buttoned his lips. Not a subtle bone in his body.

Connor laughed, oblivious, and reached for the ice pack under Clara's ankle. "Let me swap this out and then I'll hit the road."

"You don't have to do that. Ryan can help me." Her tone was soft.

He scanned the living room. "Are you sure you're going to be all right tomorrow?"

"Yeah, absolutely. I'll most likely stick around the house and see how bad the swelling gets. If it's worse, I'll figure out a way to get to the doctor's office." Ryan stood with Connor, following him to the kitchen.

"I can help out, too. If she needs to go anywhere, I can drive her. It's no problem." Ryan smiled at Connor from across the island. "So, you grew up here in town?"

"Yeah, my uncle owns the garden center where Clara and I work."

Ryan tilted his head. "That means you know Mark?" It was more a statement than a question.

Connor glanced toward the living room, his lips pressed into a rueful line. "Yeah, I do. We went to school together." He cleared his throat. "Before college... before Clara."

Ryan's eyes narrowed. Connor looked down, moving to the fridge. "Are you from Georgia?"

"Yeah, but we moved around a lot. We did holidays here with my grandma every year, though."

"Really? Who's your grandma?"

"Nurita Abbot. She has the shop—"

"*Nu Yu?*" Connor cocked his head, a smile forming. "You're kidding."

Ryan grinned, watching as Connor turned to pull open the freezer. He swapped out the ice pack and they walked back to the living room together.

Connor caught Clara's eye. "Why didn't you say he was related to Mrs. Nu?"

She sat up on the couch and slowly stood, holding onto the chair for balance. "Who is Mrs. Nu?"

"She's my grandma. Grandma Nu." Ryan reached for Clara, offering a hand. "She owns the beauty supply place on Main."

"Why didn't you ever tell me?" A frown etched Clara's face. "I knew your grandma lived here, but I've never been to her shop." She thought to herself. "Is it the blue building on the edge of town? Just before the farm?"

"Yeah." Ryan nodded. "That's the one."

"I can't believe you never said anything about it." Clara looked at Ryan, her closest confidante, feeling like she had just uncovered a new layer of their friendship. She felt terrible.

"Don't look at me like that." He shook his head, rolling his eyes. "I wouldn't ever expect you to go there. It's a mess... but she'd rather die than sell it."

Clara clutched the couch and hopped once, discomfort in her demeanor. She saw the trepidation on their faces and laughed. "I do have to learn to do this by myself... and I have to pee really bad."

They eyed her nervously as she hobbled out of sight. Connor perched on the arm of the sofa, and Ryan slid into Clara's vacant spot.

"So, Mr. Kent... Any broken hearts left behind in the Windy City?"

He let out a weak laugh, glancing toward the hallway. "No, not exactly." He slid his hands into his pockets, thinking of his conversation with Clara. "How about you? Are you seeing anyone special?"

Ryan preened. "Possibly. There are a few special someones... But only a couple I would consider special enough to be *notable*."

Connor smiled. "Well, if any of those special someones are *notable* enough by the Fourth, feel free to bring them along."

"That's very generous of you." Ryan's smile dipped. "But I don't want Clara feeling like a third wheel. You know, at such a weird time."

Connor's gaze tightened. "What do you mean?"

Ryan tilted his head, peeking at the powder room down the hall. "I know she's very sensitive about the Fourth of July... something about her ex." He rolled his eyes.

"*Ah*. The lake." Connor nodded slowly. "Does that crew still go every year?"

Ryan shrugged, "I don't know any of them... But I think that whole group still gets together." Silence hung in the air. "I invited her to come out with me and some friends because I want to make sure that she isn't alone with nothing to do. Plus..." He lowered his voice. "She needs to get back out there."

Connor's smile faded. The thought of Clara standing in a crowded bar being approached by guys was like a punch to the gut. He imagined her laughing at someone else's joke, smiling up at them while they worked out her favorite flower. His jaw clenched.

Clara slowly hopped back around the corner and raised her arms. "I did it!"

Connor got up and walked to her, stopping so that they stood face to face.

"Well, it's been a wild ride." He looked down into her eyes. "You have my number if you need anything."

Clara reached out and laid her hand on his arm for balance. At least, that's what she told herself. "Are you sure you have to go?"

"Yeah, I have some stuff to do before I leave on Monday."

Clara's eyebrows knitted together. "Oh, I didn't know you were going out of town."

"Yeah, I talked to Eli about it at the beginning of the summer. A friend and I are going to check out a stretch of the Appalachian Trail. Meet up and do some hiking."

"Will you be taking your camera?"

He smiled. "Yeah. It'll be nice to get away for a bit." Something in Connor's eyes made Clara's stomach tighten.

Clara hobbled one step closer and pulled Connor into a hug. With her arms around his waist, she felt his posture soften. "Thank you for taking care of me after my brush with death."

His chest reverberated against hers as he spoke. "You wouldn't have died. Heat stroke, *maybe*."

Clara laughed. "Well, I never did get that ice cream. I don't know who I'm going to have to shake down, but the payoff better be huge."

Connor patted her on the back and pulled away, shoving his hands into his pockets. "Just show up at the nursery in a wheelchair. Eli'll feel terrible. I'm sure he'll buy you anything you want."

Ryan stood and supported Clara as she sat down again. Walking to the door, he thanked Connor again for all his help.

"It was nothing." He smiled. "She's pretty tough."

With his hand on the knob, Ryan tugged, and the front door swung in. Connor's eyes shot to the porch. An enormous bouquet of roses stared up at them. He stood in a rigid trance as Ryan plucked a card from a tuft of baby's breath. Connor shifted his weight and moved to step around the obstruction.

Ryan scrunched his face, disgusted, and scooped up the vase as he backed into the foyer. "Bye Connor, it was really nice getting to meet you." A small smile reached his eyes. "I know it meant a lot to Clara that you stayed."

"No problem." Connor glanced at the roses between them. "So, I'll see you both on the Fourth?"

"Absolutely! We wouldn't dream of missing it!" He shut the door as Connor made his way down the porch steps to the delivery van. Ryan locked the deadbolt and peered out one last time before turning and marching back into the living room. He held up the card, and as his eyes met Clara's, he crushed the paper, balling it into a clump. She looked at him, confused, and gasped, noticing the roses.

"Where did those come from?"

Ryan pelted her with the crumpled card and set the flowers down on the coffee table. He fell into the leather club chair in the corner and propped his feet up on the ottoman, silently protesting. He watched as she uncrumpled the note.

Forgive me.

Clara's stomach dropped. She looked up, her eyes settling on the vase.

"He doesn't seriously think he has a shot in hell, does he?"

Clara glanced down at the card again, idly picking at the corner. "Who knows what he's thinking."

"Seems like a bold move." Ryan looked at her from across the room. "I don't think I could spend money like that on someone. Not unless I knew for damn sure it would be well received."

With a flick of her wrist, she ripped the crumpled card in half. She reached for her phone.

CLARA: SIGN THE PAPERS

Glaring at the roses, she sighed. "He obviously doesn't know me at all."

13

Connor looked off the side of the trail. The sun rode high, and the air was thick with humidity. Cooler than the city, but still summertime. He listened as footsteps approached to his right.

"If you keep stopping like this, we're gonna get in late."

They had hiked eight miles and still had another four to go. Connor wiped the sweat from his brow and kneeled to take in the perspective from the cliff at his feet.

He and Sam had crossed paths a little after Connor moved to Chicago. They were at a photography meet up, and he overheard Sam talking to someone about being from Georgia. They got to talking, realizing they had both just moved. Every year since, he and Sam had picked various hikes and traveled to stay in touch. Sam had dodged putting down roots for as long as he could remember, and their routine had evolved as a way to meet in the middle.

"Don't worry about me." Connor followed the line of the ridge across the ravine. The shutter clicked at his fingertips. "And—don't blame me for our pace." He adjusted the aperture. "You're the one that's out of shape." *Click.*

"Is it work stuff?" Sam came to stand at his side. "You just seem like you've got a lot on your mind." He breathed heavily, taking in the view. His words weren't a question.

Connor peered through the lens of his Pentax and tightened the focus. *Click.*

"What gives you that idea?"

"I don't know... you're a little surlier than usual." He smirked.

Connor's mouth pulled into a frown. "I'm sorry, man. I think I just needed to get out of my head."

"Nah, it's cool. Don't worry about it." He drank from the nozzle of his CamelBak. "You just seem kind of... angry."

Connor lowered the camera from his face. He stood next to his friend in silence, overlooking the ravine. Off to their right stood a redbud tree. Its heart-shaped leaves spilling over the branches like a wave of green valentines.

"Do you remember that wedding I helped you with?"

"After you moved?"

Connor grimaced. "Yeah."

"What about it?"

He ground the toe of his hiking boot against the rock at their feet. "I ran into that girl again."

"You're going to have to be more specific." Sam raised an eyebrow. "There were, like, ten bridesmaids."

"No... I ran into the *bride*."

Sam's eyes narrowed. He adjusted his pack uneasily. "So, I take it she's no longer a bride?"

"She's single now. I guess she's single... to be honest, I haven't really asked about the details." Connor secured his lens cap and slid the camera back into its neoprene sling. "I get the impression that it's over."

"So…what? Are you guys seeing each other?"

"No, we're not seeing each other." He thought of Clara, her eyes holding his from the other end of the couch that night at his apartment. The feel of her in his arms, against his chest. Connor's expression hardened. "I don't know what we're doing."

"Well, this sounds depressing." Sam studied him. "Obviously, it's something. This is the first thing you've talked about since we started this morning."

Connor shifted his weight. "I actually knew her before the wedding." Sam turned, facing him in silence. "We had a thing when we were in college." Connor grimaced. "Obviously, it didn't work out."

Sam scoffed. "A thing?"

"Yeah… *A thing*."

"Like what, you guys went on a few dates kinda thing? Or like, you guys hooked up on a futon somewhere kinda thing?" A moment stretched between them and a grin broke across Sam's mouth. He tilted his head back, a chuckle passing his lips. "Oh… *I get it*."

Connor's brow twisted. "Get what?"

"She's got you—*in here*." Sam stepped toward him, patting him hard on the chest. He pushed past, continuing on the trail. "Let me guess…"

Connor turned and followed.

Sam called out over his shoulder. "You sat next to her all freshman year, copied her homework, late nights at her dorm, *studying*." He laughed. "She's the reason you didn't flunk out."

Connor huffed. "No."

"All right." He looked off the trail at the sunlight cutting through the trees. "You… locked eyes at a pre-game. She beat your ass in flip-cup, reveled in her own victory, and now you can't forget her."

Sam turned, amusement painted on his face. He walked backward, his arms spread wide.

Connor shook his head. "No."

Sam cocked his head to the side, noting the clipped tone in his friend's voice.

Tightening his hold on his pack, Connor cleared his throat. "How about... I had a crush on her, and didn't make a move."

Sam slowed his pace and fell into step.

"I watched her date a total asshole, told her about the asshole and how he was cheating on her..." His eyes cut to Sam's. "Told her how I felt about her, made out with her after telling her about the cheating asshole, and then got disowned by all our friends."

"*Damn.*"

"Yeah." Connor looked at the steep stretch of trail in the distance. "Nearly got the shit beat out of me, too." He sighed.

Sam reached out and stopped him. "And... you didn't think to say anything to me about it?"

"What was I supposed to say?" Connor wiped the sweat from his face. "I got into town and realized she was marrying the asshole... and what? Was I supposed to walk out? I wasn't gonna leave like that again."

Sam scratched the back of his neck, chest rising and falling. "What do you mean *again*?

"Honestly," Connor lifted his sweat-soaked hat, the breeze touching his brow. "The whole thing was just really fucked up."

Sam nodded solemnly and looked at his friend. "I wish you would have said something sooner."

The nylon shook and shifted as Sam snored at his back. Connor watched the last log crumble into embers. Over the past hour, he had sat in a trance, waiting for it to cave. Sparks snapped into the air and a gentle glow touched his skin. Being with Clara felt just like that. Surprising and soothing all the same.

Her voice slid deep into his chest whenever she wrapped her lips around the syllables of his name. He closed his eyes, and felt the last bit of warmth linger against his hands and face, the chill at his back. He could see her now—with her chin tilted to the sky, laughter on her lips.

He wanted her. His chest tightened at the thought. He had spent more time than he should wondering what it would feel like to trail his fingers beneath the edge of her shirt. He wondered what she would do if he pressed his face to her neck and told her all the things he couldn't stop thinking about. Connor glared into the dark. Anything more than thinking made him hesitate.

The next day, Sam and Connor climbed the final stretch, not speaking much throughout the day. Reaching the peak, Connor stood, feeling the wind drift over him as the sun burned overhead. The breeze licked his skin where he was drenched in sweat. Sam caught up and let out a huff of exhaustion, clapping Connor on the back. Connor turned and smiled, breathing heavily. They found a spot in the shade and sat, taking in the view.

"How are things since you moved back home?"

Connor thought of the garden center. Immediately Clara came to mind. "Things are good. It was a little strange at first, but I'm getting used to it."

"And your family is doing good? Lucy talks about Kat all the time."

"I can't believe they hit it off the way they did." Connor shook his head, remembering his sister's last visit to Chicago. "She can be a little intense."

"Yeah, Lucy loved her." Sam sat back, a smile balanced on his mouth. The last time the four of them had been together, Kat had almost gotten them kicked out of a bar after a guy had grabbed Lucy's ass. "I think she was mostly sad about you moving because it meant she might not see her ever again."

"Ouch." Connor laughed. They both fell silent for a moment, looking out into the distance. Even in the shade, heat surrounded them. "And Lucy doesn't mind that you take off like this?"

"No—she's got her sisters, and her parents live nearby."

Connor nodded. "Are you excited about becoming a dad?"

Sam smiled to himself. "I can't describe it... I'm terrified, but I'm excited. And Lucy..." He paused. "She's *everything*. I can't imagine doing this with anybody else." His eyes connected with Connor's.

Sam had been a serial dater their entire friendship. Bold and shameless, he was Connor's complete opposite. After becoming a recluse, any social outing Connor participated in was more or less Sam's doing. He was shocked when Sam asked Lucy to marry him last year. Even more shocked when they announced that they were also expecting.

"How did you know?"

"About Lucy?"

Connor nodded.

Sam grinned and looked down at his boots. "It was weird. We knew each other for so long, but just never saw each other *like that*. You know, I was always traveling, and she had her own stuff going on." He pulled a granola bar from his pack. "I don't know how it happened, but it's like the stars aligned. All of a sudden, we were in all the same places at all the same times." He shook his head. "Two people who never sat still."

Sam broke the bar in half. "I'd never really met anyone that didn't have a problem with the way I wanted to live. Or the things I wanted to do."

Connor smiled, taking the offered granola.

"I'm being honest. Most girls thought the travel stuff was cool, but no one really took me seriously. I know I can be a little difficult sometimes... and I know I get these hare-brained ideas." He wiped his hands on his shorts. "But she just smiles and listens to me and shakes her head and laughs. And her laugh is like my green light. *She gets me.*"

Connor sat back, letting Sam's words settle.

"Looking back, I don't know how I missed it. All that time, we knew each other, and we didn't see it." Sam looked over at Connor. "So, what about this girl?"

"I don't know." A long breath left his chest. "I can't really decide if I can trust her."

"Well, trust is a major part of it. Honestly, it's pretty much the only thing that matters." Sam eyed him. "What makes you think you can't?"

"I just felt like I really put myself out there and I thought maybe she felt the same way." He pictured her in the dim light of the lake house, his mouth inches away from hers. The pain and the honesty from that night floated between them, tethering them together. "It was a long time ago, but I thought I knew her." He remembered the way she sank into Mark's arms as he watched through the glass. Disappointment wrenching his heart into his stomach. "Then I realized I didn't know her at all."

Sam gazed out over the cliff. "That's valid. So if you don't think you can trust her... then can I ask why she's even on your mind?"

Connor looked at his friend. A small grin broke across Sam's shameless face.

Connor rolled his eyes as Sam started laughing. "It's not like that."

"Fine." Sam lifted his hands, surrendering. "Answer me this. Is she a good person?"

Connor bit into his half granola bar, dry oats crumbling into his lap. He thought about Eli spinning Clara around the day it poured at the nursery. And the sweet way she spoke to his aunt on the phone whenever she called the front register to check in throughout the day. He thought about Ryan.

"Yeah. She is."

Sam offered a smile. "Well, maybe the timing was just wrong. People go through shit." He shrugged. "Seasons change."

Connor's brows knitted together, and he turned to look at him curiously. "Yeah. I guess they do."

Connor checked his phone again—he finally had reception. It was Thursday and Sam had just split off on the drive back. At the first glow of a gas station, Connor pulled over to get out and stretch. Pouring a black coffee that he was certain was going to taste like shit, he slid his card across the counter at the register.

"Twenty dollars on number seven, please." He set his drink down and, at the last second, snagged a bag of peanut M&M's.

Worn out, Connor slid back into the driver's seat after replacing the pump and checked his phone. Text messages and emails were pouring in.

ELI: Dinner Saturday. Your sister and cousin are coming. Bring the wine!

KAT: BROCHACHO!!! Will you be back by Saturday? Are you bringing the wine?

LORELEI: Just got the invite. I asked what to bring. Eli said my sparkling personality... Let me know if I need to pick something up!

Connor yawned and ripped open the chocolate. He hit Spotify and scrolled until something caught his eye.

RAT BASTARD

A sleepy smile pulled at the corner of his lips and he wavered, remembering the way Clara's eyes had lit up. He tapped the icon, turning the volume all the way up. American Hi-Fi blasted through the speakers as he rolled down the windows just before merging onto the interstate.

———ele———

Clara walked to the greenhouse at the far end of the nursery. She had just finished squabbling with Eli about taking her break out in the heat, but she was desperate to escape from the boring lull of the register. It was slow today and every time Eli looked at her, he apologized. She had reassured him over and over that her ankle was a complete accident, but he refused to accept her word.

As Clara neared the covered run, she stepped into the peaceful heat and sighed. One of the potting tables sat empty and Clara hoisted herself up, positioning her body in front of the industrial fan. A lukewarm breeze floated around her as she stretched out on top of the table, reveling in the silence. Staring up at the polycarbonate roof, the mimosa tree above the greenhouse swayed, dappling the plastic covering with tiny, shadowed imprints of dancing leaves.

The past week had been hell. Monday through Wednesday, Sharon had ridden her ass and Clara counted down the hours until she could get to the nursery. Sometimes she wondered if The Bug Zapper would be the death of her. She smiled, recalling the conversation she and Ryan had on Wednesday. He suggested she throw herself down the stairs when Sharon walked by, promising that he would call HR to make an anonymous report of hostility in the workplace.

Clara chuckled. But even at the nursery, she felt restless. Every time the door chimed, she looked up, hoping to see a head of waves and a familiar set of dimples. She adjusted her shoulders. Another reason she needed a minute to herself. She'd heard Eli say Connor would be gone all week, but she had gotten used to having him around. She missed his sarcasm and his incessant need to debate everything. On Sunday, when Ryan left, Clara had tidied up the living room. Her fingers grazed a piece of paper wedged deep between the cushions and she groaned, thinking of the card from Mark. Her heart skipped a beat when she saw a neat line of hieroglyphics scribbled along a yellow sticky note.

Be right back. Don't die on me.

She grinned. That same day, Clara had hobbled to the freezer for another ice pack. Her chest swelled when her eyes fell on a fresh pint of Rocky Road. Now she couldn't get him off her mind. When she was with Connor, she felt this strange sense of empowerment. Like she was finding pieces of herself that even she had forgotten she'd lost.

Every minute with him was like circling closer and closer to who she wanted to be. She watched the wind rustle the mimosa leaves once more and her eyes drifted shut, listening to them shake along the roof. Behind her lids, she envisioned the photograph of the ridge. Stone crunched underfoot and a wild breeze pushed her hair away from her face. She stepped forward, and the clouds broke overhead, scattering rays along the landscape. Everything around her became brighter. *Clearer.*

Her thoughts wandered to Connor. She thought about his lips, and the scruff of his five o'clock shadow. She imagined his hands, wanting to feel the roughness of his touch trailing along her skin. She wanted to know if kissing him would be as delicious as she remembered.

Shivering in the heat of the greenhouse, she let out a huff. Clara sat up and swung her legs to the side, gently lowering herself down from the potting table. She looked around at the seedlings tucked into rows and rows of plastic trays. The tender growth had yet to be burned by the harsh elements outside. She thought of Connor. What she wouldn't give to go back in time and do it all over again.

Stepping back into the AC, she spotted Eli, who was gazing at her with dramatic pity.

"Clara..."

"Eli, I told you, it was no one's fault." She shook her head. "It happened out of nowhere. *I'm fine.*"

"Well, in any case, Gloria is demanding that you come over tonight for dinner. So we can make it up to you."

"I really appreciate it, but you don't have to—"

Eli interjected, "No, no, we insist. We're eating at seven thirty. You've got our address—we'll be expecting you." He looked at her with finality. "Unless you have other plans, of course..."

Clara caved, waving her white flag, "*Fine.* I'll be there."

"Perfect!" He snapped his fingers.

<div align="center">~~~</div>

Clara adjusted the neckline of her dress, covering her cleavage—who was she kidding, her sternum. Switching on her blinker, Clara turned onto Conifer Court, spotting several cars parked outside Eli and Gloria's house.

"What in the world?"

She rolled into the last open spot in front of their house and cut the engine. Spotting Connor's car in the driveway, her heart skipped a beat.

"Shit."

Clara leaned over to the passenger side and snatched her bag from the floorboard. She dug around for whatever emergency makeup that sat forgotten in the black hole of her purse. Her fingers touched the slick plastic of an ancient compact—undoubtedly the wrong shade. She reached into the last pocket and found... hot pink blush... from last Halloween. *Great.* She pulled the visor down and frowned. The summer sun had tinged her cheeks and left a smattering of freckles. She had forgone mascara, which she was now regretting. *God, why didn't she put on concealer?*

She switched off the tiny light and shoved the mirror up to the roof of the car, uncapping her ChapStick.

"Hey—"

"Oh, my God!" Clara jumped in her seat.

Connor stood on the sidewalk, looking down at her through the driver's side window, confusion in his eyes. She yanked at the neckline of her dress. Grabbing her purse, Clara opened the door. Connor extended his hand and she took it, getting out of the car with his help. His fingers were warm against hers and she shifted, closing the door with her hip.

Clara turned, her heart in her throat. He looked gorgeous. Connor wore dark pants and a thin button-down shirt. He had a pensive look in his eyes as he studied her ankle, and she smiled. When he finally met her gaze, his dimples deepened to that full forty watts, turning her knees into cheap folding chairs.

"What are you doing here?" His eyes brimmed with curiosity as they trailed over her, stopping at her dress. Clara slipped her hand from his, adjusting the straps at her shoulders. His gaze warmed her skin everywhere it touched.

"You look different."

"Gee, thanks?" She shrugged.

Connor winced. "Well, you look nice... I just don't think I've seen you in anything but those cargo shorts all summer."

"You mean to tell me you haven't seen my *gardening gown?*" Clara gasped.

He shook his head, smiling. "Nope... I must have been busy that day. Sounds like I missed out."

Clara hummed. "Yes. Yes, you did. It was this huge, fabulous thing... with a hoop skirt." She nodded. "Eli was in tails and a top hat."

"*Man.* I can't believe I wasn't there." Connor's eyes went wide, playing along.

She shrugged. "I know. I guess you've only ever seen me in my *peasant clothes.*"

Connor stood laughing, finally offering his arm. Her fingers slid around the cuffed fabric of his shirtsleeve and she leaned in. He smelled like soap. Together, they walked along the stone pavers that led up to Eli and Gloria's home.

"Better hold on. Eli will have my head if he sees you walking up the stairs without backup."

"Oh, my gosh. Ever since he heard about the accident, he keeps hovering over my shoulder with these sad puppy dog eyes." Clara let out a laugh, navigating the treads carefully.

Connor slowed, letting Clara steady herself on every stair. He watched as her hand gripped along his shirtsleeve, smiling at the way she pressed herself against him. "Trust me, I got an earful." Connor's voice slid over her as they made it to the top.

They stood together in the glow of the setting sun. He seemed different. *Warmer.* "I thought you were out of town."

"Yeah, I was. I just got back yesterday. I got word that Gloria was fixing dinner, so of course, that means attendance is mandatory for me and my sister."

"I had no idea that you would be here."

Connor put his hands in his pockets. "Does that mean that you wouldn't have come if you knew I was going to be here?" The softness of his tone couldn't hide the weight of his question.

"No—that's not what I meant. It's just... I thought it was only going to be Eli, Gloria, and me." Clara watched the unconvincing tilt of his head as he nodded. He didn't believe her. She rubbed her forehead, grasping for the right words. "You caught me in the midst of an *emergency zhuzh*."

His eyes narrowed. "What is... an *emergency zhuzh*?"

"You know... in the car."

"Wait, when you were adjusting your...?" He motioned to her cleavage.

"What? No! What's wrong with you?" Clara shoved at his shoulder. "I was fixing my hair and my makeup!"

Connor glanced down at the neckline of her dress. "Oh, you were definitely—*you know.*" He shimmied his shoulders and leaned forward, his expression accusatory.

Clara's jaw dropped, and a blush crept across her skin.

A chuckle reverberated from his chest. "It's okay... I get it. I straightened my shirt before I walked over to your car."

"Did you really?"

"Yes—I did."

As the moment lingered, Connor's gaze settled on her, sending goosebumps across her skin. "You look beautiful."

Just then, the door swung open, and they stepped apart. A flash of red hair came charging forward. A second girl followed with just as much excitement and Clara stepped back, afraid to get caught in the whirlwind. An informal dogpile took place as she stood off to the side, observing the chatter that filled the porch.

"How was the hike?"

"When did you get back?"

"When is Sam's baby due? Have they picked a name yet?"

"I bet you they're going to have a girl. I can totally see Sam as a girl dad."

"Who's this?"

The pretty redhead hit Connor in the stomach with a soft punch. "Did you bring a date?"

The two girls gave each other a look. Clara steadied herself.

"Kat, Lorelei, this is Clara... Clara, this is my sister and our cousin. You can ignore them both."

Kat ignored the slight. "The question still stands... is she, or is she *not*, a date?"

Connor's eyes reached for Clara's.

"I work with Eli at the plant nursery." She watched Connor's expression unravel as she explained on his behalf. "He demanded that I come to dinner." Connor redirected his attention to the planters by the door, and her heart pinched. "I actually had no idea that you guys were all going to be here..."

Just then, Eli stepped through the doorway, opening his arms to Clara.

"Perfect timing! I'm so glad you made it! And you look so wonderful. Connor, doesn't she look wonderful?"

Connor glanced at Clara and smiled at Eli, embracing him in a quick hug. "Yeah, she cleans up nice."

Clara shrank at the flat cadence of his voice.

"Will everyone please come inside? Gloria and your mom are just finishing up."

Mom? Clara paled.

"Connor, did you bring the wine?"

"Yes, I did. Actually... I left it in the car. I got distracted on the way in and forgot to grab it." He looked at Clara once more before he turned and made his way back down the stairs.

"Everyone calls me Lo." The girls walked on either side of Clara as they all stepped into the foyer. Clara could have sworn she caught Kat rolling her eyes. "So, you work with Eli?"

"Yeah, I work there a few days a week. He and Gloria are really amazing."

"Wait—you're *Clara*." Kat's expression lit up. "Eli talks about you all the time." She touched Lo's arm, and they locked eyes. She lowered her voice. "You're married to *Mark Monroe*?"

"*Kat*." Lo glared at her cousin.

Clara's eyes went wide, embarrassment oozing from every pore of her body. "*Yes*... that would be me. But we're not together anymore."

"That's right—Eli mentioned that... he can't stand him."

Clara muttered, "yeah... him and me both." All three of them chuckled.

They walked into the kitchen where Gloria stood at the stove, with who Clara assumed was her sister. *Connor's mom*. Her hands went clammy. Clara hovered near the refrigerator door, observing the easy way Lo and Kat fell into their well-worn posts. Kat inched up onto the counter by the sink and Lo slid into a seat at a built-in desk, cluttered with junk mail and family photos. From where Clara stood, she noted shades of a golden sunset, wide cheery smiles, and the bright blue of a beach umbrella. Each a separate memory, all captured in tiny silver frames.

"Clara, dear, I'm so happy you came! Eli won't stop about your ankle. And when Connor told us the details, he was just in knots until he saw you himself."

Clara shook her head, smiling. "Honestly, my ankle is just fine. I'm sure Connor told you it was nothing."

The woman beside Gloria reached for the pepper and looked over her shoulder, eyes connecting with Clara's. "I'm just glad Connor was there with you. He was worried sick about leaving you alone to go on his trip."

Clara's lips parted, her voice dying in her throat.

The woman's eyes glittered, a smile at the curve of her cheek. "I'm Mrs. Kent... Adeline." She nodded her head toward the sink. "Kat and Connor's mom."

A nervous smile flashed across Clara's face. "It's so nice to meet you." Her heart thudded inside her chest, watching as Gloria dipped a spoon into the pot, tasting the sauce. "He was worried about me?"

"I think it needs salt." Gloria narrowed her gaze, tilting her head from side to side. "The Samsons have the most ridiculous set of stairs. I don't see how anybody survives bringing groceries into that house."

Adeline looked at her sister. "I can't understand why they ever moved out of their old place. It was adorable."

"Yeah, it was just one street over from that blue house Emma rented."

Lo shifted in her seat, her brow furrowing. "When did mom rent a place in town?"

Gloria leaned against the counter, smiling at her niece. "Oh, it was a million years ago. Before she married your dad."

"Connor was with you?" Kat interjected, pinning Clara with a look.

She turned, all of them standing around the kitchen island. A rack of copper pots hung overhead.

"Yeah, Connor and I were doing a delivery, and I fell. *But I'm totally fine,*" Clara emphasized. She should have made a sign to hang around her neck.

"Hopefully he didn't leave you for dead." Everyone laughed.

She smiled. "No, he made sure I was taken care of." Just as the words left her mouth, Connor walked into the kitchen. All the women turned.

Kat wiggled her eyebrows at him. "Made sure she was taken care of?"

Clara's cheeks went up in flames and she glanced down at the floor.

Just then, Eli stepped in from the dining room, accompanied by a guy who looked about the same age as Kat and Lo. "Table's all set. Are we ready to eat?"

Connor walked past, carrying several wine bottles. "Clara, this is Harrison."

"Nice to meet you." He politely extended his hand, and she noticed several tattoos peeking out from under his shirtsleeves.

Clara grinned, looking at him curiously. "I like your shirt." Dolly Parton's face was emblazoned across the front. *Guts, Grit & Lipstick.*

He glanced down, a smile pulling at his lips. "She's an icon."

"Yeah." Clara nodded, an affectionate laugh escaping her chest. "She really is."

"Harrison was our neighbor." Connor set down the wine, pulling out her chair before taking the seat to Clara's left. "We grew up together." The table was full, with everyone pressed in close. The warmth of Connor's leg, just inches away from her own, under the table. If she moved even just the slightest, she could touch him.

He handed Harrison the salad bowl. "How are classes going?"

"Really well. My professors are brutal, but I'm enjoying it."

Connor nodded. "Yeah, everything's more interesting when you get to the courses that are more specific to what you actually like."

Clara took the bowl from Harrison. "What are you studying?"

"Biology."

She smiled. "So, the green thumb is contagious around here."

"Yeah, except it skipped me." Kat took the bowl and dumped a pile of mixed greens on her plate. She laughed. "I kill everything I touch."

Harrison scoffed. "That's not true... you still have the snake plant I gave you last year."

"Yeah, but only because you secretly water it whenever you come over."

Clara sipped her wine, eyes dancing across the large wooden hutch on the opposite wall, lined with plates and dishware not too different from Bonnie's. She glanced down at the table, quirking a smile at the glass fly salt and pepper shakers. Connor looked at Clara, his leg aligning with hers beneath the tablecloth, from knee to waist. His eyes roamed over her face and she swallowed nervously, straightening in her seat.

"That's not true. I'm just a plant EMT. If I see something in distress, it's my obligation to save it."

Adeline patted her daughter's hand, taking a sip of wine. "She's never been great with living things."

Kat rolled her eyes. "I killed my betta fish when I was little."

"Yeah, you fed it to death." Connor taunted. "Then there was our bird, and then Mr. Jennings's dog—"

"Okay, Tweety was not my fault, and Bug was an honest accident."

"*Bug?*" Clara whispered, turning to Connor. His eyes dipped to the smile at her mouth. Her breath caught.

"That dog was ancient." Kat whined. "And how was I supposed to know that he needed all that medication?"

Gloria administered pointed looks around the table. "Honey, you were in ninth grade. It's old news... All has been forgotten." She sat back in her seat, sighing. "Truth be told, that dog was the most hateful little thing."

"Even so," Eli cleared his throat. "Jennings likes to bring it up every time he buys something at the store. I think he's always hoping for a discount."

Laughter traveled around the table and Clara turned her attention to Lo. "How about you? Do you have a green thumb too?"

She smiled wide, reaching for a roll from the breadbasket. "My parents are in agriculture..."

Clara nodded. "That's so interesting. What sort of farm—"

Kat turned her attention to her brother. "I want to hear all about Connor's trip!"

Connor took an exhausted breath and, just before speaking, placed his hand on Clara's knee. Clara jumped in her seat and everyone's eyes shot to her.

"Sorry! I think I kicked someone." She pretended to look below. "Oh, it must have been the table leg." She looked at Connor. Her eyes were bright and her heart was racing. She glared, and he smiled back at her, unfazed. He squeezed her knee, moving slightly higher over the fabric of her dress.

Kat continued while shoveling salad into her mouth. "So, what part of the trail did you guys do last week?"

Connor kept his eyes on his sister, never wavering his touch under the table. Clara was mesmerized, staring at his mouth as he spoke.

"Sam and I met up in Hot Springs and started at Standing Indian."

"That's awesome," Harrison chimed in. "Did you get to Clingman's Dome?"

"No, we didn't get that far. It was a pretty quick trip."

Clara exhaled slowly. His thumb was drawing lazy circles, the motion softly bunching and un-bunching her dress under his hand. Clara bit the inside of her lip.

"Do you hike?" Connor's mother asked.

There was a static pause that fell over the room. Clara gulped her wine and looked around the table full of expectant eyes. Adeline's expression was sweet and imploring.

"No! I mean... *Yes!* I have been hiking... But I wouldn't say that I am an *avid hiker*. Although—I do like being outdoors." Clara readjusted her position, wiggling in her seat. Connor's hand stayed put, the warmth of his touch sending electric currents up to the base of her stomach.

Eli spoke to her. "We just love that you enjoy the nursery as much as we do." His touch was gentle as he reached for Gloria's hand. "It's so rare to meet people these days who really appreciate mother nature." Clara smiled at them both before catching the distant look in Adeline's eyes.

Clara shifted. "Honestly, it wasn't until I started spending more time at the nursery that I came to realize how much goes into making things as beautiful as they are."

"I completely agree with you." Harrison spoke from across the table. "Learning about everything on a molecular and cellular level is really interesting. I was always good at biology, but I never imagined that I'd love it enough to study it."

Kat poured herself more wine and rolled her eyes. "You are such a nerd. You were always so obsessed with being at the nursery." She raised her eyebrows at her friend from above the rim of her glass.

"No, I think Harrison was just obsessed with being anywhere that you were." Connor shot her a look.

Kat chucked a piece of bread at Connor and it thumped him square in the chest. The assault garnered reactions from everyone in the room, and Connor released his hold underneath the table to retaliate.

"Okay everyone, settle down," Gloria ordered. Clara could tell the matriarch was secretly enjoying the outburst.

Clara took a breath. Everything below her waist was hot and tingly. The meal carried on and she relaxed, easing into her spot at the table. From where she sat, she watched the adoring way Eli looked at his wife every time she told a story about the kids. The two sisters chattered on about trivial bits of town gossip in hushed voices.

She listened to Lo speak with uncertainty about how she wasn't sure if she wanted to work with her parents or go out on her own. She saw how Kat and Harrison had their own hidden language. Seemingly imperceptible to the naked eye, but well established from what she could tell. Clara was thankful to be included. It had been a long time since she had felt this relaxed. As the meal came to a close, they all stood and cleared the table, carrying dishes to the kitchen.

Before getting up, Gloria put her hand on Clara's shoulder, gathering her hair so that it laid neatly at her back. Clara leaned into the maternal gesture, smiling to herself.

"Why don't you and Connor handle dessert and we can all move out to the porch? I'll get the citronella candles going so we can eat outside in peace."

Connor was already in the kitchen, digging around in a drawer next to the fridge. An ice cream scoop was balanced in his hand as he walked to the freezer and pulled out a large container of vanilla bean. Clara came to stand next to him at the counter and arranged two rows of tiny crystal dishes that Gloria had already brought down from the cabinet.

"Wow. I usually eat straight out of the carton."

Gloria patted her hand as she walked past. "I like to find reasons to celebrate and pull out the good stuff. Even if it's just for these rotten kids." She swatted in Connor's general direction.

Clara smiled. "That could be my problem. Ice cream is usually my vice."

"Nonsense. It's all perception." As Gloria headed toward the doorway, she turned and gave Clara a wink. "Every day on this earth is something to celebrate... Even the shitty ones."

Clara beamed and faced the counter. She tucked her hair behind her ear, speaking softly. "Vanilla bean has nothing on Rocky Road."

She looked up into Connor's face and watched a smile pull at his lips.

"Rocky road is a hard one to beat."

He pulled the lid off the container, setting it aside. Clara pried. "Why didn't you tell me?"

"I *did*. I left you a note." He mounded a large scoop, carefully transferring it into the first dish.

"Yes." Clara smiled. "I know you left me a note, but you didn't say anything about what you were getting."

"You're the one who fell asleep." Connor sparred. "How do you know I didn't mention it? How do you know we didn't have a long, drawn-out discussion about the merits and pitfalls of every flavor known to man?" He shook his head, keeping his focus on his work.

"You're impossible." Clara rolled her eyes. "I was exhausted *and* injured." She rotated the glasses, pushing them into a makeshift assembly line.

"Trust me, you don't have to tell me how exhausted you were... and I was also injured." He paused, looking her in the eyes. "I was nearly decapitated by a pile of books. Or did you forget?"

She looked into his very serious face. Buttoning her lips, Clara swallowed her laugh. "That's right..." She drummed her fingers. "I am terribly sorry about the near murder." He filled the last dish, and she turned, leaning her hip on the counter. They were standing close together and her arm brushed his shirt. "Why Rocky Road?"

Connor's attention didn't stray from his task. His brows knitted together. "A shot in the dark... but I felt pretty confident."

Clara didn't speak and instead waited, studying him. Closing the lid on the cardboard container, he held the scoop out, offering it to her. "It used to be your favorite."

She took the heavy metal from his hand, staring down at it. "You remember?" Out of disbelief, she really looked at him, taking in his thick locks of hair that laid in soft waves. The strong angle of his jaw. Clara felt a tightness in her chest, like a cage of butterflies.

She looked at the sliver of air between him and the counter and wondered, for a moment, what it would feel like to press herself into that space. She wanted to tuck her chin against the soft cotton of his shirt and feel his hands on her back. She raised the cold metal scoop to her lips and caught a trickle of sugary sweetness.

Ignoring her question, he brought his finger to his mouth, licking melted ice cream from the pad of his thumb. "You know, I've been thinking more about what we talked about the other day... about *delayed gratification*."

Clara stared at his lips, fixated on his tongue.

"What were you saying? About the seasons..." Connor's eyes held hers. Something heavy and warm simmered just below the surface. "The part about it being worth the wait?"

"*Y'all—*"

Clara turned. The scoop dropped from her fingers, clattering to the counter.

"Any longer and this stuff is going to be soup." Kat stepped into the kitchen, snatching several dishes before turning on her heel and walking out.

Clara backed away from the counter, trying to remember how to breathe. They grabbed as many of the dishes as they could carry and walked carefully out to the porch. Eli and Gloria sat on one side of the sprawling deck on a wooden porch swing.

Kat plopped down next to Harrison at the other end, and Lo sat at a wrought iron cafe table with an open seat beside her. Connor motioned for Clara to take it and moved past her, sitting at the very top of the stairs against the rail next to his mom. Clara smiled to herself.

The cicadas sang and her skin felt dewy. The candles were for the mosquitoes, but they flickered like tiny lanterns, turning the porch into a cozy, romantic cove. Planted baskets hung in each of the openings above the railing and brown burnished pots were stuffed to the hilt with flowers and vines along the banister at their feet. Normally, everything would be burnt to a crisp at this time of year, but it seemed that Eli and Gloria's porch offered just the right amount of reprieve from the afternoon sun. Clara ran her fingers through her hair.

All of them ate their ice cream in a quiet lull, their spoons clinking in their glasses. Lo's eyes met Clara's across the small table. "I'm sorry about earlier. It was rude. Eli just talks about you so much—"

"Don't worry about it." Clara smiled. She watched as relief washed over Lo's face.

They both looked at the far end. Eli and Gloria swung gently together, pushing with the balls of their feet. The metal links of the chains squeaked ever so slightly, adding to the layers of sounds that surrounded them. Like a tiny chime in the symphony of summer.

Clara smiled to herself, sending a new wish out to the universe. She hoped that one day she'd be lucky enough to find someone to sit with. Someone sincere. Someone sturdy and true.

She looked down at the candle between her and Lo and she glanced, catching Connor's eye as he studied her from his spot on the stairs, his mother's attention focused on the backyard. His gaze floated across the short space between them and she wondered if it was the flickering of the citronella candles, or if his eyes were glowing just for her. Lo's phone rang, and she stood to take the call inside.

Clara swallowed thickly and took her cue to leave. She watched as Eli and Gloria slowly made their way toward the kitchen and Adeline got up from the stairs to join them. Kat and Harrison both stood.

"Tell me you're coming to the housewarming on the Fourth. You *have* to be there."

Clara looked over her shoulder and saw Connor leaning against the rail, his arms crossed at his chest.

"I invited her, but she hasn't given me an answer." She saw a glimmer of something in his expression.

"All three of us will be there..." Kat wiggled her eyebrows. "And I'm sure we'll all end up going out afterward."

"Well, I actually already have plans with a friend of mine and there's a bar that he wants to go to. They're doing some sort of blast-from-the-past thing."

"Oh, my God! Is it Throwback Night? At Crazy 8? Our friend is a bartender there, and we were just talking about making Connor come out with us. He's been in such a weird funk all summer."

Unsure if they were within earshot, Clara peeked in his direction. He was gathering ice cream dishes and heading toward the kitchen.

"At least tell me you'll try," Kat pleaded.

She didn't commit, but didn't cave. "I'll try."

Clara walked into the house, placed her dirty dish on the counter by the sink, and turned to bid Gloria farewell. "This really was a special night."

"Oh honey, you're welcome anytime. I'll be by sometime this week to check on those pots that I ordered from that woman at the market last month. You'll love them."

"That sounds great." Clara smiled. "I can't wait to see them."

As she walked back through the entryway, she ran into Eli and Adeline. He leaned forward, enveloping her in a quick hug. "Thank you for coming tonight."

Clara looked at them both, sliding her purse up to her shoulder. "Thank you for talking me into it."

Adeline reached forward, smoothing her hand across Clara's arm. "I'm so glad we finally got to meet." She smiled. "I feel like we always miss each other at the nursery."

"I know." Clara nodded. "I'm only there a few days a week, but I wish I could be there more."

"Well, Eli and Gloria have always sung your praises, but now that Connor's home... I just keep hearing your name floating around."

She squeezed gently at her elbow, a warmth in her expression. "I thought, I just need to meet this girl."

Clara looked down at her feet, her throat tightening at the sentiment in Adeline's words.

"We'll do this again soon." Eli's smile stretched, reaching his eyes.

C lara slipped out the front and took her time descending the porch stairs. The pea gravel surrounding the pavers crunched beneath her feet and she heard steps following close behind.

"Clara, hold up..."

She stopped just as she got to the sidewalk and waited. Her heartbeat thrummed a little faster as Connor fell into step beside her.

"I wanted to walk you to your car. I got caught up talking with Kat about next weekend. I didn't realize you had left already."

She looked into his eyes, uncertain of what he would want to talk about. Their conversation from earlier replayed through her mind, and her stomach turned on its side. She drew in a breath, tightening her hold on her purse. Maybe he could believe in second chances the way she did. Even if most people thought she was crazy. He offered a small smile as they turned and walked the rest of the way to her car.

"Do you think you and Ryan will come next weekend?"

"Well, Ryan won't shut up about it." She sighed as they strolled, shoulder to shoulder.

He gave her a suggestive smile. "I told him that he could bring someone along if he had a date."

She laughed. "Yeah, he told me. He actually has a potential *love interest*." Clara grinned mischievously, thinking of Ryan's unusually cheerful disposition whenever he talked about Jonah. "He says they're just friends, but I think he'd like it to be more."

Reaching her car, Clara leaned against the trunk, smiling up at him. Conifer Court was silent at this time of night. Each house glowed from within, like tiny lanterns dappled along the quaint, residential street. Connor dropped off into a contemplative silence and, after a moment, placed his hand beside her on top of the warm metal. Bringing them closer.

"Summer is so different here." Connor cleared his throat. "You know, in Silas Grove." He followed her gaze down the street, lingering on his aunt and uncle's house. "I almost forgot how it felt."

Clara raised a brow. "What exactly does it feel like?" She took in his profile, tripping and skipping over every feature, her heart thudding, curious about his answer.

"It's quiet. It's something you never think about until you don't have it anymore." Tilting his chin, he looked up at the night's sky. "The air is heavy, like it's always about to rain." He faced her and his dimples deepened. "And it's so fucking hot."

Clara's lips parted. She tore her eyes from his, looking at the row of neatly clipped shrubs hovering in the distance behind Connor's shoulder. "I've never lived anywhere but Georgia." She shrugged, an easy smile balanced on her lips. "So, I'll take your word for it." Clara tucked her hair behind her ear, glancing over at him. "But for what it's worth, I've always loved summertime."

Their eyes held. Connor finally broke, glancing down at his hand on the car near her waist. "Do you ever miss it?"

Her eyes widened. "Do I miss what?"

"The lake house." His gaze met hers.

Her throat bobbed. She thought of all the things she loved about summer. How all those things felt magnified at the lake. All the pain did, too. "Sometimes."

He nodded, studying her lips. "What do you miss?"

Her chest tightened, seeing the careful way his gaze roamed her face. "Memories." Snapshots flooded her mind of parties and people. Sunshine and arguments. Being surrounded by family and feeling completely alone. "Some good, some bad."

Clara wished she could read his mind. She thought about Harrison and Kat. Connor straightened, adjusting his collar.

"I don't know if it's my place..." His brow furrowed. "But are you and Mark still..." He swallowed thickly, rubbing the back of his neck. "Are you still seeing Mark?"

Clara frowned. "No, I'm not seeing Mark." She shifted her weight. "I mean, he comes by the house from time to time, but we aren't *seeing* each other."

Connor pursed his lips. Clara watched him carefully. Desperately trying to decipher whether her answer was the right one.

"Was it him that sent the flowers?"

Clara let out an empty laugh, eyeing him. "Yes, those were from him."

"And... you're not seeing each other?"

Exasperated, Clara tilted her head, not breaking eye contact. "*No, Connor, we are not seeing each other.*"

"He just seemed to have a lot of stuff at the house. And I can't help but ask because... I think I'd like to spend more time with you."

She took his words and tucked them into her heart, if only so she could take them out and remember them years from now... when she was out of this mess. Clara's breath stilled. She couldn't screw this up—*again.*

The moment lingered and Connor stood back, inching his hand off of the trunk. "You really know how to keep a guy on his toes."

She drew in a breath, tempering the spark in her chest. "I would like that." She smiled and then looked down at her feet. Hers were together, and he stood wide—his shoes framing the outside of her wedges. "But... I don't know if it's the best idea."

"I don't either."

His words surprised her.

"That's why I wanted to talk to you about whether you two still see each other."

"He moved out months ago..." Clara traced her naked ring finger. "I told you about the letter. I'm sure it was just the tip of the iceberg." She looked at the trunk, wishing Connor would put his hand back down. "I guess I should have listened to you." Her shoulders lifted, eyes misty and defeated. "You know, back then."

He shrugged, jesting, "Yeah... *maybe*." He raised a brow, taking her lead. His chest swelled. Feeling relieved that the flowers meant nothing. That she wanted to see him, too.

Clara choked back a laugh and stood indignantly, bringing them closer together. She shoved at his shoulder, smiling and sniffling at the same time. The moment quieted. "I guess I just always want to see the best in people." Clara looked into his eyes, feeling wistful and safe. "I'm a sucker for second chances."

Connor tilted his head, pinning her with a look. "Yeah... second, and third, and fourth, and fifth..." His words were playful, but the meaning felt anything but.

Clara's posture stiffened. "That wasn't very funny."

Connor's gaze narrowed, his smile fading. "C'mon, don't be like that. I was just giving you a hard time. You know, because..." Connor straightened, scrubbing his hand through his hair.

Clara stared, waiting for him to speak. *Nothing.* "You know what? We were both right."

Connor's jaw went slack.

At his silence, Clara shoved her hand into her bag, fumbling for her keys.

Heat shot across his skin, and he sucked in a breath. "Clara—"

"No." Her eyes were trained on the inside of her purse. She made her way around to the driver's side, yanking the car door open. She stopped to look at him, anger and embarrassment in her eyes. "This *was* a bad idea." And with that, she slid behind the wheel.

There was a moment that Connor almost went to her, but he stopped himself. He realized how vindictive the words felt the second they tumbled out of his mouth, bruising the honesty that had been there only moments ago.

Connor stood alone, watching Clara's taillights disappear down the street before hanging his head and walking back toward the house. The way her demeanor changed so quickly burned a hole in his stomach. He didn't want to hurt her. Even when he'd told her about Mark all those years ago.

Maybe she was smart to call it.

———✦———

C lara chucked her purse onto the table in the foyer, slamming the front door.

She marched to the kitchen, ripped open the fridge, and stared into the abyss. She had just eaten a full meal. "What an asshole!" Clara slammed the door shut and ripped open the freezer. *Second dessert.* Immediately, her eyes fell on the container of Rocky Road and she kicked the drawer shut. She was unraveling.

Clara strode to the hallway and stood fuming. Moonlight trickled in through the window above, and she sucked in a breath. The inside of the refrigerator had been dark. She reached, flipping the light switch on the wall closest to her. *"Shit."* Clara walked back toward the foyer. She could check the fuse box. *Not that she knew what to check for.* Mark had always handled that stuff. Dread flooded her stomach. *Mark.*

CLARA: The power is out at the house.

MARK: Did you pay the bill?

Clara's chest caved. She stared at the three dots, her stomach in her throat.

MARK: Divorce isn't cheap.

You've got to be fucking kidding me. She trudged up the stairs in the dark, tripping over a pile of laundry. She dug out an old T-shirt and stripped down. At dinner, she had reveled in the feel of her dress underneath Connor's hand, sliding along her thigh. She threw the dress in the general direction of the hamper. Stumbling to the bathroom, she scrubbed her face clean, leaving no trace of emergency makeup behind.

Clara couldn't believe Connor had uttered those words. *With that stupid grin on his face.* She had gotten enough of that shit from everyone in college. As if she didn't know what people were saying behind her back when Mark proposed. *And he just stood there.* She dried her face on a hand towel and dropped it on the counter. After the wedding, the whispers became more subtle, but she knew they were all the same. *She was a fucking idiot.*

Clara moved into the bedroom and flung back the covers. She pulled the blankets up to her chin and snuggled in deep, going over every single second in her mind. Torture by rewind. She lay there in the dark, seething as heat invaded every inch of the house. Her hair began to stick at her neck and she groaned. Kicking at the heavy duvet, she rolled over, snatching her phone.

CLARA : SIGN THE PAPERS

Thank God the weekend was over.

Connor pulled into the gravel lot, his eyes scanning around the exterior of the nursery. Half hoping, half dreading he'd see Clara. She worked Monday through Wednesday at her other job and the second half of the week she worked at Grady's.

He cut the ignition and sighed. Stepping through the front door, the bell chimed and his uncle turned. Eli waved from the register as Connor made his way through the store. It felt emptier than usual. No music playing overhead. No buzz of excitement humming in the air.

Lately, he looked out from the doorway of Eli's office, hoping to catch a glimpse of Clara as she passed by to tend to customers. Or answer the phone. Or just... exist. He hadn't slept the night before. Instead, he tossed and turned until finally caving and going for a run.

Every time he closed his eyes, he saw the pain in her face. Like he'd dumped salt in a wound that had just started to heal. In the silence of his apartment, all he could hear was his voice echoing over and over in his head. Every idiotic word.

Eli tilted his head. "What are you doing here today?"

"Just wanted to see if you had any updates on the pottery Gloria mentioned?"

"Oh, that's right—she said you'd be coming by. I spoke to the manager this morning and the order should arrive today." He checked his watch. "Probably a little after noon."

Connor looked around aimlessly, searching when he knew, in fact, she wasn't there.

"Everything okay?"

Connor brought his attention back to his uncle. "Yeah, why?"

"I don't know. You just seem a little out of sorts." Eli was looking at him curiously. "We really enjoyed having everyone over on Friday. It was good of you to come. I'm sure you were worn out after getting into town."

"You know I wouldn't miss it." Connor smiled.

"You and Clara seemed to have a nice time."

A breath passed his lips, and he reached out, fidgeting with a display of paper seed packets.

"Yeah, we did. Until we didn't."

Eli crossed his arms at this chest, leaning a hip into the counter. "Well... unless I missed something, I don't think it was so bad."

"No, dinner was great." Connor shook his head. "It was nice having her there. It's just weird... how we know so much about each other—but sometimes it feels like we're strangers."

"I don't understand what you mean."

Connor turned to face Eli. "You know how at the beginning of summer, I told you we knew each other?"

"Yeah, you said that you helped take pictures at her and Mark's wedding."

"Yeah. About that—"

"And you guys had all gone to college together."

"Right, we did... We were friends, and I did something really stupid."

Eli placed his forearms on the counter, leaning forward. "Oh, I don't like the sound of this."

"I mean, stupid in retrospect. I thought I was making some heroic gesture. Mark..." Connor paused, hating that even after all these years, he was still caught in the same old shit. "Mark was just her boyfriend at the time... let's just say his behavior was about the same as it's always been." Connor glanced up.

"You know I have never liked the boy." His uncle frowned. "We've always thought Clara was too good for him, even before we got to know her. Every time they came in, he would just stand off to the side and she would roam around. Alone. He'd wander off making *work calls*." Eli rolled his eyes. "He'd even leave town without her. Stay in the city sometimes during the week." He looked at Connor, shaking his head. "People *talk*."

Connor grimaced, looking out the window behind the register. He thought about Clara walking up and down the rows of plants and all around this building. Spending hours outside, working in her yard. Existing in a town that had once been his home. All the while, he was gone.

"I told her about him."

Eli's eyes widened. "About Mark?"

"Yeah." Connor rubbed the back of his neck, remembering that night. "One summer. We were really drunk, and I told her everything."

"And what happened?"

"There was a huge fight."

"Who got into a fight? You got into a fight?"

"Mark started the fight."

"Mark fought with Clara?"

Connor scrubbed his hand through his hair. "Yeah."

"Why would Mark start something with Clara?"

"Well, that's the thing. I think she confronted him... and I don't know what happened." Connor couldn't look at his uncle, and instead looked down at his hands. His palms were flat on the counter. "We were at a party, and when Mark walked in, Clara and I were together."

"*Together.*"

"Mark came up to us when we were talking. I had just told her that he was cheating on her, and then they went outside and got into a huge fight." It wasn't a lie... but not the complete truth. He didn't add the part about how he had just kissed her. Or the part about how everyone there saw the whole fight unfold through the sliding glass doors that led out to the back deck. How Connor stood there like a coward, watching the emotions play across their faces like an old black and white film. About the sharp pain in his chest when Clara started crying, like he couldn't breathe. How his heart twisted when Mark pulled her to him and wrapped his arms around her.

"So she forgave him."

Eli's words settled between them.

He thought about the icy shift in Clara's demeanor. The shift in all their friends after that night. He shrugged. "We haven't really talked about it. I don't know that it matters."

"Of course it matters—"

"No, I don't know if it matters *now*." Connor dragged in a breath. "On Friday, I walked her to her car, and we started to talk about it." His throat bobbed. "It didn't go so well."

Eli's mouth twisted, deep in thought. He shook his head. "You guys were so damn young." He pushed himself up off the counter, slipping his hands in his pockets. "Everyone makes mistakes." He studied Connor, seeing the quiet intensity in his eyes. A look he had witnessed only a handful of times over the years. Eli's demeanor softened. "How do you feel about her?"

A tired laugh shot past his lips. "It's not that simple. I was an idiot. I thought I was being funny, and obviously, I wasn't."

"I thought you guys were getting on like a house on fire. Not to mention that you two have been making eyes at each other all summer."

Connor's stomach tightened. Eli knew him better than anyone.

"That's the thing... It was like the more time we spent together, the less the past seemed to matter. So Friday, I put myself out there."

"And? What did she say?"

"She said yes... and then I put my foot in my mouth."

"Hm. Did you apologize?"

Connor shook his head, his mouth pressing into a flat line. The sound of her jingling keys flashed across his mind. So did the slam of her car door.

"So you just let her leave?"

"It happened so fast and she was so pissed." He thought about the hurt in her eyes and winced.

"And then she just left?"

"Yes, Eli, she left."

"Have you called her?"

"No, I haven't called her."

"Have you texted her? She's really good about answering her texts."

Connor felt hot, like his feet were being held to the fire. "No, I didn't text her. I don't know what to say. You would think that it'd be easier because we already know each other. Instead, there's this weird barrier. Like the history is making it harder." Connor fell silent, deep in thought. "Would you have forgiven him?"

Eli looked across the counter. "Forgiven Mark?"

Connor nodded.

A pensive expression etched Eli's face. "I don't really know how to answer that. Some people might say it'd be foolish. Some people would say it'd be naïve." Eli shrugged, looking at his nephew. "I guess if I really wanted to see the best in someone, it'd be tempting."

Connor scowled, and Eli held his hand up. "Now, you didn't ask about right or wrong. But I can tell you that girl is no wimp. People make it sound like it's so easy to just up and leave." He shook his head, a stern look on his face. "I think it takes a lot of nerve to wake up, day in and day out, and look that person in the eye—"

"And just forgive them? Like nothing ever happened?" Connor uttered the words, bitterness coating every syllable.

"To choose them." Eli leveled. "To choose them when they aren't worth choosing."

Connor scoffed. "Why would any sane person put themselves through that?" He searched Eli's face.

"I think some people just hope." His uncle shrugged, looking up at the ceiling, grasping for an explanation that surely didn't exist. "They hope things will be different that next time around. You know..." The edge in his voice quieted. "To give it a second chance."

<hr>

Sharon hovered over Clara's shoulder for the third time that day. Clara sucked in an even breath, trying to steady her nerves. She hung up her call with a customer, gathered her composure, and turned in her office chair to face Satan herself.

"Everything okay, Sharon?"

"Clara," she raised her voice. "I've noticed that you're receiving very low performance scores on your customer satisfaction surveys." Ryan bristled in the cube next to her, curiosity and ferocity emanating in equal measures as he continued his phone call.

Clara glanced around, "Sharon... is this a conversation we could have in private?"

"I don't see why we can't just take care of this real quick. Unless you're trying to make it a bigger deal than it is?"

The hair on the back of Clara's neck stood on end. After she got home Friday night, the rest of her weekend had been shot to hell. Sunday had been a complete waste, and this morning had been nothing but a series of unfortunate events. Every single one involving Sharon.

Clara squared her shoulders. "I'm not trying to make anything a big deal. I would just appreciate some sense of courtesy if this is regarding my performance."

Sharon smirked. "If you insist on making this a formal meeting, then I suggest you swing by my office so that we can schedule a more in-depth discussion at a later date." She turned on the ball of her foot and walked away through the aisles of cubicles back to her office.

Clara stood from her desk, feeling everyone's eyes on her, and marched to the elevator, holding back tears. She smashed the down button repeatedly and waited. The metal doors opened, and she slid inside. She leaned back against the mirrored wall and looked up at the numbers flashing above, willing her tears to reabsorb into her body. A hateful reluctance twisted in her gut. Just then, Ryan ran into the elevator and stood beside her in solidarity, waiting for the doors to seal shut.

"Okay. What gives?"

Clara sucked in a shaky breath. "Sharon is such a bitch."

Ryan snorted. "Okay, besides the obvious?"

"I don't want to talk about it."

"We both know how this is going to end."

Clara turned to face her friend. His all-knowing expression stared back at her. "You're going to tell me what's wrong or I'm going to wait this out and you *will* tell me by the end of the day." He checked the time. "And seeing how we're going to lunch early, this is going to be a very quiet meal. Unless you decide to fess up so we can work on fixing this as soon as possible."

Clara smiled, running her finger below her lashes, catching a tear.

"I don't know what I was thinking... I left everything upstairs. I just had to get out of there."

He smiled at her. "I'll spot you. I'd say it's an emergency."

They reached the bottom level, and as the elevator dinged, Ryan stepped in front of her. "You should have taken your moment." Clara followed him through the lobby in confusion. He chuckled, yanking her under his arm for a hug. "We should have framed her when we had the chance."

❦

"So, you're telling me he asked you out, then insulted you, and then... he just stood there?" Ryan finished off his milkshake with a noisy slurp.

"Yeah, that's the gist of it."

His eyes narrowed as he looked at her, deep in thought. "Oh, Connor... what is happening in that beautiful head of yours?"

Clara shrugged, falling back against the booth.

"Did he think it was funny?"

"Who knows what he was thinking?" Clara reached into the plastic basket in front of her, pushing around her pile of fries.

"All I know is we were having such a nice night..." She sighed. "I really thought there was a *sliver* of a chance that things could work out."

Ryan wiped his mouth. "Did anything weird come up during dinner?"

Clara found an extra crunchy fry and pressed it between her fingers. She brought it to her lips, crushing it between her teeth. "Yes... No. I don't know.

"Hold up. I feel like you're not telling me something."

Clara looked at him, guilt staining her face. He studied her. "What happened during dinner, Clara?"

"Ryan, at this point, it's depressing to even think about. The whole thing was a mistake."

Placing his elbows on the table, he leaned in, lowering his voice. "I have to have the facts before I can help you."

She huffed. "Okay. He was flirting... shamelessly."

A smirk played at Ryan's lips, but he held his reaction back like the Hoover Dam.

"When you say *shamelessly*... did he say anything in particular?"

"It wasn't anything with his words."

His eyes widened. "Okay, Clara. Out with it." He glanced at his phone. "We have exactly ten minutes before we have to get in the car and drive back to 1-800-PRISON. I don't have time to play games. We already wasted most our lunch on Sharon The Bitch, but I refuse to let this moment pass after hearing that, arguably one of the most attractive guys I've seen all summer, shamelessly flirted with you—and now you're dangling this information in front of me like a fucking carrot."

The floodgates broke. "He put his hand on my knee during dinner."

Ryan sat up straight. "Was his hand placement..." He glanced over as the waiter walked by. "*Momentary*?"

Clara looked at him, pondering.

Ryan leaned forward. "As in *fleeting*?"

Clara scrunched her nose and shrugged, unsure.

He leaned forward even farther, his pecs meeting the table. "Was it *temporary*?"

"I know what you're asking, but I don't know how to describe it—"

Ryan threw his paper napkin on the table. "Babydoll. Use your words. Obviously, it meant *something* because you said that he was *shameless*. So what part of a hand on the knee is *shameless* unless there is some level of delicious indecency behind it?"

Clara burst out laughing and covered her face. She looked over her shoulder at the rest of the diner, relieved to see that no one was paying them any attention. Ryan glared at her, his patience wearing thin.

She thought back to the look in Connor's eyes. The pressure of his fingers over her dress. "Yes. It felt very shameless. It's just... I had come to the conclusion that he wasn't interested—so it threw me for a loop that he was being so *openly interested* the entire dinner." She dropped her shoulders. "I didn't know what to do with any of it."

"Let me get this straight." Ryan exhaled. "Connor was putting deliciously indecent, super stealthy moves on you *in front of his family,* and you, Clara Monroe, were dumbfounded. Like, you didn't know whether he liked you?"

She winced, biting the inside of her cheek. "*Possibly*?"

"Oh my God, what a *fucking waste*."

Clara retaliated, snatching the last crunchy fry out of Ryan's basket. Despite her appetite, she shoved it into her mouth out of defiance.

"I'm just saying..." Ryan laughed, swatting her hand. "I've seen it. Even a blind, deaf person would sense this man's interest in you. It's *vibrational*."

Clara suppressed a smile.

"We're talking dolphin sonar."

Clara shook her head.

He grabbed her wrist from across the table, shaking her. "We are talking, *Fly Away Home*, bird navigational patterns." She looked at him like he was crazed. He gave her one final shake before releasing her. "That man is jonesin' for you."

Clara looked straight into Ryan's face. "It doesn't matter whether he's..." she lowered her voice, "...*jonesing* for me. It was horrible. I wish you could have seen the look in his eyes when he said what he did."

"I hear you... and it sounds super shitty. *But,* is it possible..." Ryan circled, "that he genuinely had no idea it was going to sound so atrocious?"

Clara gave Ryan an ounce of respect in the moment and considered his question sincerely.

"I cannot say with 100 percent certainty that there was mal-intent behind his words. It's possible he thought he was being funny."

"So, is there any room in your heart to overlook this?"

Clara sighed. "I don't know, Ryan, what would you do?"

"Oh—this is not about me. This is Samantha Jones we're talking about. I would have those dimples on a dartboard, *and* I would have moved on to bigger and better things by now."

She glanced down at her lap. At the paper napkin covered in splotches of ketchup and French fry grease. "So, you're saying I should forget about him?"

"I didn't say that..." Ryan frowned. "I think if there's any part of you that is remotely interested in Mr. Kent, you need to address it, set some boundaries, and see where it goes."

Clara considered his suggestion and thought of her therapist, Eileen. *Yay. More boundaries.*

The corner of his mouth rose. "We'll let this simmer. We can revisit it at the end of the week before we get to the housewarming."

Clara's eyes went wide. "I am not going to the housewarming."

"*Clara.*"

"What?! I'm not going."

"You insisted I invite Jonah, even though I was adamant about it being just the two of us. We've already made plans, and it's a perfect halfway point to Crazy 8. And since we're going there anyway, it'll be a nice stop over so we can pregame."

"Well, you'll just have to go without me." The waiter stopped at their table, leaving the check.

Ryan glared at her, snatching up the bill. "Right." He mocked. "In what universe?"

━━ᥫᩣ━━

That week, Connor had texted Clara and called her once. He almost didn't make the phone call, wanting to err on the side of caution... but by Thursday, he caved. He felt out of step. Over the years, he had more or less learned to leave things alone. But after his conversation with Eli, he realized he didn't want to leave things alone—not with Clara. Even if she didn't want to be anything more than friends, he owed her an apology. He just needed to figure out what to say.

As the weekend neared, he couldn't stop thinking about her. He didn't go to the nursery, not wanting to make her uncomfortable. If she wouldn't reply to him and hear him out, he wasn't about to make her uneasy at work, especially not in front of Eli. Connor circled his desk chair, setting down a mug of coffee. He checked his phone. *One last time.*

KAT: Super pumped for this weekend! Do you need me to pick up beer?

He frowned, placing his phone face down by his laptop. He barely stepped away before it chimed again. He pivoted, snatching it up.

KAT: Is Clara coming?

He let out a frustrated breath.

CONNOR: No clue... No word. Bring beer.

KAT: Someone's in a mood.

Clara stood in front of the mirror in her walk-in closet, cringing. Tonight's conundrum was not only that it was the most patriotic holiday of the year, but that they were also going to Crazy 8 after Connor's housewarming. *Connor.* She frowned, looking at her choices. She'd been boycotting the party but began to reconsider when Ryan pulled her into a second-hand store, purchasing a couple of emergency options without trying them on. Once she divulged that Connor had called and sent her a text, Ryan gave her no choice.

He demanded that they attend, and that she dress both patriotic *and* retro... and now she was running late. Jonah had just gotten into town and they were stopping by to inspect her ensemble before heading out. It was a funny thing, knowing so much about Jonah, but never having met him. Clara grabbed a pair of denim overalls hacked off into a skirt. Pulling them up over her waist, she secured the buckles at her shoulders. Ryan had insisted that she pair it with a red tube top. Clara stepped back, assessing the nineties train wreck.

Sweat beaded along her upper lip. Since Clara had gotten the electricity bill sorted out, she had become more conservative with the AC. She pushed her hair off her shoulders and checked the time, yanking the denim overalls off. She stuck her hand into the plastic bag from Goodwill and pulled out her last option.

The doorbell rang, and she did a quick twirl, eyeing her reflection in the full-length mirror. *Middle School Clara* might actually be pretty proud. She dug out some chunky sandals and laughed at how silly she felt. The Tommy Hilfiger dress was short and bright. It was color-blocked in red, stretchy fabric, with a wide white and navy stripe running down to the hem at her thighs. She leaned toward the mirror, touched the tiny embroidered flag, and smiled.

The doorbell rang a second time, and she descended the stairs, a little wobbly in her shoes. Ryan peered through the glass at the front door and she could already hear him hollering from the porch. She couldn't help noticing the gorgeous guy standing at his side. As she opened the door, they showered her with praise.

"Oh, this is it! *Please* tell me this is the final decision. Very *Sporty* meets *Ginger* meets *Uncle Sam*."

She laughed, tugging at the hemline. "It's the only thing we bought that I'll survive in. I think I'll sweat to death if I wear the overalls."

Clara took in Ryan's Chicago Bulls jersey—number twenty-three, of course—denim blue shorts, and crisp white sneakers. Jonah was wearing an oversized, swishy, royal blue track suit, topped off with a red, white, and blue sweatband.

Clara shook her head, smiling. "I feel ridiculous."

"Fourth of July is already ridiculous. The only difference is that when we are done being ridiculous, we are going to go out. While everyone else is home watching fireworks and stuffing their faces with hotdogs, we'll be dancing the night away."

She grabbed her wallet and her purse, turning off the TV in the living room. "You're right. It's going to be fun."

Clara was not having fun.

Every ounce of Clara's confidence evaporated the closer and closer they got to Connor's apartment. She was about to walk into his loft, and introduce herself to people she didn't know, dressed like a Spice Girl.

Ryan's eyes connected with hers in the rearview. "I see that little frown you've got going on back there."

She forced her gaze out the window as they rolled to a stop in front of his industrial apartment complex.

The three of them stood together on Connor's doorstep as Ryan knocked cheerfully. "Okay, under no circumstances are we to leave her alone. We're here to show him what he's missing."

Clara looked at Ryan in disbelief, shooting a glance at Jonah.

"*Yes*—I told him. And we agree, Connor does not deserve to kiss your feet. *However*... I also disclosed that if you were still interested, I don't think it's a complete lost cause."

Clara pulled at her hemline. She was starting to sweat.

Ryan lowered his voice. "Wait—are you still interested?"

She bit the inside of her cheek. After their lunch at the diner, she had begun to consider whether the entire thing had been a misunderstanding. Every day she went back and forth, unable to make up her mind. Clara blew out a breath. "I don't know what I want."

"Well shit, this oughta be interesting." Ryan pursed his lips.

Jonah chimed in, adjusting his sweatband. "I do love a little intrigue." He gave Clara a wink.

She swallowed, a weak smile pulling at her mouth.

⟞⟞

"I can't believe he isn't even here." Ryan, Clara, and Jonah stood huddled in the corner of the kitchen.

Kat walked over to them. "Guys, I think there's just so much traffic because of the holiday. Connor should have been back by now."

Harrison stood next to her, scrolling through his phone. "Yeah, he was just running out to get charcoal for the grill."

Ryan whispered into Clara's hair. "Unless he literally needed to go into the Earth to mine it himself, I don't understand how he's missing his own party."

Clara smiled. "I'm going to get another beer. Anybody want one?"

Lo was digging around at the bottom of the cooler. She stood up as Clara approached. "Hey, I don't know what's taking Connor so long."

"Oh, it's totally fine. I wasn't here just to see him."

Lo eyed her. "You know he's crazy about you."

Just then, the door to the apartment swung open and a group of people walked in. Clara heard a loud bout of laughter and she immediately leaned forward, digging into the cooler on the floor. "Lo—which one were you looking for?"

"Uh, I was looking for an Athena, but I think they're all at the bottom." Clara crouched, up to her elbow in ice. The hem of her dress rode up, and she yanked, willing it to stay put. Connor's familiar chuckle was followed by two female voices, and her stomach tightened.

A pair of Chucks stopped at Clara's side and she followed the length of Connor's legs until their eyes met. The warmth in his face could have melted all the ice in the cooler.

"Oh, that's it!" Lo exclaimed.

Clara looked down at her hand. Her fingers had gone pink and were starting to sting. "You weren't kidding... those really were at the bottom."

"I know. We should have strategized a little better when we were filling it up." Harrison stepped forward, grabbing the bag of charcoal from Connor's arms.

Kat breezed by, "It took you long enough."

The entire time, Connor never took his gaze off of Clara. The look in his eyes sent a shiver down her spine. He offered her a hand, and she stared up at him for a moment before placing her icy fingers into his palm. He smiled, enveloping her in his warmth.

"So, I take it you're going out afterwards?" He gestured to her outfit.

Clara opened her mouth to answer and was immediately diverted by a very festive manicure snaking around the top of Connor's shoulder. Five glossy little American flags adorned each nail. Clara had never questioned her patriotism a day in her life. *Until now.*

Clara's eyes jumped from the heat in Connor's gaze to the blonde standing *very* close to him. *Touching him.* Clara stared down at her feet, sucking in a breath. *Please don't be sleeping with her.*

"Hey—where do you keep your wine bottle opener?"

"Um... should be on the counter, over by the fridge."

She smiled. "I just looked there... but no worries. I'll walk down the hall and grab one from my apartment." She traced his arm. "Do you want to come with?"

Connor's attention finally broke. "I'm sure it's in here. If you just give me a second, I'll come look for it."

Clara's eyes flitted over the woman in front of her. She was gorgeous.

"It's no trouble. Megan can come with me if you're busy." She cut a glance in Clara's direction. "I'll be right back."

Clara watched as the flags slithered down Connor's arm before floating away. Just then, a pretty brunette walked by in denim cutoffs and a red, white, and blue bikini top. They strode arm in arm toward the front door, laughing at a joke Clara wasn't in on.

Connor pointed in their general direction. "They live in the building. When they found out I had people coming over, they kind of invited themselves." He shrugged, raising his eyebrows with an easy smile.

If only he knew what that smile did to her. "So... I hear the traffic is crazy."

Connor tilted his head. "You really want to talk about *traffic*?"

Her eyes widened. His question knocked her clear off her chunky sandals. She had a million other questions that she'd much rather ask. *Like are you sleeping with your pretty neighbor?* Clara stood, cracking open her can of beer. "No, we don't have to talk about the traffic." She offered. "We can talk about the *weather*." She took a long swig and smiled at him.

"Hmm. We could talk about the weather." Connor leaned forward, plunging his hand into the ice. His gaze lingered on her bare legs and Clara stepped back, tugging at her hemline. He stood to his full height, mirroring her easy stance. He popped open his can, running his tongue across his bottom lip, catching a droplet of beer.

"Or. We can talk about the apology I owe you."

Clara swallowed at the knot in her throat.

"Connor! Come light the grill or we're all going to starve to death!"

He cringed. "Can we talk later?"

"Yeah, no problem." She nodded, tucking her hair behind her ears.

"Connor!"

He shook his head. "Kat—shut up, I'm coming."

Clara beelined to the bathroom when the front door opened and *American Hustle* returned with a wine opener. She made a hard right at the bookshelf and was accosted by Ryan and Jonah. "Who the hell are Jennifer and Megan?"

Clara jumped. "Uh, I have no idea. It sounds like they invited themselves."

"Connor should have *uninvited* them if he knew you were coming." A hot flush crept up Clara's chest.

"Well, I never responded. So it's not like he knew I would be here for sure."

"So—what? He just magically started seeing one of these two in the span of a business week?"

Clara let out a huff. "I doubt he's seeing either of them." She heard the thinly veiled desperation in her voice.

The front door opened again and three guys walked in with cases of beer and more food. Clara didn't recognize any of them.

Behind the bookshelf, the three of them stood huddled together.

"Do you think the hunky blonde is with the hunk with the buzz cut?"

"I don't know, but he just put an ice cube down the back of Jennifer's top and he's staring awfully hard at her nipples..." Ryan shrugged. "I'm still inclined to say he's batting for the other team."

"Who knows, maybe he likes Megan's nipples *and* the buzz cut."

Clara thought about what Lo had said earlier and smiled to herself. She handed her beer to Ryan. "Will you hold this for me? I have to use the ladies' room."

Clara slid into the bathroom and secured the lock, having learned her lesson from last time. After she was done, she washed her hands and looked into the mirror. A bout of laughter echoed from behind the door. Clara sighed. She placed her cold, wet palms flat against her cheeks. *You didn't make a move. He didn't do anything wrong.*

She exhaled, wiping her hands on her dress. Looking down, she pulled open the small drawer to her right—knowing what she'd find. She touched the hard plastic of Connor's deodorant.

A loud knock banged on the door.

"Just a minute!" Clara straightened her outfit and fluffed her hair. She opened the door to find Kat standing on the threshold. "I don't know where Connor meets these idiots."

"You don't know any of them?" They passed each other, swapping places in the tiny bathroom. Kat chuckled. "Nope. The dudes on the balcony are one shotgun away from puking and it's *embarrassingly early.*" Clara smiled back at her. The temptation to fish for intel sat in her stomach—but she held back. She and Connor were adults. He hurt her feelings, and she rebuffed him. He called and sent a text, offering an olive branch... and she went radio silent. Much like her past with Mark, she could handle swallowing the pain of her own mistakes. She was a big girl.

Spotting Ryan and Jonah out on the crowded balcony, Clara circled the kitchen island. They were shoulder to shoulder and pointing at something over the railing. She smirked. Ryan was a goner—even if he didn't know it yet. She filled her hand with *Cheetos*, popping one into her mouth. A familiar set of Americana claws reached forward, grabbing a handful.

"*Oh my God*, I love these..." She pushed a puff carefully between her lips. They were bright, like a candied apple. "But *Fritos* are my number one."

Clara nodded, her mouth full of delectable cheesy space dust. Anyone that preferred *Fritos* to *Cheetos* couldn't be trusted. She brushed her hands together. "I find anything in the *-ito* family to be consistently reliable..."

American Hustle looked at her curiously.

Clara straightened her shoulders. "You know... as far as snack food options go."

After a momentary pause, the other girl moved on. "So, how long have you known Connor? I've never seen you in the building."

Clara's lips parted. She covered her mouth before speaking, using her tongue to dig a Cheeto out of her back molar. "We've known each other a long time." Her eyes drifted to Connor at the grill. She smiled, seeing their alma mater logo on his backwards cap. Her stomach fluttered.

The pretty blonde contemplated her answer. "So, you guys are just friends?"

Clara's eyes darted over to Connor's couch and the flutter turned into a back flip. "Um, no..." She wiped her hands on her dress, frowning at the streak of orange she left behind. "*Shoot.* I mean, *yes.*" Clara grabbed a napkin.

Lo walked over and dumped a small pile of chips and salsa onto her plate. "Connor is taking too long with the burgers." She rolled her eyes in annoyance. "Sorry, was I interrupting?"

"I was just asking her how she knew Connor."

"How do *you* know Connor?" Lo asked, pointedly. Clara detected an edge of something in Lo's tone.

"He moved in down the hall from us in May." She smiled, glancing over toward the grill. "He's always so nice whenever we see him." Her eyes met Clara's. "And he's *fucking hot*."

Lo choked on a chip and put her hand on her sternum. Something coiled tight in Clara's stomach and she looked at the couch once more. She sucked in a breath. He *is* fucking hot.

"Come on. Don't tell me you don't find him like, absolutely delicious?"

Having recovered, Lo took a sip of her drink. "That would be incestuous. *He's my cousin*."

"*Oh my God*. Ew." Jennifer elbowed Clara in the ribs. "I mean, you know what I'm talking about, right?"

Clara's chest swelled. She *was* interested in Connor. *She was very interested.*

Lo looked at her, a smile forming on her lips. Connor walked in with a plate full of food, lowering the tray to the island in front of all three of them. "Did you call me?"

Jennifer smirked. "She was just answering a question for us."

Clara's eyes clashed with Lo's. She looked at her, pleading. Lo raised her eyebrows at Clara and popped a chip in her mouth, silently conspiring.

Clara fanned herself with her paper plate, Cheetos crumbs scattering to the counter. "I'm starving—"

"*Not so fast!* She was just answering whether I'm the only one who finds you attractive." Her tone was laced with something bold and competitive.

For a moment, Connor froze, focusing on the food. He shifted, moving platters around until he raised his gaze, settling on Clara. Her skin warmed everywhere his eyes touched, and she wet her lips. A desperate breath shot from her chest at the same time Ryan and

Jonah walked in. The group gathered as people grabbed their plates to dig in.

"I think... *objectively speaking*... it's... um..." She cleared her throat. "It's safe to say that I would agree with that statement." Clara looked at Ryan and she tensed, realizing she was still fanning herself. Her eyes locked with Connor's.

The blonde snorted. "You sound like a robot."

Clara winced, and averted her eyes, staring as all five American flags climbed Connor's bicep. She glanced at the couch again. Her blush deepening at her own dirty thoughts. Ryan stared at Jennifer's hand on Connor's arm. From across the island, he caught Clara's eye, nudging his head. The boys met her at the cooler and Ryan hunched down, fishing for a decoy drink.

"What in the hell was that?"

"While you two were out there enjoying the sights, I got cornered!" Clara ran her hand through her hair.

"What happened?!"

Clara shoveled her hand into the slush. "She forced me into talking about my personal thoughts on his... his..." she looked at them both, grasping.

"His—*what?*"

"If I think he's hot!"

Laughter erupted, nearly knocking Clara back on her butt.

Jonah ignored Ryan's outburst and looked at her, seriously. "What did she say?"

"She was obviously just trying to embarrass me!"

Ryan exhaled, calming himself. "I hate to say it, but I think she may have succeeded." He patted her on the shoulder. "I think she was feeling out the territory."

Clara huffed. "Well, what in God's name am I supposed to do? *Pee on him?*"

Jonah placed a compassionate hand on Clara's shoulder. The gesture was both endearing and heartbreaking. If Ryan didn't make his move soon, Clara would happily grovel at this man's feet.

"I know we don't know each other very well... but this doesn't seem like you."

She put her hand on top of Jonah's and looked up into his soulful, beautifully lashed eyes, and sighed. "I'm making an executive decision. You guys invited me out to have fun and we're not. Let's get out of here."

Ryan studied her. He knew her pain threshold like the back of his hand.

Clara glanced over at Connor, surrounded by people. "What time did you want to go to Crazy 8?"

Ryan stood, extending his hand. "Who cares? We can just kill time and get drinks somewhere else."

"Should we dine and dash?" Jonah asked, observing the crowded kitchen.

Clara didn't want to go back to the island, feeling like an eighth grader who just saw her crush pass another girl a note in class.

Ryan tugged her hand. "Well, come say goodbye and be gracious. Then we'll make our exit."

———e&e———

Connor stood next to the grill and overheard Clara's voice on the balcony. She was talking to Harrison and Kat.

"I don't know why you have to leave so soon. I know Connor took forever to get back, but he's here now—"

"Oh—it's not that. Ryan just really wants to go."

He could feel her standing right behind him. He ripped open a pack of hotdogs and laid them out on the grill. His stomach dipped, and he turned with the metal tongs in his hand.

"Heading out so soon?"

Clara turned away from his sister and moved to his side. Heat radiated off the charcoal.

He watched her throat work. "Ryan and Jonah are ready to head out."

Connor searched her face through his sunglasses. Whether she could see it, he didn't know.

"Well, thanks for stopping by." He leaned forward and gave her a brisk hug, devoid of any emotion, and returned his attention to the grill. Clara looked after him with a furrow creasing her brow and retreated inside.

⟞⟍⟋⟋⟋

"What the fuck was her problem? It's not like Jennifer *owns* him." Ryan spoke over his shoulder as he divvied out shots from the bar.

"Do you remember that scene from *Far And Away*?"

Clara held her shot glass in one hand, clutching her other hand over her heart. "*Oh, my God*. With the little white flag at the end?"

"*YES!*" Jonah was easily becoming her new favorite person. He did his best swoon.

"I wouldn't say that she was staking her claim *as majestically* as Nicole Kidman—but it was just as intense."

Jonah nodded in agreement. Ryan shook his head, completely lost. They had commandeered a high top table, keeping every empty shot glass and cup contained between the three of them.

Jonah draped himself across Ryan's shoulder, sipping his gin and tonic. "They lived like five million lifetimes together, *and* crossed the globe, *and* sustained bodily injuries." Four drinks in and Jonah had definitely gotten more loose-lipped. "Then they finally got to claim their gold rush land!" He pressed his face in close, and Ryan's hand shot up, steadying him.

Clara watched the nervous bob of Ryan's throat and she smirked, loving every drunken second of it.

"What I wouldn't give..." Jonah settled both elbows on the table and leaned forward. "For someone to lay a flag down on this sweet piece of *uncharted territory*." He trailed his hand over his chest in mock-ecstasy.

Clara's eyes widened, and she laughed, clashing her glass to his. "Cheers to that." She took a drink, glaring at Ryan. He tore his eyes away from Jonah, and she raised her eyebrows at him.

Ryan tilted his head back, downing another tequila shot. He grimaced, popping a lime between his lips. "I highly doubt Jennifer has journeyed across the globe or any of that shit. If anything, she's had to endure watching his *fine ass* walk up and down the hall every day." His eyes slid to Clara's, holding a stone outside her big glass house. "*But*... if anyone has lived five million lifetimes with the man, it would be Clara—"

"Connor's whereabouts are none of my business." Clara frowned, hearing the shrill pitch of her voice.

Ryan grabbed her wrist across the table. "We understand that it's technically none of our business, but it doesn't mean that we can't commentate. Plus, you're the one who said you didn't think he was dating her."

She did say that. Now she wasn't so sure.

"Can we take a second to talk about how you didn't respond to him all week?"

Clara covered her face. "I was still pissed, and I didn't know what to say... and I thought that everything I wanted to say would sound stupid over a text."

"Why in the hell did you not meet him in person?" Jonah reached the bottom of his cup and slurped noisily through his straw. "You could have had front row seats to see that beautiful specimen grovel at your feet."

Loose-lipped indeed. "I highly doubt there would have been groveling."

"He had *grovel* written all over him." Ryan poked her hard with his index finger.

Jonah nodded in tipsy agreement.

Clara laughed. Ryan pushed the two remaining tequila shots closer. They threw them back, instantly shoving lime wedges into their mouths, shaking their heads. "I don't want him to grovel. That apology—*maybe.*"

He wiped his hands on a napkin, crumpling it before tossing it onto the table. "Well, you may have missed the boat on the apology."

⸺ ✿ ⸺

They were out on the dance floor when Clara caught a glimpse of blonde hair and a wide smile. Harrison was putting his ID and wallet back in his pocket when Kat and Lo slunk in behind him. He caught Clara's eye and waved from across the room. The girls jumped up and down and pointed to the crowded bar. Clara couldn't help but look back over toward the entrance, searching.

Ryan and Jonah announced they were going to step out back for some air. Lo was on her cell phone with her hand pressed to her ear, and Kat stood on the bottom rung of a bar stool, leaning halfway over the counter, hugging a bartender with hot pink hair.

Clara motioned for Ryan and Jonah to go on without her. "I'll be there in just a sec! Do you guys want another round?" Ryan shook his head, holding up a full cup.

"We'll keep an eye out for you."

Clara turned and saw a row of shots forming along the sticky bar top.

She watched as Harrison, Kat and Lo all tipped their heads back in unison, slamming down their shot glasses and chasing them with limes. Two glasses remained. Sensing a shift behind her, goosebumps raced across Clara's skin. A tanned, muscular arm reached around, brushing the fabric of her dress.

The heat of his peppermint breath rustled her hair. "I think that one's got your name on it." His voice was low, and she loved the way it felt, heavy against the shell of her ear. Clara watched Connor's fingers wrap around the tiny glass and she looked at the lone shot sitting next to it, waiting for her.

She shifted, leaning back, and smiled to herself. From her peripheral, a hand reached out, snatching the shot. Clara's smile fell and her heart stopped. She followed the red, white, and blue and saw the Cheshire cat smile plastered on Jennifer's face. Her eyes were glued to Connor as she tossed back the tequila, placing a lime seductively between her lips.

With the warmth of his chest at her back, Clara felt a painful tug in the pit of her stomach. For the briefest moment, he'd been hers.

He had stepped into her gravitational pull. Like she was possibly strong enough to keep him.

One look at Jennifer and the way she was undressing Connor with her eyes—and it was clear she was the sun. A radiant streak of gold, glittering in the middle of the dark bar. Clara swallowed, feeling like the planet that was arguably a non-planet... until it was more recently found to have enough significance to be considered a planet. *What was its name, again? That's right—she didn't fucking know.*

Kat's face soured, and she looked at Harrison, pulling him close and cupping her hand by his ear to tell him something. Lo announced she was stepping out back, still on her phone.

Clara leapt at the chance. "I'll go with you." She glanced back, seeing Jennifer smiling up at Connor... but his eyes were trained on her. Clara's breath hitched, stealing one last look before slipping away and turning the corner.

As they stepped out to the patio, twinkle lights hung overhead and groups of people huddled along the bench seating and cafe tables. Music poured out through the heavy metal door every time it opened and shut. Clara spotted the boys laughing together in the far corner. She and Lo made their way over.

"So, the *motley crew* showed up?"

"Yeah, they just got here."

"Is our leading man in tow?"

Clara smiled and rolled her eyes. "Yes... and so is Nicole Kidman."

Their eyes went wide. "*No—*"

"*Yep.*" Clara tossed back the rest of her beer and exhaled. "She has traveled through mountains and rivers and valleys to journey here—to this far edge of the new world to stake claim—"

The boys erupted in laughter. Jonah softened his expression, drunkenly pointing a finger at her. "*You* are Nicole Kidman... *not her.*"

Clara leaned over, pulling him into a hug. "I just knew I was going to love you..."

Ryan inserted himself between them. "Okay, that's enough of that." He glared at her and she straightened, like a child scolded.

Lo ended her call and pulled out a chair, plopping down. "Sorry about that. My boyfriend couldn't be here and we're doing the whole long-distance thing." She waved a dismissive hand through the air. "What did I miss?"

Ryan and Jonah laughed, and Clara shook her head, rolling her eyes. "*Nothing*... Long distance is so tough."

Lo eyed her suspiciously, but dropped it. The door opened again and music filled the patio. She spoke above the noise. "We've been together forever. I know people think I'm an idiot, but I totally trust him." She looked at Clara and frowned. "I just miss him a ton."

Clara nodded, knowing full well what it felt like when people had their assumptions. She softened, channeling her inner Gloria. *She could be sage for Lo.* "Of course you do. When do you get to see him next?"

"He's supposed to come visit next weekend. Or I'll go see him... He goes to college out of state."

She smiled dizzily at Lo. That last shot was sneaking up on her, and Lo could see it, too. She laughed at Clara and declared that they should all go back inside, that she was in desperate need of inebriation.

Connor stood glued to the far edge of the dance floor, still technically at the bar. Jennifer was relentless, tugging on Connor's hand, trying to lure him out to sea. Clara would have been jealous, except she could see his blatant state of misery from across the room. Connor looked over, locking eyes.

He mouthed an exaggerated *help me* and she smiled, heading toward the bar.

Inching within a few feet of him and his relentless temptress, Clara ordered another beer. She felt Connor sidle up behind her.

"I said help *me*, not help *yourself*."

She leaned into him. "I'm getting another. Do you want one?"

Jennifer walked past, and Connor leaned in close, pointing at Clara's beer. "Make it two." He slid his credit card across the bar to start a tab as they both turned their backs and stood, drinking in silence. The bass shook everything around them as they surveyed the room crammed with sweaty, dancing bodies.

With both of them facing out toward the crowd, Clara smiled, spotting Ryan and Jonah. Panning to the left, she caught a glimpse of Jennifer and her friend. Megan was dancing with Harrison, and Jennifer pointed boldly, summoning Connor.

He groaned. *"Shit."*

It was too loud to hear his sigh, but Clara felt the pain wafting off of him. Twisting the sole of her chunky sandal along the sticky bar floor, she smiled, watching as Connor's feet moved to face her. Just like the night outside of Eli and Gloria's—*only closer*.

A tingle started in the back of her knees as she looked up into his eyes.

"Please let me stand here. I just want to drink my beer in peace."

Clara eyed him narrowly, silently granting him this favor. He smirked and her pulse thrummed, his dimple deepening right in front of her. Braced against the bar, her feet were planted between Connor's. Her head lolled to the side, and she smiled. She liked the feel of him. Close to her. *Over her.*

They stared at each other, and something shifted. Maybe she *was* strong.

"So, what's this I hear about an apology?"

The corner of Connor's mouth pulled into a quick frown, their faces inches apart. "Why didn't you call me back?" His gaze held hers.

"*Because*. I wasn't ready."

He mulled over her words, accepting her honesty. "I was an idiot. You know—after dinner? I shouldn't have said that..." His eyes dropped to her lips. "About the second chance stuff."

Clara's heart pounded as she looked up, seeing herself in the unknown of Connor's eyes. Neither of them knew what to do.

But she knew what she wanted.

She took another drink, steadying her nerves. "I can understand that you have a lot of complicated feelings about this," she motioned between them, grazing his chest. "But it's been a long time." She took a deep breath, straightening her shoulders. "We're not the same people we used to be."

I'm not the same.

There was an openness in his gaze, and she pushed forward. Trying to make it through the doorway before it shut. "You might not understand why I stayed. I don't expect you to." She shrugged. "Sometimes I can't even understand it myself. All I can do is accept that the gamble I took was a shitty one." Clara grappled with the truth. *Her truth*. "But I lived to tell the tale."

She watched his grip tighten on his drink, his reluctance tangible. A long silence stretched between them. She smiled and leaned in once more.

"Penny?"

The corner of his mouth lifted—and so did her heart.

He glanced down. "I don't know..."

Clara's heart stopped.

Connor turned, leaning against the bar alongside her, facing the dance floor. "Maybe we were right to call it."

She bit the inside of her lip, trying hard to hide her disappointment. He was tumbling out of orbit. They looked out to the crowd once again, and Clara felt him slipping out of reach with every second that passed. She took a deep breath and pivoted, closing him in where he stood.

A question etched his brow. "What are you doing?"

She shook her head. "I don't want to call it."

He stared down at her, his lips pressed into a hard line. Her chest rose and fell, years of indecision weighing every labored breath. Seconds lingered, and she shifted. The bravery that had swelled only a moment ago was rapidly deflating, and she moved to pull away from the bar.

Connor put his hand on top of hers. "Then keep convincing me."

The air left her lungs and the skin on her collarbone tingled where his breath had touched her. He didn't pull away.

The room was spinning and Clara clamped her lids shut, willing the room to slow.

She spoke against his jaw. "What happened was awful..." She swallowed. "Not one of my finer moments." Her eyes opened, and she was met with a small lift at the edge of Connor's mouth. It was slight, but Clara held onto it.

"The history we have—it could suffocate us. But I know that's not what I want... and I'm pretty sure that's not what you want, either." She watched the bob of his throat and she took a deep breath. "You're unsure about me, but when I'm with you, I feel like I'm a new person." She raised her eyes to his. "A stronger person."

Clara fought every urge to lean into him. To run her lips across his stubble. She could see the rise and fall of his chest. He smelled just as good as he always did. Like soap. And Peppermint. And *Connor*. She shifted, feeling his touch slide, trailing from her hand to her wrist.

He pulled her to him as he turned, his lips brushing against her hair. It was a whisper of a movement, but she felt it. The heady look in his eyes made her shiver, and a tingle skated around her stomach, diving down below.

"Is that your closing argument?" A grin tugged at his lips.

She nodded assertively. Bravely. Like she was approaching the edge of that great precipice.

Clara rose to her tiptoes. She placed her hand in the center of his chest and hovered, taking a breath before taking the plunge. Connor's grip tightened.

His lips were soft, brushing against hers. Soft but hot and firm with promise. He brought a hand to her jaw, and Clara leaned against him, reveling in how they fit together. The electricity coursed through them. Like one of those crystal balls full of little blue lightning bolts, flickering everywhere their fingers touched.

Connor deepened the kiss, drinking her in. Tilting her head, she succumbed to the pressure of his lips and she opened to him. His fingers drifted, tangling in her hair, and Clara melted, coming alive at the feel of his tongue against hers. She gasped as Connor ran his hand down the back of her dress.

Clara pulled away for air and laughed. A dull ache settled between her legs as she stared at his mouth, wanting more. "So... what will it be?"

He ran his thumb along her lips. "I guess that all depends."

"On what?"

Connor's jaw tensed. "Are you going to break my heart?"

Clara bit the inside of her cheek. The intensity in his eyes burned a hole straight through her. It was too much. She lowered her gaze, staring at the thrum of his pulse. She shook her head. "No."

Seconds passed. A heartbreaking smirk broke across his face, rising to the full forty watts. It was the most beautiful thing she had ever seen. Reaching up, she traced a dimple. "Does this mean *yes?*"

He nodded. "Yeah."

Connor crushed his mouth to hers. A sense of urgency filled the air around them.

"Oh my God."

Connor pulled back. Dazed from the sudden withdrawal of his kiss, Clara turned, now face to face with Connor's family. Harrison and Lo were laughing, and Kat feigned mock disgust. Ryan and Jonah walked off the dance floor, meeting the rest of the group. Ryan looked around, his eyes finally stopping at Clara. "What did we miss?"

Kat shook her head. "They were sucking face."

Ryan's eyes jumped to Clara's. She went to cover her face but stopped, a feeling of shamelessness washing over her. She had fought for what she wanted, and for tonight, at least, she was victorious. Clara didn't know she could feel like this. She wanted to hold on to it.

Jonah smiled and leaned in. "We were just leaving to meet up with some friends over at Looking Glass. Are you coming with us? Or do you have better plans?"

Clara grinned, turning her face into Connor's shoulder. Connor smiled sheepishly and pressed his lips to her hair, speaking against her ear. "The three of them are crashing with me this weekend."

Clara pulled back, her gaze dipping from his eyes down to his mouth, feeling that delicious tingle tightening in her stomach. "So... I'll see you at work then?"

Kat poked her finger down her throat, faux vomiting.

Connor's dimples deepened. "Yeah, I'll see you at work."

Butterflies the size of bats fluttered in her stomach.

"Y ou're sure you don't want to come with us?" Ryan rolled down the window of their Lyft.

They all stood together outside the crowded bar, splintering off as they parted ways. Kat finished programming her number into Jonah's phone and stepped toward the car, passing it to him. "Text me so I know it's you."

A couple of guys walked by, glancing at Kat bent over at the waist outside the car. Clara caught what she thought was irritation on Harrison's face just before he shifted, obstructing their view.

Everyone said goodbye as Ryan and Jonah drove away. Kat, Lo, and Harrison ambled down the street, stopping at another bar down the way. Connor pulled Clara to him, smoothing his hands across her shoulders. She pulled back, grinning up at him, drunk and dizzy.

"You're sure you don't want to come with us? I can get you a ride back home."

Clara breathed deep and shook her head softly. "That's really sweet, but I don't think I can do another stop." She closed her eyes, hypnotized by the feel of his hands over her dress.

Her ride pulled up to the curb and Connor groaned, not ready to let her go. "I'll text you." He held the car door open, closing it softly behind her, an easy smile balanced on his mouth as he stepped back onto the curb, hands in his pockets.

⸺ ⁓ ⸺

And he did. Not one second before Clara had walked around to the back porch, her phone chimed.

CONNOR: Thanks for un-calling it.

She pulled the handle of the screen door and smiled.

CLARA : Glad you decided I was worth taking a chance.

Three dots danced across the screen while she waited, standing on the back porch.

CONNOR: You were always worth it.

A shiver shot across her skin, settling between her ribs. Clara's smile beamed in the glow of her screen and she sank into her favorite chair. She felt naked, sitting in the dark alone. After the bar, everything felt muffled. But even through the buffer, summer seeped in through her skin.

The air stayed thick and the warmth of the earth continued to radiate after a full day in the sun. She sighed, tipping her head back against the wood. She closed her eyes and saw Connor's face.

The last time she had sat in this seat, she had thrown up in the backyard. She cringed and drew in a breath. Tonight, the room was spinning for a different reason. Behind her lashes, the tipsiness slowed, and she thought of Connor's lips against hers. The strength in his hands. She magnified the memory second by second, clutching onto every piece. It had been so long since she had felt the thrill of being touched.

Being wanted.

The next several days floated past like moments from a dream. The unnamed feeling of something new and untouched brewing in the air. Like the beginning of spring. Instead of reaching for the same ratty clothes, Clara stepped into her closet, running her fingers along a row of tops. *Every day is something to celebrate.*

On her drive over to Grady's, she heard her phone ding in her purse and glanced at the dashboard. *Nine o'clock sharp.* She bit the inside of her lip, holding back a smile. Connor had sent her a text every morning since Saturday. When she asked why nine a.m., he responded with a list of determining factors he had taken into serious consideration that ended, most importantly, with *I don't want to wake you if you're sleeping well.*

She pulled into the parking lot, glancing around for Connor's car. She grabbed her cell phone, opening his text.

CONNOR: Can't wait to see you.

The slow thud in her chest started racing, and she beamed, staring at his message as the air conditioning quickly faded from the car.

CLARA: What time will you be here? I can't wait either.

She stepped out of her car and made the walk to the front door, traversing the hot gravel lot. Her phone dinged.

CONNOR: Noon.

Clara went to slide her cell into her back pocket, and another message sounded.

CONNOR: Also... good morning.

She laughed, looking down at the screen. She shook her head and pushed through the front door, bell chiming overhead.

Eli complimented her new look the moment she walked in. Eyeing her blouse, he chuckled nervously. "I hope that's machine washable."

Clara smiled and got to work, busying herself through the morning, glancing at the clock every second she got. She made her way around the nursery and soaked the plants, preparing them for the long, hot day ahead. She was taking inventory and walked back to the greenhouse on the far end, the one she took her breaks in when she needed a moment to herself.

They were currently using it for a rotation of lilies and sedum. She heard the crunch of gravel behind her and turned, catching Connor's silhouette leaning back against the door. *Eleven thirty a.m.* Excitement coursed through her as she admired him in broad daylight.

"Don't let me disturb you." His mouth pulled into a grin. Clara held her clipboard to her chest, hoping to muffle the sound of her racing heart.

"I'm almost done. You're not disturbing me," she added.

"I can wait for you out here."

Clara shook her head silently, still beaming. "Don't move a muscle."

She finished up her count, trying not to lose focus. As she got to the bottom of the form, she felt Connor moving closer. Slowly approaching, like a cat going in for the kill. The disruption of the gravel under his feet sent tingles to the backs of her knees. She rushed to record the final numbers, frantic to get every last digit down. Connor's hands skated down the outside of her arms, stopping at her elbows. He placed his chin on the top of her shoulder, nuzzling her hair.

"You smell good."

Clara's pulse fluttered as she finished the last entry, not caring if her four looked like a seven. She tossed the clipboard on the table in front of them. "I smell like sweat."

She turned in his arms, her skin damp from the heat. He captured her face and tilted her jaw, dropping a kiss to her mouth. His eyes never left hers. Clara smiled against his lips. "You're here early." Just like at the bar, she rose to her toes, snaking her hands around the back of his neck. She brushed the edge of his hair and his eyes went half-mast.

"I had somewhere I needed to be." His body relaxed and he brushed another kiss to her mouth. Clara held his gaze as she opened against the sweet pressure of his lips and something hot flickered behind his eyes. He tilted his mouth over hers, a satisfied sound slipping from his chest.

At the bar, they had been surrounded by people. Here, there was no one but them. She had replayed their kiss so many times she had broken all the buttons on the VCR in her brain. Connor's hands moved down, wasting no time. Their lust was intentional, not frantic. It was only a matter of how long she had to wait before she got a taste.

He lowered his voice just above a whisper. "Tell me something you like."

Clara shook her head, losing sight in the heady, delicious fog. "I... I like gardening, obviously..."

He smiled against her cheek. She continued, "And I... like going to the movies..." His touch drifted and she sucked in a breath. "But I haven't been in a long time."

Connor chuckled and Clara looked at him, confused and hazy. He tilted her head to the side, trailing kisses down to her collarbone and spoke against her skin. "Not exactly what I was talking about... but you're giving me ideas."

"Oh." She blinked, looking up at the ceiling of the greenhouse. "I don't really know." She couldn't think of anything at the moment. Everything that wasn't his touch ceased to exist.

He brushed his lips against her shoulder, kneading her lower back in slow circular motions. *No one has ever asked.*

Connor leaned back just enough so he could look into her eyes. Dark and teasing. "I think you do."

Everything inside her tightened. She slid her hands along his biceps, contemplating as she trailed her fingers down his forearms. For the briefest moment, she had shrunk beneath his question, feeling unsure.

Looking at Connor, she didn't know why she had ever doubted herself before. Her chest swelled, filled with the need she saw in his eyes. Her touch traveled until her hands covered his at her lower back. Clara dipped her gaze from his eyes to his lips, applying light pressure to his palms... sliding them down.

A daring smirk pulled at his lips, deepening his dimples.

She brought her mouth to his. "I like this."

A soft groan slipped from the back of his throat. He flexed his fingers, grabbing her ass, pulling her even higher on her toes—tight against him. Her breath hitched and he loosened his hold, dragging her down his body. Whatever had been hovering just below the surface was pulling them both under.

Anticipation swirled in her chest. Connor lifted Clara, settling her back on the empty potting table behind them. He stepped between her legs and Clara ran her hands over his shirt, skating along the cotton and dipping below the hem. The second her fingers touched his skin, Connor caught her wrist and kissed the side of her face.

"Let me take you out."

She laughed. Sitting back on the dirty worktable, Clara sank into his gaze, submerging herself in every shade of blue. He was torn and strung tight. She knew somewhere deep inside that if she wanted to push, he would fall with her.

She looked down at his hands lightly holding her wrists. "Too good for a romp in the greenhouse?"

A smile broke across his face. "If you knew how many times I've thought about this..." Hooking his hands under her knees, he pulled her to the edge, pressing himself against her. "You wouldn't ask me that."

A flush crept up Clara's neck, flaming her cheeks. "How many times?"

Connor studied her with a shameless grin. "That's classified information."

Ohmygod.

He rested his hands on top of her thighs. "I'm asking you out on a date."

She straightened and took a breath, searching his face. "Okay."

"Good." He nodded. "Friday... Dinner and a movie?"

She looked down, watching the way his fingers dragged back and forth over her skin. "No movie." She worried the inside of her lip.

He tilted his head, a question in his eyes.

"The sooner we're done with dinner, the sooner..."

Connor shook his head. Now he was the one blushing. He towered over her from where she sat. His mouth worked in a dangerous way, biting back things he shouldn't say. "I want to do this right... and you're making it very difficult."

Her breathing was labored as she looked up into the blue. She nodded, relinquishing what little control she had. "*Fine*. What should I wear?"

His gaze lowered to her shirt, searing her skin through the fabric. "Whatever you want. You look good in anything."

Connor turned onto the private drive that led to Clara's house, grimacing at the *Monroe* nameplate on the brick mailbox. He breathed deep, a smile working its way across his mouth, spotting her car in the distance. He took a breath and cut the engine, checking his mirror before sliding out of the driver's side.

They had been relentless at the nursery. Every time he and Clara weren't together, they searched for each other. He couldn't remember the last time he had felt this needy, insistent excitement. Every day, he came in early, making excuses to stay late just to be with her. Connor smiled, thinking about the greenhouse.

After several heated debates, he relinquished. *No movie.* He grabbed the gift from the passenger seat and headed up the porch steps, taking two at a time. He rang the doorbell and stood, drumming his fingers against the side of his leg, waiting.

He smiled wide when he saw her shape through the glass inlay. The door swung in and her excitement mirrored his as they both stood, drinking each other in. Clara wore her hair down. Her wavy frizz tamed into loose curls. Her lips were shiny, and she had on a gauzy white top, tucked into a pair of cut-offs. Not used to seeing her out of work boots, Connor enjoyed the rare sighting of Clara's bare feet in heeled sandals. He let out a long, low whistle, and she shook her head, a smile on her lips.

"You clean up nice, Kent."

He had opted for a pair of dark jeans and another linen button-down. In place of his Chucks, he wore a pair of dress shoes.

Clara's eyes floated down from his smile to his hands. "Is that for me?"

"Oh—yeah. This is from that ceramicist. The one Gloria ordered from for the shop."

"Wow... I haven't seen this design."

"Yeah, I looked her up." Connor studied the look on Clara's face. "I wanted to see what her business page was like... you know, to see if there was any opportunity there. I saw that and thought it might be something you'd like."

Clara's chest expanded. The pedestal planter was timeless. She took the lime washed stone from his hands. "Did you end up talking business with her?"

"No, the site was actually pretty nice. The photos she's got showcase her pieces really well."

"So... you made a trip to her shop *just* for this?"

He watched her turn the stone planter in her hands. A warm smile reached his eyes. "Special trip for a special person."

Connor's words settled over her. Her eyes met his, not sure of what to say. All she could do was smile.

He cleared his throat. "She had it labeled as a *compote bowl* so I thought of—"

"Gloria." Clara beamed.

Every day is something to celebrate.

As they made their way outside, Connor walked behind her, trailing slowly and taking in how beautiful she looked. He stepped in front of her as they got to the car, opening her door. Before shutting it, he leaned in and dropped a soft kiss on her lips. Her eyes crinkled in the corners as she smiled up at him.

His breath caught. "You're gorgeous."

She looked down into her lap, blushing under his words.

"Have you been here before?"

Clara shook her head, taking Connor's arm as they walked into the restaurant.

"Good evening. Do you have a reservation?"

Connor nodded and Clara glanced around, taking in the dimly lit tables and tall ceilings. They followed the hostess, stepping outside to the patio. Vines covered the exposed brick and the noisy echo of dishes and flatware disappeared behind them. A warm breeze touched her face as Connor pulled out her chair.

The waiter arrived. Connor ordered his drink and looked at Clara.

"I'd take a guess, but I figure you'd probably want to pick for yourself."

As the evening carried on, they fell in and out of lulls in the conversation. They smiled at each other, enjoying the silent flirtation between them. Connor stretched out his legs and Clara moved forward so their ankles rested against one another. More than once during the meal, Connor had reached across and held her hand.

"So, you and Kat are how many years apart?"

"Two years…"

"And Lo is whose daughter?"

"Gloria, my mom, and Lo's mom are all sisters."

Clara nodded, taking in the details of their family tree. "It must have been so cool having Eli as an uncle growing up… he's so crazy and fun."

"He is." Connor smiled. "He was always a little eccentric, but we didn't really know any different. Everyone in our family is pretty laid back. Except Aunt Emma—Lorelei's mom." Connor pulled a tight smile. "She's really strict."

Clara watched the candlelight flicker, casting a glow across Connor's face.

"We were always up to no good. We'd play outside or run around in the greenhouses until we had to go home. I think Mom and Dad were just happy to have people that were always up for babysitting."

"And Eli and Gloria never wanted kids?"

His smile dipped. "I think they tried, but it never really worked out."

She leaned her leg against his under the table, and the smile returned to his face. "That explains why they fuss over you guys so much." Clara sighed. "Your childhood sounds like a dream. Like *The Secret Garden*."

"Would you believe me if I told you I could probably quote that whole stupid movie?"

Clara's eyes sparkled. She tilted her head back as a laugh bubbled up from her chest. "It is not stupid!"

"No—the movie itself is not stupid. It's just... I've probably seen it over a million times." His gaze warmed. "It was Kat's favorite when we were kids."

The image of Connor and Kat and Lo as kids all huddled up, watching one of her favorite childhood movies, made Clara's heart pinch. Even if Connor was miserable, the thought was endearing. She had been an only child, and she watched all her movies on repeat to fill the silence while her mom was at work.

"What about you?" Connor sat up in his chair, leaning on the table. "What's your family like?"

Clara creased and uncreased the napkin in her lap. "I don't really know my dad. They split when I was young. My mom worked all the time, so I pretty much lived at my neighbor's house... her family was really awesome." She took a sip of her drink. "But we lost touch when we went to college. She went to North Georgia, and I went to—"

"UGA."

Clara smiled. "Right. So, we would catch up on the holidays when we came home, but after a while we had less and less to talk about. Honestly, I think I enjoyed being at her house because it felt so... *normal*."

The compassion in Connor's eyes was almost too hard to look at.

"I don't blame my mom. She was just doing the best she could." Clara shrugged. "I understood she had to work a ton, and I just got used to not having her around as much." She drew in a breath. "What about you?"

A frown tugged at the corner of his mouth and he gazed at the candle between them. "When our dad died, things were different. Mom was so busy, and I think she was just trying to get through it all." The sadness in his eyes made sense. Like her life was closer to his than they both realized. "Sometimes I feel bad for Kat. Like I should have paid more attention."

"What do you mean?"

"She started getting into trouble." He shook his head, traveling back in time. "Some of it's funny now, but back then, none of us knew what to do. Eli started taking us camping—you know, hiking and stuff." Connor smiled softly. "It seemed to help."

Clara grinned, thinking about his sister. Gorgeous and tough. Feminine and bold. "And you're back now." Clara smiled. "I can tell she loves having you around."

He smiled and shifted in his seat, clearing his throat. "So, do you still talk to your mom?"

"Oh—probably not as much as I should. She wasn't too happy about Mark and me."

Connor nodded, glancing down at his hands. "She bummed about the divorce?"

Clara laughed. She saw the confusion on his face and straightened in her chair. "No... that's not what I meant. She was disappointed in me for being *with* Mark."

Connor's brow knitted.

"I think it hurt her to watch me put myself in a relationship like that. She was always busting her ass so that she didn't have to rely on anyone."

"Yeah, but surely she thought at some point that you were, you know... happy."

"Yeah... When we were in college, she knew that I was dating someone. And when it got serious, I introduced them. I remember the time I brought Mark home to meet her." A bitter smile touched Clara's lips. "My mom didn't like him. It was like she had some sort of intuition." Clara reached forward, turning the votive candle. "I was so fucking naïve."

Connor placed his hand on top of hers.

"It's fine." She shook her head, lowering her voice. "Over and done with."

"It's still shitty."

A bead of condensation rolled down the outside of her water glass, picking up speed before dripping to the table. Her jaw clenched. "I hate that I wasted so much time. Like if I had just opened my eyes and listened to *anyone* around me..." Her gaze held his. "Things would be different."

Connor listened to the pain in Clara's voice. She was looking down at their clasped hands.

"I bet you're just waiting to say *I told you so.*"

His mouth twisted. "That's not exactly how this works." He ran his thumb over her knuckle.

"I only mean that I'm sure you saw it from a mile away." Her nostrils flared. "I probably got what I deserved."

"Clara, I cared about you. Mark was... *Mark.*" Connor grimaced, not needing to explain what she already knew. "Even after everything went down, I only wanted the best for you." His voice was firm. "No one deserves what he did to you."

When Connor's eyes met Clara's, he saw the shimmer behind her lashes.

"You know that night at the lake? When you went outside with him?

Clara shrugged. "It was a long time ago."

"I saw the whole thing." He cleared his throat, his gaze softening. "We all did."

Her eyes widened. Memories flooding in from that night.

He stilled, remembering Mark yelling at her. Clara crying. A silent show that everyone watched. "I should have gone out there. I should have stood *with* you."

Clara swallowed the lump in her throat. It hurt too much to wonder. She squeezed his hand, a weak smile on her lips. "I wish I could get all that time back."

He lifted her hand to his mouth, brushing his lips across the space where her wedding ring used to be. "Who knows... maybe we wouldn't be here now."

She slipped her hand from his and raised her glass. Connor followed suit and waited, the trace of a dimple flashing. "To making up for lost time."

* * *

As they made their way up the steps of Clara's porch, excitement thrummed in her chest.

They reached the front door, and she dug her keys out of her purse. "If you want dessert, I think I've got some ice cream in the freezer—"

"There's no way the Rocky Road has lasted this long." It had been about three weeks since Connor bought it.

"No... that one's long gone." Clara laughed. "It's been replaced already."

He smiled.

"If you're not in the mood for ice cream, we could have another drink." She turned the key in the lock, glancing over her shoulder. Connor's gaze trailed down the backs of her legs. A warmth spread across every inch his eyes touched. Clara pushed the door open and cool air tumbled through the entrance. The chill inside the house touched her skin through her cotton blouse. She kicked off her sandals and set her purse down on the foyer table next to Connor's gift.

"I'm just going to freshen up. I'll meet you in the kitchen."

Clara stepped into her bedroom and did a once-over. She had already cleaned the house in hopeful anticipation. The day after she made out with Connor at the bar, Clara had run out and picked up a new set of king-sized sheets. She thought of Miranda from *Sex and the City*, and her attempt to change her bed karma in hopes of getting lucky.

The very thought of having sex with Connor on anything Mark touched felt like some sort of cosmic violation. Clara chewed the inside of her lip. She slipped into the bathroom and ran her hand through her curls. She fixed a tiny smudge of mascara underneath her eye and checked her deodorant.

The image of Connor backing her up onto the worktable in the greenhouse flashed through her mind and she swore out loud to herself. She needed a karmic *Kama Sutra* miracle.

———

They sat on the wicker sofa outside on the back porch. Clara stretched into Connor's lap and his hand rested on her bare ankle as they talked into the night, the tension painfully evident.

"Tell me..." Her eyes landed on his lips. "Was the date everything you hoped for?"

The corner of his mouth rose. "I had a nice time."

"There's no part of you that wishes we would have just... *kept going* in the greenhouse?" She moved her foot and his grip tensed. The easygoing look in his eyes darkened.

"You definitely gave me something to think about."

"So you *did* think about it..."

"Of course I thought about it. You propositioned me."

Her jaw dropped. "I did not *proposition* you." She sat up. "If anything, *you* walked up to *me* in my place of work!"

Connor held up both of his hands in defense, laughing. "I will admit to *starting* it."

His dimples deepened, his grin glowing to the full forty-watts. She was leaning into him, her breathing unsteady.

Connor tucked a frizzy curl behind her ear and looked at her seriously. "What if I started something now?"

Clara's heart pounded. Her eyes locked with his and she reached up to his hand, idly tracing a tendril. "I think if you start something... you better be prepared to finish it."

She heard the brazen tone of her own voice. The weight of her words floated between them, settling heavily in Connor's chest. It spread like wildfire.

All summer Connor had wanted this, even when he hadn't realized it. Every day spent under the sun, bickering with Clara. Seeing her skin glisten with sweat. The way her hair tangled, slipping from her stupid hat. Wanting her work boots wrapped around his waist.

It was only this week that he'd gotten a taste. Stolen glances between rows of trees and greedy touches in the greenhouse. All of it foreplay. None of it enough. Connor pressed his lips to hers, wanting everything, but wanting it to last. Clara sighed, and he ran his tongue along the seam of her lips, prodding her to open. She yielded and a noise of content escaped his throat at the feel of her tongue against his. Connor's hold tightened in her hair. Clara gasped, and he felt her reaction in the base of his spine.

"I like that."

He grinned against her mouth. "Noted."

Clara ran her hands down his chest, reaching for the top of his belt buckle. Connor groaned and caught her hand with his own.

He drew in a breath. "We should slow down," he whispered.

An electric current skated between her shoulder blades, raising the hair on the back of her neck. He tilted her chin with his hand and laid a trail of open-mouth kisses along her throat. Clara exhaled impatiently, glancing down at where his hand covered hers. Everything in her tightened, seeing the evidence of what she did to him.

She felt herself running closer and closer to the edge. Restless, she pulled back and looked into his eyes. Connor's chest rose and fell with controlled, even breaths as he searched her face. He placed his rough hands on her shoulders, working at the tension he found there. His warmth penetrated her blouse, and she melted under his touch.

A shaky laugh passed his lips. "We don't need to rush this." His patience was both sexy and unbearable. Clara focused beyond him, through the mesh screen, unable to look him in the eyes.

Her conversation with Ryan flashed through her mind. On Monday, she'd broken down, divulging that she'd never been with anyone but Mark. How she was nervous. How she was certain she'd mess something up. He had showered her with encouragement. Told her not to overthink it, to only do what she felt comfortable with. That it was just like riding a bike.

But, Ryan had said, if it were him, he'd rip that Band-Aid clean off.

Connor touched her jaw, forcing her to turn back to him. Clara averted her gaze, instead focusing on his lips. *Just like riding a bike.*

She took a deep breath, feeling his touch warm below her chin. *Band-Aids.* She looked down at the fullness straining against his jeans, and she swallowed. *Bikes and Band-Aids.*

She wanted him, and he laughed. His ease was unnerving. She pulled back. "I think I need some water..." Clara motioned to the kitchen, picking up their empty beer bottles before slipping inside. Connor frowned and stood up, following her. When he closed the door to the kitchen, he saw Clara standing at the sink. His chest constricted.

Connor approached, leaning down on the counter beside her. He pressed against her from shoulder to waist. Waiting. Clara exhaled, watching the cold water run over her skin. "I was excited to spend time with you... alone."

Her words were endearing and honest. Connor's smile dipped. "Was?"

"I *am.* It's just..." She cut off the tap. "It's been a while."

When she finally looked up at him, Connor swore, angry with himself. "What's a while?" he traced his thumb along her jaw.

Clara ran her tongue across her bottom lip, tamping her frustration. "This wasn't supposed to be a big deal..."

Connor looked at her thoughtfully, the realization hitting him. "Clara, I can wait." He dipped his chin, holding her gaze. "We don't have to do anything that you don't want to do."

A small smile pulled at her mouth. She shook her head. "I want to, *trust* me." Clara's eyes warmed and her voice quieted. "I think I just got a little nervous."

"Would it help if I told you..." Connor cleared his throat, brushing a tendril from her face. "That I was telling myself to slow down?"

Her throat bobbed. A feeling in her chest like a pile of fireworks sitting, waiting for a match.

"To make it last." He reached for her fingers, still cold from the tap. Enveloping her hands in his, he brought them to his chest. Connor watched her expression soften. "Because I've wanted this for a very long time."

Seconds passed, ticking by with the beat of his pulse as he studied her. Clara leaned into him, pressing a kiss to his hand. "I want this too."

"You're sure?" He whispered.

She nodded, brushing her lips against his skin.

Dropping their hands, Clara lifted the hem of her shirt, and his eyes lingered, soaking in every inch of exposed skin. Connor touched the silver closure of her shorts. Clara brought her mouth to his, slipping her hand beneath his collar, kneading the warmth of his shoulders. Making quick work of his buttons, his muscles flexed and bulged as he pulled his shirt down his arms.

Her denim shorts hung loosely at her hips, and Connor stripped them down over her thighs with a new sense of urgency. The metal of his buckle rang out like a bell in the empty house, and she stared at him, standing shirtless in her kitchen.

Seeing the hot, needy look in Clara's eyes sent him over the edge. Catching her by the waist, Connor pulled her to him, dipping his mouth to her shoulder. Sliding his hands down her body, he lifted and Clara wrapped her legs around his waist, bringing him hard against the fabric of her underwear. She gasped, and he tightened his grip, carrying her upstairs into the dark.

Clara dragged her fingers through his hair. "Second door to the left."

The windows pooled with a hazy glow from the moon, and Connor eyed the bed. His stomach twisted and he pivoted, sinking to the bench at the end of the large wooden footboard.

"What's wrong?" Her voice was breathy as she kissed along his neck.

"Nothing." He looked into her eyes and the pain in his chest eased. Connor ran his hands from her thighs up to her waist, holding her close as she straddled him. Clara tucked her chin to his shoulder, closing her eyes, shuddering at the feel of rough denim against her skin. Connor breathed into her hair, trailing his touch down her back, and she opened her eyes. In the dim light of the moon, Clara stilled, staring at the bed.

Connor sensed a shift. "We don't have to do anything if you're not ready."

Clara tore her focus from beyond his shoulder, tightening her legs around him. A breath shot from his chest, and reluctantly, he stood, taking her with him.

"Wait—what are you doing?"

Connor lowered her to her feet, and once standing, turned her in his arms. "Come here." He sat back down on the bench, pulling Clara into his lap, both of them facing away from the bed.

He sank, pressing a kiss between her shoulder blades, unhooking the fabric covering her breasts. She moved her hips, and a tortured noise slipped from his throat. Connor nipped at her soft skin with his teeth, cupping her, and Clara whimpered, covering his hands with her own. Connor held her tight, running his stubble along her spine, breathing warm air over her skin.

Clara leaned back. Connor's hands spanned her ribcage, and she sighed, arching into his touch. The sound of her approval stoked the flames inside him and he shifted, bringing her hard against him.

"Does this feel good?"

"*Yes—*" A shaky breath trailed from her lips. "Better than good."

At her back, Clara felt his smile. She knew it even in the dark.

"Tell me what you want."

He palmed her breasts, rolling the tips between his fingers. Her breath hitched.

Her head dropped back against Connor's shoulder, her voice hushed. "I want you."

"You have me." The rough calluses of his hands skated across her sensitive skin and she writhed. "Tell me what to do."

The openness of his offer sent a shiver through her body. She sat in silence, unable to speak. Earlier, she had felt bold. Audacious. With their clothes on, the directness of her words felt like child's play compared to this. Connor took her silence as obstinance.

Tilting her jaw, their lips met over her shoulder, his breath warm and laced with peppermint. "If you don't have any requests..." He kissed her deeply, a whisper of his teeth grazing her lips. Their eyes connected in the dark, and Clara felt the tension tighten between her legs.

A breath passed between them and she shook her head against his mouth, "I... I don't..."

Connor trailed his hand, reaching the edge of her underwear. Her eyes widened, and Connor moved his stubbled chin to her neck. Dipping his hand lower, he traced along the fabric seam that covered her. She sucked in a breath. "I don't know what I like."

He stilled. She felt the shift of something invisible between them. Something in the darkness that she couldn't see. Like the raging heat of embarrassment coursing through her body. Clara placed her hands along his forearms and Connor drifted, tenderly sliding her underwear to the side. He skated along the inside of her thigh, urging her gently.

Clara opened herself to him, and he covered her aching center with his palm. Her breath caught at the warmth of his hand. Connor brushed his mouth to the crook of her neck and drew on her flesh, pressing his tongue along her salty skin. Desire dripped between her thighs.

"Clara..." Her name was a sigh tumbling from his chest. He kept a firm pressure to his palm. "Do you like this?"

She found herself moving her swollen sex against his hand and she closed her eyes, nodding. Her pleasure heightened his own, and Connor groaned his approval against her skin. "Say it—"

Clara sighed. "*Yes...*"

He shifted beneath her, adjusting his hold on her body, whispering into the dark. Clara's eyes opened, feeling his hard, thick length trapped beneath his jeans. Connor breathed heavily, applying more pressure as she rolled herself against him. "I need to tell you something."

She twisted, looking into his eyes as he touched her. His motions slowed, now tracing along her crest, covered in her slick heat.

"I've always wanted you for myself."

Her eyes dropped to his lips, feeling the pull of something hot and tight, Connor's words winding around her heart... And she wanted *more. More friction. More pressure.* "Please—" He moved in tight circles between Clara's legs and she arched, no outlet for the ache building inside her. She strained, reaching between them, stroking him over his clothes. "Connor—"

A breath hissed between his teeth and he thought of the night at his apartment. The way she had jerked away from him flashed through his mind, and his throat tensed. He wouldn't survive that again. "Baby... tell me what you need."

She swallowed at the emotion his words evoked. At the power he gave her. "I need you inside of me."

He drew in a breath, one hand pulling and pinching a blushing tip as his hand at her center lowered. Clara bit the inside of her lip, feeling him circle her entrance, once, twice, his mouth dragging against her neck. Connor slipped a finger inside her and Clara clenched around him, pleasure humming through her body.

Seconds passed. Connor stilled, reveling in the wild beat of Clara's heart thrumming in his arms. He felt her move, covering his hands with her own, her voice pleading. "Please... don't stop."

Lust rolled through him as he clutched her breast, working her over, edging in and out of her body. His palm slid over her, building a rhythm that had Clara writhing with every stroke.

Connor kissed the side of her face, and his hold tightened, slowing to add a second finger. She gasped, grinding herself against the pressure. Racing, chasing, begging for release. Connor curled his touch inside of her, pressing, and Clara moaned, shuttling over the edge. Her back arched, and fireworks shimmered as she fell apart into a million tiny pieces of cinder and ash. All with Connor wrapped around her.

His breathing slowed, and he kissed her sweaty skin. She turned, bringing her lips to his, sighing. He studied her with a lazy grin, his gaze drifting over every visible trace of Clara in the moonlight.

She lifted her hand to his cheek, grazing a dimple. She felt his smile. *The full forty-watts.* "I don't know if I can stand." A laugh bubbled up from her chest and she slid from his lap, unsteady on her feet. Clara walked to the bedside table, pulling a foil packet from the drawer. Connor stood from the bench and came to her side, kissing her shoulder. "We don't have to do this yet."

She touched the waist of his jeans, hooking her finger into the space where denim met skin. The foil crinkled in her hand. "I bought these after you asked me out..." She bit her lip, unsure why she felt compelled to tell him. "And the sheets."

It was Connor's turn to laugh. He rubbed his hand across his jaw and nodded, glancing down at the bed. "I bet they're very nice."

She smiled, boldly undoing his top button. Holding Connor's gaze, she tore open the packet, watching him shove his pants down his legs. "They're very, *very* nice." Her words were hoarse and heavy as she stared at him, naked in front of her.

Connor's eyes fell closed at Clara's touch, her palm pressing against him. Taking him in her hand, she rolled the protection down his stiff length. His pulse picked up, catching the playful pull of Clara's lips. Lacing their fingers, she lowered herself to the bed, asking him to follow.

Her voice softened. "Is this okay?"

Connor's eyes darkened. A grin stretched across his mouth, and he descended, covering her body with his own. "Better than okay."

Clara turned her cheek, running her lips along his bicep, reveling in the feel of him over her, surrounding her. He caught her kiss, a hum of pleasure vibrating against her mouth as she parted her lips, his tongue seeking hers. Below him, Clara's skin was soft and warm. His touch became insistent, fanning his fingers across her breasts. Tracing her nipple, he dragged in slow, lazy motions.

Her breath hitched. "I like that—"

Connor smiled. Sliding his hand down between them, he found her hot and slick. His desire responded, like a jolt running from his chest to the base of his spine. He flattened his touch. The expanse of his hand made thrilling contact with her entire sex, spanning between her legs. Nerve endings shot off like sparklers.

He listened as her breath left her body in quick, staggered bursts, watching as pleasure clouded her eyes. Connor adjusted, looking into her face. His gaze was imploring, finding her in the haze between them. "Are you still nervous?"

Pushing her underwear down her hips, she stared up at him. Clara's heart pounded at the feel of Connor's hands covering hers before he took over, sliding the fabric down her legs. Clara reached for him a second time. She trailed her hands along his naked body, searching. She drew him close, shaking her head, brushing her lips against his. "No, I'm not nervous." She positioned his rigid length, pressing vigilantly to take him. He stilled.

The only movement she felt was the heavy rise and fall of Connor's chest. Rolling her hips, she reveled in the thick weight of him against her. Clara closed her eyes, holding onto this moment. Feeling the delicious, aching stretch, she covered his hand with her own, where his fingers rested between her legs. She pressed, urging him to touch her as she took him.

"Clara…" A rough groan slipped from his throat. "Open your eyes."

She drew her bottom lip between her teeth, her breathing sharp and short. There was something in his voice. Something laden with longing. She gazed up at him, knowing that feeling better than anyone.

His eyes held hers. "I need you to see me."

The air left Clara's lungs, and she clenched involuntarily. He slipped from her silken heat and a string of expletives rushed between Connor's lips. They both frantically reached, guiding him until he filled her—completely.

"*Fuck.*" His forehead pressed to hers, his voice no longer soft, but coarse like gravel.

Clara found his lips in the dark. Connor set a tortuous pace, easing in and out, his hand never leaving her. His body was strung tight, braced above her as he deepened the kiss, gliding his tongue against hers. The mirrored feel of him inside her was excruciating. Clara felt a coil begin to tighten. Eager, she raised her hips, begging him to pick up the pace. He answered her, stroking faster. His touch quickened between her legs, and she moaned.

"Oh, my God... just like that."

His labored breaths fell against her neck.

"*Harder,*" Clara demanded, and he whispered incoherent groans of encouragement, his control disintegrating with every thrust. Clara bowed to the pleasure, hovering right on the edge. Connor chased her, feeling her reserve slipping—just like his own. He withdrew and buried himself deep. She gasped at the friction, and her demand became a mantra. Connor met every command, slamming into Clara's body, covered in her desire. He bit the inside of his lip, willing himself to last.

He removed his touch from her center and reached, sweeping her damp tresses away from her neck. Cool air rolled over her shoulders as he twisted his hold, Clara's silken strands wrapped around his fist. Connor dropped his mouth to the smooth expanse of her throat, drawing on her skin, grazing his teeth against her. Clara gasped. The freedom he gave her, and the trust she gave him in return, was her ruin. The chord snapped within and wave after wave of delicious release rolled over her. Connor followed, and with a final thrust, he ground into her, his muscles shaking as he collapsed.

⁓ℓℓ⁓

"You're making a mess."

The metal spoon in Connor's hand clinked, scraping the bottom of the mug. A golden glow from the lamp illuminated the bed, rumpled and worn. "I wanted to use a bowl."

"The mug was a sufficient choice." The duvet twisted as Clara propped up on her elbow, swiping her finger across a bead of ice cream just about to drop. "I stand by that."

"Maybe for one person." Connor inched the cup out of reach, a grin balanced on his lips. "But there are two of us... and one of them is a hog."

Her gaze fell to the sheet draped across his torso.

Catching her eye, Connor placed the mug on the bedside table. He sat up, inching closer, looming over her. He lowered the spoon, mounded with Rocky Road. "Last bite."

A smile stretched across her face and she looked up at him, parting her lips. Connor slipped the dessert into her mouth and her eyes fell closed, heavy with delight. Watching the lamplight slide across her in that moment, warming her, his heart expanded. Connor shifted, rolling them until they were nothing but a tangle of linen, and laughter, and skin—the spoon clattering to the floor.

As the ice cream melted on her tongue, Clara tucked her face below Connor's jaw, rubbing her cheek against him. She hummed, her senses filled to the brim, wrapped in traces of sex and summer.

"Was it the truth?" Her voice floated across his chest, barely above a whisper. Clara shifted, looking into his eyes.

Connor drifted, idly touching a lock of hair at her shoulder. Absorbed in the way the light caught the colors. Clara in every shade. "The part about you being a hog?"

"*No.*" Her brow furrowed, and she pinched his side. He let out a yelp that dissolved into laughter, and after a moment he quieted, seeing the vulnerability in her gaze. "That thing you said earlier..."

Connor slipped his arm farther beneath the sheet, searching, unable to get enough. He pulled Clara close, as close as he could with bunched up blankets and crumpled sheets. The heat pressed in and the fan whirred overhead. Memories crowding the fragile space between them. Taking a deep breath, their eyes met, his mouth tilting into a small smile. "About how I wanted you for myself?"

Connor lifted himself over her, taking in the sight of Clara, flushed and warm beneath him. Her throat bobbed, and she nodded, lowering her gaze to his lips. Her fingers traced along his stubble, touching the spot where a dimple should be.

Connor watched the quick rise and fall of her chest. He touched the sheet and, with a glance into her eyes, lowered his mouth, pressing a kiss over the cotton. With his hand at her knee, Connor slowly ascended, his voice muffled against her. "Yes—I wanted you then."

He pulled the sheet away and Clara breathed in. Connor's words unraveled something inside that she hadn't known existed. Tears shimmered in her eyes, and the bedroom blurred. She swallowed tightly, feeling his lips brushing and drifting, leaving kisses across her skin. Heat curled low, settling between her legs as she ran her fingers through his hair.

Connor shivered under her touch, his breathing becoming ragged. His hands curled around Clara's hips, holding her, like something precious that could disappear.

"And I want you now."

19

The next morning, Connor unwound the crumpled sheet from around his legs. He reached, fingers skating along the cold cotton until he opened his eyes, realizing he was alone. Sunlight cut across the mattress, and he traced the satin stripes, a smirk pulling at the corner of his mouth.

The bedroom was filled with large, expensive furniture that looked very different in the light of day. He grimaced. Everything felt muted and formal. There was no color. No soft curves or worn edges. No life. No *Clara*. He sat up and his eyes fell to the nightstand, their mug from last night sitting on top. A heavy pang twisted in his gut at the thought of Mark existing in this space. Breathing the same air as her... sharing this bed.

He stood and walked to the bedroom door, hearing the clanging of pots and pans. He smiled at the muffled hum of Clara's music. Making his way to the adjoining bathroom, Connor passed the walk-in closet and noticed nearly half of the racks were empty. Undeserved relief washed through him.

He heard Clara singing, and he laughed. Connor stepped onto the tile and glanced down. He frowned briefly and straightened the area rug at his feet. Walking to the vanity, he turned on the tap. Connor took in all the bits and pieces of Clara's personal things strewn about the counter. He noticed a large clip that she used to keep her hair out of her face on most days at the nursery. He found a hot pink hair tie that he had seen her wear all summer. Like the day that she slipped on the stairs.

He leaned forward, splashing water on his face, and scooped up some to rinse. He swished the water around between his lips, hoping to ease the morning breath.

Raising his eyes to the mirror, he noticed the empty vanity at his back. He used a small towel to wipe his chin and something shiny caught his eye. He turned, his eyes falling on a small bottle of cologne sitting in the middle of the counter.

His gaze darted through the bathroom door to the bedroom, and his jaw clenched. He stood, staring at the bottle before finally stepping forward, reaching for a drawer. Connor cracked it open, seeing enough to know that it was still full.

An uneasiness slid up his spine, settling low in his gut. Placing both hands on the cold marble, he glared at the bottle looming over it. *Does she miss him?* He pursed his lips. *Had he been here?* His gut twisted. *When?*

An unsteady breath trailed from his chest, and he grabbed his pants from the bedroom floor. He made his way downstairs in his boxer briefs, suddenly feeling out of place. *She said it was over.*

He snuck around to the kitchen, stopping at the sight of Clara working her magic. A giant T-shirt grazed the tops of her thighs and her hair was messy from sleep. The image of her swaying to the song was enough to soothe the nervous pang in his chest. He leaned against the doorway, watching as she poured batter into a hissing waffle iron. A drizzle dripped down the side and onto the counter.

Clara jumped. Her heart pounded, catching Connor as he watched her with a gorgeous pull of his lips. The sleep-rumpled version of him was a dangerous thing this time in the morning.

"*Shit*—are you trying to give me a heart attack?"

Pushing away from the threshold, Connor walked toward her, finding her shape in the giant bulk of faded cotton, soft from years of wear.

"I didn't realize that our date included breakfast." He leaned down and trailed soft kisses along her jaw.

"Mm. Are you saying you would have asked me out sooner?"

He pulled away and his warm gaze settled over every inch of her tangled hair and sex-sated smile. "It would have been the first thing I did."

Clara laughed as he leaned into her, nudging her back against the cold countertop. Her breath caught, and she looked down at the jeans in his hand. "I don't think this is an *underwear only* kind of establishment."

Connor buried his lips in the crook of her neck. "I'm sorry." His hands skated over her chest, trailing down to her stomach. "I assumed *come as you are* was acceptable."

Clara sucked in a breath and eyed the steam wafting from the waffle iron. She swatted his arm and wiggled out of reach, laughing. "I can't serve you a burnt breakfast."

Connor huffed and circled the edge of the island. His linen shirt and belt draped over the back of one of the bar stools and he glanced at her, a smile reaching his eyes.

Clara watched from the refrigerator. "The wrinkles are deep." She bumped the door closed with her hip, carrying a small plastic basket of blueberries to the counter. "If I was a better woman, I would have tossed it in the dryer."

He pulled on his jeans, and Clara snuck a peek, watching the flex of his arms. She bit into a blueberry and licked her bottom lip. "You know... all these years of domesticity."

"Don't do that." Connor's voice was soft, but firm. He leaned across the counter on his forearms, his pants still unbuttoned at his hips. The sight of his shirtless physique draped across her kitchen island made her go weak in the knees. He plucked a berry from the basket and looked up at her. "Don't belittle yourself."

Her heart climbed in her chest and she tore her gaze away from his, returning to the waffle iron. It was too much.

"Tell me, Mr. Kent. How do you like your eggs in the morning? Sunny side up? Poached?" After a long silence, Clara glanced in his direction and frowned. "Don't tell me you're a *fried hard* kind of guy."

"What's wrong with fried?"

She moved a carton of eggs to the stove. "Nothing is *wrong* with fried—it's just, is that the only way you eat your eggs?"

Connor chuckled, feeling personally victimized. "Eggs are just weird... they have a weird texture."

Clara shook her head and pinched the space between her eyes. "What am I going to do with you?"

He met her at the counter and moved his hands to her waist. "Hopefully, you're not going to hold a gun to my head and force me to eat a runny egg."

Clara snorted and ladled more batter onto the iron. "What would you do?" She pressed the hinge down, listening to the sizzle. Their eyes met over her shoulder and his mouth flatlined.

"I would choose death."

She tilted her head back against his chest, the sound of her laugh bubbling up and filling the kitchen. Connor snaked his hands around Clara, pulling her close. He could drown in that sound.

Looking at the wall behind them, he grinned, watching as the clock struck nine. Pressing his face to the shell of her ear, he bunched the fabric of her shirt in his hands. "Good morning."

She matched his tone, low and sultry and laced with knowing. "Good morning to you, too."

Connor sucked in a deep breath, grazing bare skin. "I missed you."

"I'm sorry. You just looked so peaceful."

The waffle iron and the coffee pot beeped simultaneously. Clara grabbed the carton of berries and plopped a handful over the batter before closing the hinge. "Shoot." Excess batter sludged over the edge, pooling onto the counter. Just as she reached for a paper towel, her phone chimed.

Connor stepped back with a regretful smile. "What can I do to help?"

She cut the burner off on the stove, removing the eggs from the heat. "We're nearly ready if you want to get the coffee."

Her phone chimed two more times, one after the other. "Could you grab that for me? It's right behind you."

Clara had her hands full, ladling the last waffle onto the iron. She pursed her lips, strategically placing the blueberries. "Ryan is probably champing at the bit." She cut an eye toward Connor, smiling brazenly. "He made me swear to check in."

Connor walked over to the fridge and pulled out the creamer, grabbing her phone. The device lit up and vibrated twice more in his hand. He glanced at the screen. Every single notification was from Mark.

He set her phone down beside her, dropping it like something singeing his skin. Turning on his heel, he walked over to the coffee pot. "Mugs are over here?"

There was a long pause. In the silence, he imagined Clara picking up her phone. He pictured her face when she saw Mark's name and his stomach twisted.

Clara had gone radio silent. Connor noted the rigid pull of her shoulders, and his emotions shifted so quickly he felt nauseous. His thoughts drifted to the vanity.

"How do you take your coffee?"

Clara spoke, the words hollow, her tone cold. "Cream and sugar."

He heard the frantic clicking of her keyboard. *Was she responding? Fuck.*

Connor carried their drinks to the table. Gone was the playful, light tone in Clara's demeanor. She brought two plates of waffles over to the breakfast nook, setting them down with a heavy hand. Clara kept her eyes down as she trudged around the kitchen, grabbing flatware and syrup. Connor slid into the seat across from her, with no choice but to observe. The shift was tangible. "Don't tell me..."

Clara turned to face him. Her eyebrows jumping to her hairline.

"Did you let him down slowly?" He unfolded his napkin, placing it in his lap.

Clara stood still. Her expression etched with painful confusion.

"You told Ryan I was bad in bed, didn't you?"

Connor watched a breath shoot between her lips as she pulled a quick smile. He swallowed the tension in his throat. "Do you need any help with that?" Connor pointed to the pan of eggs she was carrying to the table with a trivet.

"No-not at all. Go ahead and dig in. I hope you like blueberry waffles. I didn't even ask."

He concentrated on the syrup spilling onto his plate, purposely avoiding her eyes. "Everything okay?" He couldn't crowd her with his insecurities. *Trust her.*

"Yeah, I just got a little distracted. How are the waffles?"

He hummed his approval, his mouth full of fruit, carbs, and maple.

Clara fidgeted with her fork. "What have you got going on today?"

Connor carved out another section of waffle. "Nothing much. Kat wants help putting a dresser together. Apparently, Harrison tried, and she's pretty sure he didn't do it right."

Clara crinkled her brow. "What makes her so sure?"

"She sent me a picture of a baggie of nuts and bolts. She found it after Harrison left."

"I see, so she's going to rely on her big brother to come sort it all out?" Clara took her mug of coffee and sat back against her chair.

Connor scooped his fried egg out from the pan between them and sliced into it, seeing the firm yellow center. His eyes cut to Clara's and he smiled. "Thank you, chef."

Clara feigned annoyance. "One day you'll have eggs benedict... and it'll change your life." She narrowed her eyes and laughed, watching a shiver of disgust roll through him.

"What about you? What have you got on the agenda for the day?"

Clara ruffled her hair and looked out the banquet window next to the table. She motioned with her mug. "I should do some yard work... but I don't know if I'm up to it today." Connor followed her tired gaze. In the hazy morning light, he could see her sprawling jungle.

"Is this one of those, *those who can't do, teach,* sort of things?" Her absent gaze stayed on the yard, and Connor felt himself grasping at straws. Like he was calling out to her from miles and miles away.

"I only mean to say you're like an expert gardener... So things in your own garden are a little unruly?"

Clara looked at her place setting. She sliced into her over easy egg, spilling its golden yolk. Like the sun was bleeding out on her plate. "Something like that." Disappointment fell across her face.

Connor reached across the table and touched her hand. She finally looked at him and a small smile pulled at her lips. Connor swept his thumb along the ridge of her knuckles, trying to read her mind. "What's going on in that head of yours?"

Clara breathed, her smile slipping, and his phone rang noisily on the table between them.

"It's just Kat." He went to silence the call and Clara stood.

"You should get that. She might be waiting for you." Clara turned away from him and walked to the coffee pot. The moment slipped through his fingers. Uncertainty raged in his chest. The same uncertainty he thought he had finally shaken from all those years ago.

He took his phone and stepped out to the back porch.

"Hey Loser, when are you getting here?"

"Good morning to you, too."

"Seriously, unless you're trying to run errands with me later... or if you want to be left alone to play *Ultimate LEGO Master: Furniture Edition,* then you need to come over 'cause I've got stuff to do today."

"Well, damn. Glad I could be of service."

Kat laughed, but her statement stood.

"Yeah—no, it's fine. I'm just finishing up here and I'll head over in a bit. I need to swing by my apartment."

"Oh shit. You're not even home?"

There was a pause on the line.

"Are you at a girl's house?... Are you at Clara's?"

Clara slipped out the door, bringing him a fresh mug of coffee. She smiled sweetly at him and he rolled his eyes, pointing at the phone. Her smile warmed at the reference to his sister.

"Yeah, I am... Give me about forty-five minutes. I'll be there."

Connor went to hang up the phone amid Kat's excited chirping.

"What was that about?"

"Let's just say Ryan's not the only one excited about the date."

Clara's eyes widened and pink tinged her cheeks. After a moment she retreated again, leaning against the railing, looking out beyond the porch screens.

"Penny?" Connor made one last attempt. Raising his coffee to his lips, he winced as it scalded his tongue.

She turned to look at him. The sunlight caught her hair and Connor's heart climbed to his throat. He wanted nothing but to smooth the worried wrinkle between her brows. To go back to last night. To replay it—over and over—until they were both too tired and too spent to think of anything else.

"I'm just a little stressed."

Connor closed the space between them. He set their mugs down and wrapped his arms around her.

"Will you tell me what's going on?"

Clara bit her lip. She wanted to tell him everything. About the bills piling up. About falling behind. *About falling apart.* She rubbed her cheek against his shirtless skin. *No. She got herself here. She'd get herself out.*

"I've just got a lot to do."

Connor exhaled heavily. The emptiness of her words bobbed along the surface. She was so cool and calm... but he saw through it. She was barely treading water, kicking furiously underneath.

"You would tell me if something was wrong, right?"

She pulled back from his chest and searched his face. "Yes." He felt her arms tighten around him as she tucked back into his shoulder.

He rubbed his thick five o'clock shadow against the top of her head and breathed in the scent of her. Connor closed his eyes, feeling the morning sun warming his back with Clara pressed close to his chest. What they shared the night before had flooded every space in his heart and left him at a loss for words. He trusted her. She would tell him if something was wrong.

He leaned down and whispered into her hair. "Kat is going to murder me if I don't get over there."

She laughed into his chest. "You're a good brother."

"I'm the only one she's got."

———

Later, after a painful afternoon of disassembling and reassembling Kat's dresser, they strolled the aisles of the supermarket around the corner from her place on the other side of town.

"So... I need details."

Connor scrunched his face. "I'm not giving details."

"Ew. I don't mean *those* details. I mean, where did you go? What did you eat? You know—basic information."

Connor grabbed a box of granola bars and tossed them into his side of the cart. "We went to Three Rivers."

"Very nice. How was it?" Kat was reading the back of the box he had just thrown in. "Do you realize how much sugar is in this stuff?"

He ignored her. "The restaurant was nice. It's nice being back and having everything I missed in Chicago."

"I don't know how you survived being away for so long. I would die if I had to go one day without a good biscuit."

Connor chuckled. "Biscuits aren't exactly vegan. And I'm sure you'd survive just fine."

"Whatever." She rolled her eyes. "So other than the food, the date went well?" There was a pause. "Obviously, it went well enough... because you were at her house this morning."

He frowned and shot her a glance.

"Like I said... Not asking for details. I'm talking ambience and conversation."

Connor steered them toward the produce, a small smile pulling at his mouth. "The date was good. We talked about a lot of stuff. And she asked about you." He elbowed his sister as she bagged up zucchini and yellow squash.

"I'm sure you sang my praises."

"She told me a little about her family. Sounded pretty lonely."

"Well, that's a bummer. Not everyone gets raised by a bunch of hippies in *The Secret Garden*."

Connor s, recalling the way Clara lit up. "That's her favorite movie."

Kat grinned, tossing in a bag of oranges. "I knew I liked her."

"She was basically drooling over the idea of growing up at the nursery."

"Yeah—except every single pair of pants I owned had dirt stains. I got made fun of, like, every day."

Connor smiled. He and Kat looked unkempt in all their childhood pictures.

They pushed the cart toward the meats, and Kat turned away, looking elsewhere. "So, what's your next move?"

"Not sure." Connor thought of their breakfast that morning. Seeing Clara so worried bothered him more than it should. He picked up a pack of bacon and they cut through the frozen food on the way to the register. Kat walked quickly, escaping the cold. Connor halted the cart and reached into one of the doors, snagging a container of Rocky Road.

Kat eyed him. "You never buy ice cream."

He shrugged and set it down in the shopping cart. "Actually... I might ask her if she wants to go to Seattle with me in a couple weeks."

Her eyebrows lifted in intrigue.

He frowned. "Too soon?"

Kat shrugged. She reached into the cart and began piling groceries on the conveyor belt. "Not running off to elope, I hope."

"Hey, guys."

"Oh, hey, Jeff." Kat glanced over at the store owner's son, working the checkout line. He was Connor's age, and he'd had a thing for Kat since junior year of high school. Jeff was kind and accommodating, always willing to order in every ridiculous specialty food item she requested. And she couldn't be less interested.

Kat deposited a pile of canvas shopping bags at the end of the conveyor belt, and Jeff scanned her items, smiling brightly from across the register. "Did you see that we got that nut butter you had asked about? I don't remember the brand, but they had a bunch of different kinds..."

Kat pursed her lips, looking at Connor, beseeching. She hated forced pleasantries.

"Yeah, there are a lot of varieties," Jeff gleamed.

"Sunflower—"

Beep

"Almond—"

Beep

"Hazelnut—"

Beep

"You know, there was even one made with *Brazil nuts.*" Jeff lifted his hands excitedly, shaking his head to himself. "I've never even had a Brazil nut before."

Connor busied himself staring at the magazines, leaving Kat to suffer alone.

"I mean, who knew there were so many nuts in the world?"

Kat dragged in a tired breath. She pulled out her credit card, sliding it through the reader. "Not I, Jeff... *Not I.*"

Connor took over, stepping forward in line. He gave Jeff a quick smile. The guy had gone pink and was channeling all his energy into not staring at his sister. Connor shrugged, picking up where they'd left off.

He turned to Kat. "No... Not eloping. She's just been working all summer. And other than the night we went out, I don't really know what she does for fun." He thought of the stress that tinged her eyes. "Or what she does for herself." He gripped the handle of the cart. "I don't know—I thought maybe she'd enjoy getting out of town." Away from whatever was making her so upset. *Whoever* was making her upset.

Kat slid her credit card back into her purse. "I wish someone would whisk me away for a weekend adventure." She put her hand on her hip and pouted. Jeff looked up from the register, tearing a receipt and handing it over. He swallowed, peering over at her.

Kat cleared her throat, sliding her sunglasses up her nose. "Let me know if Clara turns you down. Me and Harrison would be up for a weekend of hiking with you." She grabbed her bags and walked toward the entrance, and Connor followed behind.

"You should put him out of his misery."

Kat chuckled. "No way. Who's going to order stuff in for me? Plus…" She popped the trunk of her car, shuffling junk around. "You heard the man… There are a lot of nut butters to try."

The following week, Clara floated along with her head in the clouds. Even Sharon's dictatorship couldn't shake her. She caught herself smiling like a fool, thinking back to Connor and the night they spent together. She blushed, remembering the way he touched her. *I've always wanted you for myself.*

From the corner of her eye, Ryan waved at her, annoyance emanating from his cube. She plummeted to earth and removed her headset.

Ryan shook his head, tsk-tsking her.

Clara shrugged and looked around. "What's up?"

"You got it bad."

Clara straightened in her chair. "I thought you wanted me to give him a second chance."

"I did—*I do*. Just... pace yourself."

Clara scoffed. "Didn't we joke that I needed to take a *lover*?"

"Oh... Mr. Kent does not, *a lover,* make."

"What's that supposed to mean?"

"A *lover* is casual. There is nothing casual about the way Connor looks at you. That day with your ankle? I thought he was going to build a makeshift Baby Bjorn so you wouldn't have to lift a finger."

She smiled. "Is that really so awful?"

"He's not *lover* material... he's got way more on his mind than just getting you in the bedroom—it's obvious."

Clara let Ryan's words roll off of her. She and Connor had only gone out on one date. It's not like they were getting married. Her stomach turned. She thought of that night in her bedroom when tears soaked her pillowcase. The promise she swore to herself.

She shook her head. Connor was amazing, and patient, *and* supportive. He would understand that she needed to sort out her life. What they had was... incredible. She smiled. "Well. He's already gotten me in the bedroom. And I must say his moves are very much *lover* material."

Ryan held his palm to her face and turned away. "Trust me. No one is happier that you're getting your *well-deserved* freak on... All I'm saying is you almost cut him off cold turkey for a minor offense."

"Okay, All-Knowing Guru." She pursed her lips. "How do you know we haven't worked through it all?"

"You have *I got lucky* written all over you."

Clara's jaw dropped.

"And I love you... but you are possibly the most confrontation-averse person I know." Ryan turned back toward his desk. "Which leads me to believe that you and Connor got *very busy* this weekend, but didn't review the fine print."

Clara was reeling. Was she that transparent? She took in the smug look on Ryan's face. He knew he was right. She tucked her hair behind her ears. "I do not have *I got lucky* written all over me."

Ryan scoffed. "Oh yes, you do." He was looking at her like she was a crazy person. "All you've done since you clocked in is smile, and basically spew rainbows out your ass." Ryan wafted his hand in her direction. "Sharon can probably smell it coming off you all the way from her office."

Clara turned crimson.

"Probably why she hasn't even come over here all morning. You *reek*."

Clara tugged at her shirt, lowering her voice. "I do not have rainbows spewing out of my ass... and I do not reek."

"Oh, yeah?" Ryan grabbed his headset, typing furiously at his keyboard. All business. "Now, tell me what's different..." He adjusted his mic, taking his sweet time while sporting a ridiculous, dreamy smile plastered across his face. Clara clamped her lips, fighting a grin. Ryan cheerfully waved like a pageant queen to the cubes around them and she covered her face, mortified.

He pulled her hands away. "Oh, no... I'm not done."

As a grand finale, Ryan rolled out his chair. With one strong push of his foot, he rotated effortlessly through the air.

"God. That is sickening."

"Well, that's what I've had to look at all morning. Be thankful I told you, or else Sharon would have probably come over and made up a reason to burst your sex bubble."

"Okay. I'll dial it back..."

"Like I said, no one is happier for you. You deserve a slice of some Grade-A, All-American Beefcake. Just..." Ryan looked over at her from the corner of his eye. "Be careful."

Clara sat back. The weight of doubt fell heavily on her shoulders. It hit her in waves and she sank. His words had nicked a hole in her sex bubble armor.

Ryan looked at her. "I just need you to be 100 percent certain that he's not carrying a chip on his shoulder. You were devastated after dinner with his family. Who's to say what he's capable of if you guys have an actual argument one day... Or what if Mark shows up at the house again?"

Clara paled.

"Has he?" Ryan touched her wrist. "Please tell me he hasn't."

"No... But he's been texting me."

"Wait. What do you mean, texting you?"

She fell silent and Ryan shook his head, worried.

Clara grabbed her phone. "I've been avoiding him. When I see his name pop up, I usually just ignore it." *Except Saturday.*

Ryan scrolled. "These are bad." She saw his eyes widen. "Oh my God—this one's from when we were at the house. He saw our cars."

She knew he was approaching the texts from Saturday and picked at her slacks, watching his every move. His jaw dropped. "*Oh shit.* This was after your date?"

Clara bit the inside of her lip. "It was the next morning."

"What did Connor say?"

Clara thought about that tiny moment when she almost spilled her guts. How she almost gave in and told him everything. She reached for her phone and clicked the lock button, turning the screen black.

Ryan's smugness was gone. All that was left was worry. "*This* is the fine print I'm talking about, Clara. Please tell me he knows about Mark... About what he did?"

She swallowed tightly, drawing in a breath.

"Connor knows about that night, right?" His eyebrows rose, insistent. "At the house?"

She frowned. "Mark is my baggage, not his." Connor wanted to call it... and she didn't let him. She couldn't fuck this up—*again*. "I've wasted so much time, Ryan. It wasn't all Mark. I was there, too." Clara sighed. "I could have left whenever I wanted. I can't change what happened, but I can cut him out of my life now." She motioned to her phone in her purse. "I just want him to leave me alone."

Ryan stared at her, shaking his head. "I still think we should make a plan." The sight of Sharon straightened them at their cubicles. His voice lowered. "At least tell me you're going to the festival on Saturday."

Clara fell into a daze, thinking about her emotionally charged to-do list. "Yeah. I'll be there."

"No. Tell me you *and* Connor are coming." She turned her head while entering her password.

"What?"

"I need proof that you and Connor can be upstanding citizens and that you're not just shacked up somewhere having copious amounts of weekend sex."

They both watched as Sharon made her way to the elevators. Clara let out an exasperated breath. "You said to rip off the Band-Aid."

"Oh, Clara." Ryan glanced around before rolling his chair over to hers. "I hope you didn't do anything just because of me."

She shook her head and sighed.

"Hey—*I'm sorry*. I wasn't trying to be a buzz kill." Ryan frowned. "I shouldn't have been so harsh. This was a big deal, and I totally ruined it."

"No." Clara drew in a breath. "You didn't ruin it. I know you're just looking out for me."

Ryan tilted his head, a smirk pulling across his lips. "*So...?*"

Clara held his gaze, and she smiled, visibly melting in her chair. "The date was amazing."

"I *knew* it." He rolled his eyes. "And... what about *after* the date?"

Her eyes went wide. "I had no idea..." She chewed the inside of her lip. "I mean, it wasn't always bad with Mark." Clara shook her head. "Just nothing like this... Not even close."

Ryan stretched out, his smirk turning into a grin. He nudged her shoe with his. "I *am* happy for you."

Clara nodded, lowering her gaze to her hands in her lap. "I really want this to work."

"For what it's worth... I think you should tell him about the night Mark came by." Ryan glanced at her phone, laying facedown. "And the texts." He raised his chin, holding her eye. "If Connor is one of the good ones, he won't let you do this alone."

Her throat worked, heavy with emotion, as she rolled back to her desk. Clara took a deep breath and clicked her headset, answering a call from a customer. What she didn't see was the worried way Ryan watched as she turned back to her work.

21

By Friday, Connor and Eli got an update on the tracking for the signage. After so many weeks of no correspondence, the delivery had moved to the back burner. Eli paced around the warehouse. Connor stood behind the register in Clara's usual spot, ringing up a customer.

"I don't understand what the problem is."

Eli sighed. "The problem is that we moved the display of pavers and we've been using the section along the building as a holding area because of the shade. It's too hot. If we move those plants, they're going to scorch. It wasn't meant to be permanent.

"There should still be plenty of space for them to drive through."

"You'd think so. But the company called and gave me the dimensions the truck requires for clearance."

Connor looked at the worry etching his uncle's face and contemplated. "What if I start moving the shrubs today?"

"That fixes that... but we still need to move the pallets of shale pavers." Eli put his hands on his hips, deep in thought. "There's no way you can do that by yourself."

"Well, what about Brandon? Can we ask him to work an extra shift?"

"We can, but Brandon is only working part time as it is. He's getting ready to leave for college, so I've got the delivery guy working inside until I can hire a couple new people."

They were short-staffed, and the clock was ticking. "What if I work late tonight? And what if Kat and Lo come? Harrison can probably help, too."

"I hate to do that to you kids on a Friday night."

"We've all been looking forward to this. And that's what family is for." He smiled at Eli, offering encouragement. He thought about all the time he had missed and felt it like a pang in his chest.

"While we're at it, how about we ask them to work inside tomorrow? It'll free up Sonny, and he knows how to handle the equipment. He can move the heavy stuff while the Three Stooges manage the customers."

Eli went over to the large window by the front door, seeing Clara talking with Kenny and Steve. "Maybe Lo can handle the customers. I wouldn't want Kat to scare anyone off with her sparkling personality." He faced the register. "Do you think Clara would be willing to stay and help? I hate for you to do all this by yourself, but it would make me feel better if it was all done." They both watched as she waved goodbye to the two men outside. "The sooner the better, so we'll be ready tomorrow when the truck gets here."

Clara stepped back into the air conditioning and lifted her hat, wiping the sweat from her forehead. Connor smiled. He knew she'd do anything for Eli.

Clara pulled into the gravel lot for a second time that day. She agreed to stay late under the condition that they got to eat real food for dinner. *No granola bars.* Parking between Eli and Connor, she leaned over to the passenger seat, grinning as she grabbed two takeout bags. All week at the office, she hadn't stopped thinking about their night together.

However, the second she got to Grady's, she kept tripping over a heavy dose of doubt. Ryan's words had wedged themselves into the corner of her brain. Their conversation was hard-wired to every dirty thought she had, lighting up with warning bells whenever she looked at Connor.

He greeted her at the front door, pushing open the heavy metal handle as the bell rang overhead.

"So, what did you decide?"

Clara bit her lip, stifling a smile. "Halley's". Connor lifted the bags from her hand, the paper sacks sporting a burger in the shape of a comet.

He smiled wide, pulling her in for a hug. Halley's was one of his favorites. The simple gesture caught her off guard, and she melted. This was something new, his sudden random displays of affection. She hadn't quite gotten used to Connor reaching for her, or touching her so openly. Clara smiled into his chest. After a summer of dancing around each other, she had grown used to observing him from a distance. Now everything seemed to be up close. She liked it. *She liked it a lot.*

Eli walked out of the back office and greeted them both with a smile.

She pointed at the bags in Connor's hand. "Do you want to stay and have a bite?"

"No, thank you. I've walked Connor through the plans, and I know you know where everything should go. We mapped out the width for the truck, so as long as we get everything moved from that far wall, we should be good to hit the ground running tomorrow."

Clara tore open a ketchup packet, squirting some under the bun of her burger. "And the guys can handle moving the rest of the pallets tomorrow?"

"They'll have to use the forklift. I hate to do that with the customers around, but it's going to have to happen during business hours." Eli sighed. "Hopefully, we'll be able to get it all done in time."

Connor picked up a curly fry. "We'll get it done."

"You're a saint for staying late." Eli patted Clara on the shoulder. "I didn't want Connor up here doing this by himself."

"Many hands make light work." She bit into her burger, and Connor grinned, leaning over to wipe a napkin across her cheek.

"Right. Speaking of which, Kat said they should be here in a bit. I'm going to take off and get home to Gloria, but I'll be in first thing in the morning. You two call me if you have any problems at all, okay?"

Connor laughed and shook his head. "Eli, it's manual labor—not rocket science."

"So... What's the plan of attack?" Connor pursed his lips, sliding on his work gloves. He and Clara had taken their time closing, avoiding the worst of the heat for as long as possible. The sun was starting to set.

"I think we should probably start with all the three-gallon pots. We can move them over to the open space between the greenhouses on the far end. They're smaller and need as much shade as possible." Clara put her hands on her hips. "We'll get everything organized eventually, but for whatever reason, if we're not able to get to them early next week, at least we know they won't burn to a crisp."

"Okay—so we start with the shrubs, then the bags of soil, and then the pavers."

"Right, which is going to suck because we can't get to them very easily and those are going to be way heavier."

Connor nodded absently. Clara had on a tank top with a summer's worth of crazy tan lines on display, and one of her many pairs of worn cargo shorts. His eyes trailed down, stopping at her work boots. "I think it'll be easy enough..." The corner of his mouth rose. "I've seen you tackle worse."

There was a glint in Connor's eye as he swiveled his hat backward. Leaning forward, he pinched the black plastic between his fingers, carrying several shrubs at once. He winked, walking past her.

Clara's stomach flip-flopped. "Are you referring to *that day*?"

"Oh, I'm definitely talking about *that day.*"

She followed close behind him. "What did you think when you saw me?"

They had made it into the spot between the greenhouses, and Connor lowered his pots. Clara motioned for him to keep moving back further into the space. "I think if we start back against the fence, we'll have more room to use."

"Good idea."

She set her plants down next to Connor's. "So, what did you think?"

"Was this *before* or *after* I realized it was you?"

Clara looked at him, raising an eyebrow. "Do I want to know?"

Connor contemplated, choosing his words. "Before I knew it was you... I noticed your legs." He trailed his finger down her thigh as he bent at the waist to grab another set of pots. "And I couldn't take my eyes off of your—" Clara looked at him and he smirked. "Incredible muscles?"

"You're impossible."

"I mean, you were going after that sack of dirt like it was *Friday Night Smackdown*."

Clara laughed, following him to the holding area they were creating. "And what about *after* you realized who I was?"

He sighed. "That's a tough one."

"Tough as in *bad*..." Clara stated more than asked.

"It was a mixed bag."

They set down their pots and were now walking back between the greenhouses in silence. Connor held his tongue, not wanting to say all the wrong things.

He bumped her arm, catching her attention. "It wasn't all bad. Just a surprise."

She cracked a smile, accepting his word.

"Anyway, I'm sure it wasn't all warm and fuzzy when you saw me."

"Oh. Definitely not." Clara turned to catch his reaction. Connor was stooped over, closing the gaps.

"*Ouch*."

"Well, I was worried about some sort of lawsuit."

He grinned. "You did take me down pretty hard. But if I had tied you up in a legal battle, I don't know that we would have... *you know.*" Connor raised his eyebrows at her.

Clara's lips tilted in a hollow smile. The unsigned divorce papers flashing through her mind.

Connor read her silence as fatigue. "Hey, why don't we take a break?"

She looked at him, skepticism tinging her expression. "We just got started."

Connor pulled her into the greenhouse with a lazy smile. Clara shook her head, a resigned laugh escaping her chest.

"The others are going to be here any minute."

"And when they do, we'll hear them coming."

"What if they're walking in right now?" She glanced back at the doorway, worrying the inside of her lip.

"Then I guess we shouldn't waste any time."

Clara's heart raced as he pulled off her gloves, tossing them on the worktable behind her. Taking her face in his hands, Connor smiled against her lips. "Like I said... I've been fantasizing about this all summer."

"What happens in this fantasy of yours?"

Connor pulled back, a dark look in his eyes. "My family wouldn't be showing up anytime soon."

"Mm. So you're saying we wouldn't be rushed."

"Right." His mouth was soft against hers, his hands skating down her arms.

Clara shivered. "What happens next?"

Connor shifted, turning, so that she stood in front of him, both of them facing the industrial fan built in at the end of the run. The very spot where Clara took her breaks when she needed a moment to herself. She had no idea how many afternoons she had lain on this worktable. Some days drained, some days emotionally spent... some days, all she thought of was him.

He tugged on her ponytail at the base of her neck and she smiled, her eyes falling closed. His callused hands slipped beneath the hem of her tank top, trailing along her hot, sweaty skin. His touch lingered as it skated over her bra.

"What else?"

"There are less clothes involved." Connor's voice was laced with longing, and she breathed in. Thoughts replayed in her mind of Saturday. Clara felt the heavy weight of him pressing against her shorts and everything tightened between her legs.

"Come away with me."

Her eyes shot open. "What?"

He nuzzled her shoulder before kissing her there. "Come with me to Seattle. I was hoping to go next weekend."

Clara's heart skipped a beat at the idea of being alone and away from it all. She smiled. "What would we do?"

"There are some trails I've been wanting to check out. Amazing restaurants." Connor exhaled, a lazy hum heavy with possibilities. "If you weren't so averse to granola bars, we wouldn't even need to get out of bed."

Spending all day surrounded by nature. Waking up in Connor's arms. The backs of her eyes prickled at the very thought, and her stomach twisted. "Connor—I can't."

He hugged her tighter, holding on like something slipping from his grasp. "Fine. No granola."

Her shoulders sagged. "It's not about the granola."

His throat constricted. He didn't need to see her face, he could hear the stress in her voice. "What if I take care of it?"

Pride pinched Clara's heart. "I can't do that."

"You've been going at it non-stop, and you signed up to stay late to help my crazy family. Let me take care of it."

Clara kept her eyes on the giant fan in front of them. The blades spun lazily around and around, never stopping. It's how she felt. Like no matter how much she paddled, she was still gasping for air. One charley horse away from drowning. The late notice on her electric bill was the first tug of her muscles seizing up, ready to pull her under. She shook her head against his shoulder.

He frowned. "If you say that you can't... I won't push you. It's just a chance to get out of town. To have a little fun."

A heavy breath trailed from her lungs. His words drew her to the edge, tempting her.

Connor held her, his desire still pressed against her. "Just think about it."

She turned, wrapping her arms around his neck, and she drew his mouth to hers. Connor shifted his hands to the backs of her legs and she inched up onto the table, his teeth gently nipping at her bottom lip.

She gasped, and he smiled. "It's like you just knew I needed to get away."

Connor shrugged, lifting her hands to his chest. Her fingers bunched against the cotton, sweaty and warm. "You said you were stressed."

Clara's gaze roamed his face before sinking into the deep blue. She hovered a second time. At the sight of Connor's mouth right in front of her, courage swelled in her chest. She saw the intensity in his expression... not commanding, *but concerned*. She drew in a breath. "What were you saying about less clothing?"

Their eyes locked, his gaze smoldering as he leaned in, capturing Clara's mouth. Her fingers drifted, and she leaned back on her palms, feeling the weighted drag of his lips on hers. Connor touched her jaw and pressed, dropping her chin. Clara sighed, her skin tightening at the feel of his tongue slick against hers.

Clara made an impatient sound and Connor smiled, his eyes holding hers as he pulled back. "You're so soft."

She smiled. "I'm sticky."

"No." He shook his head, looking at her in the dim greenhouse. All shadows and fading light. His attention dipped to her mouth, drifting to the column of her neck. "You're soft everywhere."

Grinning, she wrapped her legs around his. Clara's skin warmed where his eyes touched. She glanced down, watching as Connor's fingers skated along the hem of her shorts.

He smirked, drawing in a breath. "You don't believe me?"

Reaching up, his fingers slowly trailed the path of his eyes, meeting her shoulder. Connor touched the strap of her top, pinching the fabric before slipping his fingers underneath, touching her skin. "Take this off."

"Here?" Clara's eyes widened.

His fingers traveled along the neckline of her shirt, sending goosebumps across her chest. She looked up into his eyes and her heart pounded, an ache building between her legs. Clara peeled off her tank top and bra, and Connor helped her, sucking in a breath, seeing her sitting bare before him. He stepped back, his eyes lingering across her body, and she frowned.

"Where are you going?" Her eyes darted to the door.

Reaching over, Connor stole a Shasta daisy from a tray of new growth behind them. He came to her, holding it as it glowed against the darkness, slowly enveloping them. He resumed his spot between her legs, bringing his face to hers. Clara stared, hypnotized by the hunger in his eyes as he lifted the flower to her skin.

The petals touched just below her ear, slowly inching down her neck. Clara watched Connor's jaw clench, and something heavy and hot coiled inside her. The daisy skated along her collarbone, dropping lower. Connor's eyes caught hers. Clara's lips parted as he brushed the petals to the weighted swell of her flesh, circling, drifting, before touching her nipple. "Beautiful."

Connor's throat worked, watching as she tightened, puckering under his gaze. He lowered, bringing his mouth to her skin, lightly brushing against her. Clara felt the graze of his stubble and his breath, hot and quick. She gasped. Connor dropped the flower, stroking her breast with one hand, cupping the other as his tongue laved across the tip. Clara sank, laying back on the table, feeling him pressed between her legs.

Her breath was labored as electricity sparked and flickered, humming through them both. Connor drew a blushing peak between his lips as his fingers massaged, clutching and rolling her other breast. A frantic heat clawed through her body and she wrapped her legs around his waist, bringing him hard against her center. She sighed, rotating her hips, increasing the pressure beneath her shorts. A groan slipped from his throat, ending in an amused huff.

"What's so funny?"

"Nothing." Spreading his rough palms across her chest, he stared, mesmerized, her skin glistening from his mouth. Connor hooked his hands under her legs, drifting until he touched her boots. His dimples deepened. "The fantasy."

Clara looked up at him, her tangled hair splayed on the table. Her skin smooth and exposed to the night. Her lips curled into a smile. "How does it compare?"

"You have no idea." He drew in a ragged breath, grinding himself against her. "How bad I want you."

Her eyes widened, and Connor repeated the motion, his nostrils flaring. "Then what are you waiting for?" Clara reached for Connor's hand and he went to her, covering her body with his, dragging his mouth across her chest.

"ALL RIGHT, LOVEBIRDS!"

"*Shit.*" Clara broke away. Sitting up, she reached for her bra, motioning toward the entrance. A frustrated breath shot from Connor's chest as a flood light turned on in the distance, casting the greenhouse in a stark, unnatural beam. Clara inched out of Connor's embrace, seeing the disappointment in his eyes as the moment dissolved into nothing.

He forced a smile, helping her back into her tank top. Clara quickly straightened her shirt and dropped from the table, tugging at the hem of her shorts. Grabbing their gloves, she followed him out to the storage area.

Just as they reached the door, Connor slipped his hand to her neck, lifting her hair from the back of her shirt. "Time to greet the crew."

"What were you two doing?" Connor shook his head in disapproval. "Isn't it rude to talk to your elders that way?"

"It's only rude if I'm not right in assuming that you guys were getting it on."

Clara brought the gloves up to her face in embarrassment. Desperate to change the subject, she walked back over to the rest of the plants and the pallets of fifty-pound bags that still had yet to be moved.

Clara glanced over at Connor's sister, seeing Harrison walking out to meet them from the building. "We were just talking about the Summer Shade Festival."

Kat snorted. "Right. Are you guys going tomorrow or Sunday?"

"I was planning on tomorrow." She turned to Connor and added, "our attendance is mandatory."

He raised a brow.

"Ryan's orders." Clara lowered her voice. "He's not convinced we're capable of doing anything other than..." She nodded toward the greenhouse.

Connor pulled his work gloves from Clara's hands and slipped them on. He dropped a lingering kiss on her mouth. "Maybe he's right."

She used her gloves to slap Connor across the backside as he walked by, and he jumped. Clara laughed.

"So, are you going to go after the delivery?"

"If all goes smoothly tomorrow, yeah. We'll be pretty exhausted, but I promised Ryan we'd be there."

"Harrison and I will definitely be there. Lo is still figuring out if she'll get to see Ethan this weekend." They smiled at each other, grabbing several three-gallon pots. "We should all meet up and hang out."

They made their way over to the other plants she and Connor had already moved, and Kat shrugged. "It might not be *as cool* as The Brunch Brawl but, *you know*." Kat gave Clara a sly smile, her tone sarcastic.

"I haven't been in years." Clara caught the surprise in Kat's face. She looked down, lifting her shoulders. "We went the year I moved here... but Mark didn't really care about going after that."

Kat frowned, setting down her shrubs. "That's stupid."

Clara slowed her pace, swallowing thickly.

"Mark, I mean. He's stupid for not taking you... You know, if you wanted to go." Kat shook her head. "He's the one who grew up here." She reached over, hooking her arm through Clara's. "It's a Silas tradition."

Clara pursed her lips, thinking to herself. "He didn't really like breakfast."

"What a fucking monster." They had reached the pool of light shining from the main building and Kat's eyebrows knitted together. "How in the hell did you end up marrying him in the first place?"

Connor and Harrison passed them, both carrying bags of mulch. Clara sucked in a breath, watching Connor's sweaty arms as he adjusted his hold. He caught her gaze and grinned, flashing her with a wink.

"Honestly... I have no idea."

⎯⎯ ✦ ⎯⎯

Clara, Connor, Kat, and Harrison worked over the next few hours. Harrison and Connor fell into a comfortable routine tackling the heavier items while Kat and Clara moved the smaller stuff. Both she and Connor acted as team captains.

"So, I hear you and my brother are getting out of town."

Clara smiled, no longer surprised by Kat's bluntness. "It's not decided yet. He just told me about it today."

"I'm super jealous. It's going to be gorgeous out there."

"It sounds fun." She exhaled slowly. "I've never gone on a trip like that before." *And I can't now.*

Kat and Clara walked over to a display of patio furniture, sinking into two chairs. "Like hiking? Or on a vacation?"

The pitch in Kat's voice when she said *vacation* made Clara wince. She and Mark had vacationed routinely over the years, always with his family. Attendance was expected—no exceptions. Most times, he used it as an excuse to golf all day while Clara was left to sit and listen to petty gossip with Bonnie.

No sleeping in, no adventuring, and definitely no afternoon delights. They frequented a consistent rotation of beaches and country clubs. And locations with beaches *and* country clubs. She'd never been anywhere spur of the moment.

Kat forged on. "I joked that if you turned him down, I would take your spot. Although I have a feeling he'd be bummed if you said no."

Clara smiled. "He's pretty convincing..."

Kat shot her a look of mortification and gagged. "I'm sorry. Really, I'm more evolved than this." She shot her a look. "It's just because he's my brother."

"It's fine, I get it." Clara blushed in the dark and glanced out toward the parking lot. The glow of the inside of a car was visible from where they sat. "So, what's the deal with, Lo? Is she all right?"

Harrison and Connor walked over, joining them. Connor slumped into a chair, pulling off his gloves as Harrison flopped down on the ground, panting. All four of them were sweaty and covered in dirt. Harrison groaned dramatically. "I can't feel my arms."

Kat shook her head, ignoring him. She followed Clara's gaze. "Her and Ethan were arguing on the phone before we all got in the car to head over."

"Oh…" Clara frowned. "I thought they were doing all right."

"They are. But even the best can fall."

22

"I think I managed to scrub off all 500 layers of dirt."

Exhausted, Clara lowered the towel from her hair and sighed, sliding out the lone barstool in Connor's kitchen. He pulled open the freezer door, gripping his towel at his waist, and Clara grinned in observance.

He turned around with a serious look in his eyes. "I think you missed a spot."

She frowned, looking down at her arms and hands.

"You really should have let me in there with you." A smirk played at his lips as he slid a pint of Rocky Road across the stainless steel island. "I would have inspected every inch."

Clara clapped her hands together in delight, and Connor walked over, carrying two spoons. He loved putting that smile on her face. She was wearing one of his shirts and he softened at the sight of her, pink and warm from the shower. Relaxed and comfortable in his clothes. Connor dropped a kiss on her shoulder and his heart thudded in his chest. He handed her a spoon and waited as she tore the lid off the box. They stood in silence, scooping bites straight from the carton.

Clara sighed. "I hope the delivery goes well tomorrow."

"It will." Connor gave her a quick smile. "You were painstakingly thorough."

The pull of her lips mirrored his. "We make a pretty good team."

Connor nodded, his dimples deepening. He cleared his throat. "So, do you think you'll keep working at the flower place?"

Clara scrunched her nose, apparent discontent written across her face.

He chuckled. "I only mean—is there any chance for something long-term? Are you interested in any other positions with the company?"

"No, definitely not." This was a topic she had been avoiding since her first day in The Bug Zapper. "I only took the job when it was obvious that things were over between Mark and me." She leaned forward, resting her elbows on the shiny surface. Goosebumps shot across her skin.

Connor looked at her, taking in the furrow between her brows. "Well, if I know anything, I know careers change all the time. You might not know what you want to do right this second, but that doesn't mean you can't start focusing on the things that make you happy." His expression softened. "I didn't think I could make any money off of photography, and it's definitely not my main gig right now, *but* it's more substantial than I ever would have dreamed of back in college."

Clara nodded, absorbing the wisdom in his words.

"What sort of things make you happy?"

"Obviously, you know I like Eli and the nursery."

He smiled, watching as she went after a chunk of marshmallow. "*Obviously.*"

"And Gloria really seems to think that I'm good with the arrangements."

"Do you think you'd be open to doing florals in general? Sounds like you have at least a little experience at the job that shall not be named."

A laugh bubbled up, and she carved out another scoop. "Yeah... I do think I've picked up a few things. The biggest difference is the quality. We exclusively sell cut arrangements which are different from what Eli specializes in." Clara thought out loud, "but I guess those two worlds aren't so different." The wheels started turning in her mind and her gaze caught Connor's. "Honestly, a better way to tell someone you care would be with something that lasts a long time. Rather than something that just ends up in the trash."

Connor tapped her arm with his spoon. "You're brilliant, you know that?"

Clara beamed up at him. His gaze dropped to the chill on her skin and the quick pulse at her throat. The shirt he'd given her was damp where her hair laid in heavy waves and a bit of chocolate lingered at the corner of her mouth, teasing him.

He thought about the day it poured and how this woman was now sitting in his kitchen, wearing his shirt and nothing else, licking ice cream from her lips. Knowing that if he leaned in and pressed his mouth to hers, she'd welcome him. The reality of it was enough to send him to his knees.

She followed his gaze, looking down at his shirt. "Can we swing by my place in the morning?" She shifted in her seat. "I don't want to make the wrong impression showing up in your clothes."

Connor's brow furrowed. The idea warmed something inside of him, and he swallowed hard, studying her. The image of Clara walking into work, walking around town, in anything of his. Living her life in Silas Grove with his name emblazoned across her heart. "And what impression would that be?"

He watched as the amber in her eyes warmed. Teasing and soft. "That I spent the night here." Her tone was playful. "That we're sleeping together."

His throat tightened. Clara wasn't wrong... but it didn't feel right. He drew in a breath, letting the feeling go. "That would definitely be the wrong impression." Connor leaned over the island and brought his hand to her chin, sweeping his tongue along her bottom lip. Sticky sweet. His hand drifted, touching the wet collar of his shirt. "There's not much sleeping going on here."

⸎

"**O**h my God! Are you sure he's not going to hit the gate?" Gloria's eyes went wide.

Clara stood with Gloria and Adeline under the awning just outside of Grady's. Clara walked a few feet and craned her neck, watching the truck slow and inch forward. Connor, Harrison, and Eli surrounded the delivery vehicle, all waving and signaling to each other and then to the driver.

Adeline rolled her eyes at her sister and turned, patting Clara on the arm. "They got themselves in here, so surely they can get themselves out." She leaned in, lowering her voice. "I don't know about you, but I'm going back into the air conditioning." Connor's mom smiled at her just before stepping back into the main building.

The two sisters had arrived that morning with homemade muffins and coffee in tow for everyone. Clara shot Connor a look as they pulled into the parking lot, breathing a sigh of relief that she had gone home and changed after sleeping at his place. *Well... not sleeping.* She smiled.

The day had been filled with nervous anticipation, but it was finally done. Joe was parking the forklift out back and the truck driver sounded a departing honk, pulling out onto the street. The boys trudged around the corner, drenched in sweat, and Kat and Lo came out from manning the register. Exhaustion broke across Eli's face as Gloria and Adeline joined them, passing out cold water for everyone.

"Let's make a toast!"

"We need to take a picture!"

"I've got my camera in the office. Let me go grab it."

The whole group walked out to the sign at the entrance and stood together, admiring the new addition. Clara spotted Connor, walking toward her with his camera in his hands and a warm smile balanced on his lips. "Everyone stand together."

Kat frowned. "Connor! You have to be in the shot!"

Brandon stepped forward, offering a hand. Connor looked through the viewfinder and adjusted the focus. Clara watched as he instructed the high schooler where to stand and which button to press before he jogged over to join his family. Standing in the back, Connor pulled Clara close to his chest, hanging his arm around his uncle's shoulders.

"1-2-3-CHEESE!"

Tears glistened in Gloria's eyes as they all took turns hugging and celebrating, covered in sweat and dirt. "We really couldn't have done this without you, Connor."

He looked at the emotion on his aunt's face, and his heart clenched. He hadn't realized just how much he had missed being home until the day he returned to the nursery. That day at the beginning of summer.

He watched his mother smiling and laughing with Clara, and something settled inside. Like a piece of a puzzle hidden under the couch when you'd just about given up. Eli clapped him on the back, dragging him in for a hug.

"You really saved us! If you hadn't gotten a head start last night, we never would have been ready in time." Laughter and relief surrounded them, but his uncle's words were sobering. "I bet after everything we've put you through, you're probably wondering if you should have stayed away."

Connor swallowed the lump in his throat and looked around at his sister, his cousin, and the place they grew up.

"No—it feels like I've finally come home."

Clara felt something brush her palm, and she looked down, seeing Connor's hand reaching for hers. She glanced around the crowd at the Summer Shade Festival and smiled, slipping her fingers between his. Connor squeezed, and Clara inhaled, feeling his grip around her heart. They strolled at an easy pace. Ryan and Jonah lingered, idly bumping into each other and talking. He'd shown up for an impromptu visit and Ryan was more than thrilled to have a day date—even if he was still in denial.

"This is exactly what we need." Clara tugged, pulling Connor toward a dessert truck. The four of them stood together, combing over the menu. "We've definitely earned it."

Connor snaked his arm around Clara's shoulder, pulling her in close. The last forty-eight hours had been nothing but brutal perfection. All of their hard work had paid off. The whole summer of stressing and worrying was coming to an end, and it felt like everything was falling into place. Harrison snuck up to Connor's side and jabbed him in the ribs. Connor jumped, punching him in the arm.

"*Please* tell me you're getting this tiramisu-fritter-donut-monstrosity." Kat's lips parted, her eyes like saucers.

Clara laughed. "I was looking at that one! Although... I feel like maybe I should get some actual food."

Kat turned to her brother, her brow furrowed. "Did you guys start celebrating without us?"

"No... we've just gotten the party started a little." Connor winked at Clara, touching her where their hands hung at their sides. He strengthened his hold, stepping forward and ordering a round of drinks.

Connor brushed his jaw against the top of her hair and bumped his cup to hers. "Cheers." He whispered. "To us."

She beamed up at him as they hung back from all the chatter, drinking in the fading afternoon sun. Music played in the background between the throng of vendors and tents. The sweet smell of dessert carts and greasy, deep fried fair food skated through the air. A southern summer at its finest. Clara leaned into his chest and motioned her chin toward the chalkboard.

"What'll it be? Deep fried matcha cheesecake bites?" She grinned. "Or a blueberry lavender cronut?"

"Lo just texted me." Kat looked up from her phone. "She said she's over closer to the band. Sounds like Ethan just got here, too."

They walked the short but crowded distance over to where Lo stood. Clara noticed a very tall, very rugged guy with his arm looped around her waist. Clara leaned into Kat. "Is this the infamous boyfriend?"

"*Yes*... they're *not* on the rocks."

"Good to know." Clara stood to the side as Connor greeted Ethan with a handshake and a hug.

Ethan smiled. "It sounds like y'all had quite the morning."

"Yeah, but it all paid off."

"I wish I could have been there to help."

Clara caught the sudden downturn of Lo's lips as she faced the band. They all settled in with their drinks and everyone coupled off, sitting in the grass. After a few minutes, Kat announced she wanted to go check out some local art, and Harrison got up, following behind.

"So, how's college treating you?" Clara spoke over the music. "Not long now, right?"

"Yeah, I actually finish up in May." He tilted his head and glanced at Lo. "There's a program that I'm considering applying to that's more specialized." He squeezed her shoulder, touching her hair. "The only problem is, more school means more time away from this girl." Ethan kissed Lo on the cheek, and she smiled tightly.

Clara noticed the shift. "So, what's the plan when it's all said and done?"

"The dream is to help out at the farm."

Lo leaned over, perched between Ethan's knees. Their limbs entangled in a well-learned puzzle. Clara looked down at her own feet, her legs stretched out with her ankles crossed. She and Connor sat side by side. She scooted over, closing the space between them in the grass.

"He's being modest." Lo squeezed Ethan's arm. "He'll eventually take over the farm."

Clara raised her eyebrows. "That's pretty major."

Lo and Ethan glanced at one another. A stolen moment between them, saying nothing and everything with one look. "It's the dream."

Clara sucked in a breath. They were both so unencumbered. Like Kenny and Steve bickering outside the nursery. There was something disarming about seeing people so honest and happy. So clear in what they wanted.

Her gut twisted, and she averted her gaze, looking over at the band. "I think that's amazing." Her phone buzzed in her pocket.

RYAN: JEWELRY TENT. PURPLE SIGN BY THE GERMAN FOOD CART.

She looked up and scanned the sea of vendors surrounding them.

RYAN: ASAP

Clara chuckled, kissed Connor on the cheek, and stood. "I'll be right back. Ryan wants me to come look at something."

She finally spotted Ryan and Jonah hiding between two tents, surrounded by stacks of handmade soaps. The heat and the smell were nauseating.

She looked at them curiously. "Are you buying something?"

Ryan shushed her and motioned for Clara to come closer. All three of them hunched down and peeked out. Ryan pointed to a gap between the tents, two rows over.

"Why are we hiding?"

"Because."

Clara froze. "*Holy shit*, is that—" Sharon stood fifty feet away, dressed in hot pink daisy dukes and a hot pink top bedazzled within an inch of its life. Sans office-wear she looked like a peacock outside the zoo.

Jonah crouched alongside them, staring. "Oh, my God." He didn't know Sharon but remained fully invested in the super spy extravaganza. "She looks hideous."

Clara smiled.

The crowd broke, and a disheveled man clad in lederhosen approached. Ryan clutched Clara's arm in silent enthusiasm. She teetered, her balance unsteady.

Clara gasped. "*Noooo—*"

The man approached Sharon with the biggest bratwurst she had ever seen. Like *Lady And The Tramp*, they leaned forward, holding each end. Ryan covered his mouth. Clara covered her eyes.

"This is the most wonderfully disturbing thing I've ever laid eyes on," Jonah whispered.

Clara leaned forward, bracing herself on the plastic table laden with lavender sachets. The force rattled several displays and the kiosk owner frowned. "If you're not going to buy anything, I suggest you leave."

Ryan and Clara uttered a simultaneous, "*Ohmygoshwe'resosorry.*"

Jonah shot his hand out to Clara. Ryan absently inched toward a pile of tangled power cords on the pavement. Clara reached out to Ryan and his attention leapt to Sharon, putting his hand to his chest in disgust.

Clara and Jonah both jumped. All three of them latched onto each other like a runaway train. Sharon and Kraut Daddy were getting hot and heavy in the shade of the German Food Truck. A giant blob of mustard rested ceremoniously on her very visible boob job, a half-eaten bratwurst still balanced in her palm.

Ryan's foot caught, and the three of them scattered like dominoes. The tent shook, and the vendor shot up from her folding chair as they fell into a heap on the pavement. Jonah helped Ryan up, brushing at his arms and knees.

"That was the best thing I've seen all year."

"Better than when the fire alarm went off because someone microwaved the shit out of some *break and bakes* in the employee lounge?"

"Oh. This is so much better." Clara gasped for air, her belly shaking. "I won't be able to look her in the eyes for at least another three weeks. Every time I see her, all I'm going to think about is her Kraut Daddy."

Tears streamed from her eyes. Clara stayed on the ground, laying with her ass in the dirt for a second time that summer. Oh, how different the world looked this time around.

Connor spotted them in the ruckus and made his way over, hunching down beside her. She gazed up at him, his smile like a string of holiday lights in the dark. The moment slowed, and she sighed. *Christmas in July.* Connor brushed her hair away from her face, and she sat up, covered in dust and debris.

"We've got to stop meeting like this." The glimmer in his gaze hit her square in the chest.

Connor wiped off the backside of her shorts and pulled her into his arms. Ryan smiled at her over Connor's shoulder and she closed her eyes, melting in the middle of the crowd.

Squinting against the sun, something looming caught her attention. Her stomach twisted and her bones went cold. Sweating from everything but the heat, Clara shifted into Connor's chest—but it was too late. Mark had spotted them.

"Afternoon, y'all."

Before she could utter a warning, Connor turned. She watched as his smile dipped, settling into a hardened line.

"Hey, Mark."

Connor pulled Clara's hand so that she tucked in next to him. His arm lifted, draping around her shoulders. "How's the summer treating you?"

Ryan and Jonah stood firmly at her other side.

"Things have been good." Mark's gaze slid between Connor and Clara, his tone lingering. "Looks like summer's been pretty good to you, too."

Connor stiffened. His fingers slowly traced her arm, steadying himself. Clara felt his chest rise and fall in a heavy, stifled rhythm.

"I'm surprised to see you two together..." A low chuckle left Mark's chest. "But then again, nothing seems to surprise me these days."

Clara cleared her throat, staring at Mark's boots. She looked up and met his eyes. Even through the jet black of his sunglasses, she felt the smugness there. She could see it with her eyes closed. It was burned into her brain. "What do you want, Mark?"

"No reason to be unfriendly." He scoffed. "I came by the other day to see you and noticed you had company." Mark's eyes cut to Connor. "Figured I'd come back another time."

Clara glared at him. "Why would you need to see me?"

"Well... I wanted to come over, you know, to talk about a few things."

She frowned. "What could we possibly have to talk about?"

Mark shook his head, his eyes sliding across the group. "You know. *Private matters*."

Clara touched Connor's hand. She glanced up into his face and saw the muscle flex in his jaw. She laced her fingers with his, trying to hold strong—to hold onto him.

Ryan crossed his arms over his chest. "Were you coming by to get your stuff?"

Mark's mouth twisted. A smirk laden with anger overtook his expression and he shifted. "Damn Clara, you run your mouth to just anybody?"

Ryan stood his ground. The glare he cut would have obliterated anyone into a puddle of tears—*anyone except Mark*. Clara glanced at Ryan apologetically and winced. She looked beyond her friend, to the spot in the dirt where she had just sat, laughing until she cried.

Her gut wrenched, and she drew in a shaky breath. It had taken her so long to get there.

When she turned, Mark and Connor stood facing one another, the moment tense and uncomfortable. Everything suddenly unbearable. Connor's thumb methodically traced her palm like it was the only thing grounding him.

Under Connor's arm, Clara straightened. "Anything you want to say to me, you can say in front of them."

Mark's eyes caught hers before flitting over the boys, finally meeting Connor's. "You sure you wanna do that?"

Clara's anger climbed, scaling her ribs, and her nostrils flared. Just as she stepped forward, Mark raised his voice, "I spoke to my lawyer and wanted to let you know... looks like I'll be moving back in."

"*What?*" Clara choked. Her eyes burned. Hot and full of tears she had shed too many times to count. She bit the inside of her lip, tasting blood. "*When?*"

"Soon." His eyes locked on hers. "So if you don't want to, you know, *work things out...*" He looked at Connor. "You need to find yourself somewhere else to live."

Connor's brow furrowed. *Work things out.*

Heat climbed Clara's face and she turned, feeling the acid rise from her stomach. She inched past Ryan and Jonah, and they pivoted, following right behind her.

Connor's jaw clenched as he glared at Mark, his hand flexing by his side. The corner of Mark's mouth rose in a satisfied smile. At Clara's back, he spoke, holding Connor's eye. "Give me a call when you're ready to talk."

Clara slipped away. Her breath left her chest, and she gasped, sinking below the surface. Connor's hand found hers in the crowd and just as her grip loosened, Connor's tightened. He followed, never letting go. Tears spilled down her cheeks, and she trudged in a cloud of confusion, until she couldn't walk anymore. Until she finally lost sight of where she was going.

"Yeah, she's all right—" Connor glanced over the console at Clara, her eyes trained on the windshield. He reached over to touch her hand, lowering his voice. "Ryan's asking if you want them to bring food over later." Clara looked at him in a daze, and he motioned to the dash, to the phone call she hadn't even heard.

Connor pulled into her driveway. Realization flashed in Clara's eyes, and she gave him a weak smile, shaking her head. He nodded, speaking to Ryan. "Thanks for offering—" He put the car in park. "I think we're just going to hang here." He grabbed his cell from the cupholder, disconnecting from the speaker. Connor's gaze drifted to the yard. "Yeah, I'll make sure she charges her phone." He spotted the stone squirrel, still face-down in the dirt as he hung up.

They had driven back in a suffocating silence. The car was too small for all the confusion and frustration that sat between them. Connor cut the engine, his stomach twisting. *Give me a call when you're ready to talk.*

Clara sat staring out the window of the passenger seat, her posture etched with exhaustion. Her fingers slid back and forth over the hem of her shorts—a habit that meant she was nervous. He looked over her shoulder, curious as to what held her attention. The patch of yard beyond her window was overgrown and messy. He swallowed past the knot in his throat, looking back toward the house.

Connor placed his hand on Clara's knee, and she startled. Her eyes were rimmed with red and worry tinged her brow. His chest constricted. Angered by anything that could make her feel that way.

They sat, Connor parting his lips, thinking of a million different things to say, not speaking a word. Clearing his throat, he twisted in his seat and unbuckled her seatbelt. "Let's get you inside."

Much like the car ride, they remained silent, neither one daring to speak. Throughout the evening, Connor looked to Clara for a sign. Every time he searched for answers, her expression shifted to something else entirely.

As they crawled into bed that night, Clara inched toward him, wrapping herself around him at his back. She slipped herself between his skin and the sheet, wanting so badly to sink into him. She squeezed hard, closing her eyes.

"Baby..." Connor moved, and Clara tightened her hold, pressing her face between his shoulder blades. He frowned. "Will you tell me what's going on?"

"Please."

She rubbed her cheek against his spine, her breath hot on his skin. His throat bobbed, wanting to hold her.

Clara's voice lowered to a whisper. "Just let me stay like this."

She sniffled, and the knot in Connor's gut twisted. He covered her hand with his own, shifting so that it laid over his heart. "Promise you'll tell me in the morning?"

There was a long stretch of silence, heavy with hesitation. "I promise."

Connor settled, standing firm in Clara's request. This silence was different. This silence had a purpose. This silence was what she needed... and he would give it to her. He would give her anything.

Around five a.m. Connor lay with his eyes open, staring at the ceiling. The fan moved overhead. Their limbs were tangled. He thought back to the last time he had been here and how close they had become that night.

He thought about the last forty-eight hours and how much they had shared. How monumental and bright everything had felt. And how quickly it seemed to fade. His gaze slid to the doorway of the connecting bathroom.

A frustrated breath shot from his chest, and Clara stirred beside him. He looked at her and softened. Tangled tresses spilled over her pillowcase and he watched the gentle rise and fall of her body as she breathed, deep in a dream.

The skin around her eyes matched the tip of her nose. Pink and swollen from crying. The thought of Mark coiled something inside him so tight he felt a wave of nausea roll through his body. It was too hot in this bed, and there wasn't enough room for the both of them.

Clara shifted, finding a new cold spot on the mattress, and sighed. The fan was doing nothing but pushing warm air around. Even with the AC, her bedroom faced the east, which made for a beautiful morning that was an absolute bitch in the summer.

Clara winced against the sunlight. She never slept in. The angry hum of a lawn mower grumbled just outside, and she rolled her eyes, falling back against the linens. She twisted on her side and swiped the empty space where Connor should be. She thought of the festival and winced.

Clara pulled on a pair of worn cotton shorts and a T-shirt. Making her way downstairs, she walked to the kitchen and frowned—no Connor. Alarm rising, she moved to the front door, peeking through the glass inlay. His car sat parked outside. Her mouth turned down at the corner and she heard a noise. She trudged to the back of the house, opening the door to the porch.

The noise intensified, and her heart stopped. Connor stood shirtless, in tiny shorts, wielding an electric hedge trimmer at the edge of the yard. A smile cracked wide across her lips and Clara pressed her hand against the mesh screen.

She watched as he pruned the overgrowth off the anise and the tea olives. Clippings fell around him, raining at his feet as he worked. Clara's pulse raced and the smell of licorice reached her all the way at the porch. Connor searched for his phone in the wheelbarrow, turning up the volume as the next song rolled on. Clara covered her smile with her hand.

The spring of the screen door squealed, and Clara made her way across the lawn. She saw several flower beds had been weeded. Leaves and debris sat in neat piles, and the lawn was mowed. As she got closer, she felt the sting of tears at the backs of her eyes. Connor's sweaty, naked skin glistened, and she laughed as she took in the sight of him.

He turned at her stifled chuckle, and she grinned, motioning behind him. "Is that..." The wheelbarrow curled around her playlist, filling the yard.

Connor squinted against the sun and cut the music. "Rat Bastard?" Setting the electric hedge trimmer in the grass, he wiped his hands together. He turned toward her, dimples flashing. "Maybe."

Clara smiled, pointing to the material straining across his thighs. "What are you wearing?"

He sighed. "You really don't remember, do you?"

Clara stood in contemplation, racking her brain. Suddenly, the image of young Connor flashed in her mind. Layers and layers of body paint and a sparkly shimmery wig. "Oh my God... are *those*...?"

"My lucky shorts."

Her jaw dropped. "I can't believe you still have them."

"I can't believe you didn't remember them. I wore these shorts to every winning game... they are *very* lucky."

Clara reached forward, snapping the elastic waistband. "Well, I was wearing them the day I fell, so I think the luck may have run out."

Connor hushed his voice. "You can't say that around the shorts."

"Oh, so now you're superstitious?" The thought of Connor rummaging through all his old clothes and coming up with one of the few memorable relics of their past made her chest tighten. She pursed her lips. "Where did you find them?"

"I saw them in the laundry basket by your dresser." He looked down, a lopsided grin tilting his lips. "Thanks for washing them."

Clara nodded, holding her hand up to shade her eyes. "I can't believe you did all of this." She motioned to the yard.

"No big deal." They stood side by side, admiring his work when he pressed his hip to hers. "Couldn't really sleep... so I thought I'd make myself useful." The feel of his sweaty, warm skin as it gently pushed and tugged against her was intoxicating. His voice softened. "Think you're about ready for that talk?"

Clara's smile dipped, and she lowered her gaze to the grass in front of them. Little rows of clippings laid in perfect lines, like a Zen garden.

"Let me get you something cold to drink."

They walked across the yard and Clara stepped inside. "Water? Or sweet tea?"

His dimples deepened. "Sweet tea sounds good."

Clara retreated into the kitchen, coming back with two full glasses. She sat them down and condensation instantly began to bead.

"Do you mind?" He deposited himself on the stairs, looking out over the yard.

Clara shook her head, looking at the screened-in porch behind them. "If we get eaten alive, you're to blame."

He patted the tread next to him. She sat down, feeling the heat emanating from his skin. Surveying his handiwork once more, she felt the weight on her shoulders lighten. "You're too good to me."

Connor took a swallow of his drink and ran his tongue across his lip. The salty taste of sweat mixed with sugar, and he wiped his mouth with the back of his hand. "I'm not *that* good." He smirked and her heartbeat quickened.

Clara took a breath. "About yesterday..."

Connor leaned forward, resting his forearms on his knees.

"So, you know most of it." Her tone was matter-of-fact. "Mark and I split up months ago... I found out he was having an affair and he moved out." She glanced over at Connor as he sat with his eyes down, focused on a pile of weeds he had pulled at the bottom of the stairs. The truth sat lodged, burning in her throat, and she winced.

"Actually..." Clara shook her head. "I found out about the affair a year ago." She tilted her face, looking up at the trees in the distance. "I didn't say anything about it... *to anyone.*" She blew out a breath, feeling the weight of the truth replaced with shame. "He moved out six months ago."

Her eyes darted over, seeing Connor winding the stem of a weed around his finger, his skin white where the blood couldn't flow. "He comes by to pick up his things, here and there. He just shows up out of the blue."

Clara inhaled, staring at his hands. "He had been texting me and it got to the point where I stopped responding. I didn't really know what else to do, but I think it made things worse..." She wiped her palms on her shorts. "And then yesterday happened."

In the corner of Clara's eye, she saw the flex of Connor's fingers.

"There was this one night when he stopped by. I didn't think it was any different than normal... but he made me upset and I asked him to leave." She felt him shift beside her and she sat up straight. "For some reason, he got the idea that I was seeing somebody and he... kind of lost it."

The stem snapped around Connor's finger, and she felt his eyes slide over her. She kept her attention on her hands, rolling the hem of her shorts.

"It was before you and I started seeing each other. I didn't correct him." Clara's throat worked nervously. "I don't know... part of me liked it. Like, after all of these years, I finally had something that made him lose his nerve." When Clara glanced over at Connor's expression, she saw the tightness in his jaw and the rigid line of his shoulders. But his eyes stayed soft, edged with worry.

"Anyway, he sent me those flowers... the ones you saw. All of a sudden it went from him not giving a shit, to him texting non-stop."

She chewed the inside of her lip, drawing in a breath. "That's when he started driving by the house."

"The morning after you stayed over, he sent a ton of messages." Clara stilled, remembering how Connor had held her on the porch just behind them. "I think he saw your car in the driveway and... he got mad."

Connor's mouth pressed into a flat line, and the softness in his gaze hardened. Closing her eyes, Clara swallowed, envisioning the photograph at Eileen's office. She walked up to the edge of the precipice in her mind. Staring out at the ridgeline, she took a breath. *Waiting*.

"What did he say to you?"

Clara blinked, stepping back from the cliff. "What?"

"You said he came by the house and *lost it*. What did he do?"

Her thoughts jumped to that night. To the moment fear had shot up her spine, and she had scrambled to the ground. The firm grip he had on her arm. She reached up and touched the skin just below her lip.

"He told me he didn't want anyone at the house."

Connor's eyes narrowed, his breathing ragged. His attention traveled to the spot she was idly tracing. He thought of the way Clara jumped away from him at his apartment, and he bristled. "Did he hurt you?"

"No—" A breath shot between her lips. "No, he never laid a hand on me." Memories bounced around in her head like a pinball machine. "He just... wore me down. After so long, I didn't even have my own thoughts anymore. Everything was his." Clara stood, pushing her hair from her face. "And you wanna know the worst part of it all?" She paced angrily across the pavers, shaking her head. "I let him do it."

"So, what was that about yesterday?"

Clara halted. "Ever since he moved out, he stopped paying for things. Then he got the idea that I was seeing someone... and it got worse." She motioned to the house. "It was just small stuff, like my credit card. Then it was the water bill and the electric bill." Her gaze flitted over the house behind them. "Now I need to find somewhere else to live."

Connor's jaw clenched, his hand squeezing the back of his neck. "Have you talked to a lawyer?"

Clara glared at the house, betrayal in her eyes. "Who? Bo?" She pinched the space between her brows. "He's the one who handled our prenup."

"You didn't have your own attorney?"

"I had no idea what I was doing. Bonnie made it seem like it was no big deal." She shoved a hand through her hair, bristling against the pain of all her pent up secrets. "I used my savings to pay for the lawyer I have now." Clara clenched her jaw, her voice low. "I had to ask my mom to pay for the rest."

Connor swallowed thickly. Bo Branson was a close friend of the Monroes—and the only attorney in town. "Why didn't you tell me?"

She turned to face him. Her arms crossed at her chest. "Why didn't I tell you? Because it's fucking embarrassing. *I'm* fucking embarrassing. I don't have *one* job, I have *two jobs*. And between my *two jobs*, I can't afford to live. I am a college-educated woman who can't even afford to leave—"

Connor stood at the outpouring of her words, pulling her to him. She resisted, residual anger coursing through her limbs. He tightened his hold and hot tears slid from her lashes.

"I'm drowning. I've been drowning since the day he left and I just want to take a fucking breath." The unsigned divorce papers weighed heavily on her heart. Suffocating her. "I can feel him. He's right there, holding me down—like some sick game."

Connor rubbed his jaw against her temple. He exhaled, his chest heavy with all the things Clara carried alone. His warm breath ruffled her hair. "You don't have to do this on your own."

Clara scoffed. *If only you knew.*

He pulled back and looked into her eyes. He had so many questions. Tears streaked her face, and her breathing was uneven. She had had enough. He pulled her into his lap and they sat in silence. Connor's hand ran up and down her spine, a meager attempt at easing the pain. "I know money is tight, but if you *could* move... Where would you go?"

Tucked into the crook of his shoulder, Clara sniffled. "It's more than just moving. I've never even lived by myself. I mean... I've been alone, but it's different."

She righted herself, sitting up straight. The embarrassment was too much. "You wouldn't understand. It's like, while everyone was out building their lives, I chose *this*." The severity of her self-inflicted punishment broke his heart. He wanted more than anything to bear it for her. If only she would let him.

Connor shook his head. "Clara, do you think all of us are out here, just living our lives like we've got it all figured out? I have like *three* jobs. Look at half of the people we used to be friends with. All of them either hate their jobs or they're making up some dumb shit for themselves, acting like they've got it together. We're all just pretending in some way or another."

He studied the pensive look in Clara's eyes. The play of her fingers along the hem of her shorts. "There's gotta be somewhere that'll work. We just have to find it."

The corner of her mouth lifted, then dropped, clouded by doubt. "Where? The city?"

"You'd be closer to Ryan... but farther from Grady's." He drew in a breath.

Clara looked down at Connor's fingers on her skin. Seeing the scorch of pink across his arm from the sun. "I'd be closer to you." She covered his hand with hers.

"The thing is..." His touch slowed, settling at her waist. "I was thinking I'd move back to Silas. You know, after my lease is up."

Clara's stomach dropped. "Oh..."

Connor shifted her in his arms. "It'd be good to be closer to everyone. And I could help out at the nursery more." Squeezing Clara's hip, his voice warmed. "I'd also like to see you every day."

She stilled, her heart climbing in her chest.

Connor smiled against her hair, Eli's words coming to mind. How much he admired Clara. How she wasn't a wimp. He cleared his throat, brushing his fingers against her skin. "I wouldn't blame you if you left town. But if you wanted to stay... I'd be here. We'd all be here."

He watched Clara's throat work as she gazed up at the house behind them. "I want to." She looked into his eyes, unsure. Her shoulders sagged. "I don't know if I can."

His brow furrowed. She had no idea. "You are so much stronger than you give yourself credit for." He pressed his forehead to hers, lowering his voice. "You are so fucking brave."

His words floated over her, wrapping around her heart, warming her from within. Clara brought her hands to Connor's face and locked her mouth to his.

Connor hooked his arm under her legs and stood, never breaking their kiss. Retreating into the shade of the porch, he lowered himself to the wicker sofa, with Clara in his lap. She sat up on her knees and straddled him. Clara's messy hair framed her face, grazing his naked chest as she leaned over him. "Tell me again."

She took his hands and moved them to her shoulders, following the line of her collarbone. Clara inched slowly, guiding their fingers down her chest, over the fabric of her shirt. She wasn't wearing anything underneath. His touch burned along her body, leaving a trail of goosebumps in their wake. She felt the thick pulse of Connor between her legs through her faded cotton shorts. Her eyes held his, and he smiled, drawing a heavy breath.

"You are so fucking brave."

Her chest flooded. Pressing his hands to her hips, she leaned forward, rocking against the strain between her thighs. Under her guidance, his palms moved, sliding over the swell of her backside. The weight of her breasts pressed to his chest, and his breath left his body, his fingertips biting where cotton met skin. Everything inside her coiled. He was so dangerously close to where she wanted to be touched.

"Clara."

His breath climbed, and his grip became firm. She sighed, feeling powerful. She wanted this more than she had wanted anything for as long as she could remember. She rolled her hips, and the fabric between them pressed against her center. The strength in his hands put the perfect amount of pressure on the perfect spot and she groaned into his neck. He locked her tight against him, the sensation between them pulsing with every ragged breath she took.

Connor lifted one hand back up to her neck, and with the softest touch, he kissed her temple. He challenged her, striking a match behind her eyes as he looked up at her in awe.

He adjusted, and she ground herself against his length, desperately seeking him below the thin, sweaty layers between them. An impatient noise escaped her as Connor licked the salty skin at the base of Clara's throat. His hand scorched through her T-shirt, finding her breast and teasing, brushing the cotton against her nipple. Clara gasped and sat back, never breaking eye contact. Her breathing strained as she stood.

Catching the waistband of Connor's shorts, Clara peeled them away from his legs, undressing him. Fully clothed, he was the epitome of wholesome. Stripped down, Connor's body was borderline pornographic. She shoved her shorts down around her ankles. Standing in her T-shirt and nothing else, Clara retrieved an empty glass from the stairs.

A seductive smile reached her eyes as she returned to the sofa. Tilting her chin, she drew an ice cube between her lips. Connor gazed up, skimming his hands along bare skin, meeting the hem of her shirt. He stared at the glimmer of water on Clara's mouth and a moment floated between them, surrounding them, transporting them. His eyes darkened as he clutched the faded cotton and twisted, dragging Clara down over him.

The heat of Connor's skin was intoxicating, radiating like the scorching summer sun. His mouth skated across her breasts, pulling them into tight, aching peaks through her shirt. Their lips met, and he wrapped his arms around her.

The contrast of fire and ice was tantalizing. He ran his tongue along her bottom lip before nipping it between his teeth. Clara strained, her thighs clenching his waist, and he groaned against her mouth. The drag of his kiss, hot and frantic against the melting chill of her tongue sent her into a frenzy. She couldn't get enough.

Clara reached back, pulling a condom from her shorts on the porch. The curious smirk on his lips made her blush. "*What?*... I came looking for you this morning." A laugh escaped him and he drew her close, running his lips along her jaw. Connor trailed his fingertips down her spine, and Clara shivered. He breathed into her hair in a low vibration, sending a chill across her skin.

"Put it on me."

She ripped open the foil packet, taking in the mundane spectacle of Connor Kent sitting bare ass naked on her porch. His gaze slid from her eyes and he touched her mouth, pressing his thumb along the plush cold of her lips. She stilled as he reached down, dipping his hand into the glass at their feet. He stole an ice cube, and she gasped, feeling the biting cold against her ankle. He trailed it lazily along her body, meandering as he rose. It melted completely, dripping against the sensitive skin of her thigh and she froze, unable to breathe.

Clara brushed her face against his stubble. She edged his hand between them, watching Connor's eyes as his fingers slid along her slicked flesh. His gaze went half-mast and her breath hitched from the chill of his hand.

"*Fuck.*"

Emboldened, Clara thought of the greenhouse. "Remember what I like?"

Connor's smile shot straight to her heart and his hands clutched her waist, dipping down to her ass. He rolled her forward in his lap, dragging her against him. She sighed, feeling the rush between her legs. She sat up and positioned him, their gazes never breaking. Clara pressed his rigid length against the dripping seam of her center. He clutched her shirt, barely breathing as she took him, inch by inch.

Her eyes closed and her jaw went slack. Connor's grip loosened and his hand floated beneath the cotton, laying his palm along her chest, stroking across her breasts. He cupped her, running his thumb over a blushing tip. A whimper slipped from Clara's throat and when she opened her eyes, Connor was right there with her. Watching with a wicked pull of his lips, pain and ecstasy etched into his face.

Clara winced, meeting the slightest resistance, and Connor tensed, his eyes searching hers. She raised herself, clenching around him. His head fell back against the cushions and he closed his eyes. Through a barred breath, he uttered, "Let's slow down..."

His words only made her bolder. Clara lowered herself more forcefully, and the air left Connor's lungs. She settled, taking the full length of him, reveling in the sublime stretch that bordered on pain. Leaning forward to kiss him softly on the lips, she lifted, teasing him. "Is this slow enough for you?"

Connor shifted, wrapping her legs around his waist so she'd take him further. "You don't know what you do to me—"

Connor withdrew, only to bury himself deep. A moan slid from Clara's throat and she watched the mesmerizing flex of his chest and arms as he gripped her. Connor started a slow rhythm, rolling her sensitive crest against him every time their bodies met.

Clara's eyes locked onto his. "Show me."

The swell of pressure was numbing. She fell into a trance where all that existed was pleasure and Connor. The universe dissolved into nothing. When she opened her eyes, she saw the beautiful way he was watching her. His body beaded with sweat and her muscles clenched at the sight of his restraint. He groaned, a strangled sound escaping his chest as he continued to urge into her with painful concentration. She needed more.

"*Connor...*" She touched his jaw, threading her fingers through his damp hair.

Clara pressed him back, picking up the pace. The sound of their skin, slick with sweat, only amplified their mounting race toward the edge. Connor's reserve disintegrated with every thrust, and she reveled in his loss of control.

He rasped between gritted teeth, "*—not going to last.*"

"Then don't," Clara challenged, her gaze clouded with pleasure.

Her words broke something inside him and he drove harder. Clara moaned, her head falling back as Connor stroked a place deep inside of her. Her hands reached for the back of the sofa and she clutched onto it, steadying herself as he slammed into her. "Oh my God—don't stop."

Connor reached for her, cupping her through her shirt. The fullness of her breasts filled his hands, and he pinched, the abrasive cotton pushing her straight to the edge. Clara cried out, shaking as she clenched around him. Electricity danced up her spine and she arched, sparklers glittering behind her eyelids. With a final thrust, Connor pulled her to him, burying his face in her neck as a string of expletives rushed between his lips. Clara's fingers loosened on the wicker as Connor shuddered inside her, his breath falling against her throat in hot, heavy bursts. Clara stared at the deep red lines embedded in her palms and sank, melting into Connor's arms.

On Monday, Connor and Eli walked into the main office. Sonny rang up a customer at the register. "So, you swear it's okay if me and Clara take off?"

Eli smiled warmly. "I think we'll survive without you for a few days."

"I know... she's just worried about leaving you in a bind."

"She doesn't need to worry about us. Honestly, Connor, I think she craves feeling... *necessary*." The words fell heavily between them. "I think it's been a long time since she's had a strong sense of purpose. It makes us happy for her to feel needed." Eli patted him on the shoulder. "And with that, I'm going to run out and pick up lunch. Mike's probably got it ready by now."

As Eli walked through the door, Connor turned to unpack the new order of glass bird feeders.

He checked his watch. "Hey, it's pretty slow right now. Why don't you go ahead and take your lunch? We'll switch out when Eli gets back."

Sonny pointed to the door. "I'll be out back if you need anything."

Connor stepped into the storeroom and pulled out his phone, a smile stretching across his lips.

CLARA: A little something new for the playlist...

He stopped in his tracks, thinking about their tangled, sweaty bodies, and the look in her eyes as she straddled him. The sound of his name on her lips as she melted in his arms. Clara deserved to feel needed. *She deserved everything.*

Connor tapped the first song and turned the volume up. He had barely begun with the box cutter before he heard the front door chime. Stepping out of the mess of packing supplies, he walked back into the hallway.

"How can I help you—"

Mark stood with his hip pressed against the checkout counter, leaning with his ankles crossed. He took his sunglasses off and tucked them into the collar of his shirt as his eyes snagged Connor's.

"You know, it's funny. I knew Clara was working here now..." Mark picked up a small glass self-watering bulb and twisted it in his hand as he spoke. "I was in town and imagine my surprise when I drove by and happened to see the same car that's been parked at my house—parked right outside."

Connor crossed his arms over his chest, squaring his shoulders. "Is there a particular reason you stopped by?"

"I heard you were back in Silas. Didn't think much of it until our run-in the other day." Mark shook his head, a smile tugging at the corner of his mouth.

Connor made his way toward the register, taking time to straighten the shelves along the way. He steadied himself.

"Just thought you'd like a little heads up before getting yourself too involved, is all." Mark shrugged, his attention drifting around the building. "I don't know what Clara told you… but we're working things out."

The hair on the back of Connor's neck rose. An uneasy silence washed over him, not trusting himself to speak.

"She's still a little hot about what happened, but she'll get over it." He spun the bulb in his hand and smirked. "She always does."

Connor's gut twisted. Less than twenty-four hours ago, tears were running down Clara's face. He thought of the trust between them. How it was so new. And how it could shatter like the glass in Mark's hand. Connor placed his palms flat on the counter and leaned forward into the pain. His eyes hardened.

"That's funny… she hasn't mentioned anything about that." He grimaced with an air of indifference. "She said something about you needing to get your shit out of the house, though."

Mark's nostrils flared. Connor picked at a speck of potting soil, swiping his hand across the counter. "I didn't want to bring it up, but every time I'm over, I think it's a little strange." Connor watched as anger radiated off the body standing across from him. He glanced out the window, seeing Sonny walking back toward the building from his lunch break.

Mark scoffed. "Now, why would I need to move my stuff out of my own house?" He registered the shift in Connor's body language, and he pressed. "I let Clara have her space, but we're not getting a divorce."

Connor's fists clenched at his sides behind the counter. With a smug glint in his eyes, Mark's mouth twisted, a glimpse of straight white teeth flashing.

"You know she begged me not to go?" He leaned across the counter, into Connor's face. "Did she tell you that part?"

The door chimed. Eli stood holding a to-go bag in his hands, his mouth pressed into a flat line. "Mark. What brings you in today?"

Connor's stomach was in his throat. His scalp tightened and his hands were hot at his sides. His heart pounded.

Mark slapped Connor hard on the shoulder with hollow enthusiasm. "Just thought I'd stop in to see an old friend." Their eyes met, and he lowered his voice. "She's never gonna leave."

Connor felt dizzy, watching as Mark made his way through the building, nodding to Eli as he walked past. He slid his sunglasses back up the bridge of his nose; the bell ringing overhead as he opened the door. "Tell my *wife* I stopped by, will you?"

—⁕—

Clara heard her phone buzzing below her desk and glanced around, seeing Sharon at the far end of the floor. Several more chimes dinged, and Clara reached for it, disconnecting her headset. She smiled when she saw Connor's name, then quickly frowned.

1 Missed Call
CONNOR: I need to talk to you.
Her heart dropped. Three dots raced across the screen.
CONNOR: Mark came by.

Clara stood in the parking lot, leaning against her car in the shade. The metal singed her skin through her slacks and she started to sweat. Connor pulled into the lot and parked. Their eyes connected through the windshield and her chest tightened. Walking to the passenger side, she gazed at Connor through the glass. He looked away and unlocked the door.

The AC would have normally been a welcomed luxury, but the cold she felt was from Connor. Clara slid into the seat and dread filled her stomach at the look on his face. She shut the car door, sealing them in a deafening silence.

"Mark stopped by the nursery."

Clara frowned. "What did he want?"

"He said you two are getting back together."

She scoffed.

Connor's eyes dipped to his hands on the steering wheel in front of him. "That you're working things out."

Clara was silent. Connor felt nauseous.

"It's true then..." his jaw clenched. "You're still together."

Anger pooled in her gut. "No. Connor, I gave him the papers months ago—"

"*Why* would he say that?"

"I don't know—he won't sign!"

Connor turned in his seat. His breath left his body in short, angry bursts. Clara's heart felt like it was going to split in two. Everything was crumbling.

"You said that he's been texting you." He scraped his hand over his face. "And he comes by the house."

"I told you everything." Clara shook her head, confused. "He comes by to pick up his stuff."

"Why couldn't you have just left?" Connor's stomach turned sour, and he dragged in a breath, looking out the windshield. A moment stretched between them and he scowled. "Did you beg him to stay?"

Hurt flashed in Clara's eyes, and her chest swelled with betrayal. "No." Her brow knitted at the bite in Connor's voice. "He fucking left. He left me to deal with all of this shit." Her throat was hot and tight. The letter that she carried for months was still mocking her.

Fucking disgusting.

Tears welled in her eyes and she swiped them away, furious. Furious with Mark. Furious with herself for all her mistakes. Mistakes she was still making.

"We should have fucking called it."

"We're *not* together." Clara heard the frailty in her own words.

"But you're still married to him." Connor raked his hand through his hair, a breath of incredulity passing through his lips. "And you're never going to leave."

His words stung, burrowing hard and deep below her skin and she shook her head, fighting. "Connor, please listen—"

"Listen to you? Now? I've been hanging on your every word all summer... begging for you to let me in."

Clara broke eye contact, unable to look at him. She reached for the door handle.

"I should have known this would happen."

Clara froze. Frustration coursed through her and she turned in her seat. "Do you know what he said to me?"

Connor sat silent.

"Do you?" Anger surged, and she looked him straight in the eyes. "That night at the lake. I told him what you told me and... he *laughed* at me." Her gaze narrowed, disgusted. "And when the laughing stopped, he got angry. He twisted everything." Her nostrils flared and hot tears streamed down her cheeks. "He accused me of cheating on him... *with you.*"

An icy fist reached into Connor's chest. He looked at Clara. At her wet lashes and the hopelessness in her eyes. He flexed his hands, fighting his need to reach for her.

"We had just kissed…" She blew out a breath, staring at the dash. "And I panicked."

Her words knocked the air from his lungs. Memories flooded the car, and he sat, gasping in the midst of all the things he hadn't' known.

"I should never have done that to you." Connor shook his head. Furious with himself.

A sob left Clara's throat. The color was slowly fading. "Please…" She didn't know what she was asking for.

"I don't think I can do this." Connor swallowed thickly. "Not again."

After a long, painful silence, Clara wiped her face with her hands. She drew in a breath laden with shame and regret, and straightened her shoulders. "And you shouldn't have to."

She glanced over at Connor one last time before stepping out into the heat. It enveloped her, sliding around her chilled, broken heart. Fresh tears dripped down her face as she walked across the parking lot, back toward her life in black and white.

26

"So, tell me how you've been."

Clara wiped at the snot under her nose. She shifted uneasily, glancing at Eileen. "As of yesterday... shitty."

Eileen scribbled on her notepad. "Could you tell me why you feel that way?"

Clara snorted, picking at the hem of her shorts. "Oh, let's see. I thought I was finally setting boundaries with Mark. *That backfired.* I thought I was finally starting to move on. I even started seeing someone new..." Clara smiled at her sarcastically. "And now I'm not." She held up her hands. Like some pathetic version of a magic trick.

"Okay... Let's start at the beginning. Could you explain what you mean when you say things *backfired*?"

Clara took a breath. "You know how Bonnie has been calling." Eileen nodded. "Well, Mark's texts became more frequent, and more..." Clara's eyes connected with Eileen's. "*Inappropriate.* So I decided I wasn't going to respond anymore." Eileen scribbled. "Anyway, Connor, the guy I started dating... he and Mark and I all knew each other from a long time ago. Mark realized we were seeing each other, and he basically involved himself." Clara's jaw clenched. "Now everything is a mess."

"And, *a mess,* meaning?"

Clara breathed deep, her nails digging into her palms. "Mark told him we weren't getting a divorce... he made Connor think that we're still together."

Eileen's brow arched. "How does that make you feel?"

"Angry... I feel like a fool." Clara shook her head and swallowed. "I didn't tell Connor about the divorce papers and I didn't tell him that Mark won't sign." She cleared her throat, looking down at the carpet below their feet. "He doesn't think I'll actually leave."

"What is your reaction to that?" Eileen's gaze held hers.

Bits and pieces of summer filled her thoughts. All the times she told Mark to sign. All the moments she could have told Connor everything. *Should have told him.* Her heart twisted.

Clara stared at Eileen's pen, rolling between her fingers. "I feel stuck."

"Hm. Do you truly believe that? That you're stuck?"

Clara glanced down at her hands. "For a long time I did." She thought of Connor. "I guess deep down, I don't believe it anymore... Just, right now, I feel alone."

"Let's go back. When you think about the time when you stopped feeling stuck... can you think of anything that was going on? Did anything happen?"

The corner of her mouth lifted. Clara thought about the long days at the nursery. Working nonstop. *Connor.* Her smile dipped. "I was around new people. And I was doing things differently."

"So, you had a change in routine. And a possible change in your support system."

"Yeah. In a way... yes."

"What sort of things were different about this support? What seemed to make a difference in you *not* feeling stuck?"

Clara inhaled, studying Eileen's shiny red hair. She thought of the deep red grooves that marred her palms and Connor beneath her. *Inside of her.* The words he repeated that she still carried.

"I felt empowered. Like someone... *believed in me.* You know, rather than just trying to control me."

Eileen nodded.

"It was like even though Mark was trying to keep me down, I was finally able to figure out how to do things on my own... like everyone around me wanted me to make it without him." She sniffled, thinking about Eli and Gloria. About Kat and Lo.

"And when you say you feel alone, what do you mean by that?"

"I'm not really with that guy anymore. And those people." Clara frowned. "They're *his family.* So I don't know that I'll be seeing them much anymore."

"I see. If I may, you said that you were able to figure out how to make it on your own—which is what you've been working toward, right?"

Clara's emotions felt too close to the surface. Like an ant under a magnifying glass.

"Is that fair to say?"

Clara's eyes met Eileen's. She nodded.

"And you mentioned that you don't believe you are stuck now. Is that correct?"

Clara nodded again.

"What sort of actions did you take to figure out how to do things on your own? When you felt like Mark was trying to control you?"

"Well, it started when he stopped paying the bills." Clara watched Eileen write something down. "It was small stuff at first, the water bill, then the electric bill—which was significantly higher because it's hot as hell. But I started working a ton and somehow I was able to pull it off." She sat up a little straighter, her voice lowering. "The other day, Mark said he was going to move back in." Clara bit the inside of her lip. "He said I would have to move out unless we made up."

Eileen's eyes lifted from her notepad.

"And do you want to make up?"

Clara returned her gaze. Her brow furrowed deeply. "I'd rather die."

"And why is that?"

"Because he's a terrible person... or at least a terrible person for me. I know now that I don't *have* to make up with him. The idea of living without Mark used to scare me. But now I think that, yes, it'll be shitty for a while... but I'll be *free.*"

⸎

E ileen walked Clara out to the lobby at the end of their session. Clara took one look at the art and pivoted. Her eyes settled on the photograph hanging on the far wall of the waiting area. "Eileen, where did you say you got that again?"

"Let me get the business card. I think I've got it in my desk."

Clara waited, standing in front of the ridgeline. She could feel the cool fog dissipating. Rocks crunched underfoot as she stepped onto the path in front of her. She could almost feel the sun on her face.

"Found it." Eileen had appeared at her side with her hand outstretched. Clara took the card and glanced down.

Connor Kent

"You can't be serious."

A frown creased Eileen's forehead. "Is everything all right?"

"Yeah. Everything is just fucking perfect."

Clara sat in her car, flipping the business card over in her hands. She tilted her head back on the headrest. She *would* survive this. Everything might be going to hell in a handbasket, but at least she was tough enough to make it on her own. She called into work and took a sick day. She texted Ryan and told him she wouldn't be in. She bit the inside of her lip.

CLARA: Are you up for a packing party?
RYAN: When do we start?!
CLARA: Immediately.

⸙

Clara checked her face one last time in the rearview mirror before stepping out into the parking lot. She walked briskly to the front door, keeping her eyes averted. The door chimed overhead as she stepped into the air conditioning and she was met with a very surprised pair of eyes.

"What are you doing here?"

Equally surprised at Eli's words, she tilted her head in confusion. "Working?"

"I thought you and Connor were going out of town?"

Clara glanced around the building and tucked her hair behind her ear, nervously. She thought there was a chance she'd run into him today. "No, we... we aren't going anymore."

"I don't understand. Connor left. He told me about your trip last week and he's gone. I just assumed you were with him."

Clara's stomach dropped at the idea of him leaving without her. Her mouth twisted.

"What happened? Was this because Mark was here?"

Clara's eyes widened. "You were here?"

"No, I wasn't here. I ran out to grab lunch. When I came back, he and Connor were just over there." He pointed to the register. Clara's eyes followed his hand and her heart sank.

"Did Connor say anything to you about what happened?"

Eli shook his head slowly. "No. Right after Mark pulled out of the parking lot, Connor left, saying he'd be back."

Clara fell silent, and Eli frowned, studying her. "He didn't say anything. We had a lot of work to do before y'all were scheduled to leave... you know, before the trip." There was a sadness in his eyes. "I got a text from him when the plane landed, but I haven't heard much since. Probably bad reception on the trail."

Eli took in the despair touching Clara's eyes. "Do you want to talk about it?"

Clara shook her head. "I just want to get to work."

⎯⎯ 𝓵𝓵𝓵 ⎯⎯

On her lunch break, Clara sat at one of the cafe tables on display outside. Through her sunglasses, she eyed the greenhouse in the distance and turned in her seat. She took a long swig of water, pushed her frames back up her nose, and scrolled. She had been sending Ryan a list of rental units. Her phone chimed all morning as Ryan made quick work responding to her selections.

RYAN: Did you see the bathroom in the first one?

Disgusto Barfo.

CLARA: But it's in the budget-o

RYAN: Nice try. That last listing is nice, but the area is a little... young.

CLARA: What does that mean?

RYAN: Lots of noise

RYAN: The pool will include red solo cups and vomit.

Clara wrinkled her nose and frowned.

CLARA: That's a no.

Eli stepped out into the sun and walked toward her. He smiled gently as he sank into the seat next to her. "How ya holding up?"

She grimaced. "Hanging in there. I'm actually looking at apartments."

"Oh, is that right? Are you guys selling?"

"No, we are not selling. Actually, *we* are not doing anything. But *I* am not living there anymore."

Eli cocked his head.

Clara swallowed. "Mark is moving back in... so that means I will be moving out."

"You've got to be kidding me."

Clara pursed her lips and shook her head. Refusing to feel defeated. She held up her phone. "So... I am looking at my options. I guess the only thing I have going in my favor is that I don't have a dog or a cat. A lot of landlords really seem to be anti-pet."

"Any luck so far?"

"Honestly, no. I mean, there's tons of housing, just not much that I can afford. And I need something fast."

"I see... What's your budget looking like?"

Clara sighed. "Nonexistent... I'm trying to save as much as humanly possible so I can prepare." She frowned. "I think I'll be starting from scratch when he finally decides to sign the divorce papers."

Eli's smile settled into a hard line. "I'm sure there are a few places around here." He looked off past the parking lot, to the stretch of old brick buildings in the distance. "Gloria and I could ask around. Find you something reasonable."

Clara's throat tightened. "I don't know if I can stay here... In Silas Grove." She glanced over at the greenhouses and her stomach twisted. "You know, with Mark moving into the house and Bonnie in town... And Connor will be back."

"Don't worry." Eli laid a hand on top of hers. The warmth of the iron table almost hurt. "I know you'll come out on top. It's just the way nature works."

Clara smiled at him adoringly. "I don't know, Eli, even the strongest things can snap in the dead of winter."

He looked up toward the sky, contemplating. "That might be true... but if the roots are good, there's always a chance they'll make a comeback."

Clara laughed, giving in. "You win." She thought of Connor, and her smile slipped. She missed his bickering.

"What if you come and stay with us for a bit?"

Clara's brow furrowed. "With you and Gloria?"

"Yeah." Eli looked away from her and glanced around the nursery lackadaisically. "You know we love having you around. Gloria would have my head if I didn't offer. And I know you've had a rough go of it."

The scrolled pattern on the tabletop went blurry as Clara blinked back tears. She let a slow, even breath pass through her lips.

Eli patted her hand. "Think it over. You don't have to make up your mind right now." They watched as a customer pulled a cart full of hostas toward the main building, heading for the register. Eli stood and started toward the door. He stopped and turned, smiling warmly.

"And Clara?"

Tears rolled from her eyes and hit the table.

"It would be our honor to make sure you survive the winter."

"What the hell is wrong with you?"

Connor pulled his camera down from his face and turned to Kat. "What—"

A breath of exhaustion left her chest, and she shifted her weight. She motioned around the clearing surrounding them. "All this space and you keep cutting me off. You're checked out."

Connor shook his head, resuming his concentration. He focused on what he thought was a Douglas fir, just on the other side of the lake in the distance. She walked up behind him and thumped him on the back of the head. "There is nothing happening up there."

Connor snapped a shot and checked his settings. After adjusting the aperture, several more clicks ensued. When he faced his sister, she was leaning against a fallen tree.

The landscape was incredible. It was like someone had dialed the saturation up fifty notches. Back home, everything was drying to a crisp. Here, things looked lush. Like spring all over again. He frowned, wishing Clara was here to see it.

"Sorry. I'm a little distracted."

Kat raised an eyebrow. "*Distracted* is an interesting word."

"Would you recommend something else?"

"I don't think you want to know." She stood up from the tree trunk and resumed walking in front of him. "I'm going to lead. You cut me off again and I'm going to push you right off the trail."

Connor adjusted his pack and fell in step behind his sister. Kat looked out toward a steep drop-off in the distance. It met the edge of a clearing down below. "Are you going to tell me what happened with you and Clara?"

He glowered, stifled under his sister's unrelenting questioning. "No."

Kat rolled her eyes. "Lo and Harrison and I have a bet going."

Connor cut a look toward his sister.

"Harrison thinks it could have been amicable." Kat crossed her arms, raising an eyebrow. "Lo and I think you fucked up."

Anger climbed his chest, and he turned. "You don't know what you're talking about—"

"Why are the trees so big here?" Kat deflected, raising her hand to her eyes, looking around.

Connor shook his head, just wanting a moment of peace. A breath huffed from his lungs. "Not sure."

"It's weird."

Connor held his camera up and zoomed in. He lowered the lens and squinted into the distance. He peered again a second time through the viewfinder.

A lone hiker sidled up beside them. His dog trotted along close by. Stopping at the fallen tree that Kat had just vacated a moment ago, he pulled out a Nalgene bottle.

"I mean, they're massive. It's creepy. Like they're from another world," Kat said.

Connor continued to look, zooming in even further.

"The oldest one in Seattle is about five hundred years old."

Kat and Connor both turned to face the hiker.

The man nodded at them, smiling. "Give or take a few years."

"A tree?"

"You're talking about a Douglas fir?" The man pointed out into the distance.

Connor looked over across the lake. "Yeah."

"There are older ones, of course, but different varieties. I think there's a Sitka spruce that is closer to a thousand."

Kat's eyes widened, and she mumbled under her breath. "I told you—*weird*."

"It's not weird," Connor scoffed, gazing through his camera.

The man shrugged. "There are lots of weird things in nature, but that's half the fun."

Kat dug her sunscreen out from her pack, squirting a glob into her hand.

"Just this week, I saw a flower at Bloedel Reserve. It was ten feet tall."

"A *flower*?"

"Yep. *Cardiocrinum giganteum*." The older man laughed. "Also known as the Himalayan lily. They're pretty strange looking." He knelt down and poured water into a collapsible dog bowl for his comrade.

Connor followed the drop-off, taking in the deep blue of the lake. It didn't look real.

"I think they can grow to be fifteen feet." He had finished scratching his dog behind the ears and shook out the bowl before stuffing it into the side of his pack.

Astonished, Connor continued to stare through his camera. He snapped a photo.

The man made his way over to Kat and Connor. "They're massive. The craziest part is they take seven years to bloom."

Connor lowered the camera. His heart slowed to a dull thud.

"You're shitting me."

"Real charming, Kat..."

She shrugged. "Sorry."

"It's all right." The hiker smiled. "It's unbelievable... something taking that long to come around." The man adjusted his pack and looked out over the expanse. "I was lucky to catch it. We're at the tail end of the season up here."

Connor stared out and raised his eyes to the sky, feeling tiny all of a sudden.

The man tipped his nylon sunhat to them both and went on his way, his dog following right behind him. "If you get a chance, go see them. They're impressive."

"Earth to Connor? I'd like to get back to the B and B before midnight. And we're getting pizza. I've earned it."

***

Connor and Kat climbed the stairs to the dark rental. They kicked off their hiking boots on the porch, juggling their dinner.

"I call dibs on the first shower."

Connor pulled the key fob out from his pocket. "I will not be held responsible for how much I eat."

"Shit. They put pepperoni on the whole thing."

Connor looked at his sister in disbelief. "You realize this isn't vegan by any stretch of the imagination. The meat isn't the sole culprit."

Kat glared at him before turning. "There better be half a pizza left in that box when I get out of the shower... or I will *end* you."

Connor tossed the box down and threw back the top. "What does that even mean?" Melted cheese scorched the roof of his mouth and he contorted his face, puffing out tiny, panicked breaths.

"I don't know... but it'll be awful."

Connor slumped down into the chair in front of him. He peeled off his socks and glanced at the dark line of dust and dirt around his ankles. Stretching his shoulders, he pulled his phone out of his pocket.

ELI: Clara is here at work... I thought you two were going out of town together?

ELI: Text me when you get this.

Connor checked the time. It was the middle of the night back home. They had some time to kill before their flight tomorrow, and he thought about the lilies. He shoved another bite into his mouth and remembered the pear and prosciutto.

He checked his messages one more time. Reaching over, he cracked open a beer and carried the cardboard box to the living room. He took a pull from his drink and opened Clara's never-ending playlist.

⸻ ❧ ⸻

"Y ou're going to use up all the hot water!" Two beers and five songs later, Connor was nodding off. His phone sat perched on the coffee table and he hovered off the couch, grasping for it with his fingertips. It tumbled to the ground, and he remembered the morning he was nearly decapitated. Connor looked at the screen.

Edge of Desire

He kept scrolling, seeing several of the songs Clara had added the day Mark showed up at the nursery. Kat walked out in a pair of fresh PJs with her hair soaking wet. "I can't believe you listen to this crap."

Connor looked up as she towered over him, dripping droplets onto his face. He groaned, and she assessed the pizza, making her way to the kitchen in search of a drink.

"What's wrong with this song?"

"Nothing, it's just a little... desperate."

"I think it's nice." Connor saw the surprise on his sister's face. He rolled his eyes and lay back on the couch. He didn't know the song, but he knew Clara liked it enough to put it on the list.

"I don't enjoy music that croons on and on about feeling weak and lusty." She bit into her slice crust-first. "Like... I don't want to hear anything that puts those feelings into a literal song. It's gross."

Beer sludged down the wrong pipe and Connor coughed. "*What?*"

"Just listen to it. He's all sad and mopey and, you know, *super horny*." Kat picked the pepperoni from her half of the pizza, piling them off the side. "He's saying that he'd take it all back because that's how bad he wants her."

Connor stared at his sister as she chewed with her mouth open. She wiped her chin with the back of her hand. "I could never be that weak."

⟋⟍⟋⟍

A series of muffled knocks pounded behind Connor's head. "If you don't turn that off, I'm going to throw your phone out the window!" Kat yelled from her bedroom on the other side of the wall. Connor reached for his AirPods, pulling the sheet up to his waist. The rental didn't have AC, so he slept with the window open.

Laying back against the mattress, he closed his eyes and restarted the song once more. The melody looped. He had listened to Clara's playlist so many times over the summer, but this was different.

Something had shifted. The very thought of Clara lying in bed, listening to this exact song, and possibly thinking of him was torture. Self-inflicted torture to make it worse. Connor looked up at the moon, lost in a fog of confusion and doubt. He thought for the briefest moment about what things might look like if he had stayed and fought for what he wanted.

⸺ℓℓ⸺

"**I**s that all you're going to do for the next five hours?" Connor removed one AirPod, instantly assaulted by the wails of a baby crying three rows up. Kat repeated herself. He was still listening to the song and scrolling through his shots from the hike.

Earlier that morning, while Kat slept in, Connor headed back out with his camera to track down the Himalayan lily. He had to take a ferry and barely made it back in time for their flight, but he found them. Connor flipped between the few photos he had taken on his phone before glaring at his sister.

"Are you going to tell me what's going on?"

Connor hit pause. He took a breath as the flight attendant rolled by with the beverage cart. "Well, you know how Clara and I—"

"*Broke up.*"

Connor pressed his lips into a hard line. "Right. Well, it was me... that broke up with her." He shifted, keeping his eyes on the magazine hammock in front of them. "It's complicated."

Kat flung off her sleeping eye mask, looking at him. "Lucky for you, I've got nothing but time."

He sighed, glancing around. The man to Kat's right was snoring. The couple in front of them were watching a movie. He lowered his voice. "For starters, she didn't tell me she was still married."

"To Mark."

"Yeah."

Kat shrugged. "I mean, she's obviously not with him, though, right?"

Connor cleared his throat. "Right... she said that." He scrubbed his jaw and glanced over at her. "But they're still legally married."

"Yeah, but doesn't that stuff take a long time?" She sipped her drink before setting it back down on the tray table. "She told me he moved out."

"Right." Connor felt like more and more of an idiot the deeper the conversation got. "Let me back up." Kat crossed her arms at her chest. "Me, Mark, and Clara... all of us went to college together."

She nodded. Absorbing.

"He was shitty even back then. I told Clara about what he was doing... you know, cheating on her and stuff."

Kat's eyebrows shot up. "Bold. Very bold."

"Very stupid." Connor took a sip of scalding hot tea. "Stupid because she didn't break up with him. She stayed..." Connor swallowed. "After that summer, when the whole thing came out, I stopped being friends with everyone."

"Okay..."

"And in retrospect, it was part of why I left. Why I moved. That is, until I came back. And I shot their wedding... with Sam."

"*Shiiiiiiit.*" Kat leaned forward, eyes wide. "What happened next?"

"Nothing. I mean, nothing happened between me and Clara. That morning, I went to take photos in the groom's suite—you know, with the guys. Sam was taking the bridal pictures. Anyway… they were all talking about how Mark had had someone over the night before."

"Wait, the night before the wedding?! What a piece of—"

"*I know.* And I just had to sit there and listen to all of it. From these guys I used to be friends with." Connor wiped his hands against his shorts. "For a long time, I just figured Clara made her choice." Connor shook his head, remembering how he walked out of the church. The music started and everyone stood for the bride. Connor felt like he couldn't breathe.

"So, what happened?" She scrunched her brow.

Connor swallowed tightly. "Mark showed up the other day while I was working. He uh—saw my car and recognized it… from outside their house."

Kat shook her head, stifling a smile.

"It's not funny." He grimaced. "He said they weren't getting a divorce. That they were *working things out*." Connor rotated the paper cup on his tray and he frowned.

Her brow furrowed. "Connor, he was obviously trying to get to you." She rolled her eyes. "This is Mark Monroe we're talking about. He's an asshole." She eyed him as he glanced out the window. "What did Clara say?"

The plane hit a bit a turbulence and the seatbelt light flashed overhead. He thought of the pain in her eyes that day in the car. The things he said to her. Connor straightened in his seat, his jaw tight.

"It's more than that. The day we broke up… she told me something I didn't know." Connor stretched the crick in his neck.

He hadn't slept well at all. "Clara said that summer, when she confronted Mark about what I told her, he accused *her* of cheating."

Kat scoffed. "Why didn't she tell him to fuck off?"

"Because..." Connor sighed. "I kissed her... *that night*. And she felt guilty." And he had been the one to make her dishonest. He remembered watching them argue through the glass. Clara had been so innocent. "I was an idiot, and now I feel like the worst person in the world." He looked at his sister. "I judged her for staying with him... I had no idea."

"Shit." Kat winced. She pursed her lips, deep in thought. "Well, they were together a long time. She could have left whenever she wanted."

Connor nodded, not feeling much better. "Anyway... she's got this playlist." He glanced at Kat, and she looked at him with a quirk of her lips. "I'm not sure, but I'm hoping that some of the songs she added are for me."

Kat laughed, and Connor rolled his eyes. "It's pathetic, I know."

She laughed even harder. "No Connor, it's not pathetic. *It's love.*"

28

Connor and Kat got their duffels off the plane and made their way through Hartsfield-Jackson. When they finally got to the car, he checked his phone again. No messages. Kat sank into the passenger seat, stifling a yawn.

"I'm so tired. *And hungry.*"

"Is that all you ever think about?" She had stolen his Biscoff on the plane.

She rolled her head against the headrest and looked across the console. "Let's just go straight to Eli and Gloria's. We might make it in time for dinner."

Connor froze. "I need to stop somewhere first."

"Fine. But if you take too long, I'm going to leave you on the side of the road."

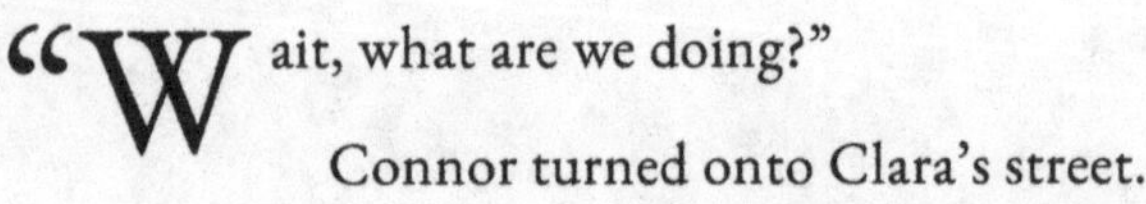

"Wait, what are we doing?"

Connor turned onto Clara's street.

Kat looked at her brother. "Don't tell me you're about to stand outside her house with a boombox."

They pulled past the entrance and into the driveway. Reaching the house, Connor cut the engine. The windows were dark. "Wish me luck."

"I don't think anyone is home."

Connor jogged up the stairs and knocked. He looked over at her car parked next to his in the driveway. He knocked once more and peered through the glass inlay. His heart twisted. The foyer was empty. Stepping back, Connor glanced up at the windows upstairs. No sign of life. No sign of Clara.

He reached for his phone.

CONNOR: I know you don't want to talk to me... but I need to see you.

He tapped his hand against his leg. *The back porch.*

He stepped toward the grass and walked along the pavers, his heart pounding. *Please be here.*

Connor stood on the grass and frowned. Squinting through the screens, there was nothing. No Clara. He heard a car honk, and he jumped, running around to the front of the house. Kat stared at him from the car.

"What the hell is wrong with you?"

She shrugged with mild indifference. "Well, if she's in there, she knows we're out here now."

He turned, searching for a clue. Looking at the steps once more, he saw the ceramic squirrel perched by the door, no longer facedown in the yard. He glanced over his shoulder at her car, seeing an envelope in the driver's seat.

"Dude. She's not coming out."

"I need to talk to her."

"Face it... you guys broke up." Realizing the bite in her tone, Kat softened. "Just give her some time."

On their way over to Eli's, Connor fell silent.

"I didn't think it was possible."

Connor shifted, tightening his grip on the steering wheel. "What?"

"I didn't think your mood could get any worse."

Connor stopped at a red light and drummed his fingers impatiently.

Kat sighed. "She'll come around."

Connor peered at his sister as she picked at her nails. "I'm not so sure."

"If those freak lilies can handle seven years, I think you'll survive."

—⁂—

They parked in the driveway of their aunt and uncle's house, unbuckling their seatbelts. Connor let out a defeated sigh.

"Do you think you could try to be slightly less unpleasant? It's going to be obnoxious if you're pouting the entire time."

Connor straightened as they walked across the lawn.

Kat pushed open the door and bumped into a stack of boxes. "What's all this?"

She shoved, and the pile shifted. "Hey guys! What's the deal with all this stuff?"

Eli and Gloria stepped out of the kitchen. "Oh, you're here! How was the flight?"

Checking his phone again, Connor frowned. No messages. He heard a noise upstairs and looked at his aunt and uncle. Then back at the boxes. He pushed back the cardboard and peered inside. Edging aside a crumpled newspaper, his fingers grazed something rough. His heart leapt as he uncovered the stone compote bowl. Eli walked over to Connor, closing the lid.

"What's this doing here?"

"This is just the stuff that wouldn't fit in the storage unit." Eli shook his head. "Poor thing is exhausted."

"I don't understand..."

"Well... maybe you should go and talk to her."

Eli patted him on the arm before turning toward the kitchen. "I don't know about you guys, but I'm starved."

Connor's eyes roamed the ceiling. He wiped his sweaty hands before walking to the stairs. His heart was in his throat as he ascended, putting one foot in front of the other. At the top of the landing, a muffled hum of music drifted from behind the door at the end of the hall. Connor stood outside, catching his breath. He knocked softly and movement stilled behind the door.

"I'll be right out!"

"Clara. It's me... Connor."

After a moment, the door cracked open and the smell of Clara's shampoo floated into the hallway. Her hair was wet from the shower, and his heart leapt at the sight of her. It quickly sank when he noticed the exhaustion in her eyes. He asked quietly, "Can I come in?"

She looked up at him and inched back from the door. Connor steadied himself and stepped into the room. The lamp on the bedside table cast the small bedroom in a soft glow. He smiled, seeing Clara's belongings in a room he had been in more times than he could count.

The rose pattern on the quilted coverlet was worn and the furniture was dated, but he had played with his Legos on the carpet under their feet. A combination TV/VCR used to sit on the chest of drawers in the corner until a few years ago, when his mother had finally convinced Gloria to donate it.

Clara wrung the water out of her hair with a towel and sat down on the edge of the bed. She pulled her knees to her chin and waited.

Connor stood by the wall with his hands in his pockets, wanting to touch her. "I went by your house."

Her eyes widened.

"I tried to get ahold of you... but I didn't hear back. I just wanted to talk."

Clara shook her head. "I'm sorry I... I just got a chance to shower and change." Her shoulders sagged. "It's been a long day."

Connor nodded.

"I moved out."

The magnitude of her words hit him hard. "So you're not—"

"No. I'm not making up with Mark." Irritation fueled her tone. "We're *not* together."

He pointed to her suitcases. "I was going to say... you're not getting your own place."

"*Oh.*" Clara shifted on the bed, rubbing her forehead. "I'm only staying for a couple days... there are a few more things I need to get from the house." She cleared her throat. "Ryan's going to let me crash at his place so we can drive to work together. You know, until I can get my own car."

Connor stared at her. "What about the nursery?"

She shook her head. "Um. I'm just going to work at the office." Looking down, she twisted the towel between her fingers. "I can save more money that way, and it'll be easier for Ryan." Clara glanced up, wincing when their eyes met. "We won't have to..." She swallowed around the knot in her throat. "It'll just be easier."

Connor clenched his hands in his pockets. The idea of stepping foot in the garden center, not seeing her face, made him dizzy. The thought of walking around town, knowing she didn't live there anymore, of her leaving Silas... he couldn't breathe.

He pushed a hand through his hair. "I thought I was over everything that happened... I didn't realize how wrong I was until it felt like it was happening all over again." His chest heaved. "I should have trusted you."

She sat in silence, shaking her head.

"Clara..."

"I should have told you about the divorce papers sooner." She looked up at him, a sad smile balanced on her lips. "I didn't say anything because I just want it to be over. And I wanted to do it on my own."

Their eyes met. After a moment, she reached for her purse. Connor stayed put, watching from his place against the wall. She pulled something from her wallet and placed it on the quilt. Connor's gaze tightened, his breath uneven. "Where did you get that?"

Clara shook her head. "My therapist got some new art."

Connor stood at the edge of the bed, their knees almost touching. He clenched his hands at his sides. The space between them hummed.

Clara laid her hand on the coverlet, tracing the card. "It's a picture of this ridgeline... and you can see the trail veering right at the bottom of the frame."

Connor smiled to himself. If he closed his eyes, he could take himself there.

"I looked at it for a long time in the waiting room the first day I saw it." Her eyes fluttered closed, her voice soft. "I don't think you could know how many times I've thought about it." Connor watched Clara's throat work as she found her words.

"I had no idea you'd moved back. It was before I knew about you and Eli, and it was before that day with the dirt." A tiny smile lifted the corner of her mouth, and Connor stared down at her, his heart pounding.

"Some of the days I thought about that picture were the shittiest days of my life." Clara pursed her lips and looked down at her hands. "Sometimes, when I was scared of being alone, I thought about standing at that cliff. What it would feel like with the sun shining down. When the power got shut off, I thought about that big open sky... and how small my problems really were."

She looked up at him with tears in her eyes. "When I was terrified of starting over..." Clara wiped her cheeks. "I promised myself that I would never rely on anyone ever again." The words reverberated in Connor's chest. His stomach was in his throat.

Clara winced, motioning to her things around them. "I'm not doing so well, you know, the *not relying on people* part... but I'm working on it." Clara sighed. "I guess I should say thank you. I know deep down that I would have survived it all, but you believed in me... and even if that's all I take away from this whole summer, I will always be grateful."

Connor's eyes went glassy.

Weariness tinged her expression. "I just hope at some point, you know, we can move past all of this." She smiled before her face crumpled. "I really love your family and... I don't want to lose you as a friend."

Connor's mouth hardened, settling into a frown. He stood in silence, his heart thrumming wildly in his chest. "I don't know if I can do that."

Clara looked up into Connor's face, her eyes searching. Unable to speak, she looked down, averting her gaze. Rejection burned a hole in her gut, and she shifted.

Connor cleared his throat. "Is this how you really feel?"

"What?"

Connor pointed to her phone, still playing just above a whisper. The song was so soft he could barely hear it. Clara reached for it and fumbled, a blush flaming her cheeks.

"Because—" He stepped forward and knelt down on one knee. Cradling her legs, Connor pulled her to the edge of the bed. He covered Clara's hands with his own and smoothed them against his chest. Her fingers bunched the thin cotton of his shirt and his breathing stalled. "Because if that's how you really feel... then I can't *just* be your friend."

Their eyes locked.

"When I thought you were going to take him back... it broke me. But then I realized it wasn't about that." Clara's hands were warm and soft beneath his. "It was the thought of not having you." He swallowed. "Of losing my chance."

His eyes brimmed with tears, and he drew in a breath. "You're everything, Clara. You're sensitive and kind and you love my crazy family. And you *are* brave. I can't just be your friend." He stared into her eyes, pleading. "I'm so sorry. I was stupid, and young, and selfish."

A smile broke across her face. The sight knocked the air out of his lungs.

"I love you." His voice was hoarse. "Please give me a second chance."

Clara slid her hands up to his jaw, and his dimples deepened. "I love you, too." Leaning forward, she brushed her lips against his.

Salty tears laced their kiss. Connor's touch was like him—strong and patient. He didn't rush her, and instead, let her come to him when she was ready.

Clara tucked her face against his shoulder, melting into his arms. She inhaled his scent, and she was right back at the ridge. The world quieted. Goosebumps raced across her body where the wind licked her skin and sunlight poured down around them. Clara could hear the ground shifting below her boots as she took her first step onto her new path.

EPILOGUE

Click.

Clara peered through her lashes. Nylon glowed around her with the first traces of morning light. Listening to the gentle purr of the zipper, she snuggled deeper into her sleeping bag, stifling a yawn.

Click.

That sound had slowly made its way into every peaceful moment of her and Connor's relationship. Sunday mornings at his apartment, she'd awake just like this. The subtle sound of the shutter within earshot, and the feel of Connor near her, somewhere. His gaze magnified by the contraption he held in his hands. She had developed a sixth sense for it. Sometimes she felt it during the quiet hours at Grady's as the day wound down. Or when she was relaxing on the porch swing at Eli and Gloria's. On hikes, where there was no one around for miles.

Click.

Bending her knees, the sleeping bag swooshed against the tent floor beneath her. She peeked down the length of her body, wincing against the burst of light illuminating the halo of waves not trapped by Connor's hat. Her eyes adjusted to the sun like the aperture inside his camera. Connor knelt at the edge of the tent, the zippered entrance half open. A chill slipped in around him and she smiled.

"You're letting in the cold."

Click.

He shifted into the tent and balanced on his knees, sprawling across the top of Clara's body. Trapping her below him in the plush sleeping bag, he brought his face closer to hers. She wiggled a hand free, touching the strands that curled at the edge of his cap above his brow. The lens in front of his face had become a regular sight.

"How long have you been awake?"

The corner of his mouth lifted. "A while."

She smiled. "You could have gotten me up."

"You were sleeping so deep." *Click.* "I didn't want to wake you."

She sighed. Late nights had become a usual occurrence. Between working her last several weeks in The Bug Zapper and preparing for her transition to full-time at Grady's, she had been burning the candle at both ends. It took a lot of preparation, making sure everything would be perfect when she handed in her notice. Connor had offered to help her out, but of course, she said no.

He hadn't expected anything different after all Clara had been through. He watched her through his viewfinder as she stifled another yawn, observing the soft tug of her lips as she settled back against the pillow. Her mouth disappeared as she hid her nose below the top of the sleeping bag. A sliver of light shot through the opening of the tent, catching the tangled mess of her hair. His dimples deepened.

"If you're not going to zip the flap, the least you could do is get in here with me." She watched the dangerous pull of his lips. The upper half of his face, covered by his camera. She reached out, blocking the lens with her palm.

"I didn't want you to miss the view." Connor sat up to unzip the flap the rest of the way, unveiling a breathtaking sunrise in the distance. He kicked off his boots.

Connor slipped into the sleeping bag, setting his camera down carefully beside them. Clara beamed and sucked in a breath as his chilled clothes met her body, disrupting the warmth of the cocoon around her. She tucked her face into his neck and they lay like that for a while. Both gazing out into the distance as the landscape became brighter under the rising sun. Clara hummed her content against his skin. Connor lifted his hand, letting her hair slip between his fingers, luxuriating in the weight of her curled into his chest.

"Are you excited?"

"I am." Clara pressed her cold nose against his jaw.

She sat up on her elbow, looking down at the playful look in Connor's eyes. "Are you nervous?"

"Why would I be nervous?"

She lifted her shoulder. "Once we're both settled in town... You'll be stuck with me." Her eyes held his. "Silas is a small place."

It had been six months since Clara moved out of the Monroe Mansion. She had crashed over at Connor's pretty regularly in the city, but between her living with Ryan, working some days at The Bug Zapper, and some days at Grady's, their life had become a series of pick-ups and drop-offs. Their love had grown in a million moments, split between a million places. "Let them talk." Connor grinned. "I don't care."

"And you're not upset that I want my own place?" Clara sank into the depths of his gaze. Her fingers trailed along the collar of his shirt. "It'll be more expensive, but it's part of my plan."

Connor smiled. His hand inched to her back, his fingers brushing in lazy circles over her shirt. He knew this was important to her. He shook his head, covering her hand with his own, pressing it over his chest.

Clara lowered and her hair slid down her shoulders, a curtain framing their faces as she brought her lips to his.

"Everything is perfect." She felt his touch slowly drifting to the hem of her shirt. His fingers slipped between the fabric and her skin, still cold. She closed her eyes.

His breath was warm against her cheek. "I just want you to feel okay about everything."

Clara's heart softened at the sentiment, knowing that he didn't want her to feel rushed. After a hefty back and forth, her divorce from Mark had finally been settled.

"Better than okay." Clara smiled, her lips brushing against his. She shifted, raising her leg over Connor's. "I love you."

He sucked in a breath, feeling her brush across the front of his jeans. Moving from her collar to the back of her hair, his fingers tangled, holding Clara close as he kissed her. Hooking his other hand below her knee, he pulled her over his body so she straddled him in the sleeping bag. "I love you, too."

Both trapped by their clothes, her teasing dissolved into want. Just below the edge of her shirt, his fingers bit into her skin. She grinned against his mouth, dragging her teeth along his bottom lip. Clara listened to the sharp intake of his breath and rolled her hips, pressing herself more firmly against him.

He groaned and his hands skated higher beneath her shirt, luxuriating in the feel of her skin as he peeled the fabric away from her body. She raised her arms, goosebumps racing as Connor lifted her shirt above her shoulders and over her head.

Connor pulled the sleeping bag higher around her as he sank back down, pressing kisses across her chest, filling his hands with her breasts. Her heart pounded, matching the dull ache building between her legs. His tongue circled her sensitive flesh before tugging a peak between his lips.

"You aren't playing fair." Clara's breath hitched, and she ground herself hard against him. "You have too many clothes on."

He smiled. "Feels pretty fair to me."

The dull ache turned into a throb and she reached between them, yanking his shirt up, exposing the expanse of his chest. She grinned, his shirt collar catching his hat as she shoved everything over his shoulders. Clara bit the inside of her lip, unable to hide the need coursing through her at that moment. His dimples edged with stubble, and his hair rumpled. The blue of his eyes illuminated by the sun glowing inside the tent.

The air was crisp and his nose was cold as he pressed his face to her skin. She wanted more. She wanted to feel him over her, surrounding her. Clara made a meager attempt at flipping them over and groaned. Connor laughed and gave in, rolling them so that she was trapped beneath him. He held Clara close, her naked skin pressed to his as the tent shook and shifted around them.

Connor eyed his camera. "Grab my lens cover, will you?"

She huffed a laugh, squirming against him. "Can't you reach it?"

"I'm busy." Connor's breath was heavy against her hair before his teeth grazed her earlobe.

Clara gasped and relinquished, poking her arm out of the sleeping bag. A chill raced across her skin as Connor pressed kisses down her throat. Her hand grappled along the nylon, meeting the rough fabric of his camera bag.

Connor sucked the patch of skin just above her collarbone and she twisted against him, trying to widen her legs. Her fingers touched the pull of a zipper. Clara inhaled. "I can't focus when you do that."

Connor had moved his hand down to her waist, lightly tracing over her pants. Clara tugged the zipper under her fingers and felt around. Her hips jerked subconsciously, chasing Connor's touch between her legs. Her breath hitched, and she bit her lip as he slipped his hand inside her pants.

He grinned, his fingers skating over the fabric that covered her center. "Baby..."

Clara dragged in a breath, her eyes falling closed.

His touch slowed. "The lens cap."

Clara groaned and Connor listened as she furiously dug around in his bag. The moment stretched on and he met the edge of her underwear.

He felt Clara's body tense and Connor's gaze darted to her pulse, then to her eyes. His heart hammered in his chest as he followed the smooth skin of her arm to her fingers. They were wrapped around a tiny velvet box.

He swallowed thickly. Removing his hand from between Clara's legs, he propped himself up above her. Her lips parted, and she blinked. Turning the box over between her fingers, Connor watched as her eyes clouded.

He cleared his throat. "May I have that, please?"

Connor's gaze dropped to her mouth, seeing the way Clara worried the inside of her lip. Goosebumps rose along her skin and she brought the box to his fingers, placing it in his hand. She tucked her arm back into the sleeping bag and gazed up at him in silence.

"I've been waiting for the right time to do this." His thumb brushed the top of the box, his mouth lifting at the corner.

"You have?"

His eyes caught hers. "You're not the only one who's got a plan." He noticed the nervous bob of her throat and his gut clenched, a hint of nerves suddenly racing through him. He drew in a breath. "I bought us a house."

He opened the box, and Clara's eyes widened.

A set of keys shimmered, light bouncing around the tent as a wrinkle etched Clara's brow.

"Well, sort of. It's not set in stone yet, and there weren't a ton of options in Silas." He smiled. "It's actually a duplex, and it needs some work... but I thought maybe you'd want to be my neighbor?"

Clara frowned, shaking her head in disbelief. A heavy silence stretched between them, and panic filled Connor's chest as he closed the box. "Baby, if you don't want to live in the unit next door, then I'll just use it as an office or something." He searched her eyes. "I can rent it out."

Clara's gaze met his. "You want me to move in... next door?"

"Yeah." Connor tucked her hair behind her ear. "You won't let me pay for anything and I was thinking... We could split everything down the middle, but you'd still have your own place." He drew in a breath, his throat tight. "Maybe it was a stupid idea."

She swallowed hard and reached out from the sleeping bag, pushing at the lid of the box. They both watched as it sprang open, her fingers tracing the set. "Why are there two?"

"It might be a little fast..." Connor shrugged. "But I wanted to give you a key to my place."

Clara blew out a heavy breath, her eyes glittering with tears. "I can't believe you did this." A smile broke across her face and she stared up at him, amazed.

Happiness flooded his chest as he pulled her to him, dropping a kiss to her naked shoulder. "You don't have to decide this second."

Relief washed over him and he breathed in, the scent of Clara filling his senses, making him dizzy. "Will you promise me something, though?"

She nodded, bringing her hand to his jaw. "Anything."

He shifted, lowering her back down to the sleeping bag. "Your plans are my plans, Clara." Something serious passed through his eyes as he took in every inch of her laying beneath him. "Your dreams are mine, too." He watched the rise and fall of her chest and the softness in her expression as he spoke. "I'll do everything in my power to make them come true... even if that means I have to wait."

A tear slipped from her lashes, and Connor pressed his lips to her cheek, catching it with his kiss. "Promise me you won't ever forget that."

She wrapped her arms around him, holding him close. "I promise."

❦

Thank you for reading Second Bloom!

Can't get enough of Connor and Clara?
Scan the QR CODE down below to get their
bonus story + a sneak peek of book two
delivered straight to your inbox!

Acknowledgments

In all seriousness, I have to start by saying that my parents and family are amazing. Mom and Dad- there isn't one memory I have where you didn't drop everything you were doing to listen to me. It didn't matter if it was trivial or time sensitive. My thoughts and whims were important because you made me feel like they were important. To this day I can call you day or night with a hairbrained idea, and I know you're on the other end of the line, turning down the TV and putting me on speakerphone. I wish everyone was so lucky to have that kind of support. I will forever be grateful.

This cast of characters would be sad, flat, and without life if it weren't for my friends. Y'all are my family. Y'all are the heartbeat of every sassy bit of dialogue, every eye roll, and every chapter that left the reader thinking, "I need a Ryan in my life." There have been so many times where I felt like I didn't know what the hell I was doing. Or where I was going. But each one of you has stuck it out, in the shade of that metaphorical homemade soap tent, laughing with me until I was crying, telling me I can conquer anything. You all have inspired me in countless ways and I'll continue to be inspired for the rest of our lives.

To my husband. Man, you're the best. When we were dating back in college, I described you to every single one of my friends as a golden retriever puppy. So sweet and endearing and a little bit of a mess. This was before I knew what a trope was. And it was before I could grasp the full meaning of what that *Golden Retriever* title truly held.

Your selflessness is unmatched. And although your love sometimes comes with forcing me to take vitamins and trying to get me to exercise more, I know it's because you love me and want me to be around for as long as humanly possible. Thank you for every incredible breakfast, every plant nursery excursion, and for every single time I reach for your hand at night and you squeeze back, even if you're fast asleep. I love you and the life we share.

For all you ragtag misfits and OGs out on the mean streets of *Romancelandia*, thank you. Thanks for sustaining a wonderful place where we can let our imaginations run wild. A place where new writers like me can find inspiration in you, just lovin' on love for love's sake. The friends that I've made through this journey have been integral in the most unexpected ways to the realization of this book. No question was ever too ridiculous, and your generosity has been unreal. I know y'all will be around for the long haul.

For anyone who picked up this book and took a chance, thank you. All my daydreaming would be nothing but that if it weren't for you, spending your time and money to read something that I wrote. I hope I never get over this feeling, because it's beautiful and surreal.

ABOUT THE AUTHOR

Eve Matthews has an affection for tiny towns and she writes about the daring women we love to see in the world. Inspired by the uncanny resilience of the human spirit, she believes that bravery is always there, within our reach. If she's not dreaming up places, she's adventuring around Georgia with the hero of her heart, rescuing plants, and searching for her next cup of coffee.

Want to know what she's got in the works?
Check out **evematthewswrites.com**
and sign up for her newsletter, *The Evening Break!*

Website : evematthewswrites.com
Instagram : evematthews.writes